TAMING HIS BRIDE

"You lied to me, O'Rourke! You and Papa double-crossed me!"

"Sorry, Kate. You'd better accept things the way they are. 'For better or for worse,' remember?"

"Oooh! I hate you, do you know that?" she railed, her fiery head thrashing in a vain effort to strike him in the face.

O'Rourke had had enough. He shut her up the fastest way he knew how. He kissed her, hard. Ravaging and pillaging forcefully, he let her know who was in charge. He kept it up even while she continued to express her low opinion of him. His tongue began a shocking assault on her senses.

"I was a fool to trust you," she raged.

"Don't give me any more lip."

"You can't make me do anything," she persisted defiantly.

O'Rourke plundered her mouth again. He could feel her shiver as his tongue came against hers, feeling her resistance waver . . .

O'ROURKE'S BRIDE

BARBARA DAN

ZEBRA BOOKS

Kensington Publishing Corp.

www.kensingtonbooks.com

Chapter 1

Virginia City, Nevada
September 21, 1864

Mary Katherine McGillacutty stared out the tall, heavily draped parlor window at a desolate view of dull, taupe-gray mountains and blinding sunshine glinting off the ugly corrugated roofs of Virginia City's mining district below her father's mansion. Blinking rapidly, her green eyes awash with something mighty close to tears, she forced down a hard lump of disappointment and gave her chin a proud little hitch.

So unfair! And monstrous unfeeling of Papa, too. If he had said even one word about having missed her, their reunion might have been so different.

On top of everything else, Papa's crass ultimatum to Mama had forced them to cancel an entire season's social calendar. This, to Katherine's way of thinking, was unforgivable. All things considered, she intended to make herself as uncooperative as possible.

Newly arrived a scant hour ago, Mary Kate was still dressed in her traveling clothes, following a horrendous journey on the Overland Stage Line from Omaha. Her trunks, full to overflowing with the latest fashions, still bore railway stickers designating her point of origin as Chicago.

Raising her pert chin, she turned to eye her sire with only revenge on her mind. The sooner he sent her and Mama packing, the better. "Really, Papa," she said, tapping her foot, "how can you possibly expect me to live in Virginia City?"

Again she peeked through the dusty parlor window at the dreadful little town. Even knowing its streets were paved with low-grade silver ore didn't change her opinion of it, or the sweaty miners plodding along B Street just below their veranda. Virginia City was a wild, barbaric place, lacking any of the proper incentives to gladden a young girl's heart, a galling place to waste her time and talents. There was simply no way she would stay when Chicago, New York, and Paris beckoned.

What could have possessed Papa to leave a thriving business in Chicago? Selling stocks and bonds certainly beat anything this crude place could offer. Of course, she couldn't fault his success, since he'd bought up several claims and formed the Lucky Strike Mining Conglomerate five years ago.

Naturally, Katherine and her mother hadn't let Homer McGillacutty's ambitions and business decisions alter their lifestyle one iota. Last summer they had taken the Grand Tour of Europe, spending their new wealth with aplomb, while "good old Homer" had continued to puff on his smelly stogies and pay the bills.

Now Homer McGillacutty considered himself a tolerant soul. As best he could, he kept up with their travels through the occasional postcard or brief scribble "sent off in haste" by his wife. (Both Mrs. McGillacutty and his fashionable daughter lived it up to their hearts' desire, knowing he was too busy making money to miss them anyway.) True to form, Homer made daily trips to the bank and twice weekly visits to a shapely young widow, whose husband had perished when one of the Lucky Strike's unluckier mine shafts had collapsed.

This tacit arrangement had gone on for some time in

apparent harmony. But in the late spring, Homer ran into an old friend from Chicago at the San Francisco Stock Exchange. While comparing notes, he learned that his wife was pushing Katherine, nearly eighteen, into the social whirlwind in hopes of finding a "suitable match." (Definition: Marry old money!)

Of course McGillacutty had nothing against money; it was the all-consuming passion of his life. But he was a self-made man, and pride was his middle name. His immediate reaction, upon hearing his little twit of a daughter's name linked with the effete Mr. Clarence Stokes of Oak Park, could be described only as mercurial. His temper flared hotter than the geothermal temperatures down in Shaft No. 9. With the speed of a Washoe zephyr, one of those sudden tornadoes that periodically ripped the roofs off Virginia City churches and houses, he set about to rectify the matter.

A flurry of correspondence ensued between Mrs. McGillacutty, formerly the beauteous Madeleine Yves-St. Suivvant of New Orleans, and the robust Scotch-Irish tycoon. Homer objected vehemently. His only child would not—repeat: *would not*—marry anyone who was afraid of "honest-to-God hard work!"

Naturally his wife didn't see eye to eye with the bombastic man who had swept her off her feet some twenty years prior. She told Homer he was old-fashioned; he had forgotten which fork to use in polite society. And then she threatened to sue him for a long-overdue divorce for harboring such an "unfeeling attitude."

Homer, in turn, promptly froze his wife's line of credit, cut her household allowance by half, and promised to sell the house in Chicago if she and Katherine weren't on the next train West.

They were on the next train West.

Madeleine McGillacutty wasn't at all sure she cared whether she ever lived with Homer again. However, she was certain she wanted to spend more of his money. And so she had come, bringing their only offspring with her. She was upstairs unpacking at this very moment.

Secretly, the feral gleam in her estranged husband's eye gave her the same unsettled feeling as a champagne buzz.

"Papa, I assure you, Clarence Stokes means nothing to me, so you needn't have bothered to send for me. Mama and I were having such a marvelous time, too." Kate gave her father a calculating smile, her green eyes brightly snapping. "Are you satisfied, now that you've heard it from my own lips?"

"No, daughter, I am not."

Scowling, Homer McGillacutty locked his big, meaty hands behind him. He and Kate were both redheads, both stubborn, both used to getting their own way. They never failed to clash when they were together, and this afternoon was no exception. He cleared his throat and, chewing the end of his fat cigar, studied the puzzle standing before him.

Looking at his daughter, Homer felt a pang of regret. He'd missed watching his little Katie grow into the finest-looking colleen he'd ever laid eyes on. "A good thing you don't take after me more than you do, Kate." He chuckled, mentally comparing his own tall, burly shape and barrel chest to her smaller-boned elegance. It was hard to see much of her mother in her, either. Perhaps she got her delicate features from Madeleine—they both had high cheekbones and that intriguing catlike slant to the eyes. But Kate's coloring and tall stature came from him.

Kate shrugged, her long, tapered fingers playing idly with the lace curtain. She knew her father had always wanted a son. When the doctor had told him that her mother shouldn't have any more children, he'd made no secret of his disappointment.

"If I'd been a boy, I suspect you'd have me down in that

mine right this minute," she said with a trace of bitterness, for she knew her father's disappointment when she was born a girl instead of a boy to carry on the family line.

"Ah, lass." He took a couple of puffs on his cigar, filling the parlor with a haze of smoke. "No use cryin' over spilled milk, I always say."

"Then why drag Mother and me out to this godforsaken place, if not to torture us? I grew up always knowing I was of no use to you, being a female. So why, all of a sudden, should you care this much"—she snapped her fingers—"whom I marry, or what I do with my life? Or what Mama does, for that matter."

"That's some chip you carry on your shoulder, missy." Homer bent his great red lion's mane, now shot through with gray, until their foreheads met. His gray-green eyes engaged her in a silent standoff.

"Is it any wonder?" Katherine's lips trembled. "You're a stranger, Papa. Five years without even a visit. Just sent your dirty old money. What did it matter if Mama and I rotted in Chicago!"

McGillacutty's freckled, sun-damaged skin flushed with anger.

"Watch out, daughter, or there'll be precious little money coming your way."

"Fine!" Kate flared. "Stuff your old money in a sock, for all I care! You've been stingy with your love. I'm sure I can survive without your money as well!"

"Proud, haughty words, Kate." Homer fought to keep the lid on his temper. "But you're not yet of age, and I'll decide what kind of a man you wed."

"How crass." Her lip curled insultingly. "Mama's right about you. You've degenerated into a money-grabbing old miser. You have no sense of refinement or culture at all!"

"Hold your tongue, young twit!" her father roared and gave her a shake. "And leave your mother out of this. She and I have our differences, but I'll take no back talk from either of you. You're a couple of ungrateful, *useless* females."

Mary Kate laughed contemptuously and pulled away. "I suspect you view all females as weak, contemptible creatures." She saw the frustration mount in her father's face and pressed on. "But perhaps I am mistaken. I hear one Virginia City whore still is of some limited use to you."

Used to living among rough men, Homer reacted without thinking. He hauled off and slapped her, knocking her sideways onto the loveseat. "Listen, Kate, I won't take that from a man, and most assuredly I won't allow such talk from my own daughter. Mrs. Bowers is a fine woman, and you'll not refer to her that way again."

Though shaken, Katherine refused to be cowed. "I don't believe I mentioned her by name," she said with a calm, deadly smile. "Can I help it if you associate the word 'whore' with her name?"

His hand drew back, ready to strike her again, then dropped to his side. "I'm sorry, Katie. I never meant to hurt you."

"Mercy sakes!" A voice with a pronounced Southern accent was heard from the doorway. "Will there never be a moment's peace between you two?"

Mary Kate and Homer, each with lips drawn back in a snarl, turned to confront the family matriarch's gentle wrath.

Peter Casey O'Rourke hooked a boot heel onto the brass foot rail at the Bucket of Blood waterhole and leaned both elbows back on the handsome mahogany bar while he checked out the local clientele. As a trained actor, he'd developed a gut instinct about people. Hopefully that skill would help him find his next meal.

The gaslight lamps gave the painted ladies from upstairs a familiar theatrical hue. *Turn up the amber lights, boys!* He wanted to shout—anything, if only to shake his growing sense of agitation.

Around him, grave-faced miners rubbed shoulders with shopkeepers on their noonday break. The whole place resembled a feeding frenzy; dark objects gnawing at each other's souls. Peter winced at the bartender's jovial banter—*so* out of place! He felt surrounded, caught in a web of falsehood and lies.

Harpies plying their trade for an ounce of silver. Appalling. A paltry, "civilizing" exercise upon pasty-faced, consumptive clients. *Mother of God!* A man couldn't sink much lower.

O'Rourke blinked through the haze of alcohol fumes and tobacco smoke. Usually blessed with a sunny disposition, he even questioned whether he might be suffering delirium tremens. Had his habit of "hail-fellow-well-met" turned to Irish moonshine and madness? He sincerely hoped not! He held out a well-manicured hand before his face. Steady as granite. No strange purple snakes slithered out of the spittoons. No mysterious handwriting on the painting over the bar of a nude's belly, either. *Praise be!* He could safely rule out the creeping terrors from some unsanitary still.

Two deeply tanned men in flannel shirts, toughcord trousers, and cleat shoes caught his eye: the only healthy specimens in the dimly lit bar. Everyone else seemed artificial as hell. Peter glanced down at his own hand, gripping a bar glass, and wondered when he had felt more like a misfit.

Nearby men half-dead of lung fever boasted of claims they'd staked and veins they had followed. For most, the elusive pot of silver and gold remained an unattainable dream at the end of some nonexistent rainbow. Those who struck it rich soon lost it in a game of cards. Young toughs killing time between grueling shifts, using their four dollars a day to drink themselves insensible. With cynical humor they laughed at the Fates, knowing it was only a matter of time before poison gases, the god-awful heat, or a cave-in snuffed out their miserable existence.

Many were his own countrymen. They'd worked

similar mines in Cornwall, Cardiff, or back in the Appalachian hills. Moles, rarely seeing the light of day, busting their backs, yet driven on by dreams of hitting a rich deposit of silver. He could see why, in the long run, those who ran the shops and gaming hells aboveground wound up with all the money.

As O'Rourke studied this fascinating cross-section of Virginia City's male population, he tried to picture himself earning a living doing what any of them did.

A novel idea: work.

He had never envisioned toiling at anything more strenuous than acting. Truthfully, he rather liked being one of those who "struts and frets his hour upon the stage" in imitation of life's players. Aye, compared with these poor unfortunates, who labored long and hard for the Yankee dollar, the twenty-five-year-old actor had lived the good life, coasting along on personality, wit, and his father's generous allowance—until recently, that is. Fast living, fancy clothes, fancier women. Since he'd packed up and left his family's estate on the Emerald Isle, he'd indulged his every whim, always hoping to satisfy a strange inner restlessness. And here he was, stranded in Virginia City. Lord, was *that* ever a comedown in the world!

Following in the footsteps of many a restless young prodigal before him, Peter had never dreamed the source of his independence and wealth would dry up, no matter how loudly his sire bellowed.

He and his biblical counterpart ran true to form: both highly imaginative, high-spirited hedonists, traveling first class as long as the money held out. Both younger sons and, oddly enough, both blessed with loving, rock-solid parents. But that was where the similarity ended. *Peter's* father, with unforgiving finality, had cut off the ungrateful scamp's allowance and denied him any further access to the family coffers.

Unfortunately, by the time Peter realized the money had stopped, he was halfway around the world, in

Philadelphia, enjoying "rave" reviews as a "younger version of Edmund Kean."

Not that the bottom immediately dropped out after his penny-pinching father cut him off without a cent. Of course not. That came later—*after* Peter, thumbing his nose at adversity, caught the first fast clipper ship bound for San Francisco, lured by tales of all the money actors were making in California's mining boom towns.

A week after landing in San Francisco, Peter was trouping the boards with a popular Irish company. He was up to his dimpled chin in pretty oysters! Drinking champagne and dancing till dawn. And splitting healthy purses with his fellow actors. Even so, Peter couldn't bring himself to live on an actor's pay. Bad for the image.

Without his father's largess to fall back on, he might have despaired, utterly, rather early in the game. Fortunately, rumors had reached the Irish Players of actors, who'd retired after a single night's engagement in Virginia City. "Eureka!" they cried. And so the troupe crossed the Sierra Nevadas to "mine" the Comstock Lode for all it was worth.

After playing to packed houses at Maguire's Opera House for three nights, it looked as if the company had hit pay dirt. O'Rourke, celebrating his good Irish luck with his usual ebullient charm, escorted three lively creatures back to his hotel for a nightcap.

When he woke up a day and a half later, his money was gone. He had a head as big as the hump on one of Colonel Runyon's camels, and a disposition as nasty. Moreover, the engagement had been cancelled, and the troupe had left for a place called Glitter Gulch to seek their fortune. Peter promptly forsook the chance to fight three hundred miles of burning desert and hostiles in order to rejoin them. He figured he was better off broke than dead.

Even so, he acknowledged, it took more than charm to live. Unlike Haley's Comet, he now seemed destined to disappear from the scene without even a trickle of gold or silver dust.

Egad! A pauper at twenty-five. It made him queasy clear to the empty pit of his stomach.

"That's life!" Peter muttered, acknowledging the sudden dirty deal Fate had handed him. He'd bounced around the world and enjoyed its sunsets on four continents. He'd spouted the Bard's lines to culture-starved convicts and their descendants "down under." He'd strolled on moonlit beaches with doe-eyed native women of the Pacific. Probably somewhere down the road, he'd regard Virginia City as simply another amusing detour in an otherwise spotty career.

As his dear mother back in Wexford used to say, "Troubles are a blessing in disguise." Aye, 'twas a pretty philosophy learned upon his mother's knee but sadly lacking in substance and coin.

Peter bit into a free pretzel and contemplated his future with astonishing sobriety, considering the amount of alcohol he'd swilled since nine o'clock. It was a pity his noble father didn't view life through the same rosy kaleidoscope his pretty mother did, or he might not now be forced to review his options. Without a proper wardrobe and now separated from the rest of the Irish Players, it was time to take stock of his life.

Aye, he chuckled, remembering. Fast thinking, a glib tongue, and fancy footwork had always served him well. But, of course, he'd never been quite so far down on his luck before. This time he would be forced to get a "real" job.

About to embark upon a new career, Peter sensed the choice he made would be no light matter.

"Father and I were just discussing the difference between useless but respectable ladies and women of easy virtue," Mary Katherine explained to her mother, taking the opportunity to get in another dig at her sire.

"Madeleine, I told you to stay upstairs. I want to discuss Katherine's future with her. Alone." His jaw jutting fiercely, Homer stared his wife down until she wilted perceptibly.

"Homer, I heard shouting," Mrs. McGillacutty objected tremulously. "Naturally I was concerned for Katherine's safety."

"Afraid I'll beat her black and blue, eh?" her husband asked, taking a menacing step in her direction.

"No, no, of course not," his wife said quickly. Homer had always treated her with the utmost kindness, despite their differences. She hoped to keep things cordial. "I meant to imply no such thing—"

"No, I'm sure you didn't," McGillacutty snarled. "But you'd turn my own daughter against me. Well, you're here now, Madeleine, so you may as well hear what I've got to say."

Madeleine McGillacutty stood in the doorway, twisting her lace hankie nervously, indecision written all over her face.

"Sit!" Homer bellowed, and his volume rattled the prisms on a gaudy crystal lamp on the piano. His wife sat obediently on the loveseat next to their daughter, who looked anything *but* submissive. He strode up and down, pinning the two banes of his existence to the brocaded fabric with his fiery gaze.

"What could you possibly want with either of us in this primitive mining town?" Madeleine sniffed resentfully.

"I intend to see our Mary Kate married to a real man, not some pantywaist from the Chicago suburbs," her husband informed her. "Someone who isn't a damn parasite."

"What?" Madeleine's eyes met his in horror, then transferred to Mary Katherine's equally alarmed gaze.

Homer rocked back on his worn boot heels. "You heard me, Maddy. I intend to get me some grandchildren off this useless heifer." Puffing away on his cigar like one of the overworked engines that ran the lifts in the Lucky Strike mine, he waited for that revelation to sink in.

Madeleine's mouth flew open, but words failed her.

She opened and closed her pretty mouth several times, too stunned to believe what she'd just heard.

Katherine had plenty to say: "'Useless heifer!' Is that how you regard me, Father?" she asked in a deceptively amiable tone, as she gathered herself together to do battle.

"You're a spoiled brat," her father told her. "But I don't entirely blame your mother. I tend to get preoccupied, and a lass like yourself is bound to get a bit headstrong, without a father's strong hand to guide her."

"Oh, I've felt your strong hand, all right." Her hands clenching and unclenching, she searched for a vulnerable spot on her father's anatomy. He was in good shape for a man his age. Physically outmatched, Kate settled for a verbal contest.

"I've already apologized, Kate," her father said gruffly. "Just don't push your luck."

"Since I'm only a 'useless heifer,' Father," Kate said, fixing him with a combative glare, "surely you know you're not going to get me to marry anyone against my will."

"I know several fine young men here in Virginia City who would make you a good husband," Homer stated, his mind made up. "My foreman, Lew Simpson, for one."

"Forget it, Father."

McGillacutty drew himself up to his full height and with hands as huge and muscled as a smithy's, grabbed Katherine up from the loveseat. Suspended in midair, she understood at once the disadvantages of her position as both a minor and a female.

"Put me down, Father. Please?" Guessing this wasn't the best time to rile his temper, Kate lowered her voice a few decibels. When her feet touched down on the carpet, she began to bargain. "I'm sure we can discuss this like two reasonable adults."

"Nothing to discuss," Homer said tersely. "I refuse to have a leach for a son-in-law. You'll take your pick from among my associates."

"And if I say no?" she responded sweetly.

"Then I'll do the picking for you," he said firmly, his cigar smoke giving him a slightly Mephisthophelean appearance.

Katherine drew herself up defiantly. Whatever her father dished up, she would do him one better. "Well then, Papa, I'd like to make a suggestion," she said, twin demons now dancing in her green eyes. "I presume any male in Virginia City is twice the man you think Clarence Stokes is?"

"Three times better," he responded, his jaw protruding and a gleam of triumph in his eye. He was glad she was ready to listen to reason.

"Why don't we walk downtown and meet your friends?" she invited. "As Mama and I came into town on the stagecoach, I noticed half the male population passed out dead-drunk in front of the saloons."

"Mary Katherine McGillacutty," her father warned, his eyes narrowing with suspicion.

Kate gave her father a withering stare. "What are we waiting for?" she goaded. "Evidently my education has been sorely neglected. According to you, I've never even seen a 'real' man."

At both her parents' sharp intake of breath, Katherine made a sweeping curtsy, as if deferring to her father's wishes. "I obey, Father. I shall pick a mate from the fabulous streets of Virginia City and resign myself to my fate."

"Another beer, my good man." Peter O'Rourke shoved his glass across for a refill, even though his pockets were empty. "Put it on my tab," he added grandly.

Old Man MacGruder raised a heavy black eyebrow. He eyed the dandy on the other side of his bar with skepticism and growled, "No credit."

Peter shrugged and gave the barkeep one of his patronizing smiles. "How's about I entertain your patrons with a few lines from *Hamlet*? Or possibly *Romeo and Juliet*," he suggested. "Or would you prefer a bit of poetry?"

"Oh, you fancy yourself an actor, do you?" MacGruder

stopped polishing the counter with his rag and gestured to the bouncer. "Show this smart Mick how we treat actors around here, Kruger."

O'Rourke looked up. A second too late, he raised his fists to defend the finely chiseled features that had made strong women weep and conquered many a maiden's heart.

He dodged to avoid a direct hit to his dimpled chin.

And felt Kruger's fist connect with his solar plexus.

"Oh, merde," Peter grunted, clutching the edge of the bar. He lost his grip and felt himself slide toward the floor.

Another blow sent him plummeting down a hole as black as any miner's cage plunging to the bottom of a deep shaft.

Somewhere in the back of his spinning brain, he realized with disgust that his fall lacked the grace he generally exhibited in his better dying scenes. He felt himself lifted bodily from the barroom floor. *Gad*, it was humiliating. He hated giving a rotten performance, especially before such a subhuman audience.

In the next moment, the bouncer gave him the yo-heave-ho out the swinging doors.

Skidding beneath the hitching post, Peter landed in a pile of horse droppings between two passed-out miners.

As the "international star" of a dozen creaking melodramas gazed up at the brilliant blue sky, he instantly grasped the irony of his inelegant surroundings. He threw back his tawny head and took a good whiff. Lord, what a bloody pigsty he'd made of his life!

His head throbbing, Peter laughed like a crazy loon. And then, for want of anything better to do, the O'Rourkes's pride-'n-joy calmly passed out.

A smile of anticipated victory curled Mary Kate's rosy lips. Her nostrils flared prettily in the heat of battle.

She'd thrown down the gauntlet, confident that her father would never push her to the limit.

"I could not be more serious," she assured him.

Snorting like a testy old bull, Homer McGillacutty cursed under his breath. So Katie wanted to play rough, did she? Well, he'd never passed up a challenge in his life, and he'd be damned if he'd back down before such a ridiculous proposal!

Marry a drunk, indeed!

He refused to be bluffed. If the little spitfire got her way, she'd wrap a sapwit like Stokes around her finger and produce an inferior strain of grandchildren. Unfit heirs, that's what they'd be! Well, he wouldn't stand for it!

"You mean it?" he demanded, giving Kate one last chance to back out gracefully.

Katherine planted her fists on her hips and tilted her chin defiantly. "Absolutely. Lead on, dear Father, so I can meet the man of my dreams."

"All right, daughter. You're on!" he growled.

CHAPTER 2

Whoever said fools rush in where angels fear to tread must have been intimately acquainted with the McGillacuttys.

Grasping her arm firmly, Homer unceremoniously dragged his daughter out of the parlor, causing her to trip over the hall rug and the ceramic Boston pug that served as a doorstop.

"Wait, Father!" Katherine shouted, trying to regain her balance. She was down on one knee, her voluminous peacock blue skirts and the corner of her fringed shawl caught beneath her.

Homer paused, ready to meet her halfway at the first sign that she was tractable. He had a lot invested in this girl. Monetarily, a fortune. Not so much emotionally, but a damn sight more than she or her mother suspected, though obviously neither cared to find out how much. "Damn it, Kate!"

Katherine's temper was raging like an underground geothermal geyser. "Take your hands off me," she snapped, shifting so that she could regain a more solid, dignified footing. She drew herself up and eyed her sire with contempt, while she straightened her gown. "There!" she said. "I'm sure whoever my prospective husband is, he'll be more predisposed to marry me if I look presentable."

"This is ridiculous! You're a mule-headed, waspish—"

"'Useless female,'" she finished. "Isn't that how it goes, Father? But why turn my head with flattery? I'm much too stupid for that." She put her hand on the knob and yanked open the door. "Well? What are we waiting for? I thought you were in a big hurry to get me married off."

Her father growled a warning. "Katie . . ."

She entirely missed the pain in his utterance.

Even quaking in her boots, Katherine felt she had no choice but to swallow her pride and march out the door. Behind her lay her mother in a dead swoon on the parlor floor. But neither father nor daughter paused to worry about such an inconsequential matter at a time like this.

Homer McGillacutty slammed the front door behind him, nearly shattering the thick panes of stained glass. In all his born days he'd never been so irritated. For his own daughter to defy him was galling! How dare she go against all the decent values and common sense he and her mother had drummed into her. "Very well, daughter. Since you insist."

A dust devil swirled at his feet, and he blinked quickly to clear his vision. He grabbed his daughter's slender arm and took off toward the center of the business district.

"Of course, you know this is going to cost you," Katherine told her father, running to keep up with his long stride.

"Not nearly as much as it's going to cost you, Kate." Homer forged ahead like a runaway engine at top speed. "But you're right, it's going to cost me."

"I-I always thought you liked to get a good investment on your money." Katherine skidded along on the backs of her soft pumps, trying to slow him down.

"Just make sure you pick one that can give me a passel of grandchildren." Homer yanked hard, and Kate came back up onto her toes. She flew along like a grebe performing its frenzied mating dance on a lake's surface.

"Grand*sons*," she corrected. "Remember, you think women are 'useless' creatures, only fit to produce heirs."

"I intend to have someone to leave my money to," he said grimly.

People were starting to notice the two redheaded firebrands racing down C Street. Homer swerved to avoid a runaway buggy. He pulled her up onto the wooden sidewalk in front of the Pioneer Drug Store, and they paused to catch their breath.

Kate turned and stared down the street. From where she stood, she could see several bars and several "potential bridegrooms" sprawled in drunken stupors on the sidewalk and in the street. Suddenly she didn't feel so brave and defiant. A tiny shiver snaked up and down her spine.

Seeing her revulsion, her father chuckled. "Let's go home. I'll introduce you to a couple of fine fellows who work for me."

"No!" Kate cried indignantly. "I am not a side of beef or a stock certificate or the deed to a mine that you can barter."

"You *will* marry, Kate. Before the week is out," McGillacutty stated flatly. "I'm tired of being dangled on the end of a puppet string, while your mother spends my money as fast as I pull it out of that goddamned hole in the ground! She's a poor excuse for a wife, Kate, and I won't have you wind up the same way."

"I'm not—" Kate started to protest. She was shocked. How could her father say such things about her mother?

"No? Look at yourself, missy. Can you cook? Can you sew?"

"No, of course not. We have servants to do that," Katherine said defensively.

A glint of triumph appeared in his keen eyes. "You and your mother are a delight to the eyes, but good for nothing else!"

"How *dare* you, Papa? I know lots of things. I'm well read. I know how to organize a dinner party. I even paint landscapes—oils," she added self-importantly. Beneath her lashes she noticed the attention they were attracting. "Please, Father—"

"What do you know about *life*, daughter?" Homer demanded, his face florid with anger.

"What is there to know?" She laughed, for he took himself too seriously. "Life is just *here*"—she shrugged—"to enjoy."

Homer McGillacutty uttered a stream of profanity that would have shamed a muleskinner. Katherine turned crimson and tried to hide her face behind her shawl from the prying stares of several passersby. "You're in worse shape than I thought," her father roared. "I pour a fortune into educating and dressing and pampering my daughter, and how does she turn out!"

Deeply stung, Katherine turned up her nose snootily. "*I* am a lady," she quietly announced.

"Humph! Depends on your definition of a lady," said her red-faced father.

"I have my definition; you have yours," Kate told him loftily.

Homer shifted his cigar stub to the other corner of his mouth. "You still want to see a 'real man'?"

"If it will complete my education," his daughter snipped, folding her arms across her chest and refusing to be intimidated.

"Ready?" McGillacutty offered his arm, and with elaborate ceremony, Kate accepted it. They marched up the block, his boots thudding like drums marking out a criminal's last walk to the gallows, and her light heels clicking on the wooden sidewalk like a fandango dancer's castanets. They had both reached the point where their primary goal was simply to irritate the hell out of each other, not find Katherine a husband.

Homer meant to bring her pride down a notch, and she intended to prove she could dish it up as good as she got.

They stopped in front of O'Toole's Saloon. The only patron on the sidewalk was an old man with most of his teeth gone; the top of his scalp was scarred.

"Poor fellow." Homer shook his head. "Scalped by Injuns, frozen by winter snows, and worn out from the mines." He glanced at his daughter and grinned devilishly. "Sorry, Kate. This one's too far gone to make you any brats. But he was a helluva man in his day."

He led her a few doors down to Cap's Place. Here it was much the same: the men were miners, two killing time till lung fever finished them off; the other using a cheap painkiller to ease his arthritis. "Extremes of temperature," Homer explained, already moving on.

Katherine glanced into the corner millinery shop window, appalled by the garish hat on display. Red cherries and bright orange feathers dripped from the brim; it was beyond comment. Her arm receiving an impatient tug, she reluctantly focused her attention on the male population strewn about in front of the Bucket of Blood Saloon.

They were a scurvy lot, all five of them. Filthy. Torn, disheveled clothing, scuffed boots, pathetic specimens. All but one were unshaven.

Katherine shrugged and started to move on, knowing that even in his present mood, her father meant only to torment and humiliate her.

"Now we come to the cream of the crop," her father said sardonically, removing a new cigar from the box under his arm. He clipped one end and chucked it at a long-legged male sleeping between two tethered horses. "Well, daughter?"

Kate yawned elaborately, the back of her slender hand politely raised to her lips.

"Sure you don't see anything you like?" Homer went over and with his boot flipped over each of the five.

"Harvey," he commented, nudging a man in buckskin with his toe. "Scout for the army. Might still have a few good years in him."

"No, thank you, Father," Katherine barely managed to sound amused; she was anything but.

"And here's old Pappy Cavanaugh. Celebrating the birth of his twelfth son, lucky dog."

The man was a strapping miner, perhaps forty. He had

a well-muscled physique. And a wedding ring—thank the Lord for that!

Katherine feigned interest. "Too bad he's married." She crouched, ostensibly to get a better look, and tweaked his limp bicep between thumb and forefinger. "Impressive."

Homer's toe nudged another drunk. "Walt Whitaker. Another one that's married."

"Too bad. Well, I guess all the good ones are spoken for. We might as well go home."

"Not so fast, missy. Sam Tillets is single." Her father bent down and raised up a grinning head by the hair. The object of their discussion belched and scratched a fly off his nose.

"Of course, Sam's a half-wit," Homer continued. He stepped off the sidewalk and moved on to his last candidate, who lay with a stupid smile on his face under the hitching post.

Katherine was getting tired of this game. "Come on, Father, you've had your little joke. You've shown me enough 'real men' for one day. It's hot, and I'm in the mood for cold lemonade, not—" She paused, her eyes sweeping over the tall, lean male sprawled beneath the hitching post.

Instantly she was struck by the unconventionality of his dress. His boots looked to be of imported soft leather, tapering over muscular calves like a second skin. His trousers were light blue and indecently tight. Mary Kate gulped, taking in the full revelation of his masculine power. Starting where his trousers rode low on narrow hips, her gaze continued past taut bulges to where long, sinewy thighs and perfect knees disappeared into the tops of his incredible boots!

With supreme effort, she forced her eyes upward.

Here, too, the gods were too cruel!

Open at the throat and loosely laced, his torn but costly looking linen shirt led her instantly to speculate upon the short golden curls on his chest and the wide shoulders beneath. The full sleeves gathered around strong, elegant-looking wrists. His hands were long and tapered, and she spied a large signet ring on his right hand.

Kate's heart surged with unexpected pleasure. This one wasn't married! She continued her perusal.

Homer McGillacutty was not blind or stupid. He saw the sudden interest in his daughter's face, and so he turned a critical eye on the stranger. "Damn greenhorn!" he ventured.

Katherine raised her eyes. "Not one of your local yokels?" she inquired sweetly.

As she had done over Paddy's body, Kate bent to take a better look. What she saw took her breath away.

Thick blond locks, waving nearly to his shoulders, framed the face of what had to be a fallen angel. His nose was medium long with a straight bridge. Lashes and brows like burnished bronze drew her eyes upward to a straight, high forehead, fair to look upon.

Licking her lips with a strange excitement she'd never felt before, Katherine's gaze dropped to a strong, wide mouth that curved almost as if its owner found the world something of a joke. His cheeks bore the imprint of dimples, and his slightly square chin sported a deep cleft.

He was godlike. Olympian! Poet and athlete combined in one gorgeous body.

Mary Katherine tottered unsteadily as she crouched beside him. She forgot her father entirely, or that the hem of her skirts collected the residue of C Street's equine population. What she looked upon rivaled the artistry of Michelangelo. This particular living sculpture left her weak and trembling inside.

Reaching out, Kate lightly touched the man's lips. Mere curiosity made her do it. She had to know what they felt like. It was the sort of thing every girl has to do once before she dies, or know she has lived in vain.

Holding her breath, Kate drew her forefinger across the divide, tracing his smile. Before she could withdraw, she felt her finger suddenly drawn—no, *sucked!*—into a warm, moist cavern. His lips closed around her finger, and she felt his tongue and teeth teasing the tip.

As if an electric shock had passed through her body, Katherine lurched backward, landing on her ruffled bottom. Her cheeks flaming with embarrassment and shock, she screeched.

"This must be your lucky day," her father rumbled behind her.

Peter Casey O'Rourke lazily opened his eyes. He found himself staring up at the most divinely endowed, rosy-cheeked creature, with lips so soft and moistly parted that his baser instincts were instantly set in motion.

Eyes of green fire brought back a fleeting memory of the Aegean Sea, where he had vacationed once with a Greek princess. She was exquisite, this wide-eyed enchantress, with masses of deep auburn hair set ablaze by the western sun behind her. Certainly no such beauty e'er trod the earth, he fantasized, oddly content to remain in the Stygian underworld to which he seemed to have been consigned.

But as O'Rourke's gaze wandered over this lovely apparition again, he began to think she might not be so ethereal and unattainable after all. Her skirts rode high around her knees, with petticoat upon petticoat swirling invitingly around slender ankles.

Peter closed his eyes for a brief second and swallowed hard. Milkmaid or goddess? he pondered. Tormenting angel or aerie sprite?

Then he saw this vision of sweetly curvaceous femininity rise to her feet. The rustle of her petticoats made him think of angel's wings. She stood framed in a circle of light, the sun blinding his senses. Somehow Peter knew he had died and gone to heaven.

But then she stuck her finger—the finger he'd sucked and caressed—in her luscious mouth! To O'Rourke, it seemed both the most incredibly innocent and wicked invitation he'd ever received. Again, a sexual charge lashed through him. He guffawed at his own too-ridiculous, too-automatic response. Truly he was a hopeless case. Couldn't even control himself before the heavenliest of beings. He assumed she was his own personally assigned angel.

"Well, daughter?" The question accompanied the impatient prod of a boot against O'Rourke's right leg.

Peter frowned up at the tall, scowling male figure standing beside the beautiful vision in peacock blue. Clouds of smoke rose about thick tufts of disheveled red hair. Glaring down at him beneath heavy dark brows were the fiercest, piercing gray-green eyes he'd ever encountered.

Peter closed his eyes and groaned. Bloody hell. Brought back to life in Virginia City! And if he knew anything about human nature, Lucifer and his daughter had something planned for him that was likely to make his life a hell on earth!

Startled out of her reverie, Katherine gave herself a mental shake to break the spell. Upon her response possibly hinged the whole of her future. This was no time to get carried away. Just because the man on the ground *looked* like every woman's dream didn't mean he might not turn into her worst nightmare!

Still, she pondered, weighing the pros and cons; she *was* in a particularly bad spot. Her father meant to marry her off, so why not have some say about her own destiny?

Despite his obvious overindulgence, the man's dimples suggested a sense of humor. Moreover, he looked fairly intelligent. Perhaps she could marry him—in name only, of *course!* She would make a deal, whereby she paid him for the temporary use of his name. Just long enough for her to get a healthy monetary settlement from her father and skip out of town. She had always wanted to visit San Francisco, she reminded herself. While there she could get an annulment and then take the train back to Chicago, where Clarence would be waiting for her.

Congratulating herself on finding a way to outsmart her father, Katherine walked around the sprawled figure, examining him carefully from all angles. At least she wouldn't have to stand up in church with a total embarrassment. He looked a little gaunt around the cheekbones; no doubt down on his luck. She should have no difficulty getting him to agree to her scheme.

Kate bent over and raised one of O'Rourke's closed eyelids. A green eye peered back at her under a lowered brow. "Very well, Father," she said in a clear loud voice, "I'll take this one."

'Take this one?' What the devil's going on? Peter asked himself, as he slowly emerged from the fog of too much grog, too little food, and definitely too much of the Bucket of Blood's brand of hospitality. He pushed himself to a sitting position, just in time for a bucketful of trough water to douse him thoroughly.

"What the hell?" he complained and lay back down.

"My daughter has picked you out as the one," a gruff voice overhead informed him.

To Peter, it sounded like the voice of doom. He opened one eye cautiously, wondering if he could have been so drunk that he'd seduced the man's daughter without even remembering.

Not a chance, he told himself. *Drunk or sober, I'd remember this one.* "You can't hang this one on me." He lay there, intending to ignore the pair until they went away. "Be off with you," he said. "I know my rights. I'm entitled to a little peace and quiet."

"We need to get him sobered up first," he heard the girl whisper.

"Good thinking, Kate," agreed her father. He meant to have a talk with the man. His daughter wasn't going to make any rash decisions without his help. "Hey, Mahoney, how's about you and Will helping me get this greenhorn up to my place?"

"Sure thing," said Mahoney.

"Sure thing," said Will.

Or was it the other way around? Peter wasn't sure, but obviously the man and his daughter weren't deterred

one iota from their private mission by his simply closing
his eyes and ignoring the whole ignorant lot.

Suddenly a half dozen pairs of hands laid hold of him.
Airborne the next minute, he felt himself falling . . .
falling . . . descending at a great rate of speed—

Into a bloody horse trough!

He came up spluttering and flapping out of the most
disagreeable bath he'd ever taken. Shaking the hair
from his eyes, he lurched to the center of the street, cold
sober.

"What the *hell* do you think you're doing?" Peter
roared in his most stentorian Shakespearean tones from
the diaphragm. His rounded vowels and clipped enun-
ciation made tin roofs rattle and wooden storefronts and
rain barrels echo in the dusty street. His fist raised, and
legs spread for steadier balance, he stood like an outraged god from Mt. Olympus, while his flashing green
eyes sought out his principle tormenters.

"I do believe he's more alert now, Papa."

Katherine strode forward, showing no more sense
than a gazelle walking up to a hungry lion. She stuck out
her hand to O'Rourke, her manner all businesslike.
"How do you do? I am Mary Katherine McGillacutty."

"Peter Casey O'Rourke, at your service." The tall
blond stranger grasped her hand, as if in friendly greeting, and pulled her toward him. As her slipper came
against his boot, he grasped her hip in his other hand
and levered her skyward.

Katherine screamed, feeling gravity fail her.

"Papa! Oh, help!" she cried. What was this maniac
doing? She clutched dizzily at O'Rourke's steel arm, as
she began to spin crazily. As he lowered her slow-motion,
she knew intuitively where she would land.

She did.

"Oh, my God!" she shrieked, feeling the trough's
green slime and debris seep through her lovely designer
gown from Paris.

Warm ooze crept through her undergarments, making

her think of creepy-crawly things that lived in ponds. Her shoe sank to the bottom of the tank. Squawking, she fished it out, and then dropped it when she saw what had already taken up residence.

"Ugh! Aah . . . *Eeeek!*"

Katherine cast away a tiny lizard. She hauled herself out of the wooden tank and emerged in a shower of muddy water.

The street was lined with men and a couple of gaudily dressed women. They were all laughing at her! Katherine glared at the man who had made her the laughing stock of this hayseed community.

Peter O'Rourke's face wore a mocking smile. "Enjoy your bath?" he asked.

Her hair was slimed. Katherine stared down at her dripping bodice. Her stomach rolled as she felt a string of green algae slide down her cheek.

"At least *you're* sobered up now," Kate remarked caustically. Feeling like a mud hen caught in a downpour, she spun on her heel and marched off to confer with Mama.

McGillacutty shook his head, laughing. Good! His daughter had finally met her comeuppance. The fellow had backbone. Homer liked that. Despite his strange way of dressing and long hair, O'Rourke should have no trouble handling his redheaded daughter.

"Young man, I expect you'd like to do the same to me," Homer told O'Rourke.

Peter regarded his cigar-smoking opponent, sizing him up. A broad dimple creased his cheek. "No, sir, I suspect I might be taking on a little more than I can handle right now."

"May I buy you a drink?" Homer offered, anxious to make amends.

"No, thanks. Never wise to drink on an empty stomach." Peter patted his lean waistline. "Haven't had much to eat lately."

McGillacutty eyed the man shrewdly. "Looking for a job are you?"

"I'd take just about anything." And O'Rourke's long fingers combed through his golden locks to neaten his appearance.

"What's your background, son?"

Peter hesitated, not quite sure how to answer. People didn't always take kindly to actors, counting them a lazy lot. He shrugged noncommittally. "I've done a little bit of everything."

"Good. I might have something for you," said Homer amiably. "But first, why don't you come up to the house and get cleaned up? Do you have any other clothes?"

"Lost all my work clothes." Peter strode along, instantly at ease beside his future employer. "I left a few things over at Mrs. Muldoon's Boarding House on B Street."

"Care to stop by there first?"

O'Rourke shook his head. "You know how it is, sir. I was a bit shy of the rent, so until I pay up, Mrs. Muldoon's not likely to part with my trunk."

"We'll send for it later," the older man decided, puffing away on his stogie. "First, we'll get you cleaned up and give you a good meal. Then we'll talk. I have a generous proposition I don't think you'll be able to refuse."

O'Rourke should have heard the warning bells. But his mind was already contemplating a plate of warm vittles. Thus he walked, as innocent of danger as original man, into the McGillacuttys's parlor late that afternoon.

After he met his future employer's charming brunette wife, Peter was ushered upstairs to a spare bedroom to clean up. As he prepared to descend, now sporting one of McGillacutty's bright plaid shirts, he ran into the daughter on the landing.

"You!" she spat out. Seconds from trying out some of her less-ladylike vocabulary on him, she remembered that Peter Casey O'Rourke, despicable as he was, might prove useful to her. She gave him a catlike smile, her green eyes devouring him with false cordiality. "How nice to see you again," she purred.

Peter could almost see her tail swish as she preened

and sized him up. He felt like a goldfish, waiting for her paw to strike. She'd done a better job of tidying up than he. Her shimmering gold silk dress, shot through with silver and blue, had a low-scooped neck. She was overdressed for a mining town, but Peter had seen enough Eastern women in similar fashions to appreciate her good taste.

"You shine like the sun, Miss McGillacutty." Peter bowed and stood aside to let her precede him down the stairs.

"I wonder—" She laid her hand on his arm, waylaying him. "I know it's rather forward of me on such short acquaintance, but could we speak privately? This will only take a minute, I assure you." Looking around furtively, Kate drew him into an alcove at the end of the upstairs hall.

"What's on your mind, Miss McGillacutty?" Peter asked, feeling like the spider's intended victim. "I believe your father is waiting for me downstairs in his study."

"My father intends to marry me off to some miner," Katherine whispered. "I have a proposition for you."

"Spare me." Peter rolled his eyes toward the ceiling. "This couldn't be the same thing your father has in mind, could it?"

"Quite possibly they are related, Mr. O'Rourke, but you see, I prefer to have you working for me." Kate squirmed uneasily, knowing she didn't have much time. She couldn't let her father get wind of her scheme. "Now all you have to do is marry me—"

"Marry you!" Now, marriage was the single-most terrifying word in the English language—at least to this Irishman. In the face of such danger, Peter Casey O'Rourke looked into her seductively slanted green eyes and laughed out loud. "Not likely."

"It would be a marriage of convenience, a temporary arrangement," Katherine hastily explained. "Just until I get to San Francisco, away from my father. I will pay you handsomely."

"Name your price," he invited, grinning rakishly. He

had no intention of accepting, but it amused him to lead her into quicksand.

Kate grabbed a figure out of the air. "A thousand dollars. How does that strike you?"

O'Rourke shrugged. "Not bad for a few minutes play at the altar, I suppose. I trust that's as far as my services would be required?"

"Naturally." She nodded vigorously, eager to reach an agreement.

"No groping in the dark?" He stared modestly down at his carefully manicured fingernails.

Katherine gasped. "Most certainly not!" she cried, clutching both hands to her wildly beating heart.

"That's good." Peter moved with graceful strength, so that Katherine stood trapped against the upstairs window in the alcove. "I've been a lot of things, but I don't much fancy being any little girl's *gigolo.*"

"*Gigolo!*" Katherine's mind reeled. What in God's name was she doing? Making a deal with the Devil? Why—why this man brought up things no gentleman would dream of saying to a lady!

"You heard me." Peter bent and kissed her softly parted lips.

His breath warmed her cheek as his mouth covered hers lightly. Katherine felt her knees collapse with shock. He didn't just kiss—oh, no, nothing so simple! This bore no resemblance to what Clarence and she did on the porch swing of a Saturday night. It was much more—well, it definitely wasn't—oh, goodness! Katherine gave up trying to analyze what he was doing.

For several delicious minutes, Peter O'Rourke continued to sample the juicy young baggage in his arms. *Such an innocent,* he laughed to himself. *Seducing her might be fun.*

Meanwhile Kate was slowly coming unraveled. A strange breathlessness threatened to destroy what good sense she had left, as confusing messages traveled all over her body, making her hot, then cold as goose bumps. What this man's kisses did wasn't decent. She would never dare confide how she felt to another living soul, let alone her personal journal.

Whatever his intentions, he certainly took his time!

He nibbled and tasted, teasing her senses until her head whirled. Katherine put both hands on her head to keep her hair from standing straight up. "W-will you *please*... marry... me?" she finally gasped, returning to their original discussion.

"Depends." His green eyes twinkled. He stood looking deeply into her eyes, while his thumb and forefinger caressed her dainty, trembling chin.

"On what?" she whispered, wrinkling her brow.

"I still haven't heard your father's proposition," he murmured, kissing her in a clandestine manner. "If he makes it worth my while, who knows?"

O'Rourke's amused expression sent Katherine's hopes plummeting. "You won't tell Papa about my plan, will you?" she asked anxiously.

"Miss McGillacutty, if you think I'm going to get myself involved in a contest of wills between two fiery-tempered people, you are sadly mistaken," Peter said. "On the other hand, if your father has a legitimate job for me and wants to throw you in to sweeten the pot, it might be worth considering."

Katherine hauled off and slapped O'Rourke across the cheek for wasting her time. "You crude, disgusting man!" she raved, raising her hand to smack him again.

O'Rourke grabbed her wrist and twisted it behind her back. His lips had gone white with anger. "I owe you one for that," he gritted, and turned her loose.

Katherine glared at him as she rubbed her wrist. "If I weren't so desperate, I would never have stooped to seeking your help," she said resentfully. "I should have known better."

"Aye, that you should. We men tend to stick together." He chuckled, his finger teasing a fiery ringlet all the way down to her soft breast before he released it.

"Imagine what you could do with a thousand dollars.

It would be the fastest marriage and annulment in the West."

Peter O'Rourke winced. On her tongue such words of careless contempt sounded uncomfortably like his own. He'd laughed his way through scores of romances with devil-may-care recklessness; always ridiculing and playing on other people's gullibility.

Suddenly, as his green eyes stared into her equally green ones, just the faintest twinge of discomfort crept into Peter's soul. He felt as if he'd caught a glimpse of himself mirrored back in feminine form. What he saw wasn't all that pretty. True, Katherine McGillacutty was still innocent and inexperienced in the ways of the world. But she was catching on a mite too fast, for his liking. Probably she was as vain and willful as the Irish rebel from Wexford who had rejected the witness of his parents' lives several years before! Somehow recognizing that fact made him really uneasy.

"Nobody believes in marriage anymore," Mary Kate reminded him silkily, perturbed by his silence.

"Take care, wench." Peter shook his finger in light admonition. "Only a fool makes light of such things." He turned and went downstairs to make a pact with the Devil himself.

CHAPTER 3

Since O'Rourke viewed Homer McGillacutty as his next meal, he figured it was incumbent upon him to get a proper fix on the man's income, interests, and motivation. If he did this correctly, he should be able to parlay himself into the winning circle.

Consequently, while he and Homer made small talk, smoked cigars, and drank bourbon together, Peter concentrated on getting to know the man seated behind the oversized desk of ponderosa pine.

Homer McGillacutty's study was probably the truest reflection of the man. Everything reflected a man preoccupied with business. His bookshelves were lined with everything from the classics and a Greek grammar to dog-eared geological and mining surveys put out by the U.S. government. Engineering reports from a company in San Francisco lay helter-skelter beside a bottle of whiskey and an unwashed shot glass.

Gleaming leather chairs and a well-worn couch made it apparent that the tycoon spent a great deal of time in this room. Probably even slept here on occasion. In one corner, an umbrella stand made out of an elephant's foot held rolled-up blueprints and specifications. A miner's helmet and lantern lay on the edge of his desk, strictly utilitarian—nothing decorative or proppish

about them. Their dented, dingy appearance told Peter
that both items probably saw frequent use on visits to the
Lucky Strike mine.

Every item in Homer's study was dusted and tidy, with
one notable exception: a college degree from Yale hung
crooked on the wall with a cobweb dripping from it. Its
owner's neglect to set it straight or dust it suggested he
regarded it as irrelevant to the way he made his living.

"Mining is the chief passion of my life," McGillacutty
admitted. He noticed that O'Rourke confined himself to
one drink and showed no signs of an insatiable thirst.

Peter browsed along shelves full of assay reports. He
scanned a report recommending an extensive hydrological
system to pipe water from the Tahoe Basin across the inter-
vening valley to Virginia City, and saw books in German,
French, and English on the latest mining techniques.

"You've read all these?" Peter asked, properly impressed.

Homer shrugged. "What I can. Sometimes run out of
time. I generally get Otto Kruger to translate the foreign
stuff."

"Kruger? You mean the bouncer at the saloon?"
O'Rourke shook his head in amazement. "Who'd have
thought that bruiser had anything going for him, other
than a vicious left hook?"

"Ran into him, did you?" McGillacutty chuckled. "Actually, Kruger is surprisingly well read. Used to be a
schoolteacher before he lost his wife to cholera on the
way out to the gold fields. He's never been the same
since."

"These Western United States do attract dreamers,"
Peter remarked, lifting a copy of *The History of the Paiutes:
Its People and Traditions* from the shelf. A newspaper clip-
ping fell out, and he found himself looking at a tintype
photograph of an Indian warrior. He put it back carefully, noting from the article that an uprising had taken
place only a few years prior.

"Tell me, O'Rourke, what brings you West? Gold? Or
are you just another man trying to forget his past?" the

wily old tycoon asked, studying his tall, lean-muscled guest. So far O'Rourke had asked a lot of questions but volunteered very little about himself.

"Neither. Curiosity, as much as anything, brought me out West."

"Every man is either running toward or from something," McGillacutty observed.

"I'm not running from anything. At least nobody has a price on my head. And I suspect any irate fathers have long ago stopped trying to chase me down," Peter said, making light of an ambitionless past.

"Haven't left a string of wives behind?" McGillacutty asked. "No broken hearts?"

Peter laughed. "A few slightly bruised hearts, perhaps, but nothing serious. Definitely no wives." He changed the subject, gesturing to the bookshelves. "You certainly have a wide variety of interests, sir."

Homer knew an artful dodger when he saw one. "So how have you been making a living, lad?"

"I'm a jack-of-all-trades, master of none." Peter decided all this was getting neither of them anywhere. "Look, sir, I know you invited me here for a reason. You want to know about me? Very well. I come from Wexford, Ireland. My family have lived on the same land for seven generations. They're fairly well off, and you could say I never had to worry about where my next meal was coming from." A sigh slipped out. "However, my carefree traveling days are over. My father has cut off my allowance, and I'm dead broke."

Grinning, Peter settled into one of the leather chairs, his left arm draped over the back. "If you have a job for a bum like me, I'd be pleased to accept."

McGillacutty eyed Peter O'Rourke speculatively. "You ever work in a mine?"

"No, sir, and I can't say I'm crazy about the idea," Peter replied with astonishing candor. What the hell? he figured. No point telling the man he'd enjoy sweating his balls off in a bloody mine. "I'll take sunshine over lung fever every time."

"Who wouldn't?" McGillacutty snorted. "But sometimes beggars can't be choosers."

"That's a fact, sir."

Oh, Gawd! Peter thought, *here it comes!* Well, maybe he could handle it long enough to get a couple of paychecks under his belt. Then he'd buy a stagecoach ticket and hightail it back to 'Frisco.

Or maybe he should reconsider Kate McGillacutty's offer. Easy money, no work. Still, he reminded himself, he hadn't sunk that low—yet.

"All my miners belong to the union," said Homer, purposely dragging out the suspense. "So that's out."

"I'm willing to work my way from the ground up," Peter said, meaning it literally.

The old redhead squinted through the smoke of his cigar. "Not interested in my daughter's proposition, I take it?"

O'Rourke's fingers stopped drumming on the arm of the leather chair. "You know she offered me money to marry her?"

"Hell, yes." McGillacutty walked to a small wooden door set into the side of the wall next to his desk. "You see this? Laundry chute passes right past my office, so I cut a hole in the wall. Whenever I want to know if the maid is making off with the linens or the laundress in the basement is earning her wages, I open the chute. I can even hear every uncharitable thought my wife mutters under her breath about me. Dandy invention."

Peter chuckled. "My hat goes off to you, sir."

"On occasion, I eavesdrop on houseguests. I've already put my own interpretation on certain lengthy silences in your conversation with my daughter, Mr. O'Rourke." Homer raised an eyebrow. "Perhaps you'd care to explain them to me?"

Peter nearly fell off his chair laughing. The old devil didn't miss a trick. "You've got me dead to rights, sir.

However, your daughter's virtue is intact. A few stolen kisses. No harm done," he said lightly.

"I take it you've had some experience with women?"

"In all honesty, 'tis probably one of the few skills I've managed to perfect thus far."

"A specialist, so to speak?"

O'Rourke saw the way the conversation was headed. McGillacutty looked as if he meant to hire him on as a stud. Quickly Peter reversed his strategy, deciding to downplay his offstage hobby. He needed a *job*. He did *not* want to get stuck with a spoiled rotten brat! Surely the best tactic was to convince McGillacutty that he was incapable of fidelity.

"More a weakness. Women have been a problem since I turned three." He sighed with great melancholy, putting his heart and soul into it. "I can still remember the day I peeked under the upstairs maid's petticoat. One flash of her beguiling thighs and ruffled rump, and I had my first erection. I'm afraid it's an incurable affliction."

"Bull!" McGillacutty snubbed out his cigar impatiently.

"'Tis the honest-to-God truth, sir!" Peter jumped to his feet, stuffing his hands in his pockets, for just the memory evoked a familiar gonadal response. "I've been fighting the urge for women ever since."

"I'm sure you have, O'Rourke." Homer broke into an affable grin. "But you have a few scruples left, it seems."

"I don't follow, sir."

"I mean, you're a devotee of the sport, yet reject the idea of being a kept man. I like that." McGillacutty strode over to the laundry chute door and flung it open. "Maddy, set the table for four tonight. Mr. O'Rourke is staying to dinner. And make it snappy!" his voice thundered through the metal shaft. He closed the chute, a humorous gleam in his eye. "That ought to keep my wife and daughter shaking in their boots until dinner."

"I'm sure they heard you, sir." Peter found himself liking this man more and more. "Uh, could we set aside the subject of women and, more specifically, your daughter? I'd be honored to work for you, if you have an opening, preferably aboveground."

"As it happens, I do have something." McGillacutty went to a map thumbtacked to the wall and tapped various places on the map while he described his holdings. They were as diverse as the man's library, and as ambitious and in touch with the local economy as the man himself.

"I don't often make a mistake about where I put my money, whether it be in a mine, machinery, horses—or men." He paused to fix O'Rourke with a keen look, as if to say he expected a great deal from anyone who worked for him. "I always get my money's worth."

"I'm a quick study," said Peter. "Show me once what you want done, and I'll do it."

Homer looked up suspiciously. It seemed to him that O'Rourke had an odd way of stating his willingness to learn the lumber business. But the meaning was clear enough, so he let it slide. He clapped a meaty hand on Peter's shoulder with the force of a hundred-pound hammer slamming down on an anvil.

"Good! Well, let's get to it, shall we? Right now, the mines are crying for timber. Can't keep 'em supplied fast enough. So I bought over three thousand acres of virgin forest, stretching all across the Sierra Nevada range"—he indicated the Tahoe Basin on the map—"and including lands up through the redwoods near Arcata and Mendocino."

O'Rourke's ears perked up. His own father had done well in timber, and he knew there was a fortune to be made. "I'd like to be a part of that," he affirmed, studying the vast territory the crusty old redhead had circled.

Smiling, McGillacutty lit up another cigar. "Ever do any logging, son?"

"No, but I can learn."

Homer stuck out his hand, and they shook. "You start for the logging camp next Monday. Meanwhile I'll take you around and show you how the timber is put to use in my mines and at the mill. I'll give you a lot of reading material, too. I presume you like to read?"

"Anything I can get my hands on, sir."

"I'll pay you thirty-six dollars for a six-day week. You're going to work your tail off to get it," McGillacutty warned.

Peter shrugged. "Hell, anything's better than being a miner."

"Don't ever say that around the Lucky Strike, lad. Mining is my life's blood. I need those men. But to keep 'em, I require strong timbers that will hold up." McGillacutty looped a friendly arm around O'Rourke's shoulders. "First off, you'll have to set up a sawmill to process raw timber. I'll lend you a book on that, too."

O'Rourke wondered if everything he needed to know lay between the pages of government booklets and pamphlets. Somehow he doubted it. "Thank you, sir. I can see I've got a lot to learn."

"And to sweeten the pot, I'll throw in Mary Kate." He squinted shrewdly, watching for O'Rourke's reaction.

Peter cleared his throat uncomfortably, then shook his head firmly. No way in hell was he going to get stuck with a bad-tempered redhead. Better to starve! "Sorry, sir, I can't. I appreciate the job, but not if it means *that*."

"I thought you told Kate you'd consider it, if I gave you a 'real job,'" McGillacutty said with a cagey grin.

"I said it, but I wasn't serious!"

"She needs a strong hand to keep her in line." McGillacutty scratched his head, as if the problem was beyond his ken.

"She plans to use marriage as a quick way to escape," Peter countered. "Trust me, sir. She plans to fly the coop."

"Take off, leave me high and dry, you think?" Thoughtfully chewing on his cigar, McGillacutty stared through a smoke ring.

"Exactly, sir. She'd take your money, pay off the poor numbskull who married her, and head for the nearest lawyer for an annulment." Peter was glad he was getting through to Homer McGillacutty. Aye, he decided, better to keep things completely aboveboard. "Naturally I refuse to be part of such a scheme," he added, crossing his arms over his chest.

"Somebody ought to teach that little twit a lesson, don't you agree?" Homer glanced up to find a scowl on O'Rourke's face, as stern and disapproving of his daughter as his own.

"She needs a good paddling, sir." Peter agreed that McGillacutty should set his household in order without delay. Clearly the man had let his beautiful daughter get away with entirely too much already. "Best nip it in the bud, sir."

"O'Rourke, I'm glad we've had this little chat." Kate's father clasped his hands behind his back, looking mighty relieved. "I'm a busy man with heavy responsibilities. The welfare of hundreds of men hangs over my head daily. What if Kate slips something over on me, while my back's turned?" He shook his head.

"I don't know what I could do." Peter shrugged. "I'll be up in the mountains, setting up a sawmill and logging."

Homer walked up and down, his brow furrowed deeply. "O'Rourke, you're a young man with a good head on your shoulders. You recognize a problem the minute you see it."

Peter smiled triumphantly. "I like to think I do."

"And my daughter's definitely a problem."

"No doubt about it, boss."

"She's a problem to me, O'Rourke, so I'm giving her to you. Now that she's your problem, what do you propose to do with her?"

McGillacutty's question produced a silence so profound that if a pin had dropped on his office floor it would have sounded like dynamite going off at the Comstock mine. Peter Casey O'Rourke heard the blood rush like a tornado through his ears, and his heart beat like voodoo drums—or quite possibly those were his knees knocking. *Oh, merde!* Peter agonized. *This man actually expects me to marry his daughter. I can't do it. I won't!* Tumble her? Maybe. But marriage? In Peter's book, that stood in a class all by itself.

"She's—ahem!—more of a problem than I'm prepared to take on." He gulped. "I'm really . . . not . . . the marrying kind."

"Not even as a favor to her old man? Look, O'Rourke, I can see you have your scruples." McGillacutty fixed a steady bead on Peter, his eyes flinty with purpose. "You could've taken my daughter up on her hare-brained scheme and walked out with a lot of cash, but you didn't."

"No, sir." Peter cleared his throat, now convinced he was an amateur player coming up against a casino dealer with a crooked deck. He shook his head to clear his brain.

"If you convinced Kate you'd be willing to go along with her bogus marriage, it would help me a great deal."

"I don't see how." Peter's voice bristled with skepticism. He could almost hear his beard grow while he contemplated his doom.

"It would give me time to deal with my wife, don't you see?" McGillacutty explained. "Maddy and I need time alone to iron out our differences. Now, if you'd just play along with Kate and say the words over at St. Mary's—"

Oh, Gawd! Peter groaned inwardly. *Here it comes. I'm about to pay for all my sins.*

McGillacutty consulted a big gold pocket watch, then stuck it back in his vest pocket. "Just take her off my hands for a month or two. She wants to go to San Francisco, so tell her you'll take her there. Only you take her into the High Sierras instead. Once she's there, lay down the law. Put her to work as a cook and laundress." The mining tycoon chortled, rubbing his hands together with unnecessary fiendishness, or so it seemed to O'Rourke. "Make her earn her keep."

"That's all very well for you to say, sir. But it's my neck on the chopping block, not yours," Peter reminded him. "Besides, marriage—well, 'tis not a frivolous matter, to be entered into lightly." He thought about his own parents,

who'd been married thirty years and were still very much
in love. What he'd seen of Mary Katherine McGillacutty
convinced him she was more capable of mayhem than of
being a helpmeet. His survival instincts still intact, Peter
stubbornly shook his head. "No, thank you, sir."

Homer eyed the reluctant suitor with mixed feelings.
He was glad to hear that O'Rourke, though an obvious
bounder, respected the institution of marriage. However, his resistance was irksome.

"Ah, but as long as the marriage isn't consummated,
it wouldn't be legally binding, now would it?" he argued.
"String her along, lad. Tell her you're as eager for an annulment as she is. By the time you bring her into line, I'll
have my domestic affairs whipped into shape here in Virginia City. You bring Kate back, she gets her damned
annulment, and I'll marry her off to my foreman."

"Why not marry her off to the foreman in the first
place?" O'Rourke wondered, searching for an out.

Homer shook his head. "Kate's dead set against anything I suggest. But she picked you. Think about it,
O'Rourke. Kate's willing to pay a thousand bucks. Consider that a bonus on top of your wages."

"My soul won't be worth a plugged nickel after a
month with your daughter." Peter smiled ruefully. "But
I'm going to make good on this job, and I appreciate the
chance to prove myself."

A devilish twinkle entered McGillacutty's eyes as he
squinted through cigar smoke at his future son-in-law.
"You'll make good. I feel it in my bones," he said cheerfully. "Though you've got your work cut out for you."

Emotionally O'Rourke felt like a well that had been
pumped dry. "To tell you the truth, Mr. McGillacutty,
all this talking has worked up a ferocious appetite."

"Glad to hear it, son." Homer put an arm around
Pete's shoulder, leading him toward the door. "Now, remember, don't let Kate suspect her old man's had
anything to do with you accepting her offer."

Peter grinned. "I can truthfully say this is one acting job I'm going to enjoy."

McGillacutty winked. "We'll teach her a thing or two, won't we, lad?"

"Absolutely, sir," Peter assured his employer, wondering if a master of deceit like McGillacutty really knew his daughter at all. If he was a gambling man, he'd lay heavy odds that Kate was going to be harder to deal with than a hungry bear looking for vittles in early spring.

The girl and her mother awaited them in the parlor. They were in a heated discussion of their own, which both immediately dropped as the two men crossed the threshold. Homer escorted his wife into the dining room, leaving Peter to do the honors for his daughter.

Digging her fingers into his rock-solid arm, Katherine scanned Peter's face anxiously. "Well?" she asked.

"He offered me a job, is all."

"Nothing else?" she persisted.

"Nothing as tempting as your offer, I assure you. Thirty-six dollars a week. I grabbed it."

"Fool!"

Holding her chair, he bent near. "I like to eat," he whispered in her ear. He lost no time in proving it, either, once they were all seated. Having settled the urgent question of a job, Peter loaded his plate three times and still had room left over for two slices of apple pie.

"Delicious," Peter said, rising afterward. "This is the best meal I've had in some time, and I fear I've overindulged. I believe a walk after supper would do me a world of good."

"Good idea." Homer turned to his daughter. "What about you, Kate? Perhaps you could show Mr. O'Rourke some of the local sights."

Kate's lip curled. "I just arrived from Chicago today," she reminded her father. "What could I show Mr. O'Rourke that he hasn't seen already? Unless there's another saloon or trough he'd care to drop into?"

Peter gave Kate an amiable smile. "Perhaps your daughter will be pleased to learn there are more cultural diversions in Virginia City than generally meet the eye." He turned to Mrs. McGillacutty. "There's a fine newspaper, the *Territorial Enterprise,* famous for its editorials and scathing theatrical reviews. Or perhaps Miss Kate would care to visit Maguire's Opera House."

"Opera!" Now Kate was surprised.

"I'd be happy to take you on a tour backstage, if you'd care to accompany me?" Peter crooked his arm invitingly.

Kate looked at her father, trying to fathom what was going on behind his bland expression.

"Take a light wrap, daughter," Homer suggested, as if he didn't have a lot riding on the pair. "It gets cool after sundown."

"I imagine we shall be gone no more than half an hour, sir," Peter said.

Homer's gray-green eyes met the younger man's clear green gaze in silent communication. "Take all the time you need, son," was all he said.

"Where did you say . . . this . . . opera house . . . is?" Kate panted, trotting along at his side like a puppy. "Slow down, will you? I thought this was going to be . . . a walk."

O'Rourke paused at the corner and looked down at her. "Have you seen me do anything but walk?" he asked pleasantly.

Katherine clutched her right side, which had a stitch from running after a heavy meal. "Damn you, O'Rourke!" she gasped. "Have you no manners at all?"

"No more than you, miss." Peter assumed a more conversational pace. "So how's your plan to outwit your father going? Find another accomplice yet?" he asked casually.

"No, I—well, you practically turned me down," Kate complained.

"Rethinking your strategy?"

"I may have to," she admitted. "One thing's certain. I'm getting out of Virginia City, with or without your help."

Peter peered inside the pharmacy, which had a few tables and a refreshment counter. "I wonder if they serve ices?" he speculated out loud. "Shall we find out?"

Kate nodded, glad for a chance to rest. "I'll pay," she said.

Oh, you'll pay, darlin', he snickered to himself. *Through the nose.* "Come on, little girl," he said and bowed her inside with cavalier politeness.

The shop was small and dingy, lit by two kerosene lamps. They seated themselves at a table with a checkered oilcloth.

"Two sarsaparillas, please," Peter ordered with aplomb.

"Mr. O'Rourke, I don't drink," Kate primly informed him.

Peter grinned. "A teetotaler, my, my," he said. When they were served, he waved toward her glass. "Go ahead. I'm not trying to get you drunk or anything."

"I never said you were," she said crossly, and to prove she could hold her liquor, she took a gingerly sip. The drink was delicious and definitely nonalcoholic. She looked at him as if he had intentionally deceived her.

Peter raised his eyebrows. "Trust me, Katherine," he said silkily. "Would I mislead you?"

"One sarsaparilla isn't much upon which to build a foundation of trust."

"True, but it's a beginning." He leaned forward on his elbows. "Tell you what: because I have a weak spot for damsels in distress, I've decided to come to your rescue."

"Meaning?" Kate drained her glass thirstily and ordered another.

"I'm prepared to make the supreme sacrifice and offer my hand in marriage." He laughed, and his dimples leapt out at her disconcertingly. It was one of his trademarks, and he knew how to use them to good effect.

"You've got that backwards. The bride's father gives her hand in marriage," she whispered, confident of her etiquette. She glanced around, hoping they hadn't been overheard.

"Ordinarily, but let's leave Papa out of this. You did the proposing," Peter reminded her. "I'm just accepting."

"Strictly a formality. Agreed?"

"I wouldn't have it any other way," he said, meaning every word. "So when do I get my thousand dollars?"

"After the wedding, when you put me on the stage for San Francisco." Her green eyes sparkled with mischief.

Peter finished his beverage and stood. "Pay the man, Miss McGillacutty, and let's be on our way."

She fished around in her tiny purse, found some coins, and left them on the table. Startled when he casually placed her wrap around her, she looked up at him over her shoulder. To Peter, it seemed the most natural thing in the world to do, so he kissed her. Right there, in front of the proprietor and four other patrons, Peter kissed her right on the lips.

"Mr. O'Rourke!" Kate protested, drawing back.

"You've just been impossibly compromised," he informed her. "Now your father will be forced to let us marry."

She saw at once that he'd done it before witnesses for her benefit. "Yes." She uttered a dramatic sigh. "I suspect you're correct."

"Resign yourself to your fate, Mary Kathcrinc McGillacutty," Peter said in his best villain's voice. He led her out onto the sidewalk and looked up and down the street. A brilliant sunset of russets and pinks and purples blazed across the sky. O'Rourke took a deep breath, expanding his chest, and slowly letting it out. *That was the easy part,* he told himself. *The worst is yet to come.*

"What shall we do next?" Katherine slipped her hand beneath his arm. She looked truly relieved, now that he'd agreed to assist in her escape from her father and this town.

"We're off to Maguire's! If we go back too soon and

spring this marriage idea on your parents, they might get suspicious."

Katherine looked up at her accomplice with shining eyes. "Lead on, Macduff," she said, unaware that her words caused O'Rourke to do a double take.

"With pleasure." Peter tucked her woolen wrap around her chin.

Just leading a lamb to the slaughter, he told himself, feeling quite wolfish.

CHAPTER 4

It was still early, and Maguire's curtain didn't go up until eight. That left him a full hour and a half to take Miss McGillacutty on a leisurely backstage tour and still get her back home at a decent hour.

As soon as he took her up on her "business proposition," Peter noticed an immediate change in her attitude toward him. Evidently she considered him someone she could take into her confidence. Almost a trusted friend. Peter considered that extremely naive of her. He smiled, watching her chat animatedly about San Francisco.

"When you get to San Francisco, you must visit the Jenny Lind Theatre," said O'Rourke, as they turned into the dimly lit alley behind the Opera House.

"Is it very grand?" Kate asked. "I mean, I saw a couple of plays in London and Paris last year. Will it be anything like that?" She looked up at him, wide-eyed, and Peter chuckled. She was so eager! Putting this scheme of her father's over on her was going to be so easy, it was almost immoral, he thought, seeing himself as a sort of double agent.

"Don't get your hopes too high," he cautioned. "Few playhouses I've seen in the States rival the great opera houses of Vienna, Paris, or Milan even remotely." He nodded pleasantly to the man at the stage door entrance. "Good evening, Tucker."

Tucker looked surprised. "Mr. O'Rourke? Why, sir, what a surprise!"

"Mind if I show Miss McGillacutty around backstage?" Peter indicated his female companion. "She's come all the way from Chicago just to see what Maguire's looks like," he added, with a wink to Kate.

"Of course, of course!" The man hastily opened the door and scurried into the corridor ahead of them. He turned up the lamp on the wall. "I'll fire up the footlights, so your lady friend can get a proper look at the stage." Tucker disappeared behind a stack of scenery flats.

"You liar!" Katherine whispered, lightly striking O'Rourke's arm. "You know perfectly well I didn't come from Chicago to—"

"Sshhh! It makes the old fellow feel important, so what's the harm?" Peter led her into the wings, where for several minutes he demonstrated how various levers controlled the flies and curtains.

"How do you know so much about what goes on backstage?" Kate asked, clearly awed with the way he could change scenes with a few strong pulls on the ropes.

"I used to watch a friend perform from the wings. Anyone can learn. Here," he took her hand and placed it on a lever. He kept his hand on hers, and she stared at their joined hands, nearly forgetting what he was explaining.

"That's remarkable," she murmured, and a hot flush crept into her cheeks because he stood so near.

O'Rourke was busy looking up toward the darkened catwalk, checking to make sure everything was properly rigged. "This lever runs a set of gears. See? It activates the pulleys that move scenery across."

Katherine licked her lips excitedly. "What would

happen if I moved this?" she whispered, looking intently up at him.

"It creates the illusion of a panorama. The actors simulate some action, such as running or swimming, or . . . Here, let me show you." Peter stepped behind a flat and reappeared behind a four-foot wall of painted waves. He had stripped off his shirt, baring his chest. Beyond him lay a backdrop of ocean.

"What are you doing?" called Katherine, as he bent forward and began to move his arms like a swimmer.

"Swimming. Not very convincing, right? But if you move that lever forward—all the way, Kate! There!" he called as the machine kicked in. He performed a series of swimming strokes. "How's that?"

Katherine stood enthralled by the near realism. It was exciting to watch him fling his magnificent mane and breathe to the side. The muscles of his shoulders and arms bulged rhythmically as he defied the ocean's mighty waves.

Suddenly Peter began to flounder. He bobbed up and down. For an instant he vanished entirely from her sight, then shot to the surface. He struck out, desperately—or so it seemed to Kate—trying to save himself. He gasped, "A-a shark! I'm drowning . . . For the love of God, Kate! Don't just stand there. Save me!"

Caught up in the drama, Katherine rushed onstage from the wings. "Peter!" she cried, in a panic. "What must I do?"

O'Rourke stopped clowning and casually leaned against the moving wall of painted scenery. "Not a damn thing," he smirked. "Just turn off the bloody machine."

Katherine, her face turning hot, rushed to pull back on the lever. The machine came to a halt with a slight grind of metal gears.

Pulling his shirt back on, Peter sauntered over to

where she stood, covering her embarrassment with a show of anger.

"Realistic, isn't it?" He laughed. "Maybe you've heard of Adah Mencken? She was a smash hit here in Virginia City last spring. Rode a horse across this stage in front of a painted scrim of dangerous-looking mountain trails and crevices. The audience went wild, because of the special effects. Of course, she was half-naked. That could account for some of her popularity." O'Rourke gave Kate an appraising once-over, the look in his eyes unmistakable. "Adah's about your height, only heftier."

His fingers reached for a curl behind Kate's ear. She stepped back with a yelp and tripped over a loose coil of rope behind her. Grabbing it to steady herself, she triggered a lever. A fly rose in the air, and a sandbag crashed nearby.

"My gracious! Are you quite certain it's safe to be here?" She nervously moistened her lips.

"Don't worry. I'll save you," he teased. His arm swept around her waist, and he led her to center stage.

"Where . . . Where are we going?" Kate tried to pull away. His shirt was wide open, and she nervously eyed the fair hair curling around his small, dark nipples. Suddenly uneasy, Kate did her best not to notice his extraordinary chest muscles.

"I promised you the grand tour, remember?" Peter's dimples and white teeth flashed her a broad smile. He led Kate over to a swing and seated her. "I saw Lola Montez perform at the California Theater in 'Frisco." He placed both hands on the ornately decorated swing, rocking Kate back and forth. "She came down from the flies, singing a bawdy little song and swinging her legs in pretty pink tights."

He glanced down and read Mary Kate's mind as easily as a map. She looked petrified, as if she expected to be ravished on the spot. With the gas footlights casting long shadows, Kate looked like the pale heroine in a third-rate melodrama. Her soft mouth trembled delicately, as she stared up at him as if he was the dastardly villain.

Peter laughed softly. Possibly there was a way to get out of marrying this spitfire, no matter how much she and her father had their hearts set upon it. The trick was to get Kate to back out, without jeopardizing his job.

But how? Peter studied his beautiful companion for clues. Obviously the little minx had a good imagination. Now *that* he could easily turn to his advantage! All he had to do was give her a bad-enough scare. Her father would never blame him if she rejected him as a suitor. Why not try? He'd be off the hook, and the job would soon be his. Besides, it would serve them right for involving him in their family squabbles.

Peter flipped Kate's skirts up over her knees and ran his hands up her calves. Before she could do more than utter a frightened shriek, he touched a button on the swing. The button controlled the motion of the apparatus, as did the guide wire he now grasped in his hands.

Kate kicked her feet, unintentionally giving him an enticing glimpse of trim ankles and calves. "O'Rourke, stop this machine!" she yelled, rising distressingly fast above the stage floor. Her eyes grew round as Peter pulled lustily on the wire. She went sailing out past the footlights and proscenium arch, over the front rows of the darkened theater.

"*Eeeiiahh!* Peter O'Rourke, let me down this instant!"

Peter steeled himself against her pleas. He yanked again, and she whizzed erratically toward stage left and back out again.

Kate's initial fright disappeared almost the instant it surfaced. A strange sense of elation came over her, as his strong tug propelled her higher. As she flew back and forth, she held on for dear life. But when she realized nothing worse was likely to happen to her, she laughed out loud and kicked her toes. Her bottom began to slide from the seat, and she quickly righted herself. Keeping a secure grip on the rope, she glared down at Peter.

The blackguard stood below her with a roguish smile on his face and began serenading her with a risqué song. Wretched fiend! Katherine gritted her teeth in the semblance of a smile. So he hoped to scare her, did he? Kate didn't know how she knew exactly, but she did. Well! she decided. She couldn't let him get away with it.

By releasing one hand from her death grip on the rope, she was able to lean way back, so that her head was lower than her bottom. Her auburn hair streamed behind her like a blazing banner. She waved her hand at him as she flew by overhead.

"Higher, O'Rourke," she demanded gamely. "This . . . is . . . marvelous!" Of course, it was a terrible lie. The knot in the pit of her stomach tightened, and Kate winged a silent prayer that she wouldn't lose her dinner. The ceiling raced crazily by, and she gasped as O'Rourke sent her into a sudden, spinning spiral.

Katherine closed her eyes, certain that she had turned five shades of bilious green. "This . . . is . . . fun!" she insisted weakly.

"Oh, hell!" O'Rourke said, relenting. It wasn't his plan to murder the twit, just scare the living bejesus out of her. He brought the swing speedily to the stage floor.

Suddenly Kate went limp as she spun dizzily in her descent. Five feet before she hit the floor, Peter dropped the cable and caught her in his arms, thoroughly ashamed of himself.

Mary Katherine leaned against him for support, while he gently set her feet on the ground. She was still wobbly and pale, her breathing shallow. Peter spotted the faint sprinkle of freckles across her nose and the pale sheen of perspiration on her delicate, milk-white skin, just before she turned her face against his bare chest.

Peter kept a steadying arm around her as she burrowed her feminine softness into his lean torso. Unconsciously she fit herself to him like the other half of a whole, and he felt instantly protective, and strangely vulnerable. Beneath his splayed fingers on her back, he made a mental note that she wasn't wearing the rigid whalebone corset into which most ladies of fashion trussed themselves. Her waist was wasp thin, but above it, pressed hotly against his racing heart, were young budding breasts, thrusting like tiny flaming arrows.

He couldn't accuse her, resting quietly in his arms, of being deliberately provocative, yet everything about her oozed seduction. Either that, or his mind was playing a cruel trick on him. This was the one female he mustn't get involved with, if he wanted to eat regularly.

Even so, out of habit he made an inventory of what she wore. The skimpy undergarments that lay between his hand and her bare skin were sheer gossamer beneath the silken gown. Already beset by sexual fever, this young despoiler of feminine charms caught the faint whiff of her lilac toilet water and groaned. In those few seconds while Kate clung to him, collecting her composure, O'Rourke nearly lost his completely.

Abruptly he recoiled, giving her shoulders a little shake. Katherine, her head lolling on her white swan's neck, turned slightly glazed green eyes on him, full of moot questions. Her lips parted softly—clearly an invitation to trouble!

Peter cleared his throat, torn between appeasing his natural appetites and preserving his sanity. "Uh, how would you like to see the costume and prop department?" he suggested with a boyish smile.

Ordinarily Peter might have sought out the privacy of a dressing room or the prompter's box beneath the stage. Both had played a prominent role in his offstage recreation with the fairer sex. Tonight, however, he prided himself on saving them both from a terrible mistake; he chose a room with nowhere to sit or lie down. He had to keep her moving, on her toes at all times. Aye, he would yet free himself from this snare.

Kate's mother had warned her to beware of wolves in sheep's clothing, but never a word about dashing Irish charmers with blond hair and bold green eyes. So naturally Kate promptly forgave the fright Peter had given her on the swing. How was he to know heights affected her?

Besides, the minute Peter O'Rourke's arms slipped around her, she felt safe again. An innocent set loose in a world of glamour, Kate took his invitation upstairs at face value. With such a handsome smile, how could she doubt Peter had anything but her best interests at heart? After all, he had agreed to help her out of a jam with her father. He was merely seeking to entertain her and keep her spirits up.

"You still look a little green around the gills," Peter observed with a satisfied smile, as he guided her toward a flight of narrow, winding stairs.

"You took me down a little too fast, that's all." Still wobbly, though happy for some unexplainable reason, Kate tried to act nonchalant beneath his amused gaze. "Just when I was starting to like it, too," she lied and, hiking her skirts, preceded him up the stairs.

"You'll like this much better," O'Rourke told her. "Don't look down if heights bother you."

Of course, the instant he said that, Kate glanced down. They were again in a spiral, but this time at least there was a solid step beneath her arch. Her heart gave a flutter of excitement, whether because of the altitude or his body pressed against her back she could not tell. They stood a second, while she recovered her breath; then she took the few remaining steps quickly.

The large, dark room they entered smelled musty and close.

"Ah, the smell of greasepaint." Peter turned up a gas jet on the wall. The lamplight played over his features, giving his dimples and cleft chin a somewhat diabolical aspect. He glanced around, pleased by his surroundings. "In all the world, there's no smell quite like it."

"My, you seem to know where everything is," Kate noticed, as he snatched a cape from the end of a rack of costumes, covering his golden chest with a flourish. In the next instant he plopped a broad cavalier's plumed hat upon his shining hair, and bowed low.

"Official costume for conducting milady through the costume department," he explained.

O'Rourke led Kate past several tall scenery flats, pointing out various costumes and telling her who had worn them for which role. Coming across a skimpy tunic of white gauze trimmed in gold, he held it up in front of her. "Adah Mencken's costume when she played in *Mazeppa*."

Katherine sniffed. "Hardly decent," was her only comment.

"Excuse me," Peter taunted. "I forgot what a paragon you are."

Katherine swung around, stung by his condescension. "I'm sure you and I have very different standards when it comes to women, Mr. O'Rourke."

He laughed, going around to the other side of the rack. "As a matter of fact, I tend to be picky. Nothing overripe or too green." He looked at her pointedly.

"Is that so!" Kate snapped, rising to her own defense.

Peter quirked an eyebrow at her and strolled to a rack of brocades, satins, and gaudy fabrics. He pulled out a simple, creamy-white gown and held it under her chin. "This is more your style, Kate. Virginal, yet tempting in its simplicity. Marie Sullivan wore this last," he told her with a big grin. "About your size, though not as well endowed on top." He tossed it, and she caught the dress, rather than let the shimmering folds become soiled on the loft's dusty floor.

"Here, try it on."

"I-I'd rather not," she stammered, backing away from him. She looked down at the beautiful dress. The skirt fell in smooth folds over the hip with none of the full, gathered look she was used to wearing. "It is beautiful," she admitted, stroking the satin between her fingers. "What character would wear a gown like this?"

"Juliet, a sweet heroine whose beauty quite stole away her lover's heart." He shrugged. "Both innocents, they were, with none of the defenses needed to ward off the world's cruelty and harsh reality."

Something of his own cynicism penetrated Kate's absorption with the gown. She looked up, surprised. "Why . . . You envy them, don't you, Peter? Romeo and Juliet, I mean."

If her concern touched him at all, Peter gave no sign. The corners of his mouth twisted in gentle irony, as he inclined his head toward the gown. "Try it on, Kate. Perhaps, just for a moment you, too, can shuffle off this mortal coil of nonsense we call adult sophistication." He glided behind her and began to unfasten her dress with light, practiced fingers.

"No, wait! You can't do that!" Kate protested, but he paid her no heed, merely holding her around the waist so she couldn't escape, while he worked the tiny buttons expertly. She felt a slight draft on her back as her gold silk gown suddenly swirled to the floor at her feet. Kate whirled, clutching the Juliet gown to her breasts. "Mr. O'Rourke, this is an outrage!"

"Don't be frightened, Miss McGillacutty." Aware he had her in a panic, his desire for sweet revenge resurfaced. "I'm your fiancé, remember?"

"Yes, but you needn't think that gives you any special

privileges." She ran her little pink tongue over her lips and blinked nervously.

"Skittish, Kate?" O'Rourke laughed, his glance taking in the soft, ripe swell of milk-white breasts. He could just see the coral nipples, already taut and puckered beneath her lacy chemise. "Put on the gown. I want to see what a total innocent looks like." His low, silky voice caressed her like warm sun dancing over her skin. "Think back to when you were fifteen or sixteen, Kate. Remember what it was like?"

He stalked closer, and Kate cringed, sure now that he had evil designs on her. O'Rourke hesitated. She looked so uncertain of herself. "How old are you, anyway?" He grasped her chin gently, searching out the truth in her eyes.

His whisper made shivers run up and down the backs of her legs. Katherine, struggling fiercely within herself, wondered what manner of man he was to toy with her, showing kindness one minute and deliberately trying to frighten her the next.

"Mr. O'Rourke, I'm nearly eighteen." She raised her chin bravely to show him she wasn't afraid of him. "I am not a child, and this game of yours doesn't interest me."

"This is no game," he assured her. "Put on the gown, Kate, or I shall be forced to believe you have designs on me."

Katherine's eyes grew round with dismay. "What!" She hastily threw the Juliet gown over her head and yanked it down. "There! Are you satisfied? Now kindly banish such foolish talk, this instant!"

"Ah, Juliet!" He reached out to straighten the golden kirtle around her hips, then led her to a large mirror. "Behold, all that's lacking is the bloom of innocence."

Peter picked up a brush on the dressing table, intending to add a touch of powdered rouge. But as his arm brushed in haste against her breast, nature added the touch he was seeking.

In that artless moment, she *was* Juliet—to his Romeo.

Gaping like a clumsy schoolboy, O'Rourke felt as if he'd recaptured a tiny part of his own lost innocence. Kate was divine in her simplicity, her pale skin surrounded by a fiery mass of tumbling auburn curls. Unexpectedly a lump tightened in his throat. He grappled for speech, as helpless as an actor whose lines had gone up in smoke. Desperate to cover his lapse, he turned to the Bard's familiar lines. He doffed his plumed hat and placed it over his heart.

"Alas, I have lost myself; I am not here;
This is not Romeo, he's some other where . . ."

Still in character, Peter turned Kate once more to the mirror, holding her by the shoulders. His voice a hypnotic, breathless whisper, he said,

"Look you at such a one,
She hath sworn that she will live chaste,
And in that sparing makes huge waste,
For beauty starved with her severity
Cuts beauty off from all posterity . . .
She hath forsworn to love, and in that vow
Do I live dead that live to tell it now."

Kate trembled as his bold eyes met hers in the glass. She scarcely dared to breathe. She knew he was only reciting the lines of some poet long dead and buried, yet it seemed a messenger's arrow had gone straight to her heart. For one heart-tripping second, she felt the world stand still. But then she saw his lips tighten into an amused smile.

"Such an innocent," Peter sighed and dropped his hands. "Alas, too green for picking." He returned the cape and hat to a peg, thus breaking the spell.

Kate pivoted hesitatingly toward him. Peter could see

the inevitable question in her eyes. "You . . . You do that extremely well," she said softly.

"I took a few elocution lessons in school," he said modestly. "But enough! It's time you got dressed. I'll wait downstairs." He frowned. "Hurry now. Mustn't keep your father waiting."

"But, O'Rourke," Kate began, confused by the abrupt change in his manner, "is there no more you wish to show me?"

Peter looked her up and down with a quirky smile on his lips. "Miss McGillacutty, you may find this entertaining, but frankly our little game has begun to bore me."

Katherine bit her lip, watching him disappear into the darkness. For just a second he'd almost had her convinced that he found her irresistible. *What a gift for acting he has,* she thought. Perhaps after they were married, she should suggest he accompany her to San Francisco. He could try out for the stage. Of course, she wasn't experienced in such matters, but surely a man with his exceptional good looks and thrilling voice could go far.

Sighing, she stepped out of the Juliet costume, carefully replacing it on the rack. She was just slipping into her own dress when she heard a rustle behind her. Thinking O'Rourke had returned to help her with her buttons, she blurted out, "Oh, thank goodness you're here. Could you help me?"

And then her eager smile faded.

Across the room she spied a man of perhaps thirty-five studying her. He wasn't nearly as tall as Peter, although he exuded an air of confidence with his thin mustache. He had dark brown hair and eyes, and he was coming straight toward her.

"Well, well, our new ingenue," the man purred, walking around her. "You make Miss Sullivan look like cold leftovers, my dear."

Kate clutched the front of her dress close and glared. "I don't know who you are, but—"

"Thomas Duncan of the San Francisco Repertory Company, at your service," he said with a mocking bow. His arm compassed her waist, and he pulled her up against him. At the same time, his free hand plucked her gown away so he could view her breasts. "Very nice, my dear."

Katherine slammed both fists against his chest and yanked herself from his grasp. "Take your filthy hands off me!" she yelled.

She whirled to quit the room before he could regain a hold on her, but he was too quick. He caught her wrists and brought them behind her back, pinning her to his barrel chest.

"Help! Peter, help me!" she screamed, kicking and thrashing.

"A prima donna, eh? Relax, sweet thing."

Indeed, the actor's appetite seemed whetted rather than dampened by her resistance. He laughed and lowered his head to kiss her.

"Ugh! Don't you dare touch me," Kate raged, dodging to avoid his encroaching kisses. "Oh, you filthy, rotten—" She kicked him in the shins.

"Be nice to me, kitten, and I'll see that your acting career goes far," Duncan promised as an incentive.

"You *idiot!* I only want to get as far from the likes of you as I can," Kate hollered.

Going on the offensive, she launched a mean assault of kicks and slaps, shoving and mauling the actor. While she defended herself against his unwelcome advances, she began to edge toward the door. Kate landed a particularly painful kick to his crotch, enough off center so as not to cripple him permanently, but agonizing nonetheless.

Dropping his cavalier attitude, Thomas Duncan flew into a rage and slapped her. Kate screamed wildly, more frightened than hurt. She was convinced she was fighting for her life—and her honor. As she staggered back from the blow, the actor grabbed her again, and her sleeve tore.

"Damn you!" she yelled and hit him in the solar plexus. Momentarily breathless, Duncan fell on top of her.

"Bitch!"

"Dog meat!"

"Enough," came a lazy drawl from the doorway. "Duncan, I believe my fiancée is trying to tell you she's not interested."

Duncan's head jerked around. He stared in confusion, trying to connect the disheveled redhead beneath him to the tall figure lounging against the wall.

"O'Rourke! What the hell are you doing here?"

"Just keeping an eye on the woman I plan to marry," Peter said calmly. He sauntered forward, his manner deceptively mild and civilized.

"Do you need any help, honey?" he asked Kate in an overly familiar tone.

Duncan, who knew when to back out of a fight, threw up his hands in a placating gesture. O'Rourke was taller and reputedly handy with his fists, although an amiable bloke when not provoked.

Kate squirmed out from under her assailant. "You two know each other?" she asked incredulously.

"We've met," Peter said casually. "Duncan, you've annoyed the lady long enough. Out." He jerked his thumb toward the door in a gesture of curt dismissal.

Thomas Duncan made as dignified an exit as he could, under the circumstances. "O'Rourke, you're welcome to her, Irish temper and all."

Peter leaned his broad shoulder against the doorjamb and studied the redheaded scrapper with new admiration. "Nice footwork," he commented. "Are you all right?"

"All right?" Kate snapped. She looked in the glass at her torn dress and bedraggled hair. "I look dreadful. My Paris gown is in tatters. I've lost one of my shoes, and I will probably never hear the end of this from my mother."

"She doesn't approve of you brawling?" Peter teased lightly. Coming over, he pulled together the back of her dress and began to button it. When he saw the rough red marks of Duncan's hand on her shoulder, he lowered his head to kiss the spot, wetting her skin with his tongue.

Katherine gasped, swung around angrily, and slapped at him, but he dodged away.

"Not you, too!"

"I was just trying to kiss away the pain," he grinned. Then he repented, deciding she'd had enough excitement for one evening. "Where's your wrap?"

"I don't know. Somewhere," she said, looking about her helplessly.

Peter retrieved the wool pelisse from the floor and brought it to her. "Dammit, I didn't mean for you to get such a nasty scare," he said gruffly.

He felt genuinely ashamed of himself for putting her in the path of danger. It wasn't his style to terrorize the gentler sex. Of course, he'd never felt disposed to give a female such a strong dose of her own medicine before, but Duncan's rough treatment was inexcusable. He had wanted only to keep Kate slightly off balance, so she would withdraw her offer.

By way of apology, Peter gave her shoulders a friendly little squeeze, then led her down the stairs and out the stage door.

The wind had risen, causing a considerable drop in the evening temperature. As he felt her lurch against him, O'Rourke steadied her with an arm around her waist.

Kate looked up at him dolefully. "I lost my shoe."

"I'll go back for it," he volunteered.

"No, please! Don't leave me here alone," Kate said.

Peter followed her gaze to the bold-eyed miners queued up in front of the theater on D Street.

"Right you are," he said and scooped her up in his arms.

"O'Rourke, put me down. I can walk."

"Like hell you can," O'Rourke contradicted and set off down the street, carrying what appeared to be a shopworn young doxy.

"I feel so conspicuous," Kate objected. Both arms

around his neck, she tried not to notice the catcalls they received from bystanders.

"Never mind." Peter walked briskly, ignoring the tickle of red curls on his neck. "I'll have you home in a trice."

Katherine snuggled close, absorbing comfort from the warmth exuding from his body. The wind was sharp, tugging at her clothing. She buried her face in Peter's shoulder, acquainting herself with his clean, masculine scent. A peek through her long russet lashes assured her that O'Rourke was interested only in taking her home as fast as his long stride could take them there.

"I hope I'm not too heavy," she whispered minutes later. She felt as light as thistledown and utterly safe in his strong arms.

Peter didn't answer, because he could already see her father standing on the veranda. The glow of McGillacutty's foul-smelling cigar flared like an incendiary bomb about to explode. Backing through the wooden picket gate, he shifted his prize and started to mount the porch steps. Out of the shadows a cigar butt soared like a meteor. Just as Peter reached the halfway point, an overhead gaslight spilled over the pair.

O'Rourke paused, slightly out of breath. He fully expected an improvisation with her father, but surely not what came next.

With a wounded roar, Homer McGillacutty's fist slammed into Peter's shoulder, nearly taking the three of them off the stairs backwards. Peter staggered and set down his burden.

Trying to regain her balance, Kate clutched at O'Rourke, her arms encircling his lean waist. "Father! What are you doing?" she protested.

One look at his daughter's disheveled appearance was all the damning evidence McGillacutty needed. His face flushed with the rage of betrayal, he gripped the banister, and glowered. "O'Rourke, what the hell did you do to my daughter?"

CHAPTER 5

McGillacutty advanced, rolling up his sleeves. "So this is the thanks I get for giving you a responsible job!"

Moving with the fast footwork of a man who excelled at stage swordplay, O'Rourke ducked behind a wide pillar on the veranda. McGillacutty wasn't such a bad actor himself, he decided; in all probability this was a ploy to enable him to bring up the bogus marriage.

Homer glared at the young man, whose lithe movements kept one step ahead of his own. He lunged clumsily forward to grasp O'Rourke, and missed. "Dammit, hold still, you young varmint!" he bellowed.

"Sir, your daughter and I—" Peter bounded over the porch railing to safety on the lawn below. "Be reasonable, Mr. McGillacutty. I assure you, my intentions are entirely honorable."

McGillacutty was too busy pursuing his daughter's apparent seducer through the shrubbery for more than incoherent rumbling sounds and a few curse words. O'Rourke might think it was a laughing matter, but Homer McGillacutty was deadly serious about defending his daughter's honor.

Kate came running down the steps behind her father. "Father, what's the matter with you?" she cried, completely taken aback by her father's actions. "Why are you doing this?"

Peter nearly burst out laughing. Homer was really overdoing his role as the Indignant Father. *Sliced ham,* he chuckled under his breath, neatly evading the red-faced, redheaded man.

Homer charged through a low-lying hydrangea, intent upon getting his hands on the upstart who had rewarded his generosity by attacking his daughter. "You seducing swine!" he raged, huffing and puffing angrily, while Kate hung on his back, trying to slow him down. "Don't interfere, Kate. Run get the sheriff."

"Papa, stop it, this instant!" pleaded Katherine, close to tears. "You're embarrassing me!" She pointed to their neighbors across the street, who were watching the free-for-all from their porch swing.

To Peter and Kate's relief, Homer decided not to put on a show for the whole town. With a mighty effort he pulled himself together. After all, he had a reputation to uphold. Homer never minded attracting attention if he was on the winning side of an argument. But to make a perfect ass of himself in public was something else!

Still glaring intimidatingly, McGillacutty swaggered his bulky shoulders and planted his feet on the lawn, as if defending his home turf, come hell or high water. He stuck out his jaw menacingly, reminding O'Rourke of a giant condor about to feast on a tiny chick. He laughed out loud, for his new employer could certainly use a few acting lessons. It wasn't necessary to get *this* worked up in order to put across this marriage idea to his feisty daughter.

Peter tried to give the Old Man a signal to cool down. But, for some reason, Homer took his levity the wrong way. Peter ducked as he saw the veins in his employer's neck bulge and his fists ball. *Egad!* The old redhead acted as if he really *had* seduced his daughter!

"Father, I don't know why you're so angry," Kate said, hoping to calm down her father. "Mr. O'Rourke showed me a very pleasant time. He even rescued me." She shot O'Rourke a glance to show she was on his side.

Homer looked unconvinced. A few feet away, O'Rourke remained poised on the balls of his feet, ready to take flight. The young scoundrel looked unruffled, neat in fact, and unnecessarily amused. Whereas his delicate Kate—! It made Homer's blood boil just to look at his daughter. She had left the house looking like a fashion plate. And now, after he'd entrusted her to O'Rourke, Katherine looked no better than a slattern who'd gotten into a Saturday-night bawdy-house brawl.

Homer pointedly ignored his wife, Madeleine, who stood in the doorway, wringing her hands. He stomped inside and stood waiting in the hall for the pair. "All right, you two. Come inside. And you'd better have a good explanation, or there's going to be some quick justice."

Katherine grinned encouragingly at Peter. "His bark is worse than his bite," she lied.

Peter shook his head. "I wonder if working for him is worth all this aggravation."

Kate pinched his arm to get him moving. "Remember, we made a deal," she whispered.

O'Rourke rolled his eyes heavenward and trudged up the porch steps. He sensed how a condemned man felt, walking that last mile to the gallows. *Why, God?* Why had he gotten involved with this family? If only he hadn't gotten rolled by those harpies a few days ago. If only he didn't have such a soft spot in his heart for women.

Women! he groaned inwardly. *They'll be the ruin of me yet!*

Bringing up the rear guard, Madeleine McGillacutty discreetly closed the front door and went to the kitchen to order lemonade.

"Perhaps it will cool a few tempers," she told the maid and returned to the parlor to await the explosion. Dynamite blasting at the mine had disturbed her peace all afternoon, but it was nothing to the noise coming from her husband's study.

Perhaps curiosity kept Peter from throwing up his hands on the whole impossible family and heading back into town. He had always been interested in what made human nature work. It was a natural result of years spent as an actor. At least that's what he told himself, as he watched father and daughter square off the minute McGillacutty sequestered them in his office.

The fiery old miner inspected Katherine's disheveled exterior with the thoroughness of a Pinkerton agent searching out a crime. He walked around her, taking into account the askew drape of her torn gown, the faint bruise on her shoulder, and the smudge on her cheek. He grunted at her shoeless foot and torn stocking, and sighed over her tumbling auburn curls. After a tense silence, he turned the full power of his accusing stare on O'Rourke.

"Of course you can explain all this?" he asked in mock politeness.

Kate felt it was her job to defend her appearance. "Father, it's all perfectly simple. Mr. O'Rourke took me for a walk and when we went to Maguire's, he put me on a swing, and my hair got all messy, don't you see? And then we went upstairs—"

"Upstairs?" Homer choked; his suspicious mind was way ahead of her. "*Where* upstairs? Surely not the International Hotel?"

"Don't be absurd, Papa." Kate gave her father an indignant look. "I took off my clothes to try on a costume."

"Hold it right there!" Her father held up his hand, not wanting to hear any more. He clasped his perspiring forehead with a genuinely pained expression. "You fought him off, didn't you, Kate?" he said hopefully. "Tell me that's how you came to look like this."

Kate giggled at the absurd conclusions to which he

was leaping. "No, Papa, Mr. O'Rourke let me try on a Juliet costume. You know—*Romeo and Juliet?* He recited the most divine poetry!" She included Peter in her mischievous smile. "You should have heard him, Papa."

Groaning, her father sank despondently into his leather desk chair. He passed his hands over his eyes, as if trying to blot out the mental picture of his sweet, innocent daughter being seduced by the handsome rake lounging nonchalantly against his office wall. O'Rourke seemed to be enjoying the recounting of his conquest. For a moment, Homer was tempted to haul his Colt .45 from the left-hand drawer of his desk and—

But Kate was blithely continuing her narrative.

For once too heartsick even to light up a cigar, McGillacutty grudgingly decided to delay the young man's ignoble end. But only until he determined how many bullets to waste on him, and where to fire them.

"Anyway, *afterward* Peter told me to get dressed, so I—" Kate turned to Peter, who cocked an eyebrow at her, as if even he was incredulous at her guileless stupidity. "Am I telling it right, Peter?" she asked.

If ever a man felt condemned by innuendo, Peter knew he was that man. However, he was determined not to go down in defeat without saying a few words in his own defense. "Your daughter has a truly amazing way with words, sir," O'Rourke cut in smoothly. "I beg you not to jump to any wrong conclusions."

"Surely you don't expect me to believe nothing happened?" McGillacutty snorted, gesturing to his daughter's untidy appearance. "What do you take me for?"

"I admit she looks a little rough around the edges, Mr. McGillacutty, but still intact." Peter gave his employer a significant look. "I assure you, sir, after our discussion this afternoon, I would never lay a hand on her."

"Well, that's not exactly true," Kate qualified, suddenly aware how all this might work to her advantage. "You *did* kiss me, Peter. You can't deny that." She flashed him a blinding smile. "Remember? You kissed me at the drugstore in front

of all those people. And later at the theater you kissed my
shoulder . . . and my neck. And you held me in your arms
and . . ."

Kate let her voice trail off suggestively. Her eyes
sparkled with triumph, as O'Rourke's face turned ashen,
and her father's face turned a deep shade of purple.
Now her father would have to let her marry O'Rourke,
and she would be free of his autocratic rule at last!

Homer bounded to his feet with a thud, and his big
fist pounded the desk. "O'Rourke! This is intolerable!"

"Sir, your daughter has twisted things all out of proportion." Peter felt like a man caught in a bear trap.

Both redheads were tricky devils, he realized too late.
He wished to hell he'd never laid eyes on either of them.
It made no difference that they'd seen him first. Deal or
no deal, job or no job, he wanted out—and badly!

"You dare to accuse my daughter of lying?" Homer's
gray-green eyes turned yellow in his anger. Like a
wounded old mountain lion on the prowl, he came out
from behind his desk to stalk Peter.

"Don't let him get away with it," Kate prompted,
happy to see her father so worked up.

Peter couldn't tell whose side she was on.

Homer was so intent upon defending her chastity, he
couldn't see straight. He grabbed O'Rourke's shirt—
actually, the one he'd lent the lad—and bellowed in his
face, "You took my little girl's virginity, you scoundrel!"

"No, sir, I did nothing of the kind." This was the first
time Peter had ever had to defend himself when he was
not guilty, and he went into shock. "I-I'm completely
blameless."

"Father, don't kill him!" Katherine screamed, seeing
that her father was bent on committing mayhem.

At this juncture, Madeleine McGillacutty threw open
the study door. "Homer! Stop this right now." She
rushed forward, her dark blue eyes flashing. Dainty but
feisty herself, she threw herself into the fray, pounding

on her estranged husband's broad back with a volley of ineffectual blows.

Just the fact that anything could restore such passion to a woman who had managed to hide behind a cool, ladylike façade for the past sixteen years stopped Homer dead in his tracks. No bull moose ever dropped faster during a charge against his opponent. Homer staggered back against his desk, knocking Madeleine to the floor. "Maddy," he said huskily, reaching to retrieve his wife.

Madeleine slapped away his great paw and rose gracefully in a swirl of rustling crinolines and silk. "Never mind me, Homer. You cannot kill this young man! If he did take advantage of Mary Kate, it's too late for violence."

Katherine caught sight of O'Rourke backing away toward the door. If she wasn't quick about it, he would be gone, and she would forever have herself to blame. She couldn't marry her father's foreman and spend the rest of her days in Virginia City! Seeing the error of her ways, she rushed forward and grasped O'Rourke's arm.

"Wait! Mother, Father, Mr. O'Rourke didn't seduce me," she said hastily. "I-I know how easily one could jump to that conclusion, but—"

"So you admit it." Peter's lips curled in wicked triumph.

Mr. and Mrs. McGillacutty stared dumbfounded at their daughter and the man whose arm she clasped to her bosom. They glanced at each other, as if to say, "What can a body believe anymore?"

Katherine talked fast. "I think I got a little carried away with enthusiasm, because you see—Mr. O'Rourke has persuaded me to be his wife."

"After all this? Nay, I withdraw my offer," Peter interrupted, trying to shake her off.

But Kate hung on with more tenacity than a terrier to a rat. "He kissed me in the drugstore *after* I consented to marry him." She modestly lowered her thick russet lashes for effect.

"Oh, my," whispered Madeleine. "Engaged, and so publicly."

"We'll send round for Father Manogue in the morning," Homer announced, looking immensely relieved. "I'm glad you're prepared to do the decent thing, O'Rourke."

"Sir, you know I'm not the marrying kind," Peter argued. Any second, he expected to become an ex-employee. "I've changed my mind."

And indeed he had! This wasn't the kind of family he wanted any part of. Why, oh, *why* hadn't he listened to his parents and settled down to farming back in Wexford? he lamented, looking from one fighting McGillacutty to another.

"Whether you tossed my daughter's skirts or not, she's been seriously compromised." McGillacutty reached for his favorite prop, a cheap cigar. "God only knows how many people in this town saw the two of you carrying on."

"And you, Mary Kate," her mother chided, "for shame! Such wanton disregard for your reputation!"

Peter groaned. "We weren't carrying on."

Katherine pressed her soft breast against his arm and looked up with adoring green eyes. "Peter, how can you go back on your word?" she whispered. "You *promised.*"

O'Rourke heard the night shift whistle blow in the distance. It seemed to sound his death knell. But it also reminded him of his desire to eat regularly. "Aye," he sighed, "you would remind me of that, Miss McGillacutty."

Why should he feel honor bound when Mary Katherine was such a conniving little liar? he asked himself. And how could he make promises before a priest to a spitfire who didn't know the meaning of the word *honor,* let alone *love* and *obey.*

Peter had always been conscientious about never signing his name on a contract unless he meant to perform. And now he'd given verbal consent to both Kate and her father. Under duress, to be sure, but—*ouch!* He should have walked away this afternoon, instead of digging himself in deeper. *"Listening to the devil is the first step on that long journey to hell,"* his sweet mother used to warn him.

Aye, Peter cursed himself for not seeing past his stomach. It just showed what happened when a man placed too much stock in three squares and a paycheck.

"If you don't go through with it, lad, I'll sue you for breach of promise," McGillacutty growled. "Or shoot you."

Madeleine McGillacutty, remembering the social amenities, stepped forward and took Peter's other arm, making him doubly a prisoner. "Mr. O'Rourke, I perceive that you're a man of breeding, even if you have fallen on hard times," she said in her soft Southern accent. "That you have done our daughter the honor of asking her hand in marriage speaks well of you."

O'Rourke despaired in silence. Mrs. McGillacutty seemed by far the most civilized of the clan, but he was too depressed to feel an excess of sympathy for any woman who'd get mixed up with Homer McGillacutty. She'd made her bed; let her lie in it! As for himself, he thought he might almost prefer a quick fall down a long mine shaft to a month of living with Mary Kate. He was already counting the minutes until he could return her to her father.

"Come, sir," Madeleine held out her hand to Homer with a smile. "We have lemonade and cookies waiting in the parlor. This calls for a celebration, does it not?"

Homer generally preferred a double Scotch on the rocks, but he decided the family had had enough domestic excitement for one evening, without getting in a row with his wife over his drinking habits. "Sounds like a grand idea, Maddy." He tucked his wife's hand under his arm and led the way across the hall to the parlor, leaving Peter to bring up the rear with Kate.

"Far be it from me to strangle the goose that lays the golden egg," Peter whispered in Mary Kate's ear.

"What's that?" asked Homer, sharp-eared. Standing before the fireplace, lemonade glass and cigar in hand, he looked very much the contented man.

Give the man what he wants, whether it be a new cigar or a temporary son-in-law, and he instantly loses his killer instincts and reverts to civilized blackmail. Whatever I do, Peter thought, *I mustn't underestimate the man.*

"Mr. O'Rourke was speaking metaphorically," Kate informed her puzzled parents. "He's quite the poet." She perched on a petit point chair and sipped her lemonade like a docile child.

Homer shrugged. "If you say so, daughter. O'Rourke, you'll not regret your decision to marry Kate."

"God works in mysterious ways, his wonders to perform," Madeleine mused aloud.

"Honestly, Mother," said Kate.

"Why blame God for man's stupidity?" Peter knew he had no one to kick but himself.

"Listen to the man!" Kate laughed nervously. "To hear him talk, you'd never guess that getting married is supposed to be a happy occasion."

"'True love is like ghosts, which everybody talks about and few have seen,'" Peter volunteered with an ironic smile.

Madeleine regarded her future son-in-law with awe. "My, you are well read," she said, "a philosopher *and* a poet."

"No, madam," he corrected. "Only a fool." He bowed in Kate's direction. "Like Romeo, 'I am Fortune's fool.'"

McGillacutty swallowed a seed from his lemonade. "Somehow, I don't see you and Kate as star-crossed lovers." He pulled his pocket watch from his vest pocket. "Nearly midnight, folks. Time for us all to sleep on the subject. By the way, O'Rourke, I had your trunk brought over from Mrs. Muldoon's. You'll stay as our guest, of course."

So there's no escaping my fate, thought Peter.

Homer clapped a heavy hand on Peter's shoulder. "We start early around here, lad. You and I will breakfast at five."

Peter groaned inwardly. He was used to cast parties that lasted till five in the morning; changing careers was going to take a wee bit of getting used to. "I'd appreciate a tap on the door, sir, just to make sure I'm up and moving about livelylike," he said with a lopsided grin.

"Four-thirty all right?"

"Perfect, sir," Peter said, more heartily than he felt. "I'll call it a night, then. If you'll excuse me?" Hand over heart, he bent over Mrs. McGillacutty's hand. He nodded less cordially toward Kate. "Miss McGillacutty."

Morning came around quickly. Peter staggered to his feet, bumping into things, in a strange room in the middle of the night. "Damn! Even roosters don't get up this early," he told his bleary-eyed image in the mirror, as he shaved by candlelight. If he'd known that being a reformed man meant getting up at such an ungodly hour, he never would have become one.

In Ireland, he'd rebelled against being a gentleman farmer—renting out land to tenants and sleeping in till eight—as quite appalling. Yet here he was, rising up to assault trees in the dead of night. A lumberman's hours were almost as bad as being an old dog with weak kidneys. Fortunately, even at four thirty-seven in the morning O'Rourke still retained his sense of humor, a bit tarnished perhaps, but intact. Regardless of how much his body protested, Peter was determined to give the first day of his new "career" a damn good go of it.

He rushed through his grooming, nicking himself twice. Then he tiptoed downstairs, only to find Homer had beat him. The old redhead stood by the stove, pouring himself a jolt of the thickest coffee Peter had ever seen. Homer wore a gray shirt with red suspenders, his mining helmet, black trousers, and heavy boots.

"Morning, son," he said cheerfully. "Grab a cup."

Peter obeyed, his reflexes slow, even though his spirit was willing. Right off, he saw where he'd have to do something about his wardrobe. He again wore McGillacutty's plaid shirt, for want of anything vaguely resembling work clothes. All his trousers were tight fitting, finely cut to give

the ladies a bit of excitement, and not fit for labor. His
boots were thin leather, strictly theatrical. Peter was just
working up toward asking for an advance on his salary to
buy clothing when Homer broached the subject.

"Anyone brave enough to drink my coffee deserves
some friendly advice." McGillacutty eyed his latest pro-
tégé critically.

O'Rourke tried to make light of the brew. "'Tis not
so bad, sir." Gamely he poured half a bowl of sugar into
the murky concoction and stirred vigorously, wondering
if the spoon might dissolve.

"This stuff's strong enough to strip paint off the metal
casings on mining equipment." McGillacutty chuckled.
"I hope you won't take offense, but"—he nodded toward
Peter's clothing—"you won't last long in those greenhorn duds if you wear 'em around my men."

"I was about to bring that up, sir."

"When in Rome," Homer suggested, "or be prepared
to use your fists a lot."

Peter sat eating overcooked pancakes and sausages
and sipping molasses-thick coffee with McGillacutty until
six thirty, when the rest of the family began to stir. By
then he realized that everything his employer did had a
dollar sign attached. In fact, McGillacutty's talent for
crazy-making was motivated by an insatiable desire to
expand his wealth. A master of intimidation, the man
left little to chance.

"Kate's not going to marry any Chicago playboy."
Homer fixed O'Rourke with a fiery gaze. "I've worked
too damned hard to see my money frittered away on
fancy French chapeaux and hot air balloon rides."

Peter avoided comment, knowing that McGillacutty
would probably disqualify him as a future employee and
temporary son-in-law if he ever got wind of his theatrical
background. In any event, Peter planned to stay with
McGillacutty only long-enough to learn everything there
was to learn about timber. One thing he could *not* envision was any long-range association with the man.

Even so, Homer McGillacutty's financial backing and other connections might prove useful in opening some important doors. If he played his cards right, he might be able to make himself a tidy fortune in a burgeoning industry. And then, as soon as he shook this wild carnivore and his clan off his back, he would leave, without so much as a backward glance.

That morning O'Rourke and McGillacutty toured the stamping mills, the steam-hoisting works, and the engine and pumping stations. Peter, on his own, revisited the carpentry shop and the battery. He asked questions of everyone, until he understood not only what transpired in the sorting and distribution departments, the ore house, the drying furnace, and the smelting and retorting rooms, but also how the men felt about their jobs and their boss. With growing interest, Peter learned the various steps involved, from extracting the raw ore all the way through the amalgamation processes.

The next day, following the miners' lead, he stripped down to work boots and a loin cloth and inspected mine shafts on various levels. He experienced the 125- to 150-degree heat firsthand. Later he read up on new technologies to reduce temperatures within the mines.

For three days he walked through Philip Deidesheimer's honeycomb system of supports with McGillacutty's foreman, Lew Simpson. Evenings he and Homer talked about projected lumber requirements to construct square sets in the mine, for Homer was as concerned about safety in the mines as he was about expansion.

Everywhere he went that week, O'Rourke saw things in terms of timber, all broken down into specifications and usages: firewood, flumes, building materials, bracing beams.

Peter had always had an eye for detail and had used it well in studying people. Now he used that same skill to advantage. He began to see his job not merely in terms of

serving the mine owner's needs but also for improving the
workers' living standards and homes. Virginia City was in
its infancy, as were Gold Hill, Silver City, and the silver and
gold mining camps springing up all over Gold Canyon.
Hundreds of prospectors, adventurers, and laborers were
coming across the Sierras from California every month.
Many lived in canvas tents; they would need houses before
the first snows fell. It couldn't be done overnight, but he
saw this influx as a potential source of vast wealth. In fact,
within the span of a few days O'Rourke underwent a profound change, as he realized that more money could be
made in a year in lumber than any band of touring actors
could earn in a lifetime.

Inspired by the chance to make a fortune, O'Rourke's
imagination took off. He read everything he could lay
his hands on from McGillacutty's library. He visited Joe
Goodman at the *Territorial Enterprise* about mining legis-
lation that was pending in Carson City. He saw Adolph
Sutro about the tunnel he was trying to raise money to
build; and he visited the Yellow Jacket Mine when he
heard about the owner's plans to expand.

Peter's "quick study" methods as an actor kept him so
busy absorbing information that the subject of marrying
Miss Mary Katherine McGillacutty conveniently slipped
his mind. He and Homer were up and out of the house
so early and returned so late each evening that Kate's existence never seriously intruded upon O'Rourke's
thinking. With neither the leisure nor the opportunity
to dwell on thoughts of the fairer sex, and thanks to
Homer's dedicated tutelage, he ate, drank, and dreamed
about timber, both raw and processed.

All week, bulk food supplies, clothes, tools, logging
and sawmill equipment were sent on ahead by ox-drawn
wagons to a base camp in the High Sierras. And on
Monday, September 26th, Peter knew, he was scheduled
to take the stagecoach to Strawberry Point, where he
would be met by veteran logger Jigger Jansen. From

there, they would travel on horseback and mule into some of the wildest country in the West.

Time was of the essence, and O'Rourke made every minute count. He took notes, listened to those with experience, and asked questions. By the time he fell into bed each night, he could barely remember his own name, much less worry about a certain scheming redhead, even after their engagement was announced in the local paper on Thursday evening. Indeed, the very fact that Homer McGillacutty never mentioned his daughter all week may have lulled O'Rourke into a false sense of security.

On Saturday evening, September 24th, all false hopes flew out the window.

Peter was enjoying a perfectly peaceful bath in the little room off the kitchen, soaking away a week's grime and tension in a hot tub. Humming contentedly, he puffed away on one of his employer's cigars, while he contemplated his left big toe from several angles.

Aahhh! It was a truly sublime moment.

He had earned his first week's pay—really earned it! After purchasing a pair of logger's cleats, a warm jacket, flannel shirts, and long underwear for the higher altitudes, he had splurged on a bar of fine English soap. And wonder of wonders, he still had eleven dollars left. Not much, but enough to open a small account at the Wells Fargo Bank.

Well on his way to prosperity, he congratulated himself.

Suddenly McGillacutty stuck his head in the doorway. "Father Manogue says he can fit you and Katie in at two o'clock tomorrow afternoon."

That bit of news damn near finished all his dreams of becoming a timber tycoon overnight.

Sloshing around in a tidal wave of alkaline water and silver dust, Peter barely saved himself from an untimely end. The soap flew out of his hands and skidded across the floor. His long, hairy legs flailed, as Peter considered his options: he could drown himself, or . . .

Take the marital dive!

He sank beneath the waves, tempted to end it all. But then years of reckless living surfaced to bolster his courage. Hell! No woman had ever yet sunk her hooks into the crafty younger son of Edward and Anne O'Rourke, he reasoned with lightning-witted agility.

Besides, his lungs were ready to burst!

Peter surfaced and squinted one eye at his employer. "Good, sir," he spluttered, "two o'clock sounds"—he gulped—"uh, fine. Could you hand me that towel?"

Homer grinned down at the blond giraffe in his bathtub. "Sorry I startled you, O'Rourke."

Peter laughed, a test of his bravado. "Startled? Who, me, sir? Actually I've been . . . looking forward to it," he lied.

Somehow Peter emerged from the tub unscathed, except for a bruise on his right shin. *Lord, save me from the scheming McGillacuttys,* he prayed, as he toweled himself down.

Peter might be a lot of things, but he was no fool. His behavior hadn't exactly put him in good standing with his Maker. He didn't expect any last-minute reprieve.

Doomed, that's what he was. His sins had finally caught up with him.

CHAPTER 6

Sunday, September 25th—a day destined to live on in infamy.

To most Storey County residents, it dawned like any other Indian summer day. But up on B Street, Mary Katherine McGillacutty was wringing her hands. O'Rourke had kept her awake half the night with his pacing, occasional muttering—and his odd silences, which were especially unsettling on the other side of the wall separating their bedrooms. Once she could almost have sworn he was praying! But of course she quickly dismissed *that* silly notion. Peter O'Rourke was much too cynical and worldly-wise for that.

Still, Kate was worried. What could possibly be causing him such unrest? What if he'd had a change of heart? She had to know, because if O'Rourke didn't help her escape this dreary little town, her father would surely marry her off to his mine foreman.

She stamped her foot, hearing her partner-in-crime curse again. She would wring his handsome neck if he failed her now. A promise was a promise, and she meant to hold him to it.

But this pacing like a tiger! Was he going to leave her high and dry at the altar?

Again Kate pressed her ear to the wall. She imagined

what might be going on in O'Rourke's head. Surely a
man like him would breeze through the ceremony, take
her money, and laugh all the way to the bank. It should
be the easiest money he'd ever made!

Calm down, she told herself, pausing to check herself
out in the mirror. Her large, luminous eyes had the
haunted look of a desperate woman. Well, no wonder.
This was not the first time she'd defied her father, and
while tricking Papa bothered Kate—a little—he left her
no choice. She was no pawn to be manipulated on a
chessboard! Papa could preach duty and submission till
his mine caved in. It would do him no good.

Anyway, what did he know about making a woman happy?
Kate thought rebelliously. *Look at Mother, shaking in her
boots and having to sneak around behind his back to have any
fun at all.* Well, no man was going to dictate to her.
Women had as much right to happiness as men did. She
shivered with excitement, thinking about her life in San
Francisco. She would have nobody to dictate who her
friends were, and nobody to complain about how much
money she spent, either. Being on her own was starting
to sound better and better!

Emphatically she would prove she wasn't a "useless
female" like Papa claimed. It might take awhile to discover her latent talents and carve a niche for herself in
this unmannered wasteland, but she knew she could suc-
ceed. Even after she paid off O'Rourke, she would have
enough of her marriage settlement left to give her a—
what had Father called it? Oh, yes, a grubstake!

Her spirits reviving, Katherine darted to her armoire
and pulled out the bridal gown she and her mother had
finally decided on. Her mother had insisted that she be
married in the finest wedding satin money could buy, so
off they had gone for an entire day's shopping in Carson
City. Despite all those trunks full of Paris fashions, how
could she resist one last splurge? Even if it *was* a silly old
wedding dress, the feather stole made her look like a
Christmas angel floating on a cloud.

Next door O'Rourke's voice rose just enough that she realized that he *was* praying! "Lord, I promise never to look at another woman, especially redheads, if only . . ." His voice drifted off.

Mary Kate's head whipped around so fast her neck popped. She glared at the wall. She'd had enough of O'Rourke's snide remarks, even if they were directed to the Almighty! Did he find helping her such a chore? Was she so unappealing to him, then? She ground her teeth, fighting to keep from telling him off—for a lady does not eavesdrop! But how could she not hear?

"If it be possible, let this cup pass," he groaned.

And there followed the most unbearable silence.

Kate smacked the wall as if it was his devilishly handsome face. "Damn you, O'Rourke!" she yelled. Then, turning scared, she laid her cheek to the cool, smooth surface and whispered, "You promised, you bastard. Don't you dare let me down."

A resounding thud was the only answer she got. As she slumped against the wall, she heard him resume pacing again. The faint odor of a cigar wafted through the air. It annoyed her no end. Must Peter O'Rourke acquire *all* her father's nasty habits?

"Do you have to smoke?" she complained, sliding down the wall onto her ruffled rump.

"You don't own me, Mary Kate." His low growl was so close that she actually looked to make sure he was still on his side of the wall. "I'll do as I damn well please," he told her.

"You could show me *some* consideration, at least till after we're married." And then she clapped her hand over her mouth, realizing what she'd said.

A good thing this isn't a real marriage, she told herself. Rising, she tossed the last petticoat over her head. She viciously yanked the tapes around her waist. That was just the problem with most marriages, she thought: lack of consideration. *Look at Papa.*

Thank God, she decided, *I am not as other women, falling*

all over myself to catch a male! Smiling, she went to preen
before her mirror, posing and gesturing to catch her
best angles. Her pearly soft skin glowed with health. She
tossed her fiery auburn tresses coquettishly, a gesture
often practiced for her own amusement and, with a
secret little laugh, she daringly touched the perfume
stopper to the cleft between her swelling breasts.

Men were so gullible! she mused. So easily ensnared.
Look at silly old Clarence back in Chicago. Well, she had
certainly left him howling for unrequited love. She giggled and made a face at her mirrored image. *Yes, Katherine
McGillacutty,* she congratulated herself, *you certainly know
how to use your charms.*

But then she thought about Peter O'Rourke. A worthy
target, if ever she saw one. Much more worldly and exciting than Clarence. Too bad she wouldn't have time to
practice her wiles on him. *Oh, my, isn't that the truth,* Kate
sighed, recalling O'Rourke's smoldering looks backstage
at Maguire's. The way he kissed positively set her on fire!

Peering more closely at her own reflection in the
mirror, she imagined that her eyes were Peter's gazing
back at her. The glint in his green eyes made her feel
all wild and fluttery inside, and his touch felt divine.
Kate shivered, sensing an almost telepathic connection.
It didn't take a genius to realize how easily O'Rourke
could sweep a girl off her feet, if he chose.

But Katherine didn't consider herself such a fool. She
was more than a match for Mr. Peter Casey O'Rourke; of
that she was quite certain. Still, it would have been amusing
to pit her beauty against his and beat him at his own game!

Suddenly Katherine heard the front door slam downstairs.

"Maddy, start closing windows!" her father shouted,
bounding up the stairs. He barged into her room, raced
to the window, and slammed it shut. "Wind storm," he explained and disappeared to close other upstairs windows.

Glancing outside, Kate saw a solid wall of brown
swirling. Suddenly nothing existed outside her window

but the deafening sound of sand and leaves assaulting
the shutters.

"Father!" she called, recalling Midwestern tornadoes.
"Do we have a storm cellar?" She stood undecided in her
undergarments, wondering if she was about to be blown
away. Should she flee? Get under a bed? What?

"Get dressed, Mary Kate," her father ordered, coming
back. "You and O'Rourke are getting married at two
o'clock, remember?"

"We can't get married in a tornado!" Kate screamed
over the wind's insane roar. The house stood firm, but for
how long? Perhaps this was a sign of God's strong displeasure. After all, she had defied Papa. Maybe like Jonah, she
was really meant to go to Nineveh. (Broadly interpreted,
this meant her father's foreman.) "Oh, help!" she cried.

"It isn't a tornado," her father informed her sternly.
"Just a little wind. Stop your fussing." He grabbed her
arm, spun her about, and dropped her wedding dress
over her head.

Kate looked up at him doubtfully. He was chuffing
away on his cigar like an old steam engine and, surprisingly, his matter-of-factness had a calming effect. If he
could call this a "little wind," who was she to argue?

Sighing, she submitted to her father's clumsy attempt
to fasten the pearl buttons down the back of her gown.

"Thank you, Papa," Kate said, when he had finished
the task. On impulse she rose on tiptoe and kissed his
cheek, mostly for giving her back her courage.

"You're welcome," said Homer. He turned his daughter between his big, meaty hands and embraced her
awkwardly.

As Katherine stood in the circle of his arms, a warmth
stole over her that she hadn't experienced in many
years. The sudden glimmer of pride in his shrewd gaze
strangely touched her. Normally her father was preoccupied and gruff, always in a hurry.

"Be happy, Katherine." He patted her cheek and
stepped back, letting her go.

With his retreat to a safer emotional distance, the spell was broken for Kate. His affection, once desperately longed for, came too late. It was also much too brief.

"If that is what you want, Father," she said calmly, not in response to his good wishes but because once again she felt isolated, with no shoulder to rest her head upon, and no one to love her for herself.

For a second she felt like the little girl who had seen her father off at the Chicago train depot nine years before. She had pleaded with him not to leave her and Mother, but he had gone just the same. "You don't love me, Papa. You only love your money," the little girl had sobbed, and nothing had changed between them since. After that, when he came to visit in Chicago, she kept a careful distance, polite but detached. Oh, she showed off to him her latest dresses and one time even managed a pleased smile over an expensive bracelet he gave her. But after he left, she dropped his gift overboard, while boating on Lake Michigan with one of Mama's friends.

Homer motioned for Kate to turn for a final inspection. "Not bad. Almost as pretty a bride as your mother was."

His manner was so patronizing, Mary Katherine was tempted to refuse to go through with the wedding. If it wasn't for the fact that it wasn't a real marriage, she would have. The last thing she wanted was to give her father what he wanted!

"We can't go to church until the wind dies down," she said, stalling.

"Wind or no wind, we leave for the church at two," he told her. "You'd better pray this blows over, that's all."

Katherine glared at his retreating back, silently mimicking his words. The howl of sand scraped and buffeted the house, as if some angry god had not been appeased. *This could go on for hours,* she thought, wringing her hands. She couldn't see the tree in the front yard, let alone the nosy neighbor's house. Downstairs she heard the crash of glass and her mother's muffled scream.

"Homer! A shutter's torn loose," Madeleine called, a

note of panic in her cultured Southern accent. "The parlor window broke."

"Oh, hell!" McGillacutty stomped downstairs. "I'll get some boards." Kate heard her father slam his way through the house to the back porch. A moment later loud hammering in the front parlor told Kate that a "little wind" was not going to interfere with Homer McGillacutty's plans.

When the storm hit, covering the Comstock Lode with a cloud, Peter felt much like the Egyptians when judgment brought a swarm of locusts to devour the land. There was no place to hide. With every tick of the clock, this marriage thing was closing in on him. He felt almost claustrophobic! He had barely slept a wink, his palms were sweaty, and he couldn't concentrate.

Only the scent of Katherine's perfume, wafting through the paper-thin walls, along with every word of her conversation with her father, kept him from bolting, as any sane man would.

Of course, the weather was the perfect excuse for postponing the wedding. Indefinitely. But something held him back, kept him from giving way to panic.

If only he could regard the wedding as a farce.

But he couldn't. It went too much against the grain.

"Words are like the wind," he tried to convince himself, as he stared blankly out his bedroom window. Why couldn't he accept the fact that he would be repeating words—not promises—before Father Manogue, whom he'd met briefly at the mine on Friday. If only his conscience hadn't surfaced.

Ah, sweet Savior! Which stuck in his craw most? Committing fraud before one of God's servants, taking money under false pretenses, or collusion with Kate's father? Surely, after the life he'd led, it was a little late for scruples. What were a few more lies?

But a man had to draw the line somewhere.

If he let those two willful redheads keep him pinned

between a rock and a hard place, he would never be able to look himself in the mirror again.

Peter picked up the lumberman's manual he'd been scanning and slung it onto the bed. Good information on the operation of a sawmill, but it wasn't going to help him do what he had to do right now.

If my word is no good, what's left? he asked himself.

Aye, well—he would be damned if that little spitfire was going to manipulate and make him lie for her anymore.

Nor was her father going to intimidate him.

This wasn't merely a case of whose side he was on. It was a matter of conscience. A test of what kind of man he really was. And what he hoped to become.

He was going to have to make a stand. Even if it meant groping his way to church through a twister! He had to be his own man. Even if it made the McGillacuttys mad as hell.

As soon as Peter Casey O'Rourke took his leap of faith, the storm subsided into a gentle summer breeze. The sun came out, along with half of Virginia City's disbelieving citizens. Nobody had ever seen a zephyr come up out of nowhere and vanish so suddenly before. All over town, people tiptoed around their yards, checking for damage and lost children. They remarked to their neighbors that they had never witnessed a stranger storm. And those in the know laid a finger to their lips with a furtive whisper: "Tommyknockers."

The wee folk, some called them. They dwelt in the depths of the mines, by and large a peaceful lot. Oh, to be sure, they occasionally forgot themselves and skipped about in the dark. Most of the mysterious rumblings that rose from the bowels of the earth were their doing. But always before, they had stayed below and minded their own business.

Whether caused by Tommyknockers or an Act of God,

the storm was over. On cue. Perfectly timed, like a good omen. At least, that's how Peter viewed it.

Making up for his indecision earlier, Peter shaved quickly. He trimmed his side whiskers and parted his blond hair off center, using a light pomade to keep it in place. In case the wind came up again. A man couldn't be too careful about his appearance.

Even a reluctant bridegroom should dress the part. Command performance. He donned his handsome pearl-gray frock coat and trousers, buttoned his ruffled linen shirt, straightened his black silk cravat, and eyed himself with satisfaction.

Ready. He loaded his pockets carefully and went downstairs.

"Sir, I'll meet you and Mrs. McGillacutty and your daughter at the church," he informed his employer. Before Homer could respond, Peter was out the door.

The bride, too, had gone to great lengths to do the occasion up right. Exquisitely gowned in white satin, with a neckline edged in boa feathers, Kate paused in the upper hallway while her mother attached the satin train, edged with lace and pearls. In place of the traditional veil, she had chosen a Juliet cap, like the one she'd tried on at Maguire's. It was trimmed with the same lace and pearls as her train.

"How beautiful you are." Her mother sighed, handing Kate a tiny white Bible decorated with satin rosettes, fresh blooms being scarce in Virginia City. "You would only outshine your flowers anyway." Madeleine kissed her daughter and dashed away a tear, remembering her own wedding.

Clinging briefly to her mother, Kate felt remiss for not sharing her guilty secret. But she couldn't spoil her mother's joy. In fact, Kate found it hard not to share her excitement, it was so contagious. "What now?" she asked, suddenly fidgety.

"Your father will be ready in a minute, darling. I'll check to see how preparations for the reception are coming along." Madeleine glided down the stairs with the busy rustle of skirts Kate always associated with her petite mother.

"I'll miss you, Mama," Katherine said. But the last thing she needed was to start bawling like a calf separated from its mother. She blinked quickly, dispelling the sudden urge to weep.

Straying to the alcove window, she spotted Peter, halfway down the block. He was walking fast, as if he intended his legs to cover a good long distance in a very short time.

Oh, no, you don't, O'Rourke! Katherine's temper flared. To her, Peter looked like an elegant fugitive on the run.

Throwing her train over her arm, she hiked up her skirts and took the stairs with reckless disregard for her safety. Her tiny satin slippers padded frantically, barely slowing when she ran into her father at the bottom.

"Father, I'm ready!" she announced, heading around him toward the heavy front door. "Unless you're going right now, I'm leaving without you." She flung the door wide and rushed out onto the veranda.

"Whoa there, daughter. What's your hurry?" Homer demanded. Moving faster than was his custom, he pounced, stopping her in midflight.

"He's getting away!" Katherine squawked. Biting her lip, she craned her neck to see the last of Peter O'Rourke rounding the corner a block away.

"We'll catch up," her father assured her with a chuckle. Never had he seen his daughter so eager to do his bidding! "We must wait for your mother."

Arms crossed, Kate drummed her fingers on her satin sleeves. "This was your idea, Father," she informed him crossly. "If anything goes wrong, I shall hold you personally responsible."

Homer bellowed for Madeleine to join them. "Bring

your parasol, Maddy," he advised and lit a fresh cigar. "Looks like the sun is back, full strength."

"Don't rush me, Homer," Madeleine fussed, getting herself together. She took his arm and looked out toward the street. "Where's the carriage?" she asked expectantly.

McGillacutty's face grew flushed with annoyance. "Simmer down, woman! The church is only three blocks away. Who needs a carriage on a splendid day like this?"

Madeleine fixed her husband with a pitying look and reached to straighten his tie. "It's not proper for the bride to arrive at church on foot. Polite social custom requires a carriage. Really, Homer, where have your manners flown to?"

"I see nothing wrong with walking," Homer argued, forgetting Kate's tapping foot and the reason for their outing. His lip curled in a lewd grin. "I daresay, it's better etiquette than a bride choosing a groom from among a bunch of drunks passed out along C Street."

"Homer McGillacutty, lower your voice!" Madeleine shrilled, striking her husband with her parasol. "We'll be socially ruined!"

Katherine looked glumly down the street. O'Rourke was nowhere to be seen. And from the sound of things, her parents would be busy thrashing out their domestic differences for the next two hundred years. She had to act now, or take the consequences.

"I'm walking," she announced, and took off running.

CHAPTER 7

"Anyone would think you were in a powerful big hurry to get married."

Kate's feet clattered to a stop. Looking around, she straightened her Juliet cap, while she located her tormenter.

A lopsided grin on his face, O'Rourke strolled from the depths of the church portico, hands in pockets. He lounged gracefully against a sunlit pillar, while he took in her heaving bosom and the disheveled fussiness of her wedding finery. His insulting chuckle infuriated Katherine still further.

"I am not in a hurry," she huffed.

Dropping her skirts, she adjusted her feathers to cover her breasts more modestly, all the while hoping to see her father and mother roll into sight. How long could it take to harness a horse and buggy anyway? she fumed. This miserable rake's leisurely perusal of her person was almost more than she could bear.

"Spare me your thoughts," she snapped, when she saw how hard he was struggling not to laugh.

"I've never seen such a contradiction in petticoats," he admitted with a wide, sensuous grin. "You run like a tomboy and dress like a duchess. My, but you do give yourself airs, Miss McGillacutty."

"Don't you know it's bad luck to see the bride before

the wedding?" Kate stomped past him into the church. He followed with a theatrical yawn.

"I've decided redheads are bad luck in general," he observed casually.

In the dim sanctuary, prayer candles and candelabra brightened the gloom and bathed the altar in soft light. Twinkling rays of sunlight beamed through a single stained glass window, chasing infinitesimal dust particles and casting an aspect of reverence over the sanctuary's softly gleaming dark wood.

For all its simplicity, it *was* a house of God. Mary Katherine felt it strongly and glanced uneasily at the tall man standing at her side. She wasn't about to let his remark about redheads pass, but neither could she disregard their surroundings.

Tugging on Peter's arm, she led him into a dark alcove where they could speak privately. "Just remember our bargain and that your luck is about to change," she said, alluding to the tidy sum that would soon be jingling in his pockets.

"I intend that it shall." Peter drew her toward one of the confessional booths. "How about it?" he suggested, half-teasingly. He inclined his head toward the curtained cubicle. "Any great sins you'd like to confess before we head down the aisle together?"

Katherine pulled away from the warm hand on her sleeve. "Don't be absurd, O'Rourke," she whispered fiercely.

"There's still time to change your mind." He bent his head to sniff her fragrance with an exaggerated sigh. "Mmm, expensive," he said, and his fingers slowly explored her swanlike neck.

Kate dodged his hand. "Don't! No matter how much you try, I won't let you back out of our agreement, O'Rourke." She tossed her head. Damn! she thought; he really knew how to keep her off balance. The quicker she got this over with and sent him on his way, the better.

She decided to try being a little more conciliatory. "I'm

sorry to put you out, O'Rourke. It's just that, well, you're the best I could come up with on such short notice."

"What with your father pressuring you and all?" he sympathized, running a long, tapered finger along the edge of her boa.

"Oh, please! I know this is all a big joke to you," Kate said loftily. "I wouldn't inconvenience you for the world, if I didn't have to."

O'Rourke nodded understandingly. "Terrible, what dire straits necessity can bring a person to."

Kate jumped as his thumb lightly stroked her cheek, then captured her chin. "Exactly. Now, if I were in Chicago—"

"Let me guess." His green eyes lazily drifted over her curves. "Any number of gentlemen would have gladly come to your rescue, for the privilege of one of your beauteous smiles."

"Of course." She brightened, glad he finally understood.

"Yet, out of hundreds—perhaps thousands—of potential victims, you chose me." His chuckle was full of irony.

Apparently Peter wasn't all that eager to marry her, even for money! Mary Katherine lifted her chin to show his remark didn't bother her in the least. Even so, his words rankled.

"I don't exactly consider you a victim," Kate snapped. "But a paid-and-willing participant."

"Under the circumstances, I suppose I should do the sporting thing," Peter said.

Kate raised her slanted green eyes to his. If she didn't need his help, she would have slapped the supercilious smirk off his face. But he *was* essential to her plan, so she bit her tongue.

"I would appreciate your cooperation," she said stiffly.

"Even though I'm a cad?" he asked, giving her yet another reason to back out gracefully.

"I shall just have to make the best of things," she told him coolly. She only hoped he wasn't going to make the entire marriage, which she estimated would last less than twenty-four hours, a thoroughly annoying experience.

"Ah, there you are, Miss McGillacutty," said Father Manogue, stepping out of the confessional booth. He came forward with a kindly twinkle in his eyes. "After speaking to your fiancé, I feel as if I already know you."

Katherine inclined her head respectfully. Inside, a terrible sinking feeling hit her in the pit of her stomach, like a sudden attack of conscience. Hopefully the priest wanted only to know her preferences regarding the service. "I expect your customary wedding service will be lovely. Nothing special, please."

"Any concerns you might wish to share?" the understanding cleric suggested. He paused, not pushing exactly, but waiting nonetheless.

"No, nothing!" Kate's eyes flew to O'Rourke's amused gaze, then lowered in guilty haste.

"I see," said the priest, and Katherine heard her heart thunk.

She cleared her throat. "Excuse me, Father, but d-do you suppose I could speak privately to my . . . um, fiancé for a moment?"

"Of course, my child." Father Manogue smiled and, pausing to genuflect briefly, approached the altar to arrange the sacraments on the table.

Both hands tightly grasping the pew, Kate shakily lowered herself onto the hard wooden seat. Peter casually flexed a knee and slid in beside her. Kate, her small hands balled into fists and her head down, cast him a nervous, sidelong glance.

"You told him, didn't you?" she whispered hoarsely.

Peter stretched his long legs in front of him and draped both arms over the back of the pew. Grinning at her discomfort, he nodded.

"Oh, my God! How could you?" Her whisper died in a croak.

He leaned in close, his lips disturbing the curls next to her ear. "How could I not?"

Katherine turned her head so fast their lips nearly met. "You never meant to help me, did you?"

"Listen, Katherine, I couldn't very well lie my way through the wedding service without easing my conscience—now, could I?" Serious for once, he looked her directly in the eyes.

"Why couldn't you have confessed afterwards?" Kate whispered. "Now he'll tell my father!" She bit her soft lips together to keep from crying. "Oh, don't you see? Now I'll have no say about who I marry."

Peter indolently touched the edge of her Juliet cap. His fingers toyed with her auburn tresses. "Silly child," he reminded her, "the good padre won't tell your father anything. What I told him was in strictest confidence. He cannot violate his sacred trust."

Through her tears, her mouth soft and trembling, Katherine tilted her chin and gazed at Peter. "You mean—?"

O'Rourke nodded. He smoothed away a teardrop from her dark russet lashes, then put his thumb in his mouth, tasting her salty tear. His lips curled in that secret sensual smile of his, just as a sunbeam chanced to flood the rear pew. Katherine's breath caught in her throat as she stared up at him, enthralled by so much masculine beauty. *Perhaps he's my prayer come true,* she thought. *Perhaps there's still hope.*

But then reality brought her down to earth. "You went to confession?" she asked in disbelief.

"Not something I do every day," Peter admitted with candor. "But I needed to get a few things off my chest," he said as his glance went heavenward, "if I want to remain on friendly terms with myself and"—he pointed up—"with you-know-Who."

Narrowing her eyes, Kate searched his face for signs of defection. How could he act so calm, when she felt so miserable? She dropped her head against the top of the pew in front of her. "I suppose this means you won't help me," she said brokenly. She bumped her head on the wooden pew twice, lightly. "Oh, God, I'm lost!"

His low chuckle and the warm arm around her shoulder brought her out of her youthful despondency. "You probably are," Peter agreed and gave her a gentle shake. "But no more than me, I suspect."

As Kate's head came up to regard him solemnly, he dropped a kiss on her soft mouth, as light as two butterflies' wings brushing in midflight.

"I'll still marry you, if you wish," he offered.

Gazing up at her rescuer, who sat enveloped in a golden beam of stained glass prisms and sunlight, Katherine's first reaction—which she fortunately resisted—was to prostrate herself at his feet. O'Rourke's strongly chiseled features and shoulder-length golden hair curling around his neck made him the classic knight errant. He looked magnificent in his gray frock coat and trousers. Now that he wasn't busy mocking her, she could even admit that he would have been quite a catch, if only she was in the market for a husband.

Even though that wasn't the case, she was grateful. Impulsively, she pulled his face down to hers and kissed him full on the lips. "Thank you, Peter. I shall never forget you for this!" And she buried her face in his shirt, quite overcome by his generosity.

"Oh, I'm quite certain of that," her champion replied drily.

The clatter of a woman's dainty heels and a heavier tread caused them to break apart guiltily. "Mother! Papa!" Katherine jumped to her feet, her eyes glowing. "Come, Mr. O'Rourke," she said, "now that my parents have arrived, let's go see Father Manogue."

Homer cocked a bushy eyebrow at Peter. "I see she's not giving you any difficulty," he said in a low aside.

"Everything's under control," O'Rourke said with a conspiratorial grin. "If you will excuse me, sir, your daughter's growing a trifle impatient, and I suppose I should humor her, at least where the wedding's concerned."

Stuffing his hands in his pockets, McGillacutty turned to his wife. "There goes a man after my own heart."

"Homer McGillacutty." Maddy gave her husband a suspicious look. "I do hope we're doing the right thing."

Providentially the wedding guests started to trickle in, thus sparing Homer any serious interrogation. With a noncommittal grunt, he moved to greet his guests, mostly business associates and their wives.

"Welcome!" He beamed. "Have you met my darling wife, recently arrived from Chicago? Maddy, this is John Mackay and his partner Jim Fair from the Virginia Consolidated Mine. And this is Bill Sharon, in charge of the Bank of California branch here in town."

Madeleine McGillacutty cordially greeted the men and their wives. "We really must get together," she told Mrs. Sharon and the willowy young wife of a mining superintendent, whose name she hadn't caught. "Perhaps we could start a ladies' social club." Already the prospect of living in Virginia City seemed less dismal, knowing that these fine ladies shared her lot.

In minutes, their guests were assembled in the front five pews. Homer collected his daughter, Mary Kate, and stood at the rear of the church, prepared to do his duty. Up front, Peter O'Rourke fidgeted with the pearl stud in his cravat. After a long silence, Father Manogue, the only truly calm soul present, signaled the organist to begin.

The wedding prelude and processional would never rival the Votivkirche in Vienna or the Cathedral in Cologne. In all honesty, Peter couldn't say that he'd ever heard anything like the organist's squeaky rendition of the wedding march. Somehow he managed not to wince. Instead, he thought of the old stone church in Wexford, where his older brother, his sister, and he had worshipped as children with his parents. *Memories,* Peter thought, closing his ears. *Aye, memories to sweeten even the sourest notes in life.*

His Irish heart perceptibly mellow, he took his stance and awaited his bride's approach.

In truth, the setting did strain the imagination. The organ bellows hissed and wheezed with every step

Homer McGillacutty took. By the time he'd walked Mary
Kate down the aisle, he was so grateful to hear the last
strains of the wedding march expire that he planted a
kiss on Katherine's pale cheek.

Surprised, she looked up and saw the tear in his eye.
"Papa?" she whispered.

"Get along with you now," Homer responded in a gruff
whisper. Then he transferred his gaze to O'Rourke, and
their eyes met in silent understanding.

Peter stepped forward, hand extended, and Katherine's heart began to trip a little faster. Her eyes moved
upward from their clasped hands and paused uncertainly
at his mouth, which remained unsmiling in a face so
charismatic that he made her insides wilt with the heat his
eyes generated. Katherine raised her gaze higher to find
him studying her. He licked his lips slowly, deliberately, as
if he knew exactly her innermost feelings. Suddenly fear-
ful, Katherine blushed and looked down again.

Father Manogue drew them forward. They knelt
facing the altar, heads bowed, hands clasped. "Dearly
beloved, we are gathered here in the sight of God and
these witnesses . . ."

Almost at once, Kate's mind drifted. She stared feverishly at O'Rourke's hand; his fingers entwined with hers,
long and graceful. She tried to wiggle free and found
her hand locked securely in his.

Was it really necessary to hold hands during the entire
prayer? she chafed. This was torture; their hands would
be permanently forged together if the priest didn't
hurry up!

As they repeated the Our Father portion of their re-
sponses, she focused on the hand that held hers. His
skin was pliant and smooth, yet tougher than hers, his
nails well manicured. The hands of a gentleman. Oh, if
only—!

". . . Amen."

As Peter helped her rise, Katherine's wandering
thoughts evaporated, and she looked up in confusion,

wondering where they were in the service. She found
Peter's eyes on her. His thumbnail scraped her palm,
producing a tantalizing tickle. He rewarded her puzzled
frown with a show of dimples, then redirected his attention to the priest.

"I, Peter Casey O'Rourke, take you, Mary Katherine . . ."

Mercy! They were already to the vows. Suddenly the
truth of what they were doing hit Kate like ice water.
O'Rourke was right, they *should* be worried! These
weren't just words but promises they never meant to
keep. Horrified, she held onto O'Rourke's hand for
dear life.

". . . forsaking all others, till death do us part."
O'Rourke's voice didn't waver one iota.

Assailed by guilt, Kate was almost tempted to believe
that he meant them! The priest turned to her, and her
mouth went dry with apprehension. She began to
wonder how long she would spend in purgatory. *Here
goes!* Kate glanced up at O'Rourke nervously and received a reassuring hand squeeze.

"Thank you," she whispered.

You're welcome, he mouthed.

Father Manogue cleared his throat, and Katherine's head
whipped around to meet his steady gaze. "Repeat after me:
'I, Mary Katherine McGillacutty, do take you, Peter Casey
O'Rourke, as my lawfully wedded husband . . .'"

Katherine's lips began to move, but the words had difficulty getting past her vocal chords. She faltered,
cleared her throat, and tried again. Still nothing came
out of her mouth.

The congregation sat forward, waiting to hear the
words that never ceased to tug at the human heart.

Darting a frightened look past the priest, Katherine's
eyes fastened on the crucifix. *Oh, Lord Jesus!* Her legs
buckled, and she would have crashed to her knees in a
pile of rumpled satin, if O'Rourke's strong arm hadn't
been holding her up.

She felt faint. No! She mustn't panic. What would

people think if she ran screaming from the church? Would it even matter? Her father would probably give her a lecture for embarrassing him in front of his friends and make her go through with it anyway. Oh, God! What a predicament!

A hushed murmur rose from the congregation behind her. Kate heard her father's fiery breathing, like a blacksmith's bellows, pumping away.

O'Rourke looked genuinely concerned. "Are you sure you're up to this, Mary Katherine?" he asked gravely.

Like a drowning woman, Kate clung to his arm. "Yes, yes, I-I'm fine," she squeaked. "Umm . . ." She glanced about distractedly. "I-It's just so d-dry after that w-w-wind storm," she whispered. "If I might have some water?" she asked the padre.

"Certainly, my child," Father Manogue said. Instead he presented her with a chalice of wine.

Katherine drank greedily. The spirits revived her quickly, supplying the courage she lacked. "Thank you, Father."

Manogue took the cup, raised it, and offered a blessing on the couple. "May God sustain you both to your life's end." Then he offered it to Peter.

Peter, finding that his bride had drained the cup, raised it to his lips and quaffed the empty chalice with proper solemnity, giving a creditable performance. "Dry wine," he couldn't resist murmuring in her ear.

"Now, shall we continue the vows?" the priest asked, giving Katherine a kindly smile. "'I, Mary Katherine McGillacutty, take you, Peter Casey O'Rourke . . .'"

Feeling her father's eyes boring into her back, Kate squared her shoulders resolutely. "I, Mary Katherine McGillacutty, take you, Peter Casey O'Rourke, as my lawfully wedded husband, to have and to hold, from this day forward . . ."

Her voice rang out like a sweetly tempered bell, as she pledged herself in marriage. Her eyes glittered with unshed tears of humiliation and anger, but her gaze never left Peter's. She was grateful that he had stood by her.

". . . till death do us part." Her words trailed off in a whisper, and her gaze dropped once more to their hands.

The rest passed like a dream before her. She watched O'Rourke remove the ring from his right hand and place it on the third finger of her left hand. "I'll get you one that fits later, if you want," he whispered.

It fit her finger loosely, but what did it matter? Kate thought. It was only temporary.

Then the priest pronounced them man and wife and introduced them to the congregation as "Mr. and Mrs. Peter Casey O'Rourke."

It was over! A wave of enormous relief swept over Katherine. Vaguely she was aware of Peter's perfunctory kiss for the benefit of those present. Then he tucked her hand under his arm and while the organist pumped out the most forlorn recessional Katherine had ever heard, she let her bridegroom escort her back up the aisle.

Attributing her momentary lapse to unnecessarily childish guilt, Katherine dismissed all assistance from Peter and climbed up into her father's carriage. She felt inordinately cross with the world, though why she could not say, because her scheme had worked perfectly. She should be happy! And maybe she would be, if O'Rourke stopped his infernal grinning.

Wretch! Crossing her arms, she settled against the cushions, careful to avoid O'Rourke's amused gaze. Let him think what he wished! She would soon be rid of him. It would be worth a thousand dollars never to set eyes on him again.

A minute later, her father handed up her mother and, climbing into the driver's seat, took up the reins. As if it wasn't already the most nerve-wracking day of her entire existence, Peter leapt aboard and seated himself beside her, whistling "Greensleeves." When she curled her lip, he shrugged and made a study of his cuticles. "All set for the reception, love?" he asked.

"Oh, be quiet," she groaned.

"Anything you say, my sweet," he said, all amiability, and took out a cigar. He leaned past Mrs. McGillacutty to tap Homer on the shoulder. "Got a light, sir?"

Katherine snatched the stogie from his hand and threw it in the street. "Never mind, Father," she snapped. "O'Rourke is giving up smoking." Then her eyes met her mother's. "Oh, don't look so disapproving, Mother!"

"You should treat your husband with respect," was her mother's only comment.

"Oh, dear, I forgot," Kate retorted. "You and Father never say a cross word to each other, do you?"

"Mary Katherine—" Her mother's eyes flashed a warning.

O'Rourke reached over and reassuringly patted his mother-in-law's gloved hand. "That's all right, Mrs. McGillacutty—or should I call you 'Mother'? Katherine's just a bit high strung right now. Getting married can be such a strain."

"You can say that again." Kate looked away, biting her lip to keep from going hysterical.

"I'm sure you will both be very happy," said Madeleine, fanning herself.

"Do you think so?" Peter asked. "I've heard marriage is looked upon by some as having little more consequence than a trip to the Chinese laundry or the purchase of a new hat." He nailed Kate with a provocative glance.

Katherine's face turned crimson. "How fortunate that we don't know anyone that shallow," she said, her green eyes glittering dangerously.

"Your daughter is such an innocent," O'Rourke told Madeleine with a platitudinous smile. "'Tis a good thing I'll be looking out for her from now on."

Homer drew up in front of the house and handed the reins to his stable boy. He'd listened to all the nonsense he could stand. "Enough of this bickering," he said. "We have guests coming, so let's all act civilized, shall we?"

Peter smiled. "Whatever you say, sir. It's your show, and we are merely here to play our parts. Shall we go inside, ladies?"

"Smile, O'Rourke. Papa's watching," Kate said, leaning into him so that her skirt swallowed up his right shoe. Smiling, she stomped on his instep.

Peter's smile didn't falter, although his arm tightened around her middle. "That's two I owe you for," he promised.

"I owe you more," she said through her teeth, trying to pry loose his iron fingers without attracting undue attention.

"Ah, payday! I shall enjoy watching you pay up." O'Rourke gave her an insolent smile and then turned to bow over Mrs. Sutro's jeweled hand. "What a charming chapeau, madame."

They had been circulating and chatting up her father's friends for nearly two hours. Those attending her wedding reception were extremely gracious and friendly, and seemed to be having a delightful time. But not Kate. If anyone had asked her, she could not have said what made her so incensed. She knew only that Peter, with his polished manners and unfailing smile, was getting on her nerves to the point where she could barely restrain herself from hand-to-hand combat!

Suddenly her father materialized, beaming at the newlyweds.

"Well, well! It appears you two are getting along famously," he boomed.

Peter helped himself to champagne being passed around by the butler and raised his glass for a toast. "I predict this marriage will never grow old."

"Yes, Father, Peter and I have so much in common," Kate said, trying to trip her husband under cover of her voluminous skirts.

Green eyes gleaming, the couple glared at each other like two jungle cats. Wisely, McGillacutty stepped between the pair, before anything too physical could transpire. He cleared his throat and paused till every eye dutifully turned for the inevitable toast to the bride and groom.

"This is a proud moment," Homer announced. "My little Kate has married a fine man, and Mrs. McGillacutty and I could not be more pleased. I haven't lost a daughter; I've gained a son."

"Here, here," Mr. Farley spoke up from across the room. A number of the other guests murmured in polite accord.

Mrs. Sutro sighed. "They make such a splendid couple."

"What beautiful children they will have," said Mrs. Costello.

Embarrassed, Kate raised her eyes to Peter, who only shrugged, as if to say this was the price to be paid for their folly.

Homer guffawed and pounded his son-in-law on the back. Then he drew a key from his pocket and waved it overhead. "My first gift to the newlyweds," he announced. "The key to the honeymoon suite at the International Hotel!"

Katherine choked, watching the key pass from her father to her husband. It disappeared with magician-quick ease into O'Rourke's frock coat pocket.

"Thank you, sir." Peter gave her a wink, and Katherine knew she was supposed to play along, but she couldn't. She was numb inside. This wasn't a real marriage. It had never occurred to her until now that she wouldn't sleep in her own bed as usual, eat breakfast, and then take the stage to San Francisco in the morning. She emptied her glass in one gulp and set it down shakily.

"What a . . . surprise," she managed to say.

Whereupon Homer pulled out another key and brandished it with a laugh. "Don't make too much noise, young'ns. Mrs. McGillacutty and I have taken the suite right next door."

That announcement proved too much. Both Madeleine and Katherine stared at each other, speechless.

Smiling benignly, Peter raised his champagne glass. "To second honeymoons," he said, toasting her parents with a bow.

Chapter 8

Peter stepped into the hotel corridor, taking a brief respite from the war on nerves they'd both been waging for the past hour. To say that things had become a bit awkward in the honeymoon suite didn't begin to describe it. Katherine had locked herself in the dressing room and refused to come out or listen to reason, even though he'd told her he wouldn't lay a finger on her. But there was no convincing her of that! She thought he meant to claim his marital rights, and there was no persuading her otherwise.

So what was he to do? With McGillacutty's eye to the keyhole, a stick of petrified wood had a better chance of coming alive than the one burning in his shorts.

Aye, this marriage was one of God's better jokes.

While pacing, O'Rourke pivoted and collided with Homer McGillacutty as he stepped out of the adjoining suite. Now that really irked O'Rourke. Couldn't the old gaffer wait until Katherine screamed bloody murder?

Carefully concealing his irritation, he nodded to his father-in-law.

"Women!" Homer shook his fist at the door he'd just exited.

O'Rourke nodded in a show of sympathy. Old Man McGillacutty had every right to screw his wife to his heart's content, once he got past the barricaded door. Peter was up No Dice Creek, and well he knew it. If he made any major moves on Mary Kate before the stage-coach reached Strawberry Point, where they would be joining the mule caravan, it would tip his hand, make her suspicious.

"The luggage is loaded and ready to leave first thing tomorrow," Homer told him in a low, conspiratorial tone.

"Thank you, sir," O'Rourke said as the two men proceeded to wear out the carpet together. "I hope Kate's got something more practical to wear than the dresses I've seen so far?"

Homer nodded. "I picked up some long johns and three plain woolen dresses, plus a small man's jacket that should fit her. It gets cold in the mountains."

"Much obliged," O'Rourke said. "I'll take good care of her, sir. We should be back before the first snows fly."

"See that you are." Homer narrowed his eyes at O'Rourke. "She's my only child, and I won't have her unhappy, y'hear?"

"Sir," Peter reminded his father-in-law, "she's going to be very unhappy the minute she finds out where I'm taking her."

McGillacutty waved that off impatiently. "Not the kind of unhappy I mean. You're only following my instructions on that. You know damn well what I'm referring to."

Peter reserved judgment as to Homer's true intentions. His demand that Mary Katherine be returned intact might or might not have been a ruse. Whatever the case, he was her legal husband now and, like it or not, the matter was out of McGillacutty's hands.

"She'll be fine," was all Peter would say. "Well, happy second honeymoon, sir." He smiled, watching Homer sniff around his wife's bedroom door like a stiff-legged hound after a bitch in season.

"Homer?" came a small feminine voice from behind the door only seconds later.

"Wish me luck, lad?" Homer grinned and straightened his tie.

"Luck, sir." They shook hands, the older man's palm sweaty, Peter's dry and steady. Then Homer slipped through the door and closed it.

With the hall to himself, Peter decided there wasn't much use hanging around. Not till Katherine got over her honeymoon jitters, anyway. Shoving his hands in his pockets, he descended to the lobby and ambled into the elegantly appointed saloon next door. Anticipating a long night, Peter nursed a watered-down whiskey for awhile. He would have liked somebody to pass the time with, but it was Sunday night and the place had pretty much emptied out.

Suddenly struck by inspiration, he snapped his fingers to summon the bartender. "Find me a deck of cards, will you, friend?"

"Sure thing." The barkeep finished drawing a head of beer, then produced a freshly wrapped deck from beneath the counter.

"Thanks. Put it on—"

"I know: put it on Old Man McGillacutty's bill."

"Aye. This night's on him." He stuck the cards in his pocket and left, whistling "Pappy Was A Miner."

Peter's light rap was followed by the quick rustle of crinoline. Mary Katherine opened the door of the honeymoon suite a crack.

"Aren't you going to invite me in?" he asked.

Katherine moved aside but kept a wary eye on him, lest he make any wild moves, coming through the door. She was still dressed; even the Juliet cap was primly in place.

"Mary Kate, you look like the Virgin Mother in all that white," he remarked, arching an amused eyebrow. "Why not get comfortable? Let down your hair. Relax."

"My hair is already down," she informed him and, pulling up a chair, seated herself behind a small table.

"So it is," he agreed, loosening his cravat. "Since there's nothing to do until I put you on the morning stage"—he threw the deck on the table—"what say we play some cards?"

"Cards?" Kate echoed.

"Poker, to be exact. One of the many vices picked up in my travels." Peter sprawled in the chair opposite hers at the table. He broke open the wrapper and gave the cards a quick shuffle.

Katherine eyed him suspiciously. "I've never played."

Peter spread the cards face down, cut them, and did some light finger gymnastics. "I'd be happy to teach you," he said nonchalantly, not even glancing her way.

"Well, all right," she said reluctantly. "I suppose there's no harm in it."

"None at all. We won't even play for money. Agreed?"

"Agreed." Kate gave him a baleful look. "You're making enough off this marriage as it is."

"Ah, Kate, you wouldn't be wanting to welsh on me, would you?" Peter teased.

"Not at all. A deal is a deal." She watched his hands skillfully flip cards back and forth between his fingers. He had beautiful hands, quick, strong, and supple. "I-I'm most grateful to you."

"Your heart's overflowing with gratitude." He laughed sardonically.

Katherine glared at him. "You're getting paid handsomely," she reminded him stiffly.

"So I am." Peter smiled cheerfully, his dimples leaping out at her, as he plunked the deck on the table before her. "You cut."

She stared at him, then at the neat stack of cards. "Cut?"

He demonstrated, shuffled, and set down the pack again.

Gingerly Katherine reached over and divided the cards. "Like this?"

"You catch on fast." He gathered the cards, dealt them each five cards, so fast that her eyes bulged. He slapped down the rest of the deck and examined his hand. "There are various ways to play poker, my little pigeon, but to start off, I dealt you five cards down. It's called Draw."

Katherine cautiously picked up her cards. "How do I know you won't cheat?" she asked.

"We're not playing for money, remember? Just a friendly game between friends," he said, rearranging his hand.

"We're not friends," she corrected him.

"Oh, that's right, I nearly forgot," Peter said with a crooked grin. "We're married. That does eliminate the possibility of friendship, now doesn't it?" He frowned at his cards, as if making a difficult decision. He tapped a front tooth with his fingernail, drawing Kate's attention to his flawless teeth. "What about you?" he asked, looking up suddenly. "Do you need any new cards?"

Kate put down her cards. "Look, this isn't going to work. I don't know the first thing about poker."

His free hand reached across the table and covered hers. "Let me help you, Kate." He took her cards and turned them over. "We won't count this hand." He pulled two forward. "Why, Mary Kate, you have two jacks!" he exclaimed. "That would have beaten my two trays."

"Trays?" What on earth was he talking about, she wondered.

"Tray means three," he said, exposing his own cards. "You beat me! How about that? Beginner's luck, my dear." Gesturing toward the ice bucket of champagne on the night table, he offered her champagne. "Kate?"

"I had three glasses at the reception, thank you," she said, hands primly folded in her lap.

He shrugged. "Hours ago," and he was on his feet in a flash.

Startled, Katherine's eyes grew wide as he tore off the seal with his teeth. His green eyes held hers boldly for an instant of primitive enjoyment. He shook his head like a big mountain lion, tossing the wrapping in the ice bucket.

Without missing a beat, he settled the bottle against his groin and set to work on the final seal. Kate sat, lost

in fascination. She noticed the muscular line of his long
legs as he worked the cork between his fingers. He gently
wiggled the cork back and forth, up and down. She
wasn't sure why the sight of him and that oversized dark
green bottle filled her with such excitement, but it did.
She swallowed deeply, watching the play of his shoulder
muscles and the taut line of his jaw as he concentrated
on the task.

He wasn't just opening a bottle of sparkling wine.
O'Rourke was an artist at what he was doing. His every
move was a calculated seduction! Katherine knew she
should hurl some rebuke, tell him she was on to him.
Even throw him out. Instead she sat enthralled, open-
mouthed and admiring.

The cork popped and a spurt of foam flew, a tiny fleck
catching her in the eye. Kate gasped, and then they
broke out laughing, green eyes fixed on green. She felt
wildly exhilarated, as if she'd participated in something
secret and forbidden.

O'Rourke leaned over the table until she felt his
breath on her cheek. She knew she should move out of
range, but she could neither look away nor flinch. He
touched the tip of his tongue to her cheek, where a drop
of champagne clung like a lazy teardrop.

"Mustn't let any go to waste." He smiled, then withdrew.
Katherine uttered a shaky laugh. Her heart was flop-
ping hopelessly in her chest, like a bird trying to take off
with only one wing. She felt cold and hot, at once tight
and strangely loose. It was the most helpless feeling, worse
than any noon zephyr rushing to take her breath away.

O'Rourke, his right knee cocked, slowly twirled a
goblet by the stem. His expression was one of pure
amusement. "Care for a glass?" he asked.

"Yes, of course. Certainly." To cover her embarrassment, Kate grabbed the glass from him and drained it in
a single gulp.

"Slowly, Kate," he cautioned. "I don't want you drunk."

"No, I realize that," she stammered. "You were explaining how to play cards?"

Taking a small sip, Peter set his own glass aside. Then, with lightning speed he shuffled the cards several times, until Kate began to think he was a Mississippi riverboat gambler.

"Back to our friendly little game," he said. "Let's play a couple of hands so you can get the hang of things." He set out various combinations and explained the rules, starting with deuces and pairs.

Kate nodded, careful to watch the cards and not the intense light in his eyes behind those long, thick lashes of his.

"Three of a kind." He flipped three kings over for her to see.

She gasped, surprised how fast he'd found three of a kind in the deck.

"How did you do that so fast?"

"Practice," he said with a smile. "You can do anything well with practice."

Blushing, Katherine wondered if he wasn't talking about something besides cards. She watched Peter flip a 5, 6, 7, 8, and 9 of varying suits onto the table. "A straight, five in a row, any suit."

She nibbled on her finger. "What beats a straight?"

"A flush." He demonstrated five random cards of the same suit. "They must be the same suit, but in any order."

Katherine sighed. "I'll never remember all this."

"It's not difficult. Here, take three of a kind and a pair." Peter moved three kings and two sevens together. "A full house. It beats a flush. Of course, three aces is the best flush you can get."

She gave him an exasperated look. "O'Rourke, I'm never going to need to know all this."

"Don't be too sure. A young lady wandering around San Francisco alone without any useful skills soon learns she has two choices." He shot her a piercing glance. "Especially if she rules out marriage."

"What?" she asked, curious to know a woman's prospects for employment.

"She can make her living on her back—"

Kate flew out of her seat. "That's disgusting, O'Rourke."

He laughed—and ducked, because she looked ready to strike. "Wait, hear me out, Kate. The other possibility, if she's really good at it . . . " Katherine paused, her fist still raised, but O'Rourke made her wait while he carefully laid out a straight flush. "She might get a job as a dealer in a gambling hall."

Katherine sat back down, propped her chin in her hands. "How long does it take to learn?"

"It takes practice." He tapped his forefinger on the five cards in front of him. "This, sweet innocent, is a straight flush: 3, 4, 5, 6, and 7. Five cards in consecutive order, all the same suit—in this case, diamonds." He went through the various possible hands for her, pointing to them, and making her call them out. She got confused only once.

"You've found your niche," Peter told her and gathered up the cards.

"That's all there is to know?"

"Basically. The highest straight flush is a royal flush: ace, king, queen, jack, and 10—again, all in the same suit. Ready to play?"

She nodded and he dealt. He let her win four hands in a row, even though it meant throwing away some of his best cards. Elated, Katherine clapped her hands. "O'Rourke, you're an experienced player, yet I've won every time," she crowed, leaning her breasts against the table.

Grinning at the fetching sight, Peter let her cut the cards. "Cocky wench. Remember, beginner's luck."

"Oh, fiddle," she said, making a face. "Hey! Don't I get to deal?"

Peter raised an eyebrow. "Be my guest." He slid the cards across. Katherine fumbled and slowly bent the deck in half, managing a sloppy shuffle. Peter winced, but said nothing, as he cut. "Deal, wife."

She did an adequate job of slapping down five cards for each of them. Taking up her hand, she arranged and rearranged, nibbling her lip and frowning.

"Your face is a dead giveaway," he laughed. "I'll take three cards." He surrendered three and got three new ones.

"I'll take four," she decided, sounding miffed. Then she really looked worried. She stared at her new cards, searching for a winning combination. "O'Rourke—"

"Peter. Call me Peter."

"All right. Peter, what do you do, if you . . . well, if you don't . . . oh, damn!" She threw down her cards. "I don't have a single thing in my hand." She looked ready to cry.

"You fold. Just don't bet, if it's a betting game. Or you try to outbluff the other person." O'Rourke's hand was as uninspiring as hers, so he decided to show her what he meant. "Normally, I wouldn't know what's in your hand. And, remember, you don't know what's in mine, either."

"Well, you must hold all the good cards, because I have terrible cards." Sulking, she picked up her champagne glass again. It was her third since they'd started playing.

"Is that so?" Peter laid out his cards, face up.

"Why—you tricked me!"

"No, you tricked yourself, by making assumptions about me as a player and about my hand, based on nothing more than how poor a hand you'd been dealt." He looked over her cards and then his own. "Neither of us has anything. But you win again."

"How do you figure that?" she asked, pouring herself a fourth glass.

"The value of the cards in your hand is higher than mine." O'Rourke swept up the cards. "Let's play Seven Card Stud."

A little light-headed, Katherine stifled a yawn. "What

time is it?" she asked, wishing it was morning so she could board the stagecoach and sleep all the way to San Francisco.

"Ten." Peter laughed, dealing each of them two cards down and one card face up. "Check your cards, Kate. If you like what you've got, keep them. Otherwise, discard."

She looked. "I'll keep what I've got, thank you." She polished off the champagne, went to pour, and found the bottle empty. "Oh, Peter, it's all gone."

"Good. You've had enough anyway." He dealt them each another three cards up and a last one down.

"It's hot in here," she complained. Pulling the boa trim away from her breasts, she fanned herself.

Peter caught sight of a coral bud and forced his eyes back to his cards. "Must be all that damn clothing you're wearing."

Katherine stared blankly at her cards. "What am I supposed to do, Peter?" she asked.

"Discard your two worst cards, and show me what you've got."

Two cards dropped on the table, face up.

"Damn, Kate. You're not supposed to let your opponent see what you're throwing away."

"Oh, pooh, I've had too much to drink." She struggled to her feet, as gawky as a puppet on strings, her breasts peeking over the top of her gown like rising popovers.

"You're drunk, Katherine." O'Rourke rose to steady her. "Here, let me put you to bed," he volunteered.

"No, I want to play poker." Giggling, she evaded him and, lurching, made it back to her chair. "In fact, I insist." She waved a finger in front of his face and hiccuped.

The night was young and nobody told a man of O'Rourke's passionate nature how he should entertain a willful vixen like Mary Kate, including the lady herself! Especially when they were virtually forced to keep each other company until morning.

O'Rourke studied the novice poker player scrambling cards, making her the object of his own special brand of meditation. A body like hers could well nigh reduce a strong man to tears and make a weak man throw himself under a moving train to gain her favors.

Of course, Peter wasn't going to do either, but he wasn't above a little harmless entertainment. *Why not?* he asked himself. As long as he didn't let the game get out of hand, why not keep his skills polished? With the imps of his past playing upon his desires, Peter's hands began to itch. Before he put them where they didn't belong, he scooped up the cards.

"You want fun?" he asked. "Perhaps, Katherine, you'd care to make a wager?"

"I'm not going to play for money," she told him flatly. "Besides, I have money, and you don't."

"But we both have things to barter." Peter's eyes flickered with a devilish spark. He shuffled three times and began to deal Seven Card Stud again.

"Such as?"

"I'll wager you—" He quickly calculated how many pieces of clothing she was probably wearing and divided them into a thousand dollars. *She's wearing three, maybe four petticoats, pantalettes, a chemise, a corset, stockings, garters, shoes. What else? I'm looking right at it—the Juliet cap and—damn! The bridal train. And the dress, of course. Better figure on fourteen . . . no, fifteen garments, to be safe. No wonder she's hot!*

Peter chuckled. "I'll owe you eighty dollars if I lose. You take off one piece of clothing if you lose."

"One?" She looked down at herself. "Which one?" she asked suspiciously.

"To start with, your cap." He finished dealing and rested his elbows on the table. "Well, what do you say? I'll deduct eighty dollars from what you owe me, if I lose."

"Hah! Aren't you the fool?" Kate picked up her cards and promptly discarded two. "My cap against your eighty dollars?" she confirmed.

Peter spread his hand. "Three jacks and two fives."

"I have—what is that again? A full house! How about

this?" She laid down two kings and three eights. "Kings are higher than jacks."

"Not so fast. The best three of a kind wins." He collected the cards. "Off with the hat, Juliet."

She laughed, her cat's eyes gleaming. "You didn't win much, O'Rourke."

"It's a start." He snapped his fingers. "Hand it over."

"I will not!" She took it off and laid it carefully on her lap. Peter retrieved it and sent it sailing onto the bed. Katherine propped her chin on her hand and watched him deal. "What shall we wager next? Your eighty dollars against my what?"

Lord, but this girl is setting herself up for a fleecing! Peter suppressed a laugh. He was tempted to skip the appetizers and get right to the main course. *My thousand dollars for your virginity,* he wanted to say, but something held him back. Somehow it seemed wiser to confine himself for the night to a little strip poker. He allowed his eyes to wander over her. He didn't want to make the stakes too threatening, just intriguing.

"Let's see . . . You name it, Kate."

"How about my stockings?"

Peter shook his head. "Not a fair trade. Eighty dollars against a pair of silk stockings? Have a heart!"

"What if I throw in the garters?" she offered with a giggle.

O'Rourke feigned shock. "Fair lady, I've no desire to be so cruel, at least not this early in the game. How about your bridal train?"

"You're not as daring as I thought, O'Rourke," said Katherine, agreeing to his proposition. "Deal."

He won with a couple of pairs. "Would you like to deal?" he asked, offering the cards.

She dealt and lost her shoes and gloves.

"Now it begins to get interesting," he said with a gleam in his eye. Katherine sat across from him, pouting. "My eighty dollars for your dress, Mrs. O'Rourke."

"Don't call me that!" she said, clearly more upset by

her new name than by the thought of losing her dress. "All right, the dress, but not for eighty dollars."

"A hundred?"

"Yes, and this time I'm going to win!" she declared.

And she did. It took Peter two more tries before he took the dress from her.

CHAPTER 9

She stood behind a screen in the corner, struggling to undo the buttons on the back of her gown.

"You're playing with fire," he told her.

"Maybe so, but I only owe you eight hundred now." Finally she managed, after a good deal of commotion, to free herself from the dress. She threw it over the screen. "There's your old dress! Now pass me my robe, please," she said imperiously. "It's in my trunk."

"That would defeat the purpose of getting you out of that dress," Peter said over his shoulder and began to deal another hand. "Come on out, Kate. I promise not to lay a finger on you."

"Not on your life!" she squealed.

"You can't see your cards from way over there."

He picked up his cards and groaned, clasping his brow, to convince her that his hand was a grave disappointment.

"Maybe I don't want to play anymore," she said.

"Sore loser?"

"I'm not! I'm just tired of childish games." She stood pouting at him over the top of the screen.

Peter rose to his feet, hands on lean hips, and looked her in the eye. "You're a damn liar, Kate. You're scared to death of letting me see you without your dress on."

Katherine could not deny it, because it was true. Even her vocal chords were in knots.

He stood only a few feet away. Wringing her hands, she tried to think her way out of this difficulty. "If you sit down, I'll just move this screen over to the table," she proposed.

"Game's over, Kate. You're obviously not woman enough to be a gambler." Peter sat back down, swept up the cards, and slipped them in his breast pocket. Tilting back his chair, he closed his eyes and folded his arms across his chest, affecting boredom.

Kate wavered uncertainly behind the screen, waiting for him to move. She shifted uneasily, then wiggled her nose to suppress a sneeze. Must she stand half-naked in the corner all night?

"Peter?" she whispered finally, fearing he had fallen asleep.

He didn't answer.

She tried again. "Peter!" she called softly.

Still he ignored her, except for a slow sigh.

Finally she could stand it no longer. He *had* gone to sleep, she decided. She looked longingly toward her trunk. It would take only a second to scurry over and snatch on her robe. Like a mouse on a midnight foray for cheese, she tiptoed out from behind the screen. Licking her lips, she reached for her robe.

"You touch that, Mary Kate, and you forfeit the two hundred you won from me," a low masculine voice growled in her ear.

With a shriek, Katherine snatched the robe and bolted around to the other side of the bed.

"Don't you come near me," she warned.

"Drop it," Peter ordered, advancing with a menacing smile.

Covering her breasts as best she could, Kate stood shivering with delicious fright. O'Rourke looked awesome towering over her. He held out his hand for the robe, and she handed it over with an audible gulp.

"What are you going to do?" she whispered, her mouth suddenly gone dry.

Peter couldn't help himself. He plucked one of her hands from her breast, kissed the fingers lightly, one by one, and looked deep in her eyes.

"Oh," Mary Kate said, swallowing with great difficulty. "Oh. Oh, my . . ."

Suddenly O'Rourke laughed. "It's your choice. Shall we play more strip poker?"

Kate nodded, eager to agree with him, as long as he didn't . . . well, just as long as he didn't. She ran her pink tongue around her trembling lips and followed him back to the table like an obedient little puppy. He pointed to her chair, and she sat.

Huddling as low as she could behind the tabletop, Kate cursed herself for being such a coward. O'Rourke hadn't touched her, despite her scanty attire. Yet his smile made her all tight and tingly inside, like on her trip out to Nevada, when the bandits had chased their stagecoach in Colorado, and their driver nearly drove off a cliff to save them.

She knew she'd be sorry, but she didn't exactly want to run from O'Rourke. Maybe it was because he aroused her curiosity as much as he caused her confusion. Though nothing like this had ever happened to her before, she likened it to being on a teeter-totter, up in the air one minute, hitting bottom the next. Either way, she knew, she was in for a nasty jolt.

The Devil rode on his back as Peter studied the spitfire glaring at him across the table, her teeth chattering. What a paradox! He cursed the circumstances that made him hesitate. After all, she was his wife! And Mary Kate clearly felt the chemistry between them as strongly as he did. All the old instincts that had made him a natural at the seduction game now surfaced.

"Now, Kate," he said, his voice heavy with irony, "I'll

name the stakes this time. All your petticoats for the two hundred dollars I lost to you."

Kate stared at him, the light dawning: O'Rourke meant to strip her bare!

"Peter, you can keep the money, if you'll just give me back my clothes," she whimpered.

"No, Kate, my bonny Kate, my superdainty Kate, the sweetest Kate in all of Christendom," O'Rourke waxed eloquent, one hand to his heart. "I won them fair and square." He began to shuffle again, his bold gaze never leaving her face.

A tiny mewling noise escaped her throat, not so much a plea as an animal sound, acknowledging her powerlessness. "Remember, I'm new to the game," she said, meaning poker.

"We all have to learn the rules some time," he said with apparent indifference, his mind focused upon the swelling curve of her breasts. The old familiar ache of carnal desire prodded him into pursuing his devilish game of mutual torment.

Kate leaned forward, watching his fingers skim over the cards. She felt like a thirsting bee drawn into the center of a carnivorous plant, knowing she could be devoured alive, yet willing to participate in her own death.

Somewhere in this war of nerves, Kate crossed an invisible line. If he did intend to seduce her before turning her loose in the morning, she didn't want him to get the last laugh. There would be no victim, no vanquished. Or, if there was, it wouldn't be her, she decided. From deep inside, that feminine instinct that makes women superior in any contest of the sexes emerged. Kate tossed her head, issuing an unspoken invitation to the battle royal.

Discarding two cards, O'Rourke glanced up confidently and noticed the subtle change in his beautiful opponent. She no longer cowered like a virginal ninny. She sat erect, her eyes scanning her cards like a veteran cardsharp. Her bare shoulders and breasts gleamed enticingly in the soft yellow gaslight.

"Tell you what, Peter," Kate said, made bold by too much champagne and the recklessness of youth and inexperience. "Let's not drag out the suspense. Your two hundred dollars and that frock coat, shirt, boots, and trousers for my petticoats, stockings, and garters."

"The monetary values are hardly equal," he reminded her. Dash it all! He hadn't expected her to turn the tables on him.

"Oh, pooh," she giggled, throwing down her discards. "The risks ought to be equal. I mean, all you've put up all evening is my money, whereas we both know the price for my virtue and good name."

"Aye, you're quite right." Peter nodded, as if wanting to remain fair-minded, when all the while he held a royal flush with ace high.

"Let's see how you like losing some of your clothes," Kate said, too innocent to realize that nudity in the presence of the fairer sex posed no great punishment to her opponent. Her daring was spurred on by the four eights she'd been dealt.

"I warn you, Mary Kate, if I lose this wager, it will take me down to my drawers," he said, straight-faced, frowning at his cards.

Her delicious laugh rippled like a mischievous aria. She wriggled with glee, her lucky cards clutched to her warm breasts. "Then we shall be even."

"If you insist," Peter groaned, drumming his fingertips on the table and looking quite distraught.

"Show your cards, or fold," she told him and thrust her chin forward in a challenge.

"Very well," he said slowly, laying each of his cards carefully before her, one at a time. "Read them and weep."

Mary Katherine's smile faded faster than a prairie dog taking cover in its burrow. All her hopes of showing him up evaporated like hot steam on a cold rock. The blood draining from her face, Kate laid down her cards in stunned silence.

"Not quite good enough," Peter said sympathetically.

"You don't actually expect me to disrobe?" she choked.

"Time to pay up." His voice hinted at all the things she most feared and knew the least about. Where was her bravado now? she thought desperately. Licking her lips, she looked around the room for a hole to crawl into.

"Of course, if you don't honor your debts—" Peter taunted her, collecting the cards.

"I never go back on my word," she said dismally. She could hear the clock ticking on the vanity across the room, it was so quiet.

"Is that so?" he asked sarcastically, thinking how lightly she took her marriage vows. But he had enough compassion not to rub salt into her wounded pride.

Her fair shoulders slumping, Katherine rose and walked toward the folding screen.

"No, you don't, Kate." The implicit command in his voice made her turn like a marionette on strings. "If you had won our little wager, I doubt you'd have let me scamper behind that modesty screen."

With a dejected nod, Kate fumbled at the tapes that held up her petticoats. One by one they fell, O'Rourke unable to take his eyes off the pink perfection of her, Kate already certain what her forfeit would cost her.

The fourth petticoat fell. Kate faced him in her corset, chemise, and pantalettes. Silk stockings with embroidered rosettes and blue garters showed off the prettiest legs Peter had ever seen—and he'd seen so many he'd lost count years ago!

"There," she said, crossing her arms protectively over her low cleavage. "Are you satisfied now?"

"Silly goose," he told her, his own folly near driving him over the brink into insanity. "This only whets my appetite for more."

"Have a care, O'Rourke," she pleaded, great tears welling up in her wide, swamp-green eyes.

"Your wager included the stockings and garters," he couldn't resist reminding her. "Fair and square, my love."

Watching her retreat to the edge of the bed, Peter saw

the rapid pulse on her slender swan's neck and wondered
if his own heart raced any less frantically. He knew he
should stop this madness before it did them both in.
Knowing the contest of wills ahead of him on the morrow,
he had to see this game to the end. He couldn't show her
mercy now.

Katherine wanted to rip the stockings off her legs and
throw them in his face. But the wild mix of emotions
raging in her heart rendered her incapable of quickness.
Slowly, her trembling fingers slipped the first garter past
her knee. She hesitated, unwilling, yet compelled to pay
the piper. Again the blue lace descended until it reached
her ankle. Never taking her eyes off the Prince of Darkness, whose golden hair had lured her into this brash
gamble, Kate drew it off and threw it at him.

Peter caught it and snapped it over his left bicep.
"Take your time," he urged, his voice thick with desire.

"I'm hurrying, believe me." She moistened her lips
nervously. Instead of throwing the second garter in a
show of temper, Kate let it drop from her fingers beside
the bed.

Without meaning to, her eyes dropped to the front of
his trousers and the telltale bulge. The suspense was
killing her by inches. *Oh, God!* she thought, *what is he
waiting for?*

Since her worst fears weren't immediately rewarded by
Peter burying her beneath him on the mattress, she
summoned the last of her flagging courage to meet his
gaze.

"Stand up, Katherine," O'Rourke said, sprawled in his
chair.

Kate looked at him, puzzled. What more did he want?
If he meant to take her . . . She was sitting on the edge
of the bed. Wasn't that where women lost their virtue?

"You're still wearing that damned corset," he reminded her and shuffled. The sound scraped like a ratchet against her soul.

"Never mind," she said, ready to capitulate. "You can have the corset, too. Only no more cards . . . *please.*"

Unhesitating, she stood to untie the strings. She'd always loathed the garment—until that moment. She unlaced it, let it fall to the carpet. Her hands clasped in unconscious supplication, she stared down at the whalebone foundation, as if it was all that stood between her and complete ruin.

O'Rourke rose, drawn by the bewitching creature standing in nothing but her silk chemise and ruffled pantalettes; her thick auburn hair tumbled around her shoulders. The contest was over. He had won. Kate stood shivering before him. Aye, the half-spooked anticipation, the latent passion were there in her eyes. She wouldn't fight him; he felt it in his bones. Too far gone for that. So what was he waiting for?

Strike the match, man. Light the fire!

O'Rourke moved toward her, unable to stop himself.

"Ah, Kate, 'tis a dangerous woman you are," he whispered, and bending, caught a whiff of the intoxicating, gut-wrenching scent that was Woman.

'Tis said that animals can smell fear, even when humans cannot, for all their powers of perception. Suddenly O'Rourke could smell it, and it stopped him. He raised his head like a wild stallion nickering into the wind, catching the warning scent of a natural enemy. And he found it—within himself.

Christ! What was he doing? Was he such a rutting fool, to let sheer, primitive need rule over his higher self? Whatever he decided about Mary Kate, he couldn't let it interfere with his longer-range goals. Suddenly he realized that the real danger lay not in this tantalizing bundle of woman's flesh but in his inherent selfishness. There had to be a more solid basis upon which to build a marriage than sex, great as that was. If they didn't find that common ground, then it would be best to let her go, or return her to her father, as he'd agreed.

If Mary Katherine McGillacutty O'Rourke was feeling confused, so was Peter. She was every inch a woman, from the top of her flaming tresses to her nervously twitching toes. Yet so untried. He didn't often stoop to rob the cradle.

Physically, only seven-and-a-half years lay between them in age, but a vast chasm separated them in terms of life experience. He could see she was attracted—fascinated out of her mind by every move he made. But she was also emotionally unprepared, and perhaps he was, too, to take the next step. Hell, she didn't even see him as a husband! If he toyed with her now, they could wind up permanently estranged. He wasn't quite sure what he wanted out of the relationship, but it wasn't the armed truce that existed between her parents.

How the hell did I get myself into this? Peter thought as he stood before her, rifling the cards back and forth. He looked down at his hands and wondered if life wasn't something like a shuffle. A man had to take the cards he was dealt and play the game. Win or lose.

He put the cards back in his breast pocket.

"Give me your hands, Mary Katherine," he said softly.

After a brief hesitation, she placed them in his, and he kissed each palm tenderly. "I apologize," he said, "for getting a bit carried away." He raised his eyes to hers, and she saw a curious mixture of regret and frustration. "You're perfectly safe with me."

"I . . . I know that," she said, wondering at the shift in his mood. One minute he was aggressive and teasingly seductive; the next, intense but guarded. Right now, he looked so serious!

Peter reached past her and pulled down the bed covers. "Get in," he said quietly. "You need a good night's sleep before we leave in the morning. I'll sleep in the chair."

Katherine looked up at him, more puzzled than ever. "Peter?"

He smiled wryly and, taking her by the shoulders, made her sit on the edge of the bed. He raised her feet and legs, then drew the covers up to her chin. Dimming the gas jet, he kissed her forehead the way a nanny might comfort a child. "Good night."

Retreating to an easy chair and ottoman, Peter shrugged out of his frock coat and folded it carefully. Loosening the top button of his shirt, he used the boot-jack and set his boots in the hall for a shine. Then he dropped down in his chair, stretched out his legs, and closed his eyes.

Across the room, Kate frowned. She found Peter O'Rourke completely beyond comprehension. For a brief moment, she had seen his behavior become unbelievably tender and caring, almost as if he sensed an unspoken need within her. The strangest feeling crept over her; an unexplained yearning stirred, drawing her toward this gentler side of O'Rourke.

She didn't understand it, or where it came from, but like one soul creeping slowly through the dark to touch another, it left her strangely comforted.

It was pushing four o'clock in the afternoon when the stage, having rattled and jolted its way over the pass, finally pulled into Strawberry Point.

Grateful for a forty-minute stop while the horses were changed, Katherine surrendered herself without a murmur into the strong arms that lifted her from the coach.

"Mercy!" Kate sighed, clinging to O'Rourke's neck. "I do believe we hit every tree stump and pothole between here and Virginia City."

"That driver is one of the best," Peter said, as he set her on her feet. He escorted her to the hosteller's cabin, where the driver, Hank Monk, had said travelers might get a free cup of coffee. Not exactly the most irresistible offer Kate had ever had, but at least for a few minutes she could rest. So far, the trip had bounced her around like a miner's shiny agate being agitated and pulverized to remove all the impurities.

The cabin lay in a clearing surrounded by tall ponderosas, Douglas fir, and Jeffrey pine. High mountain peaks rose on every side, drawing her gaze to an intensely blue sky with a few wispy clouds. A trickling stream ran beside the cabin, and two Indian children, dressed in calico and soft buckskin, played along its bank. A huge kettle hung on a crane over an open fire. The smell of wood smoke and rendered hog fat and lye drifted across to where Kate stood enjoying the rustic scene.

"I'll be back in a minute," Peter said abruptly and crossed the yard to speak with a man no taller than herself. The man was barefoot, dressed in blue canvas overalls, a flannel shirt, and a knitted cap. When he spat in the dirt, Kate turned away with revulsion.

A group of men, two trappers or explorer scouts, four in blue military uniform, and at least a dozen unkempt woodsmen loitered in the yard. Approximately twenty mules with packs and a few saddled horses stood tethered at the edge of the clearing.

Close by, corralled horses kicked up dust, wheeling and snorting, as the hosteller and driver cut out fresh animals for the drive to Placerville.

The cabin itself was a ramshackle affair, rough-hewn boards slapped up and caulked with clay mixed with pine nettles. Burlap sacking covered the small windows, and smoke curled from the chimney, adding to the rustic atmosphere. It was the first time Kate had ever been exposed to life reduced to the barest necessities. To her, it seemed incomprehensible how people could give up all that the East offered to live in such a place. Why, her family's homes in Chicago and Virginia City were palaces, compared with this poor hut!

"Come set a spell," invited an Indian woman in braids. Her appearance was neat but threadbare. "Coffee, missus?"

"Yes. Please." Katherine took her place on the crude planks that served as benches. Determined to make the best of an uncomfortable journey, she found a pair of solemn black eyes watching her across the table.

Uneasy, Kate set down her cup. "You live here?" she asked politely.

"Yes, my husband is head wrangler for the Overland Stage. We live here three years," the Indian woman explained. "Very happy."

"How . . . nice," Katherine murmured. A tiny, convulsive shiver ricocheted through her, but she tried not to show her disdain. After all, not everybody had her advantages. Tomorrow she would reach San Francisco, where every luxury was available, to those who could afford it.

She rose abruptly. "Thank you for the coffee," she told the woman.

"You go now?" the hosteller's wife asked.

"No, but I want to stretch my legs and get some fresh air."

"Good luck." The woman gave Kate a sly smile and went to the wooden sink in the corner.

Poor woman! I am not the one who needs luck, Kate thought, skirts sweeping grandly as she walked away. She shaded her eyes and looked around. O'Rourke was laughing and joking with a group of the most disreputable-looking roughnecks she'd ever laid eyes on. And then she noticed that he had changed clothes. He was dressed much like the others.

What on earth? Kate wondered.

Suddenly O'Rourke threw back his head and spat a long stream of tobacco juice at a lizard. The short woodsman she'd noticed when they first arrived slapped Peter on the back.

"Bull's-eye!" he yelled.

Oh, for goodness sake, O'Rourke! she gasped, disparaging his rapid descent from urbane manners. He was such a chameleon.

As if her brain had sent a telepathic message to his, Peter waved to her, spoke to a couple of the men briefly, then headed toward her. "All set?" he asked.

Katherine, arms crossed and fingers drumming, tapped her toe impatiently. "Really, O'Rourke, such an uncouth exhibition."

He shrugged. "'When in Rome,' Kate."

"This is a disgusting, low place," she told him, "and I for one shall be delighted to get back on that stage and—"

"Sorry, Mrs. O'Rourke. This is the end of the line," Peter said, knowing the time had come to break the news.

"Don't call me that, and don't joke!" Katherine snapped, whirling haughtily away.

His hand on her arm stopped her. "You're not going to San Francisco, Kate. You're coming with me."

"Unhand me this instant!" she flared, fighting his possessive grip. "I'm not going anywhere with you!"

"Think again, Kate. You're my wife, and where I go, you go. Now, I'm heading up into the high country. You've heard me mention the Diablo Camp." He had her by both shoulders; she had no trouble seeing the fierce set of his jaw.

"Wrong, O'Rourke. Our agreement—" Kate took a deep breath and tried again, just knowing this was a really bad joke. "I paid you when you put me on the stage in Virginia City. We're quits of each other, remember? You go your way, I go mine."

"Wrong. You're going with me to Diablo Camp."

"Like hell I am!"

"Watch your language, Kate." Peter laughed softly, and his mouth crushed down on hers.

She went perfectly still, until he stopped kissing her.

"I'm getting back on that stagecoach," she informed him, straining to free herself.

Peter swore under his breath. "I knew you'd be trouble the minute I laid eyes on you. Unfortunately, I don't have a lot of time to argue." Without further ado, he grabbed her around the waist and half-walked, half-dragged her toward a mule. "Your luggage." He nodded at it tersely. "And you are coming, too, like it or not!"

"O'Rourke, stop this!" Kate screamed, swinging at him with both fists. "Oh, help, somebody! This man is kidnapping me—" She looked around frantically for assistance. She spotted the loggers behind them, laughing at her. Actually laughing! What kind of men *were* they, not to lift a finger in her defense? Outraged, she whirled around, straining against Peter's arm, and dragged her heels to slow his progress toward the mules. "My God, O'Rourke, you're insane! I am . . . not . . . going!"

"We'll just see about that, Katie O'Rourke." Hardening himself against her pleas, Peter threw her over his shoulder and kept walking.

"Wait till I tell my father," she threatened, clawing at him like a hundred-and-twenty-pound bobcat on a tear. "He'll chop you in little pieces and . . . and use you for fish bait! He'll hang you by your thumbs," she raved.

"Sorry to disillusion you. This is his idea, just as marrying me was yours." Peter grunted as she landed a lucky punch. "If the choice had been mine, you'd be married to that mine foreman right now. Lucky devil," he added.

He backed her into a burro, and Kate sprang at him, kicking and punching in a frenzy of temper. "Damn you, O'Rourke. You won't get away with this!"

She sank her teeth into his arm, and Peter slapped her. "Bitch!" he cursed, prying open her jaws.

"I'll kill you, O'Rourke," she vowed, gnawing his heavy wool shirt between her teeth.

"I predict we'll be the death of each other," Peter agreed, salvaging his shirt, minus one button.

Kate spat it out. "To the death, then."

"Aye, till death do us part," he agreed sardonically.

Jesus, she could fight! He'd never seen a woman like her! No wonder her father wanted a younger man to take over the job of trying to tame her!

Unexpectedly, Kate barreled into his midsection, using

her head as a battering ram. "Ouch!" Her head connected with taut, lean muscle, and she swore at him again.

Fed up, O'Rourke yanked her to him roughly, trying to wrestle her into submission. He felt his body turn to hard, pulsing steel as she strove in vain to inflict bodily harm. He groaned aloud. He must be insane. All her struggling only seemed to torment him more with desire.

"You lied to me, O'Rourke! You and Papa double-crossed me," she swore at him furiously. "Dammit, let me go! You lied, you—"

"Sorry, Kate. You'd better accept things the way they are. 'For better or for worse,' remember?"

"Oooh! I hate you, do you know that?" she railed, her fiery head thrashing in a vain effort to strike him in the face, possibly break his nose.

O'Rourke had had enough. He grabbed her by the hair and shut her up the fastest way he knew how. He kissed her, hard. Ravaging and pillaging forcefully, he let her know who was in charge. He kept it up even while she continued to express her low opinion of him. His tongue began a shocking assault on her senses. Kate shrilled in his ear and pulled his hair. When she wrapped her legs around his waist, Peter staggered backward into a string of mules.

"Settle down, Katherine. I'm warning you," Peter growled and swatted her rump—not even worth the effort, for all her petticoats.

She opened her mouth and uttered a scream so wild even the loggers looked around, as if expecting a cougar attack at Strawberry Point's stagecoach stop in broad daylight.

"I hate you, Peter O'Rourke," she sobbed.

"An honest emotion, Kate O'Rourke," he panted. "I'm not too crazy about you, either. Now, stop your fussing and get on that mule."

"No!" She glowered helplessly up at him, clearly appalled that he meant to kidnap her against her will.

His hair fell across his brow, and he shook it back

impatiently, raising his face to the sky. *Lord, this isn't going to be easy,* he silently admitted, needing an ally. She was so damn witchy and wild! And yet, in an exasperating way, almost lovable.

"I was a fool to trust you," she raged.

"Don't give me any more lip," he said through clenched teeth.

"You can't make me do anything," she persisted defiantly.

"All right, you asked for it."

O'Rourke plundered and raped her mouth again. He could feel her shiver, as his tongue came against hers in combat, two hotheads locked in a struggle for survival and supremacy. He parried and thrust deeply. Feeling her resistance waver, Peter put more tongue into it, to show her that he meant to shove every wicked, intemperate word she growled right back down her throat.

Suddenly Kate went limp in his arms. Alarmed, Peter drew back. Had she fainted? She had not. She lay panting shallowly, her eyes glazed with passion, her lips swollen and moist. Clearly in the throes of sexual arousal.

"Any more arguments?" he asked in his most menacing tone.

Mary Kate shook her head, not especially anxious to find out what else he would do if she said another word.

"I mean it, Kate," he said sternly. "There will be hell to pay, if you step out of line."

They glared at each other like two savages competing for scalps.

Two mules away, a logger coughed discreetly, and Peter turned to acknowledge the man's evident concern. "Still on our honeymoon, Jansen." He winked. "The wife here is still making a few adjustments to married life."

Jansen, catching on, nodded. He moved out, a string of three mules in tow behind him.

"Oh, help," Kate said faintly, as O'Rourke slung her over the backside of a mule. Indeed, she had felt a little faint in her husband's arms, and not because of the altitude, either. She was beset by the most terrible sinking feeling. She and O'Rourke were the absolute worst two people to have been thrown together. Oh, surely God was playing this ghastly joke on her for lying at the altar!

CHAPTER 10

The caravan of men and supplies headed in a north-easterly direction, taking a jagged path through the soaring giants of the forest. Her back rigid with anger, Katherine rode with them, battling the growing conviction that she might never see civilization again. In minutes, her whole world of privilege and comfort had been wrenched from her. And here she was, an unwilling captive being carried into a desolate wilderness, surrounded by hostile elements and danger, not the least of which were these raucous loggers—and O'Rourke, whom she had foolishly trusted. If she had cause to resent her father before, this latest betrayal had wounded her deeply.

Vowing that her father and O'Rourke would pay dearly, Kate tried to keep track of their progress through the dry brush and grasses along the stream. She would have marked the trail, but she was afraid that either the man called Jigger or Peter—who had the gall to call himself a husband!—might see her do it. She would just have to remember the trail, that was all.

She couldn't rely on anyone coming after her. Probably no one knew or cared what happened to her. Certainly not her father, if O'Rourke was to be believed.

She would simply have to get herself out of this. It was like a bad dream. But somehow she would escape.

Long afternoon shadows faded into twilight, and still they climbed, higher and higher toward the summit, and the lonely screech of a hawk circling high above only heightened Kate's sense of isolation. Ponderosa pines and fir trees shut out the sky overhead as the silent caravan made its way into the high country. As the late sun was cut off by heavy foliage and high canyon walls, her heart grew cold and still.

When she set out that morning for San Francisco without a care in the world, her plaid muslin dress and matching parasol had seemed so perfect. But with every lurch of the smelly mule, the unsuitability of her garb and her unfitness for this mode of travel became more apparent. Saddle sore and physically miserable, Katherine fought to keep her wits about her. Finally darkness conspired with the plodding rhythm of the caravan, as it proceeded up a steep trail on the west rim. Her body slumped over the mule's neck and, as they moved into the tall timber, for a time even the frightening whispers of the forest were no more . . .

Pulling up short in front of Katherine's mount, Jigger Jansen brought the caravan to an abrupt halt. Jerking awake, Kate found herself in a clearing once populated by tall ponderosas but now an open meadowland with a few burnt stumps and scrubby bushes. They had crossed so many gullies and ravines that Strawberry Point might as well be on the other side of the world.

"We stop here for the night," Jigger announced, signaling the men to dismount.

In the dim moonlight, O'Rourke saw Kate reel in her saddle and go limp. Uttering a quick oath, he spurred his horse forward and caught her before she pitched on her head. Dismounting, he laid her down in a thick patch of wildflowers.

Still groggy and confused, she pulled away, weaving unsteadily to her feet. "Leave me along, you dirty bas—"

Before she could say another word, Peter clapped a hand over her mouth. "Watch your language." He leaned close, filling her vision with silver moonbeams glinting in his hair. "Awake now?" he asked silkily, and removed his hand.

Moaning, Kate hopped around to restore circulation to her limbs. As her feet revived, the painful prickling sensation subsided, but her fears grew. The men moved like shadows around her, gathering firewood, rummaging in packs for food and cooking pots, and hobbling the animals; a few disappeared into the dark to take care of private business.

Kate didn't need anyone to tell her what terrible danger she was in. She glared at O'Rourke, too tired and hungry to engage him in battle. But she promised herself, if she survived the night, she was going to get even, if it was the last thing she ever did.

"Moonlight becomes you," Peter said and led Kate to a log, where he made her sit down.

She didn't fight him. What was the point? she thought dejectedly. He and her father obviously meant to ruin her life. A wave of self-pity swept over her, almost choking her with misery. What had she ever done to deserve such an injustice? She had never murdered or stolen or intentionally harmed anybody. Surely Peter O'Rourke was the most unfeeling person she had ever met. With the exception of her father, of course.

She flinched at O'Rourke's touch through the thin muslin that was her only protection against the cold. "Get away," she warned.

"Katherine, you're shivering. Why didn't you say something?" Without another word, he strode to a pack animal and returned with a warm woolen jacket. "Here, put this on. You're half-frozen."

After all he had put her through, how dare he pretend he was concerned? Kate raged inwardly. She pulled away and threw the garment on the ground. "I don't want your coat," she snarled, "or your pity. I just want to get as far away from you as—"

Peter's face hardened. "I know—San Francisco. Sorry, but setting an innocent like you loose in a wide-open city wouldn't be in your best interests."

"That's for me to decide." Kate dashed the back of her hand across her tear-streaked face, refusing to look at him.

"Take it as sound advice offered by one prodigal to another." Peter hunkered down in front of her. This time she let him stick her arms in the sleeves, but she didn't help. He buttoned her coat and pulled the collar up around her chin. "There! At least you won't catch your death of cold."

"Who cares?" Katherine asked glumly. "Father couldn't love me, or he never would have done this to me."

O'Rourke laughed softly and, taking her hands, chafed them till they were warm. "Don't be so hard on him. You probably drove him to it. In his clumsy way, I suspect he's trying to look out for you."

"That hardly excuses the two of you plotting behind my back," Kate said, her head bowed. She realized Peter was still holding her hands and she gazed longingly toward the fire, which leapt and crackled against the darkened sky. "I have a good deal more sense than either of you thinks. I could have managed on my own. I have money."

With mixed emotions Peter studied the young woman now in his charge. "Perhaps," he conceded, "as long as your money held out. How much have you got on you, anyway?"

Kate sprang to her feet. "Wouldn't you like to know," she bristled. "I-I have . . . enough, you scoundrel, even after paying you more than you're worth!"

But then, in her feverish desire to be free, an idea came to her: maybe he would return her home, or at least to Strawberry Point, if she offered him more. "Oh, all right. I have eight hundred left. But I could get more. I'm sure I could." She knew her mother would help, once she knew what had happened. "How much do you want, O'Rourke? If it's ransom money you want, I'll get it for you."

"Save your breath. I'm not interested." Peter dropped her hands and stared moodily into the fire. "Damn your mercenary soul, Kate! Is money all you and your father ever think about?"

His rebuff caught Katherine unawares. She had hardly expected him to turn her down. "No, but if money will buy my way out of this predicament, I'm willing to talk price."

For a second, Peter was tempted to tell her he would take her back to Strawberry Point in the morning. But he knew he couldn't. He felt an obligation to her father—and most of all to her as his wife, like it or not. His own conscience, though newly awakened, made him want to see this through. What good was it to pull himself out of the miry clay if at the same time he shirked his responsibility to Kate?

The fire popped, landing a burning coal at his feet. Peter kicked dirt over it, extinguishing it. By the same token, he clamped a lid on his temper.

"Surely you can be bought," Kate sneered.

"Christ Almighty, you are a corrupt little bitch," he told her in a low voice, so no one else could hear. "Sorry, but I can't be bought. I went along with you before, for reasons of my own." He gave her shoulder a quick squeeze. "Legally you're my headache now. I accepted that burden when I made my vows at the altar."

Katherine began to shake; even her teeth chattered, as she began to absorb his meaning. "You can't mean that! I'm *not* your wife! I won't *be* your wife! What we agreed to wasn't marriage. It was—" She closed her eyes and swallowed hard. She must be losing her mind. She couldn't face those piercing green eyes again! What did it matter that he was the handsomest man she'd ever laid eyes on? He had tricked her!

"This is outrageous, O'Rourke," she whispered.

"We have a legal contract, Kate. I intend to keep my word to you, as long as it's humanly possible."

"Oh, God!" she moaned. "O'Rourke, I didn't agree to any of this."

"I know that, spitfire, but it's no less binding, just because you're a piker."

"I'm a . . . *what?*"

"A damn piker. A person whose word isn't worth spit." He glared down at her, his features softening only when he saw her eyes widen with fright.

"I can see I've spat in the wind once too often." Kate meant it as a macabre joke, but neither of them saw the humor in it. "Only this time, it's landed in my face," she ended lamely.

"Believe me, I'm no more thrilled about this than you," Peter said. "I dislike intensely having marriage rammed down my throat."

"What? Am I supposed to cry?" Kate sneered. He could burn in hell for eternity, and it still wouldn't make up for double-crossing her.

The aroma of strong coffee had drawn the men to the cook fire. Peter, anxious not to come to blows, excused himself to fetch them each a cup. Returning, he handed Kate's over and drew her aside, where they could talk privately. "Let's get this straight: I'm not insisting on conjugal rights—nothing like that—so relax. You can keep your precious virginity," he told her under his breath.

"Thank you very much," Kate said stiffly. While she sipped her coffee, she studied him out of the corner of her eye, wondering if that was why he hadn't touched her on their wedding night. Of course, it was too ridiculous even to speculate. She should be *grateful* that he wanted to leave her alone. And she was—*she was!* All this talk of keeping promises and protecting her innocence! Oh, la! Was that why he wouldn't let her go to San Francisco? Or was he merely her father's flunky?

"You'd like me to think kidnapping me and all the rest

of it is because you're really a noble character, right?"
Her words dripped with sarcasm.

"Quite the opposite. I've lived a very self-centered life
for longer than I care to remember." He laughed mirth-
lessly. "I'm the prodigal son who squandered so much of
the family fortune that my old man refuses to welcome
me home with open arms, for fear he will be taken advantage of again. Aye, and given the chance, I probably
would. Who knows?"

Katherine's jaw dropped. She had a hard time believing anyone would admit so brazenly to a wasted life.
Could this be the man who initially refused her bribe?
Who preferred working for her father for wages? What
kind of a man was she dealing with?

Peter chuckled grimly. "If only you could see the look
on your face!" He skimmed the backs of his fingertips
down her flushed cheek. "Nobody hates drunks more
than a reformed alcoholic, and I guess that goes for
bums, too."

"You don't approve of me, do you, O'Rourke?" Kate
asked, the light suddenly dawning.

"I find nothing to disapprove in you," he told her
gently and brushed a flaming curl back from her forehead. "You could say I'm tempted to nip things in the
bud, if I can. On that, at least, your father and I are not
too far divided."

Kate tossed her head, growing impatient of such talk.
"What makes you think I'd ever become a prodigal like
you, O'Rourke?"

"Simple deduction. It takes one to know one. But it's
a helluva lot harder for a girl to climb out of the pigpen
than for a fellow." He lowered his head, planting a kiss
on her pert nose. "Relax, Kate. Supper's almost ready,"
he said and left her huddled in the shadows to think
over what he had said.

Kate didn't know what to make of O'Rourke's self-
revelation. He seemed adamant about keeping her with

him in the woods, though why, she had no idea. It certainly wasn't because he *liked* her!

Blowing a curl from her forehead, she watched her sworn enemy chatting amiably with the logging crew. No, she decided, it just wasn't normal for a man of O'Rourke's background and habits not to have wicked designs on her. Unmitigated liar! A reformed prodigal he was not.

But that still didn't explain why he was holding her prisoner. He and her father were in cahoots, all right. She had better not lower her guard, or trust him as far as she could throw him.

Seething with a savage desire for revenge, Katherine paced, warming her hands on the coffee cup and examining her options. She knew it was neither prudent nor possible to slip away from him in the dark. The way her luck had run all day, she would probably fall off a cliff and break her neck. Or be eaten by some wild animal.

No, better to play along with O'Rourke for now.

Once he dropped his guard, she would lose him and make her way across the mountains to California. Oh, wouldn't that just tie a knot in Papa's plans to marry her off! Old hurts and resentments toward her father resurfaced, and Kate began to wonder if the Lucky Strike mine had fallen on hard times. She had heard of mines being flooded out. Surely her father wasn't so desperate that he'd taken out a life insurance policy on her? But if that was the case, he could have dropped her down a mine shaft. *Watch out, Katie McGillacutty,* she told herself, her green cat's eyes glinting in the firelight. *You can't afford to trust anybody.*

"Come'n git it!" called a toothless old man. He stood, ladle in hand, dipping into the pot and filling the men's plates.

Katherine came over, her stomach in such a state she

would have eaten a bear, if it had wandered into camp by accident.

"Kate, this is the foreman, Jigger Jansen." Peter indicated the barefoot individualist to whom the crew openly deferred.

"Ma'am." Jigger's tight-lipped smile didn't reach his eyes. One glance communicated volumes to Kate: he considered women bad luck in camp; they should stay home where they belonged. He didn't like having a greenhorn boss, either, and she could just guess what he thought of Peter for bringing along a wife to interfere.

"Hell, it ain't none of my business, 'course," he told O'Rourke, "but do you have any idee what you're lettin' yer wife in for? It's better if the men forget about women till they hit town in the spring."

"I can handle it," Peter said calmly. "My wife will pull her own weight around camp, I guarantee it."

"Huh," Jansen said noncommittally and aimed a spurt of Bull Durham at the fire. "I was thinkin', Casey, what if we give you and the missus the scaler's cabin? It's off to itself; probably has less bugs, too."

Casey? Kate raised her eyebrows. Did her jack-of-all-trades husband have an alias? But then she remembered that he used Casey as his middle name during the wedding ceremony. Just remembering their vows before Father Manogue made her stomach queasy.

Forcing a smile, Kate told Jansen, "Please don't inconvenience anyone on my account."

"No trouble. Widow-maker tree did in old Hinman last spring. Ain't got around to replacin' him yet." He squinted at her, testing her mettle.

"Oh, well, in that case, if Mr. O'Rourke thinks it will be suitable, that will be—fine by me." Kate swallowed, trying not to show how upset she was with the idea of sharing a cabin.

Peter casually looped his arm around her shoulders and gave her a hug. "I'm sure we can make do in any place," he told the camp ramrod.

"Good. It's settled, then." Jansen turned to introduce his logging crew.

As they lined up, Peter tweaked one of her curls. "Mind your manners, Kate," he muttered in her ear. Gritting her teeth, she tried to respond cordially, although in the firelight they looked like a bunch of unshaven thugs.

After the formalities, everybody fell silent and ate. Most of the men stood or squatted, shoveling in beans and sourdough biscuits as if their lives depended on it. Katherine wandered over to a fallen log with a metal plate piled high with beans, biscuits, and beef jerky. She ate quickly to fortify herself against the long night ahead. Her muscles were stiff, and the prospect of getting on a mule again in the morning left her less than thrilled. But she supposed it was inevitable. She heard the men talk about reaching Diablo Camp by late tomorrow. The camp seemed well named, considering her escort!

O'Rourke ate with the men, then pulled out a plug of tobacco and joined in some light-hearted banter for awhile. Shivering and wondering if she was expected to spend the night huddled on a log, Kate tried to block out the loggers' ribald jokes and the way "Casey" O'Rourke acted right at home with the outfit.

The swine puts on a different face for every occasion, she thought morosely, plinking beans at the knothole in the log she was sitting on.

"Mrs. O'Rourke," Peter suddenly called. "How about giving Al a hand with the dishes?"

Katherine's chin went up a notch. "You must be mistaken, Casey darling," she said, her teeth clenched in a brittle smile. "My housekeeping skills are *nil*. Or didn't my father tell you how useless I am?"

To her dismay, Peter jerked a thumb toward Al, the cook. "No excuses, Kate. Everybody in this outfit works for their food, and that includes you."

Peter almost lost his authoritative scowl when Katherine did a perfect double-take. She was superb, he thought; missed her calling. But he couldn't let her get away with that spoiled-brat routine. The men were lounging about, sizing him up. If he couldn't run his wife, he knew they wouldn't work for him, either.

Their green eyes clashed silently across the clearing. The camp grew quiet, and she knew he was waiting. He crossed his arms over his broad chest and shifted his long-legged stance. She was faced with a choice. She diverted her gaze to the pile of dirty dishes and Al. "All right, I wouldn't want to do anything to displease my husband, now would I?" she asked, getting up and walking over to the dish tub.

To a man, the loggers breathed an audible sigh. O'Rourke hadn't taken any guff from his woman, and that had put him in good stead with the entire crew. The man from the head office might be a greenhorn, but his stock went up several points that night.

"Remind me to put you on the payroll, Kate," Peter said, giving her a playful swat on the bottom as she marched past him.

Swinging around, Katherine uttered a startled squawk. He was closer than she anticipated. His mouth captured her lips in a quick buss. "I'll put up the tent while you wash the dishes," and the wicked gleam in his eye wasn't missed by his loggers, either.

"I'm afraid I've never done this before," she told the cook with a helpless shrug.

Al gave her a toothless grin and took the sponge. He threw naphtha flakes in the water, stirred it around with his finger, then demonstrated the fine art of dishwashing. "Nuthin' to it, ma'am," he assured her, placing the sponge in her dainty white hands.

To Kate's immense relief, dishwashing didn't require exceptional talent, just a little splashing, dunking, and rubbing. Halfway through, the grease floated to the surface and the suds disappeared. Concerned, Kate turned to the cook. "Do I need more soap bubbles?" she asked.

Al turned from wiping out a large kettle. Lifting the

dishpan, he threw the water into the outer darkness. Then, with a resounding clang he set the pan on the stump he used as a worktable. "There's hot water on the fire." He handed her a thick pot holder. "Help yerself, ma'am."

Katherine decided to put in the soap flakes first, then pour the water in on top. Carefully she lifted the heavy cast-iron pot from the fire and refilled the pan. A simple chore, yet when she finished scrubbing the dishes clean, she felt a tiny sense of accomplishment. Kate refilled the small tub once more and dipped in all the dishes to rinse off any soapy residue. Then, following the cook's example, she flung the water into the bushes.

"Joseph, Mary, and Jesus!" someone hollered from the darkness. "Can't a man take a leak without gettin' scalded to death?"

The man's blasphemy was met by shouts of laughter from his companions, who lewdly began to speculate on the long-range effects scalding water might have on the man's love life.

"Too bad! Ruby's sure gonna miss you, Big Jack."

"Not as much as I'm gonna miss her," the man groaned, thrashing around in the underbrush.

"A little horse liniment, an' you'll be good as new," another predicted.

"Hell, he drinks a pint o' that every day. Ain't done him no good yet." Jigger laughed, knocking a firefly out of the air with a juicy spurt of Bull Durham.

Katherine wished the ground would open and swallow her up. "I-I'm really sorry," she stammered, her pride dashed to the ground.

Surprisingly, the men seemed to bear her no ill will, but it would be a while before she got carried away again by her new-found gift for washing dishes. Thoroughly upset, she threw down her dish towel and plunged into the darkness to find O'Rourke. At least his language was an improvement over these loggers!

She stumbled over a tent stake and clutched her toe,

hopping. "O'Rourke? Where are you?" she whispered frantically. She didn't want to commit another faux pas by entering the wrong tent.

A hand reached out of the dark and grabbed her. "We're over here," Peter's voice said. He pulled her along through the pitch-black forest. The scent of pine was strong around her as she held onto his arm with both hands, ducking her head when long pine needles brushed her cheek.

"Where are we going? Ouch, Peter, stop. I can't see!"

"We're off by ourselves. Less temptation for the men that way," he said and stopped so suddenly that Katherine bumped into his back.

"Are you sure this is safe?" she whispered. "I mean, what about wild animals?"

"The only wild animals to worry about are those men," he told her, guiding her in her blind search for the tent flaps. "Don't get too friendly, and you should be all right."

"How fortunate that I have nothing to worry about, where you're concerned," she couldn't resist saying.

"No, I have a gun." He chuckled. "I can fight off any advances you make, Mrs. O'Rourke, so keep your hands to yourself. Come on, get in." He started to push her from behind.

"Stop it, O'Rourke," she balked. "I-I need to—well, must I spell it out for you? Men aren't the only ones who have to answer a call of nature."

"Why didn't you say so in the first place? Come on." Peter began pulling her through a clump of tangled undergrowth.

"You can't come with me!" Kate screeched. "O'Rourke, go away. Stand guard—over by the tent."

He laughed. "Sure you can find your way back?"

"I'll manage," Kate said crisply and promptly fell over a tree root. Peter crashed through the thicket and helped her up. Biting her lip to stifle the pain of a scraped knee, she was glad she didn't have a mirror to confirm her wretched appearance. "You may go now," she told him coolly.

She waited until she was certain he had retreated a polite distance. On her return, she halted in her tracks, sensing his presence. "Didn't sit in any poison oak, I trust?" he taunted.

"Oh, you'd love that, wouldn't you?" Kate snapped and without further ado, crawled into the small canvas tent. Feeling around, she located a blanket spread over pine boughs and nettles. The aroma was unexpectedly fresh and inviting. But then she realized she wasn't alone. "Wait a minute! You can't come in here." Kate tried to sit up, but his arm circled her waist, weighing her down.

He pulled her close, arranging the blankets over them both. "I'm providing body warmth, nothing more, Mrs. O'Rourke," Peter murmured in her ear.

"Please . . ." Kate wet her lips, glad the dark hid her flaming face. "Don't . . . Please don't touch me, O'Rourke."

She was trembling beneath his arm like leaves in a windstorm. "If I don't sleep here, Katherine, how long do you think it'll be before those randy loggers decide to keep you company?" he asked.

"What did I ever do to you?" Katherine asked in a strangled little voice. She was mashed up against him, her face against his flannel shirt. Her nostrils picked up his male scent, along with the faint smell of leather and wood smoke. *No matter what happens, don't let him take away your pride,* she told herself. She struggled to put distance between them, but O'Rourke only wrapped his arms around her tighter than ever and settled his chin on her head with a yawn.

Kate fought sleep as long as she could. She listened to a coyote serenade on a nearby hill. The cry of an owl's prey sent a shiver down her spine, and long after the camp had gone deadly quiet, one of the men roused himself to chase off a wild animal.

Finally she couldn't hold out any longer. Nestled in the warm embrace of her worst enemy, Katherine entered the dreamless sleep of exhaustion.

* * *

"Up, slug!"

Mary Kate feebly swatted at the hand that was intent upon disturbing her slumber. "I'm tired," she mumbled, rolling onto her stomach.

O'Rourke shook her again. "Kate, you're the cook's helper. Now get up and pull your own weight, or must I take you down and throw you in the creek?"

Katherine looked up through her tangled curls and groaned. Almost she would sell her soul never to set eyes on O'Rourke again. "Don't boss me around," she warned. "I may be your prisoner, but I am not your slave."

"Wrong," Peter informed her and flung her out of the tent ahead of him.

She landed on all fours in the dirt. "Bully!"

"Make it easy on yourself, Kate," he said, standing over her prostrate body. "Help out and you eat. Otherwise—" He left the rest of his threat unspoken.

"If you help me up," she said, "perhaps we can discuss this like two civilized people."

"Be my guest," he said, moving to one side with a bow.

Katherine lurched to her feet. She hauled off and slugged him in the gut. Her knuckles crunched painfully, but she wouldn't give him the satisfaction of knowing how much it hurt.

"That's three I owe you, Katie O'Rourke," he warned.

"Why stop at three?" she raged, winding up and landing another blow, this time on his jaw.

"Dammit, woman!" Peter grabbed her, his foot neatly tripping her. They fell to the dirt together, Katherine underneath. They rolled back and forth, raising clouds of dust, but she couldn't shake him. She kicked and screamed, hurling insults as freely as dirt clods.

Keeping her pinned, his eyes dangerous, O'Rourke grabbed her chin and took her down in a long, probing kiss. By now he knew the quickest way to subdue her was to use her own volatile nature against her. The instant

Kate stopped fighting and began to respond, he withdrew from the kiss. He put his hand on her breast and gave the tip a light squeeze, watching her eyes dilate at his touch. "Shall we go back in the tent, Kate?" he suggested. "Or are you ready to get to work?"

"I'll . . . I'll work! Dammit, let me go, O'Rourke. You don't have to ask twice."

She scrambled to her feet the instant he released her and fled with O'Rourke's insolent laughter ringing in her ears.

It was one of the toughest performances he'd ever had to give.

CHAPTER 11

The edge of dawn was barely creeping over the east ridge when Mary Kate stuffed the breakfast dishes back into the cook's supply pack. She scooted over to her own mule, avoiding O'Rourke's amused gaze, and flung herself into the saddle.

Admittedly, she was a desperate woman, but at least she'd come up with a strategy: as long as she did her work and stayed out of O'Rourke's way, she might still have half a chance of escaping unscathed. If it wasn't for her father's insane notion that he needed a male heir to leave his millions to, this whole travesty would never have happened, and she would never have gotten mixed up with such a scoundrel. What poppycock! She could have spent his money, and done a much better job of it, too, than most men!

But now she didn't even have her eight hundred dollars, and until she found out where O'Rourke had hidden it while she slept, she would have to play along with him. No wonder she hated him so much.

In the afternoon they came over a ridge and saw smoke lazily curling from the bunkhouse stovepipe below. A number of men were coming down the opposite

slope behind a skid of logs drawn by six oxen. As they
rode in, Kate heard the *whang* and *chong* of the camp's
saw-and-tool sharpener.

So this was Diablo Camp, she thought with a sinking
feeling.

"That's our filer, Charlie," said the young half-breed
riding at her side on a scruffy mustang. "I'm Bobbie
White Feather, ma'am. I'm a bucker."

Katherine nodded, not knowing what a bucker was,
but sure he was dying to tell her. "I'm glad to meet you,
Mr. White Feather."

"Yessiree," he said, his black eyes dancing. "My job is
to saw trees into logs."

"Sounds fascinating," she said, not really interested,
but not wanting to make enemies. Hadn't she heard
about an Indian uprising a couple of years ago in Washoe
Valley? "Is it dangerous work?"

"Ain't nothin' about loggin' that isn't," he said modestly. He rolled up his sleeve and showed her a long
white scar on his dark forearm.

Kate winced. It was hideously disfigured. "It must have
hurt terribly," she said, glancing away quickly.

"Naw, not after they got me all lickered up." He
laughed at her reaction. "Old Jigger just poured wood alcohol over it and wrapped it in baling wire."

"I should think my father would have a doctor in
camp," was all Kate could think to say.

"Jigger and Al got me over the worst of it. Nothin' like
clear grain alcohol." And Bobbie patted his stomach.

"You drank raw alcohol? That could have killed you!"

"Shee-it, ma'am, that and a little horse liniment fixed
me up good as new."

To her relief, Bobbie buttoned up his shirtsleeve at
the wrist.

"Ask Jigs. Swears by wood-grain alcohol. Says it keeps
him warm all winter." He tipped his hat and nudged his
mustang forward. "'Bye, ma'am."

Tall tales? Katherine cautiously looked around, shaking her head in wonderment. Loggers were a strange breed. They had to be, to live in crude line shacks and climb trees. Over by the bunkhouse, Jigger Jansen was introducing the other buckers, fallers, and the camp blacksmith to O'Rourke. Good, she thought; the less she saw of him, the better.

Seeing the cook disappear into a large cabin, she headed in that direction, knowing it probably housed the kitchen and dining hall. With supper only hours away, she decided as Al's new "cookee," or assistant, she had better lend a hand.

"Mr. Al," she called, bringing her mule to a stop by the steps. "I'm sorry, but I don't know your last name. How should I address you?"

"I give up last names back in '52," he said with a mysterious wink. He started unloading flour sacks from a mule. "Open that door fer me, will you, ma'am?"

"Yes, of course." Kate hurried to do as he asked and followed him inside. The walls were lined with shelves, and at one end was the largest wood-burning stove she had ever seen. She saw him head toward the storeroom and moved to open that door for him as well.

"Thank you, ma'am," Al said, heaving the flour sack on top of a barrel. It was a hundred-pound sack. Al was no longer young, but he handled those sacks with ease. He walked back outside, leaving her to get acquainted with the storeroom. A moment later he was back with another flour sack. And another.

Astonished by so much of one staple, Kate looked at three hundred pounds of flour and then at Al. "Mr. . . . er, Al, how will you ever use that much flour?" she asked.

"Can't have too much flour, ma'am," he said with a chuckle. Kate followed him back and forth, while he brought in not three, but five hundred pounds of beans. He spent the next hour restocking supplies. "'Course, a little always gits et by the mice and other varmints whut live under the cookhouse," he grunted, rolling a small barrel of grease into one corner. "The men eat pert near

anythin' you set before 'em. Pancakes is a favorite, an'
pies—Lord, how they go fer my apple and gooseberry
pies!"

Katherine counted lentils and dried peas, sacks of un-
refined sugar, and a barrel of molasses, which was used
for syrup and for sweetening of all sorts of hearty fare including pork and beans. She was astounded by the huge
quantities of oats, corn flour, and potatoes. There were
crates of dried apples, peaches, and raisins. Salt came in
a twenty-five-pound sack. And there were kegs of rum
and a whiskey barrel—"fer medicinal purposes," Al assured her with a wink.

Next, a strange contraption with a copper kettle,
tubing, and a vent stack out the side of the building
caught her eye. "And what might that be, Mr. Al?" she
asked, watching the dark liquid simmer within a glass vat.

"Gen-u-wine Kentucky still," Al told her proudly, pausing in his labors to wipe his neck with a red kerchief.
"That's the only thing I managed to bring West in '52
after my wife up'n died."

"What's in it?" Kate asked, seeing it was the man's
pride and joy.

"Bourbon. My own recipe." He tinkered needlessly
with a tube. "Only blew up once."

"That's a mercy." Katherine walked out into the dining
hall and surveyed the drafty room with its crude benches
and boards laid over sawhorses. The floor was filthy with
dust and crumbs. She bent to inspect a large, dark stain
on the floor, then straightened.

"If you'll tell me where to start, Mr. Al? I could wash
the floor, if you'd like," she volunteered, astounding
even herself.

"It'd only git dirty agin," he said and aimed a quick
squirt of juicy tobacco out the door.

Katherine shrugged. "Maybe I'll clean up afterward."

"Tell you whut, Mrs. O'Rourke." Al scratched his
head. Kate noticed that most of the men scratched fre-
quently. She wondered if they had anything catching.

"Golly, damn, but I feel bad to be askin', seein' as you're the brains' wife 'n all . . . "

"Brains?" Kate echoed. "Oh, you mean . . . O'Rourke?" She was tempted, but decided there was no point in disillusioning an unlearned hillbilly about his new boss.

"Sure. We always call the man from the front office the 'brains,' don't you see? Anyway, every other cookee I've had fetched water, so I kin boil potatoes."

"Since my . . . er, husband"—Oh! How that word stuck in her craw!—"well, since Mr. O'Rourke expects everyone to work around here, Mr. Al, you mustn't treat me any differently than your other cookees."

Al looked relieved. "Mrs. O'Rourke, I thank you fer them kind words. We'll git along jus' fine, an' I'll try not to make yer job too hard."

"Thank you, Mr. Al." Kate smiled warmly. He was a crude, unlearned man, but his kindness pleased her. "I hope you'll make allowances for my shortcomings. I-I've never cooked anything in my life. Perhaps you could teach me?"

Katherine's words brought a light to the old man's eyes. It had been a long time since anyone had treated him like anything but the low-down rumsoak he was. Al decided to make her stay in camp as pleasant as possible. "This isn't much of a place for a perty lady like you, Mrs. O'Rourke," he confided. "I'll pass the word, an' maybe some of them sour-bellies kin give ye a hand from time to time."

"Oh, no, Mr. Al, I don't believe my"—Damn! she thought, there's that word again—"my husband would approve."

"What wouldn't I approve, my love?"

Katherine whirled around and saw Peter O'Rourke's long, lank torso leaning up against the wall. He hadn't shaved that morning, she noticed. In fact, she'd done such a good job of avoiding him, she hadn't taken a good look at him all day. He was wearing inch-long cleats, whipcord canvas trousers, and another flannel shirt. He looked like a logger. Cleaner and with better speech, but obviously trying to fit in.

She gave him a tight little smile and the evil eye. "Good afternoon," she said warily.

Al tied on his none-too-clean apron and started bustling about. He didn't want to appear lazy in front of the main boss, especially right off. "Me and yer missus was just discussin' chores. I always had a boy cookee before," he said. "Mrs. O'Rourke is such a delicate, refined lady—"

"Mrs. O'Rourke *is* a lady, to be sure," Peter agreed, "but she's also no shirker. Are you worried that some chores might be too heavy for her?"

Al cleared his throat. "Totin' water from the lake, choppin' kindlin', sloppin' the hogs with leftovers, skinnin' rabbits and small game, that's not easy work, Mr. O'Rourke."

"Slopping hogs?" *How appropriate,* Peter thought, and flashed Kate one of his million-dollar smiles. "You don't object to that, do you, my love?" His green eyes pierced like a dagger, sending a silent warning against rebellion.

"Why, of course not, *darling*," Kate gritted out. "There's dignity in all work, I've heard my father say." Kate turned to the cook with a kindly smile. "Mr. Al, I want to do my fair share." She turned back to O'Rourke with a smirk. "Was there anything else?" she asked with sweet sarcasm.

"Nothing, my love," Peter said, surprised that she hadn't fired off another of her biting remarks. "I just stopped by to say that your luggage is in the scaler's cabin."

"Thank you," Kate said coolly. "Now, if you'll excuse me, I was just on my way to get Mr. Al some water to boil potatoes in."

Peter narrowed his eyes, full of suspicion. She was just too damn cooperative. Even in fairy tales, nobody turned from a witch to a lowly scullery maid this quickly!

To be sure, a few scullery maids had become beautiful princesses, but never the other way around.

Katherine picked up two buckets, let Al adjust a light wooden yoke on her shoulders, and marched toward the door. Her green eyes flared with sheer orneriness as she stepped sideways to pass in front of Peter. "See you at supper," she cooed, thinking she'd poison him, if only she could manage it without killing a lot of innocent men.

"I can hardly wait, my turtledove." Peter followed her outside, watching her hips sway provocatively as she descended toward the lake. Even during her meanest, most cussed moments, Katie O'Rourke had a way about her that set his blood to racing.

Peter jogged down the skid road toward the cabin he and Kate were sharing. He cursed himself for letting her get under his skin. *Damn her!* And damn these sudden pangs of conscience, anyway! He had best keep his distance, he decided, or O'Rourke the Invincible might fall, mortally wounded on the field of love.

O'Rourke checked out the scaler's cabin again, more thoroughly this time. Jansen was a brick to suggest it. It was solidly built, certainly better than what he'd expected. The bunkhouse fairly crawled with lice, and the camp was in dire need of repairs and reorganization before snowfall. With so much needing attention, he was sure he could steer clear of his redheaded wife!

"I don't mean to lose any sleep over you, Katie O'Rourke," he said aloud, moving the few pieces of furniture around. First, the bed. That was sure to create problems, unless he came up with a workable solution right away.

He hauled the heavy bed away from the wall. A mouse scurried out from beneath, and he made a note to give Kate one of the kittens he'd seen at the foot of Raimey Griswold's bunk. The mama cat had enough little mousers to eliminate any major problem. Al needed one or two as well. And the wangan lumber office could use a couple.

Resourceful, O'Rourke, that's what you have to be around here, he told himself.

Grabbing the tick mattress, he took it outdoors. He hung it on a tree limb and beat out the dust with a stick. He felt like a bloody housemaid, but he couldn't expect Kate to do it; the mattress was too heavy for her to pick up. But that was the *only* concession he was prepared to make.

Once the tick was well aired, Peter returned it to the bed frame and contemplated his next move. *I know,* he laughed to himself, *I'll make the little witch stay on her side of the cabin. That way we won't get in each other's hair.*

Impressed with his brilliant plan, O'Rourke rushed over to the wangan building. He rummaged through the office drawers till he found a piece of yellow chalk. *Just the thing,* he thought, hurrying back to the cabin. He paced off the length, settled on an equitable division, giving himself two feet more, and drew a line down the middle. Perfect!

Except for one thing: there was only one bed.

Of course, among so many loggers, there had to be at least one carpenter who could build him another bed. Cheered by the thought, Peter went down the road to the office again. Out back was a pile of long planks.

But he still needed some nails. So Peter loped over to the filer's shack. Charlie Mason had a foot-driven stone sharpener going, and he barely glanced up as he tread-led. The saw he was sharpening was at least twelve feet long.

"Hope I'm not interrupting anything," Peter said, stooping to enter the workshop.

"How kin I help you?" the man's tempo never missed a beat.

"I need a hammer and nails," Peter yelled over the din of scraping metal and stone.

Charlie indicated with a nod where Peter could find them.

"Thanks, Charlie." O'Rourke picked up a long board about fifteen inches wide and started back to the cabin. He was just mounting the steps when the dinner bell rang. "Damnation!"

Peter laid down the board, nails, and a heavy claw hammer. Reluctantly he decided to finish up after supper.

One of the cook's rules was that nobody was late to meals, unless they wanted to go hungry. Another rule was that nobody talked during meals. Loggers regarded eating as serious business. They could have as many helpings as they wanted, but the cook didn't want to be stuck in the kitchen cleaning till midnight. Since good chow was essential for a man doing a hard day's work, nobody, but nobody, wanted to make the cook mad. Else he'd up and quit.

Peter ate heartily, but one large serving of elk rump steak, pork and beans, mashed potatoes, and apple cobbler was all he could hold. Jigger ate three plates piled high, as did a strapping, black-haired Dane by the moniker of Lance van Ecklund. In all, two dozen men dedicatedly restoked their bodies for the work that lay ahead the next morning.

Standing to one side was Kate, ready to fetch more of whatever the men ran out of. She and Al took turns refilling bowls and platters and checking the huge pots of warm food on the stove. Bread disappeared faster than anything, along with great quantities of gravy.

Kate kept to herself, taking her job seriously—something that surprised Peter.

When the men finished, they dragged back their benches noisily and filed out silently. As they passed, the number of nods and belches helped the cook judge the success of his efforts.

Peter stayed behind after everyone had left. It was dark outside, and he meant to walk Kate home. After she wiped down the oilcloths, she swept the floor, gathering the debris on a piece of stiff cardboard, and threw it out the door. Not once did she look in Peter's direction.

"I'll wash the dishes," Al said in a low voice, not wanting to delay her, since her husband was present.

"No, that's my job," Mary Kate said, for the first time shooting a peevish look at Peter. She took her sweet time scraping plates and emptying leftovers into a pail. She dragged out the whole process of soaking, scrubbing, rinsing, and drying, until Peter thought he'd go mad.

"Dammit, Mary Kate, hurry up!" he blurted out when the foreman's lights-out whistle blew at nine o'clock.

"What's that, *dear?*" Kate asked, acting dumb. "Are you waiting for me? Li'l old me?" she asked, imitating her mother's Southern accent.

"You know damn well I am," said Peter, rising. There was obvious menace in his studied walk as he crossed the kitchen to tower over her at the wooden sink.

Al bustled over from the stove, anxious not to cause any problems. "Mrs. O'Rourke, none of my cookees stay past nine o'clock. Please! Go with your husband."

Kate uttered a reluctant sigh. "Very well, since *you* insist, Mr. Al." She folded her apron neatly and set it on the kitchen table. "See you in the morning."

Peter nodded curtly to Al. He grabbed Katherine's hand and whisked her out of the cookhouse so fast her feet had trouble staying on the ground. He was fuming but determined to keep his Irish temper under control.

"You are a royal pain, Mrs. O'Rourke."

"Why, thank you, Mr. O'Rourke. Such compliments!" Kate snarled. "How shall I ever stay humble, if you keep flattering me so?"

Peter gritted his teeth, glad he'd come to a few decisions regarding his mouthy wife. He would not argue—no! Why bother? He would never get the last word, anyway. The silent treatment was what this marriage called for. Aye. Just as soon as he explained their sleeping arrangements, and the yellow chalk line down the middle of the cabin.

* * *

"Really, O'Rourke," Kate panted, stumbling up the cabin steps. "I've had quite enough for one day of your rudeness!"

"The same goes for me, Kate." Peter lit a kerosene lamp and set it on the dusty table on his side of the room. "For one thing, I'm fed up with you calling me 'O'Rourke.' Call me Peter or—"

"Or Casey?" she suggested sidling up to him. "What's all this 'Casey' business? Ever since you got off the stage at Strawberry Point, you've turned into a total boor."

She swaggered around him, hands on hips, studying his attire. "Just look at you! Telling vile jokes and spitting tobacco!" Katherine swiped at his unshaven face and rolled her eyes in disgust. "What next, Casey? I mean, besides your wicked treatment of me. Hmmm? I suppose you plan to take up scratching, like those flea-bitten apes in the bunkhouse!"

"Lice, Kate, not fleas," he corrected.

"Ugh!" she shivered, making a terrible face.

In spite of her insults, Peter's sense of humor suddenly got the better of him. "Ah, Kate," he shook his head, "you're a corker, do you know that?" He collapsed into a chair, holding his diaphragm and waiting for the spasms of laughter to subside.

"I'm glad you're amused!" Katherine stormed, standing over him with balled fists.

"I don't owe you any explanations, but to show my heart's in the right place, I'll tell you why I'm 'Casey' to these men and not 'Peter.'" He slapped his hands on his knees, drawing Kate's gaze to his long, muscular thighs. Peter didn't notice the distraction as he rose and started pacing. "I'm a total greenhorn, and these men know it. They resent me, because I'm your father's man, sent to check up on them. So I'm hoping by becoming their friend and treating them with respect, they'll help me make a go of it in the lumber business. I need to learn everything there is to know, don't you see, Kate?"

Katherine saw very well. "What's wrong with the name Peter?" she asked.

"Nothing. But when you're up against a wild man like Jigger Jansen, who actually drinks wood grain alcohol to get himself out of bed every morning—"

"No!" She clapped her hand over her mouth.

"Yes," Peter confirmed. "The man's got a cast-iron stomach, from what I hear."

Kate frowned. "I hope you're not going to acquire a taste for the stuff."

"Saints preserve us, Kate! I'm not a total fool."

"You couldn't prove it by me," Kate sniped.

"Hold your tongue, woman!" He shook his finger under her nose. "Anyway, you can see why Casey goes over better with a crowd like this."

"All right, I'll concede you may have a point."

Peter made a little mocking bow. "Thank you, wife. Now, as to the beard, I'll let you decide." He rubbed his stubble, and the rasp drew Kate's attention once more to his rugged good looks. "Should I grow one for the winter, or not?"

Had he not mentioned winter, Kate might have dismissed the subject by telling him to shave. But at supper she'd overheard several men speak of working through to the first spring thaw. "Are you telling me that you plan to keep me in this godforsaken hovel all winter?" she asked in a broken whisper.

"Your father did mention bringing you back in a month or two," he said, watching closely for her reaction.

"O'Rourke, I know we're not friends, but would you please tell me why my father's so intent upon making me unhappy?" Her green eyes filled with tears, and Peter felt a lump form in the center of his chest. "Why are you both doing this?"

A curious mixture of compassion and something much stronger made O'Rourke wish he'd never embarked on this present course. "Your father figures that in a month, you'll be so sick of roughing it, you'll come home, meek as a tabby, and marry his foreman. It's that simple."

After a long silence, Katherine smiled wryly and raised her dishpan hands for Peter to see. "A month of washing dishes, and even his foreman won't want me," she said, turning questioning eyes on the tall, handsome man standing before her.

"'Tis your father's intent that I return you"—Peter cleared his throat—"intact. A virgin, if you will," he added, seeing her look of astonishment.

She choked. "I never heard of anything so absurd! I mean, isn't Father a bit naive? To send me off with a world-class bounder?"

Peter shook his head. "That's the most left-handed compliment I've had in a long time. Nevertheless, those were his instructions."

Kate gulped, careful not to look him in the eye. "You've already confessed what a rogue you are."

"So I have." His lips twisted in a semblance of a smile. "But your father prefers that I not mix business and pleasure. He has heavy demands on his time right now, or you and Lew Simpson would no doubt already be married."

"Well, Papa can't marry me off to his foreman!" she objected strenuously. "I'm already married to you."

"I thought you couldn't stand being married to me," Peter said in a teasing way. Forgetting his vow not to touch her, he reached out and stroked her soft cheek with his fingertips.

Flustered, Kate turned to fidget with the glass chimney on the lamp. "I'd like it even less to be married to some filthy old miner."

"Simpson's not such a bad fellow," Peter conceded. His hands gently closed around her slumped shoulders, pulling her back against him for a brief second. She left the scent of lavender in his nostrils before she skittered out of range.

"Please don't touch me, Peter," she said, eying him warily, as she retreated to the other side of the cabin.

As she crossed the yellow dividing line, O'Rourke remembered his original mission. "Wait! I nearly forgot. We need to discuss a few rules. Then—I promise!—I won't bother you at all. I won't touch you, talk to you, or . . . anything." He smiled mischievously. "You can pretend I'm invisible, if you like."

Katherine cocked her head, skeptical as always. "O'Rourke, what *are* you talking about?"

"I've come up with the perfect solution. Now, for obvious reasons, I need to give you my protection as long as we're in camp." Kate nodded, still suspicious, as he dragged a ten-foot plank into the center of the room. "So I've divided the cabin in two. You're on your side, by the way, and I'll stay here on my side."

"Fair enough," Katherine said and clasped her hands primly, waiting to hear more.

Peter pointed to the bed, which stood half on her side, half on his. "I've even come up with a temporary solution to our sleeping arrangements." He plunked the plank down the middle of the bed and balanced it on its side. He made a sweeping gesture, inviting her inspection.

"This is just until I have another bed made, mind you. Here, hold this," he ordered, indicating that she was to steady the board. Crossing with his tools, he drove a few nails into the board, securing it to the headboard.

Katherine clapped her hand over her mouth with a giggle. "Sorry, Peter, but you are no carpenter." She stood on her side, watching him hit his thumb, swear, and bend nails. After a few abortive attempts, he did better. At least the board didn't wobble. It stood like a miniature of the Great Wall of China, a barricade against passion.

"Well, what do you think?" Peter asked eagerly, proud of his ingenious handling of a sticky situation. There! He felt better already, knowing that even in his sleep he wouldn't bump into her. This was one temptation he was going to beat, he assured himself.

Katherine looked into his shining eyes and then at the bed. Each side had two feet. Not much. Still, she was willing to put up with a little discomfort. It was better than fighting off a sex maniac.

"It reminds me of a bundling board," she said, biting back a nervous giggle.

Peter thought, *The little witch! Laughing at my efforts, when I could easily have*—he scowled and banished *that* thought before it destroyed him. "I think it's an excellent way to handle our problem," he said with all the dignity he could muster.

"Oh, I do, too." She went over and tested the mattress on her side. "Have you never heard of bundling boards?" she asked chattily. Stretching out, she folded her hands behind her flaming tresses and sighed. Despite her complete indifference to him, Kate had no trouble noticing that while O'Rourke might be a villain, he was certainly handsome enough to be a matinee idol.

"In New England, due to the bitter cold and long distances," she said for his edification, "young men and women used to do their courting in bundling beds. Under the parents' strict supervision, of course."

Seeing him swallow deeply, Katherine sat up and patted his side with a teasing gleam in her eye. "Try it, Peter. After all, you're bigger. I wouldn't want you to be uncomfortable."

Her concern for his comfort made Peter blanche. "Fifty-fifty's good enough," he informed her and went to stand in the cabin doorway.

"As you wish." Smiling, Kate got up and began to explore her side of the room. "Could you slide my trunks over to my side, Peter?" she asked after a long silence.

Her trunks were safely delivered across the boundary.

Humming off-key, Katherine checked to make sure the contents of her luggage were intact. She considered the limitations of space versus the number of gowns. "Too bad I have nowhere to wear all my pretty dresses," she sighed—not really talking to Peter but made to feel awkward by his silence. She turned to find him seated at the table, drumming his fingers and staring at the lamp wick.

Peter forced himself to look her way. "Your father bought you three wool dresses. Perfect for up here in the high country. You'll find them in that black case." He pointed.

"Merci, monsieur!" Katherine waltzed over to the prescribed apparel. Soon she had the drab, high-necked dresses on exhibition. "This is more like it," she chirped, holding up a severe black wool gown. "Widow's weeds. Tell me, Peter Casey O'Rourke, is it my father's hope that a tree will fall on you and make me a widow? Or is he merely trying to turn me into a hideous frump?" She tossed the offending items in the corner and swung around for his response, her toe tapping angrily.

Peter sighed. "I'm not a mind reader, Kate. If your father wants to turn you into a pioneer scrub woman, that's his business, I suppose. Personally, I like my women soft as silk and meltingly beautiful." Peter leaned back on the chair runs. "Clean, too," he added, looking at the dress she had worn two days in a row. "That one's about ready for the dust bin."

"Thank you," she went to rummaging in her trunk again. "I'm sorry I don't quite live up to your high standards. I cannot imagine what possessed me to go traipsing all over the country on the back of a mule." She pulled out a nightgown, and then another.

When she found the most demure item in her wardrobe, she waved a scrap of lace to get his attention. "O'Rourke, even though we're sharing this lovely cabin, there will be times when I require a degree of privacy."

He rose immediately. "I'll go outside."

Katherine suddenly noticed there were no curtains on the windows. Hearing his footsteps heading toward the door, she whirled. "Wait! How am I to keep Peeping Toms from looking in?"

Peter paused by the door. "Kate, I am not a Peeping Tom!"

"Not you, silly. The rest of the camp."

"Oh, for crying out loud, Kate! We'll figure it out in the morning." He clomped outside and stood on the steps, gulping giant breaths of cool mountain air into his lungs.

The stars were tiny, flawless diamonds in the sky, and the moon was . . . *oh, Christ!* It was gorgeous and full, perfect for driving a man insane! Especially when there was a beautiful redhead right behind him, pulling on her nightgown, not twelve feet away!

Peter couldn't help himself. Through the dingy window he spied a flash of bare skin and one perfect breast, full and firm. Groaning, Peter doubled over the railing, trying to ignore his body's turgid response, but the fates wouldn't let him.

In desperation he decided to take a walk. Maybe a dip in the lake. He cast another furtive glance through the open door. Mary Kate was decent again. Thank God! He could relax.

Instead he was tenser than ever. It was that nightgown!

"Katherine," he called out, his tongue thick with desire, "close and bolt the door. I'm going for a swim."

Peter's breath caught as Kate spun around in her modest white gown. She called forth all the untamed passions that raged within him. The kerosene lamp's warm glow created a fiery waterfall of dancing lights in her long tresses.

She took a tentative step toward him, a question in her hypnotic gaze. "Peter?"

O'Rourke immediately realized his mistake. He should never have gazed upon the vestal fire. "Don't come any closer," he whispered, backing up. And then he broke and ran.

CHAPTER 12

Dismissing O'Rourke's strange behavior as that of a madman, Kate took one look at the full moon and, closing the door, slipped the bolt. Suddenly feeling the strain of the past two days, she crawled into bed. Her lumpy pillow smelled of wood smoke. She squirmed around, trying to get comfortable, and banged her elbow on the dividing board.

Damn O'Rourke! She would be black and blue by morning. Hadn't he done enough rotten things without forcing her to sleep in this ridiculous bed?

Smarting with indignation, she began to analyze the Great Conspiracy between her father and O'Rourke. What would cause a man like O'Rourke to carry out such a scheme, when she had paid him handsomely to help her break free? Oh, he was a scoundrel, all right. She would never forgive him. Never! Katherine flopped over and stared at the divider. For all of Peter O'Rourke's fine talk of keeping promises, he obviously had no intention of trying to make this a real marriage. The bundling board was prime proof of that!

So what was he really up to?

Katherine thrashed around restlessly. He was certainly confident of his ability to control her with a kiss, or with the threat of taking other liberties. And, oh, it would be so easy to succumb in a moment of weakness. But she couldn't let that happen. Hadn't she heard his confession of past indiscretions? If ever she lost her heart to such a man, she just knew he would break her heart.

But, on the other hand . . . Kate sat up in bed. She knew how to get back at O'Rourke. Two could play the game! Why not? What was to keep her from turning the tables on him? He deserved to suffer for what he'd done to her! The idea took hold in Kate's fertile imagination, and she began to work out a devious plan of action.

Women had been the downfall of men since time began. She wasn't going to be the only miserable person in Diablo Camp. By the time she finished with him, Mr. Peter Casey O'Rourke would give back her thousand dollars and pay any price to be rid of her.

Comforted by the perverse merits of revenge, Katherine snuggled down beneath the coarse woolen blanket and closed her eyes. She was nearly asleep when the strange scurry of tiny running feet—no, claws!—made her sit bolt upright.

A gray squirrel with beady black eyes reared up, staring at her from the top of her trunk, its nose twitching. Its front paws held a shiny bracelet of hers. Suddenly it jumped to the wall and scrambled up the logs to the rafters.

Clutching the blanket to her breasts, Katherine gazed upward. Any minute she expected the rodent to lose its footing and fall on her head.

Sliding out of bed, she tiptoed to the door, hoping to shoo the intruder out. The kerosene lamp still gave off a comforting light, as did the full moon, for which she was grateful, for she had no desire to step on the dreadful creature in the dark. Mary Kate slipped the bolt and eased open the door. Hoping the squirrel would take the hint if she got away from the entrance, she drew up her nightgown around her knees and scampered onto the bed. Her path took her on a shortcut over O'Rourke's side.

Only she never made it to the other side.

The squirrel chose that precise moment to drop onto the bed.

In a desperate rush for freedom, its tiny sharp claws sank into Kate's bare left foot. She dropped her gown, her hands flying to her mouth, and she screamed bloody murder. Of course, the squirrel panicked. Its bushy tail circled her ankle, and she uttered another piercing shriek.

His passions properly subdued by a teeth-rattling plunge in the cold mountain lake, Peter was just emerging from the woods when he heard Katherine's screams.

The cabin door stood wide, the light on. Another muffled scream reached his already strung-out nerves, and he could only assume the worst. Someone had broken in and was taking advantage of his wife!

"I'm coming, Kate!" Peter yelled. He took off running across the short clearing to the cabin. As his bare feet hit the porch, a blur of gray fur whizzed past.

Katherine was standing on one leg—on his side of the bed—both hands clapped over her mouth and eyes closed. She was shaking like a leaf. She was in absolutely no danger whatsoever.

Dropping his boots with a resounding thud, O'Rourke slammed the door and bolted it. He strode to the bed, suddenly angry because she'd managed to scare him out of a year's growth.

His noisy entrance caused Katherine's eyes to fly open with alarm. She smiled, seeing that reinforcements had arrived, and she was about to thank him.

But Peter lit into her, rather than negate all the good effects of his icy swim. "Dammit, Mary Katherine, what the hell are you doing on my side of the bed?" he bellowed, planting his fists on his hips and glaring at her.

Kate pointed toward the door with an unsteady arm. As a pantomimist she was hopeless, O'Rourke thought sardonically. She gave a pathetic imitation of Lady Macbeth's mad scene, her frightened gaze fixed on the door, as if she expected the ghosts of jilted victims of her beauty to materialize any second.

"It . . ." Her little pink tongue darted out to wet her lips, and a little shudder racked her body. To Peter's immense discomfort, her full breasts jiggled noticeably.

"It . . . touched . . . me," she explained.

"Well, it's gone now," he said caustically. "Now, get on your side of the bed, lie down, and be quiet." He turned his back to her and rummaged in his trunk for a towel. There was none. "Damn!" he muttered, surprised; there wasn't a single souvenir from all the hotels he'd stayed in.

When he had a sufficient hold on himself, he turned around.

Katherine still hadn't moved. "You're all wet," she said.

"I know that, you twit," Peter growled, thinking it was all her fault. He stood dripping on the floorboards.

"I have a towel," she offered timidly, not wanting to provoke his temper, "if you don't mind sharing."

"Well, get it!" he snapped. "I can't very well dry myself off with the blanket, or we'll both freeze."

Katherine stepped gracefully across the board, exposing trim ankles and strong, perfect calves. Crossing to her trunk, she retrieved the big, fluffy white towel she'd filched from her father's huge supply of linens. She handed it over and stood watching him dry his face and hair.

She clasped her hands in front, where her fig leaf would have been, had she been the original Eve, and gave him the benefit of her perusal. O'Rourke's clothes were plastered to him like a second skin. She could see or imagine just about everything.

When she continued to stand there, waiting for him to shed his wet clothing, Peter felt his Irish blood begin to stir. "This is no damn peep show, Katherine."

Startled out of her mischief, Mary Kate jumped under the covers, her face crimson, and pulled her share of the blanket over her head.

"I'm sorry I annoy you so much," came a timid voice from her side of the bed.

O'Rourke froze, as he stood buck-naked, the towel between his legs. The hair on the back of his neck suddenly bristled. "Don't talk, Mary Kate," he commanded in the stern voice of a parent whose patience was at the breaking point.

Katherine smiled to herself.

Two minutes later, as he was slipping into a pair of long johns, she thought of something else to say. "As long as we're sharing living quarters, I shall try to avoid making any demands on you, except when it's absolutely necessary."

"Thank you," Peter ground out, his eyes moving to the blanketed mummy as she lay there, talking to the wall. As a devotee of beauty and art, he reminded himself that it was only natural to notice the sweet curve of her hip.

"I shall stay out of your way as much as possible," she continued hitching her little bottom to get comfortable.

"Uh-huh!" Peter extinguished the light and got into bed on his own side. The moon filtered through the window, giving the cabin an eery atmosphere. As he stretched out and tried to put his hands behind his neck, his elbow hit the plank.

Katherine giggled in the dark.

"It's not funny, witch."

"You could have had the whole bed to yourself if you hadn't kidnapped me," she reminded him.

"My mistake. Just one more in a long list of miscalculations." He sighed, lying ramrod stiff, arms at attention by his sides, his body hanging over the side and foot of the bed. Suddenly he realized that something else was at attention. *Sonuvabitch!* This was going to be harder than he'd thought.

"Oh, I expect you'll make a lot more mistakes before you're finished," Katherine's voice sweetly informed him in the semigloom.

Peter groaned. She wasn't going to stop needling him till he stuck his foot in his ear.

"Aye, well, don't hold your breath, Katie O'Rourke," he said drily.

Kate hummed a few bars of "Buffalo Gals, Won't You Come Out Tonight?" Off-key. Couldn't carry a tune worth a damn. Her fingers started tapping out the tempo on the board next to his head.

"Are you doing that just to annoy me?" he finally asked, rearing up and glaring over the side.

Katherine looked up at him, the moonlight spilling over her pale features and the bright splash of her hair. Batting her eyelashes, she smiled, all innocence. "I know how tired you are, Peter, and not knowing a suitable lullaby—"

He sank back down and closed his eyes. "You can dispense with the serenade, Kate."

"Just trying to be an accommodating wife."

"Like hell you are."

"Good night, Peter."

He didn't answer. He lay there, arms folded over his chest.

"Peter?"

"What, dammit!" His eyes flew open. Katherine was peeking over the board. Her hair cascaded over the side, tickling his throat. "Can't a man get any sleep?"

"You needn't be rude." Kate made a stab at looking deeply offended. "If we're going to share the same bed, we should at least observe the barest civilities, don't you think?"

"Meaning?" If only she'd get her damn flowing hair on her side of the bundling board.

Kate noticed Peter's hand reach up to brush her auburn curls away. She smiled and tossed her head. Despite her apparent attempt to get her hair out of his way, more of the rich, fragrant strands settled across his face and neck.

"We should keep the conversation general, polite, and cordial," she lectured him sweetly.

Peter grabbed a fistful of her waist-length hair and pulled her face within an inch of his mouth.

"Ouch, Peter!" Kate protested, raising up to avoid getting snatched bald. In the process, her entire upper torso dangled invitingly over the board.

"Stay on your own side, Mary Kate!" Peter ordered savagely, his loins tightening as the seductive swell of her breasts came at him in the dim light.

Katherine, noting the direction of his gaze, suddenly realized the power she had over him. Instead of retreating, she stuck out her chest and laughed. "I'm not bothering you, am I, Peter?"

"Not . . . at all," he rasped, now thoroughly miserable. "Now, you either lie down and hush up, or I'm going to stop your jabbering, once and for all."

She tilted her head flirtatiously. She knew she was treading on thin ice, but couldn't resist the chance to make him suffer. "Nothing you say can stop me."

He grinned up at her, his dimples leaping out at her in bold relief. "Actions speak louder than words, or have you forgotten?"

Katherine's heart tumbled and swelled in her chest. "No, I haven't forgotten," she said in a hushed voice.

"Then, Mrs. O'Rourke, close your mouth," Peter growled and was relieved to see her withdraw to her own side. Her eyes had grown round and as dark as limes when he alluded to kissing her.

Katherine curled into a tense ball beneath the blanket. She rubbed the frayed edge against her lips, unconsciously comparing it to the texture of his mouth against hers. Strangely affected by his addressing her as his wife, Kate wondered what significance it held for him. Why did he persist in doing it? Did he do it because he knew it annoyed her?

Finally her curiosity got the best of her. "O'Rourke?"

He didn't answer, but Kate knew he wasn't asleep. Not with her chattering like a magpie.

"Peter, would you *please* not call me 'Mrs. O'Rourke'?"

"It's your name, isn't it?"

"No, it is not!"

"I suggest you get some sleep, Mary Kate." It wasn't a suggestion; it was a command.

Kate sighed. At least he hadn't called her "Mrs." again. She closed her eyes.

"Good night, Peter."

He chuckled. "Good night, Mrs. O'Rourke."

Kate stood shivering in the dark, stuffing the corners of a sheet into the log chinks to form a privacy curtain across the corner on her side of the cabin. She washed furtively and dressed, then slipped outside, all without waking Peter.

If getting up so early was the price she had to pay to avoid her cabinmate, so be it. She walked down the skid road to the outhouse. It was close to freezing and, standing third in line, she watched her breath and Isaac Yancey's rise in the lantern light. Behind Yancey, Jigger Jansen was chug-a-lugging something that smelled like turpentine.

"Ladies next," said Joe Burns, giving her a chance to cut to the head of the line.

"Thank you, Mr. Burns, but I'll wait my turn."

"Hell, while you two talk about it, I'm goin'," growled Smitty, and disappeared into the cubicle. He let the door close with a loud bang.

"Oops!" Katherine laughed apologetically to Joe Burns. "I guess that taught us both a good lesson."

"Yup, never look a gift horse in the mouth." The rough old logger guffawed and, ruffling his hair sleepily, he slouched back to the bunkhouse.

"Ain't hardly worth fightin' over a hole in the ground," Jigger said and wiped his mouth with the back of his hand.

"Does anyone know the time?" asked Kate, trying to steer the conversation toward more polite topics.

"Three-thirty. Al's chili beans last night gave us all the trots," joined in a voice from inside the shack.

"Oh, mercy!" In spite of herself, Katherine had to laugh. It seemed nothing was sacred with these men. What a sight, she thought. Seven men huddled against the cold in long-sleeved flannel undershirts and trousers. Swilling hundred-proof raw alcohol, dancing a jig, and grousing about the cook. They were funny without even trying.

To avoid more shenanigans, she waived the democratic process and cut in front of Joe Burns. After that, she raced for the warm dining hall. "Oh, thank goodness!" she exclaimed, bursting through the door, and stretched her hands over the stove. Mr. Al had stocked the cookstove with firewood, until it was fairly jumping with heat.

Lured by a desire for fresh coffee and a good roaring fire, Katherine had hoped to stay longer, but Mr. Al hadn't forgotten the camp rules O'Rourke had laid down. "Here," he grumbled, handing her the buckets and yoke.

"Already?" Kate groaned, recognizing the gesture as a work order.

"Hard to boil coffee without water." Al looked at her through his bushy eyebrows. "Unless you know a better way."

And so her day officially began. Out in the cold before she had a chance to get warm.

Before the sun crept over the mountain, Katherine had made three trips to the lake for water. She fetched kindling, stacking a neat pile near the kitchen door. Holding her nose, she slopped the hogs next.

Returning, she found Al flipping pancakes high in the air and joking with Bobbie White Feather and Lance van Ecklund. She set down the slop pail with a clatter and huddled next to the stove, hoping the rest of her chores would be indoors.

Without missing a double flapjack somersault, handled with two spatulas, Al nodded toward a pail hung on a nail the size of a railroad spike. "Wake up ole Bessie,

Mrs. O'Rourke, an' git us some nice warm cream fer the men's coffee."

Kate looked blankly at the cook. "Who's 'ole Bessie'?" she finally got out, seeing the men share an amused wink.

"Bessie's one helluva milker," said Bobbie.

"Better git a move on," Al suggested, pouring batter amidst the skittering lumps of butter on the griddle. "There's a good girl."

"You expect *me* to milk a cow?" Her breathless laugh conveyed more incredulity than a demand for clarification. The longer she was around Mr. Al, the more she realized how much she had never learned to do in her short life. But this was definitely not something she wanted to learn!

Lance van Ecklund's dancing blue eyes instantly spotted her reluctance—and her bright cheeks, made rosy by the cold. She was the best-looking woman he'd ever seen, in or out of a logging camp, but a greenhorn, he decided; newly married and probably only half-broke in.

Lifting the bucket from the nail, van Ecklund moved with the natural grace of an athlete toward Katherine, his smile offering encouragement. "C'mon, lady," he jerked his head toward the open door, "let me show you how it's done."

Just then, Kate saw Peter walk into the dining hall. Their green eyes met in a gut-wrenching jolt. She didn't know how, but even across a roomful of hungry, impatiently waiting men, he could throw her into a dither.

Fists jammed in his pockets, frost streaming from his nostrils, he nodded. Peter's territorial posture was unmistakable, as was his warning scowl.

Until he showed up, Kate was ready to wheedle, bully, or charm her way out of milking. But his challenging stare changed her mind. She was almost sure he was jealous.

Seizing the chance to test her powers, she smiled at Lance. "Thank you . . . Mr. van Ecklund, is it?"

"Call me Lance," he said, taking her arm. Quickly the tall Dane led Katherine across to the milking shed.

Using the tinderbox from his pocket, he lit the lantern, pulled up a milking stool to the swayback bovine, and sat down. "City girl?" Making no secret of his interest, Lance let his eyes drift over her body.

Kate watched him rub his hands together to warm them before he put them on the cow's udder. Now that they were alone, she hoped he understood her only interest was in milking the cow. "I think Mr. Al wants to serve breakfast right away," she said to hurry him along.

"*Ja*, we shall return soon. But first I show you." Van Ecklund laughed, sensing her nervousness. "Watch my hands."

He worked rhythmically, easing the fluid down the teats. The cold bucket rang out as warm steam and white milk hit the metal. "You must have lived on a farm," she said, watching the ease with which the logger gently wrung the rich liquid from Bessie.

"*Ja*, till I was sixteen." His eyes sparkled. "Every morning my father and my brother, Hans, and I. Up before the sun."

Katherine hoped that if she kept him talking a little longer, she could avoid the task altogether, but when the pail was three-fourths full, he stood up. "You try it now."

When she sat on the stool, Lance hunkered down behind her, his thighs on the outside of her skirts, and reached around to guide her hands to the cow's udder.

Katherine knew the instant he pressed his body against hers that van Ecklund had more than a milking lesson in mind. "Mr. van Ecklund, I think . . . I-I am sure I can figure this out by myself." Her voice quavered. Lance's breath was warm against her ear and, coupled with the gesture his hand performed on Bessie's still-swollen teat, it was clear what he intended.

Van Ecklund laughed. "Don't be so nervous, Mrs. O'Rourke." His fingers pressed hers, bringing down a warm stream of milk.

"I'm not nervous!" Kate snapped, anger replacing her confusion. She shrugged in a vain effort to free herself from his encroaching embrace. "Please stop! There isn't enough room. I can manage better alone."

Paying no heed, van Ecklund laid his hand on her flaming cheek. "Sure'n I get one small kiss for giving you a lesson, *ja?*" He laughed again, enjoying her flustered manner.

Katherine tried to bolt to the other side of the cow. Seeing van Ecklund coming around the hind end of the cow, she grabbed a rope halter and threw it at him. "Get away from me!" she cried. "My . . . My husband will kill you!"

Grabbing her, he hauled her close. "He is the jealous type, *ja?*" van Ecklund teased. His foot went between hers, tripping her, and she fell to the dirt floor beneath him.

"Damn right, I'm jealous," Katherine heard in a familiar Irish accent.

Abruptly, Lance van Ecklund's tall body was hauled off of her. The wind knocked out of her, Katherine sat up in time to see her husband pull van Ecklund to his feet. Her jaw dropped. She could not believe her eyes! Instead of pummeling the man to within an inch of death's door, Peter merely laughed and helped Lance dust off his trousers. Not only wasn't O'Rourke jealous, he acted as if the Dane's behavior was a big joke!

"Fun's over, Lance. My wife is a bit naive, and no doubt you mistook her eagerness to learn how to milk this sad-looking creature for something else."

"No hard feelings?" Lance asked, surprised that his behavior hadn't caused a fistfight or gotten him fired.

"A natural misunderstanding," Peter said cheerfully, picking up the milk pail. He walked van Ecklund to the door. "Do me a favor and take this to the cook?"

"Sure thing, Mr. O'Rourke," Lance agreed, not quite sure what made his new boss tick. O'Rourke either didn't care, was a total coward, or—more likely—had such a murderous temper that he was afraid to unleash it.

"Just don't let it happen again," Peter said, friendly but firm.

Peter didn't turn back to where Kate sprawled in the straw until he saw van Ecklund enter the cookshack.

"How kind of you to act as if it was all my fault," Kate said hotly. "My reputation means nothing, I suppose."

"Don't give me that, Kate. You were flirting, or he never would have come at you that way," he said, secretly relieved that Kate was unharmed but not about to let her know it.

"You could have at least struck him," Kate complained.

O'Rourke raised an eyebrow. "What? And risk getting trampled by that crazy Dane's cleats? No thanks, Kate! I don't plan to acquire any facial tattoos over a harmless flirtation."

"It wouldn't have been so harmless, if you hadn't come along when you did."

"True enough." Peter plucked strands of broken straw from her disheveled hair. "Behave yourself, or heaven help you! What if I'm not around next time? You might wind up with a dozen men on top of you."

Kate knew he spoke the truth. Her little scheme to stir up Peter had backfired, and it was too risky to resort to such tactics again. "I'll be careful, Peter."

"See that you are." He gruffly shoved her away. "Now, get back to the kitchen. Al was pitching a fit because his helper can't keep her mind on her work."

Katherine stumbled toward the shed door, blinded by angry tears. How dare he act as if she had encouraged that logger? But what else could she expect from a man who didn't love her and wouldn't defend her?

If O'Rourke's rejection hurt, her sense of humiliation grew worse a few minutes later. As she entered the dining room to face a roomful of loggers, a platter with flapjacks precariously balanced in her arms, she felt every eye turn her way. The room grew silent, as if they were a courtroom of jurors passing judgment on her. Kate swallowed hard. If she had a scarlet A carved on her forehead, she couldn't have felt more conspicuous.

Carefully avoiding eye contact, she slunk back to the kitchen to get the bowls of hominy and sausage. After she served the eggs, she couldn't stand the silence anymore. She crept into the storage room, closed the door, and let the tears flow.

Kate didn't come out until she heard the last heavy tread of boots leave the dining hall. Wiping her eyes on her apron, she stepped to the long tables and began to clear plates.

You'd think I was the one at fault, she thought bitterly and bent to pick up a broken cup from the floor.

Al looked up when she brought the third stack of dishes to the kitchen. "Somethin' botherin' you, missus?" he asked, noticing her swollen eyelids.

"It's pretty obvious, Mr. Al." Kate bit her lip to keep from breaking down. "You saw how quiet it was in here."

Al threw her a puzzled look. "Glory be! I wish it was that quiet all the time," he said.

And *then* Katherine remembered the cook's rule about silence. She almost laughed with relief. She had misconstrued the men's silence, conjured it all up in her head. The only thing she wasn't mistaken about was Peter's callous indifference. There wasn't a jealous bone in his body. She would just have to work harder to find his weak spot. Somehow she meant to get even.

CHAPTER 13

All morning Peter leafed through ledgers and payroll records, trying to get an idea how McGillacutty ran his logging enterprise. He was well acquainted with rudimentary bookkeeping, having cut his eyeteeth on his father's account books in Ireland. This skill hadn't grown rusty during his theater days, either, for any actor worthy of his billing soon learned to look after his own interests, or fell victim to unscrupulous theater managers. These two separate experiences, plus a general aptitude for figures and a prep school education—imposed against his will—had at least taught him how to think.

Consequently, Peter could read between the lines of the smudged, rather sloppily kept office records at Diablo Camp. He knew both how his father-in-law wanted the camp run and how it actually was run: slipshod. Both methods he rejected at once as unacceptable.

McGillacutty charged his men for everything from the special soap the men used to cut grease and pine tar to the tools they required to ply their trade. The wangan was half office and paymaster's quarters, half general company store. Blankets, adzes, shirts, boots, trousers, socks, towels, razors, and chewing tobacco didn't come cheap. Checking back and forth between payroll ledgers and the men's accounts at the company store, he found ample proof of malfeasance: for a man to stay out of debt was well nigh impossible, unless he did without, reducing himself to the level of an eating, sleeping, working animal.

Monthly "medical services" were deducted routinely from the men's pay. How Homer McGillacutty could justify this, considering he didn't provide a camp doctor, was beyond O'Rourke's comprehension.

The former camp clerk had run a shoddy operation, as his frequent erasures and price changes clearly indicated. Probably done out of fear that the men might turn against him, or so Peter suspected, for loggers were notorious for their tendency to solve conflicts with their fists.

In the few days he'd been mingling with the men on the trail, in camp, and in the woods, Peter had seen enough to convince himself that they were a volatile lot. Several bore permanent scars inflicted by loggers' cleats embedded in their flesh during bunkhouse and barroom brawls. They wore these "tattoos" the way a soldier wore medals, or a member of a secret order used a password. It gave status, proving they were members of a wild breed who put their lives on the line every time they went into the forest.

Peter felt a grudging admiration for men who could take so much abuse in the line of duty. But he also suspected some of the anger they vented on each other might be eased, if the wangan boss adopted a fairer policy. He had no intention of giving the outfit the impression that he'd "gone soft." Not at all. He had a job to do. But that didn't preclude giving the men incentives.

Two hours into examining the books, he ordered all company clothing, tools, and personal articles slashed by fifty percent. He figured that what Old Man McGillacutty didn't know—yet—wouldn't hurt in the long run. The working conditions for these men weren't much better than those for the dumb ox that brought the timber down the slopes. They slaved from before sunup until

sundown, risking their lives to make another, smarter
bastard rich.

At least they could receive a few more creature comforts and have enough money jingling in their pockets
to make those infrequent trips to town worth "blowin'
in" for.

Around ten thirty that morning, Peter was going over
the weekly tally of harvested board feet, when he heard
a loud shout. Dropping his pencil on the open page, he
strode to the window. Here came Smitty, barreling into
camp with that rolling gait of his, yelling at the top of his
lungs. The camp wrangler and Al emerged from the
cookhouse just as Peter appeared in the doorway.

"They're bringin' in Raimey!" Smitty hollered, shoving past O'Rourke and heading straight for the company
store supplies.

Peter followed the man back in. "What's wrong?"

"Widow maker." Smitty went rummaging in a large
box of bandages.

"What is this 'widow maker' everybody keeps talking
about?" Peter demanded, irked that he still didn't know
what was going on.

"Bad news," Smitty said, still out of breath. He handed
O'Rourke a stack of bandages, a bottle of carbolic acid, and
a twenty-pound sack of plaster of paris. "Follow me, boss."

Loaded up, O'Rourke went with the cantankerous old
logger. As he passed the cookhouse, he saw Kate on the
back stoop, peeling potatoes, and waved.

Smitty shouted to Al, "We'll need lots of water."

Charlie Mason and Joe Burns drove up in a buckboard hitched to two huge draft horses.

Al wiped his hands on his apron and came over to
examine the patient. "Bad, huh?"

"Could be worse."

"Raimey ain't taking it so good," Burns said.

Al disappeared into the cookhouse to fetch whiskey
while Peter, Smitty, and the wrangler, Hoss Lauken, followed the wagon to the bunkhouse. Mason and Burns

piled out and, almost as if they were attacking Raimey Griswold, hauled him, groaning and cursing, from the bed of the wagon. He was nearly out of his head with pain.

"Hey, easy, men," O'Rourke protested, watching Mason and Burns's ungentle handling of the patient.

Raimey Griswold was covered with pine pitch, tree bark, and red dirt. His left trouser leg was split to the thigh, exposing a leg swollen to twice its normal size. He threw a wild punch at Burns as he was being borne to his cot.

"Sonuvabitch!" he screamed, wrestling his tormenters. "Knock me out, goddammit!"

"Sure thing," and Mason obligingly landed a haymaker on Raimey's jaw. Griswold immediately went limp.

Peter regarded the loggers' unorthodox medical treatment with alarm. If the man's condition wasn't so serious, he might have been tempted to laugh. But despite its comedic aspects, this was no slapstick situation. These men were in deadly earnest. And despite their brutal handling, he sensed the comradery. They all faced the same dangers out here in the woods. They *had* to be tough to survive.

Still, there was a limit, he thought, to what a man should be forced to endure in the name of friendship. "Here, let me take a look at him," he said, pushing through the cluster of men. He tossed the rolled bandages, plaster, and carbolic on a nearby cot and examined Griswold's leg.

Mason shook his head. "Schoolmarm split in two and fell on him."

Frowning, Peter lifted the leg and immediately discerned that it was a clean break in the shank, midway between knee and ankle. "I thought you said it was a widow maker," he said.

"It were both," said Hoss.

"Would somebody explain the difference?" he asked, probing the swelling to see if there was any other damage. Except for helping a stableman wrap a horse's torn tendon a couple of times in Ireland, he knew nothing about doctoring legs.

Mason spat, making the spittoon ring. "That's easy, boss. A schoolmarm is a crotched tree. When the one that hit ole Raimey split, it damn near became a sneaky widow maker."

"Thank God it didn't," said O'Rourke, relieved that it wasn't more serious.

Hoss nodded toward the leg. "How bad is it? Will he be out of action the whole season?"

"However long it takes his leg to mend," Peter said vaguely. He didn't know how long it took a broken leg to heal, any more than he understood loggers' jargon. He glanced up to see Katherine and Al file in with buckets of hot and cold water.

"Tough break," said Al, shaking his head. "It's gonna be a long, hungry winter for Raimey's wife an' three kids."

"Not if he stays on payroll." Peter noted the men's look of surprise. "Nobody around here gets paid without working, but we'll find things he can do and still stay off his leg," he added, so he wouldn't find himself saddled with a bunch of freeloaders.

Katherine, her left hand resting lightly on Peter's shoulder, bent over the cot. "We need to get that swelling down," she observed.

"Kate, I don't know," he said doubtfully. It seemed a poor time for two greenhorns to attempt any heroics in front of these men. "Maybe you should leave this to me and the men."

"I brought water from the lake, ice cold," she said calmly. Brushing past Peter, she ignored everyone but the man lying unconscious before her. She dipped a clean cloth in the bucket and laid it across Griswold's lower leg.

Rough and unsentimental to a fault with each other, Hoss Lauken, Charlie Mason, Joe Burns, Al, and Smitty huddled around her like moths to a flame. None of them saw the uncertain tremor in her fingers as she ministered to their comrade. For a young woman of her obvious gentility to roll up her sleeves and care for their fallen friend revived nearly forgotten memories of a gentle mother's touch, or a sister's compassion.

Peter watched them fall all over themselves to do her bidding. Mary Kate had them lift the injured leg, so she could slip a folded blanket and clean towel under it. She washed off the debris. Then, unable to remove a patch of pine pitch any other way, she blushingly asked Charlie Mason to shave the patient's hairy leg.

When she smiled her approval of his barbering skill, Charlie beamed.

"Thank you, Mr. Mason," she said. "I knew a man who fixes tools would be able to do a difficult job like this."

"Glad to help, ma'am," the burly filer stammered.

O'Rourke rolled his eyes toward the rafters. *Kiss the Blarney Stone!* he thought. "Before we set Griswold's leg, perhaps we should shave the whole leg," he suggested.

"That's the idea!" Hoss slapped his thigh. "I 'member when Arnie broke his arm in '61. We had a devil of a time gittin' his cast off."

Al chuckled. "Damn near ripped the hide off that sidewinder."

"Mr. Mason?" Katherine gestured toward the tough, sinewy leg on the bed.

"I'd be dee-lighted, ma'am." Charlie Mason gave a few licks on his razor strop. His cheek bulging with a tobacco plug, he bent to the task.

Kate's hand restrained him. "Use soap, Mr. Mason," she gently reminded him and then stood back, while the saw filer scraped inch-long fur off Griswold's leg from knee to ankle. "Now," she said, turning to Peter, "perhaps you and I should set this leg."

Peter hesitated. "Anyone here ever set bones?" he asked, willing to share the honor with a more-qualified man.

Al stepped forward. "Sure thing."

Griswold was conscious by this time, so Burns and

Hoss got busy anesthetizing the patient with liberal doses of whiskey. Meanwhile Katherine rewashed the leg. Between her, Peter, and the cook, they reset the leg and wrapped torn strips of muslin around the injured member and then, using more strips, dipped in plaster, formed a cast.

When they were finished, Kate caught Peter's eye across the cot. "Well done," she said with a merry twinkle.

While she gathered up the leftover medical supplies, Peter emptied her water pail out the bunkhouse window. Seeing that Griswold was feeling no pain, he turned to praise his comrades. "Quick action, men."

"We'll be gettin' back now," said Hoss, sidling toward the door.

Al scratched his belly. "Stay to lunch. Then you, Joe, an' Charlie here kin take the grub out to the other men in the buckboard. It'll save me a goldang trip."

As they departed for the office, taking the bandages and plaster back to the wangan, Peter impulsively threw his arm around his wife's shoulder. "Thanks, Kate. You had Charlie eating out of your palm. All of them, in fact."

"They *are* human, after all," she joked.

"So are you, I'm happy to say," Peter returned.

"Was there ever any doubt?" Kate tossed her curls. He noticed she didn't pull away.

She stopped in front of the wangan. "We did quite splendidly, you and me, don't you think?"

They went inside chatting while he returned supplies to shelves and drawers. Finishing up, he paused to give her a hug.

"What was that for?" she demanded, instantly suspicious.

"For keeping a cool head when it was needed."

"Oh." She sounded pleased by the compliment.

In the distance, the clang of Al's big spoon beating on a pan signaled lunch.

Katherine straightened her shoulders. "I guess I'll be

needed," she said. At the door she glanced back at him uncertainly.

"Wait and I'll go with you." Peter shrugged into his jacket. He took Kate's arm and smiled down at the little girl masquerading behind her slanted, grown-up eyes. It struck him that he had a good deal to learn about his wife. Things even she didn't yet know about herself.

After lunch the O'Rourkes went their separate ways. Katherine milked the cow again, and then Al taught her how to make a huge batch of tapioca pudding. "A mite sticky, but you'll do better next time," was his verdict. To Kate, who had never cooked before, that was high praise.

Since coming to Diablo, Kate had been kept too busy to feel sorry for herself. Al kept her trotting back and forth between the spring beside the lake and fetching firewood whenever she wasn't chopping, cleaning, washing, or drying. By day's end, she was so tired she didn't even have the energy to launch a verbal assault on her cabinmate.

After finishing the supper dishes, she trudged docilely up the path beside Peter. She brushed her hair a perfunctory hundred strokes instead of her usual two hundred. Doffing her clothes behind the sheet in the corner, she put on her nightgown and hopped into bed.

Before Peter even got his boots off, Kate was fast asleep.

For the next few days, Al ran Katherine through her paces like a circus dog rehearsing for center ring. The only thing he wouldn't let her do was take food to Raimey Griswold by herself. Strangely protective, Al and Charlie Mason insisted on accompanying her on errands any time the other men were in camp.

With Katherine occupied, Peter concentrated on familiarizing himself with Diablo Camp's operations and men. As soon as Raimey could hobble to a chair on crutches, Peter had him peeling potatoes, helping Charlie Mason sharpen saws and, in spare moments, they inventoried the company stores together.

Peter spotted the troublemakers and split them up, giving assignments that kept them apart. In addition, he revised a number of McGillacutty's policies, thereby eliminating several areas of legitimate grievance and improving the men's morale.

Encouraged by O'Rourke's fair-mindedness, Jigger Jansen made suggestions about how to better handle the crews. He began dropping around the office in the evenings to discuss ways they might improve Diablo's productivity. When his brother in Vermont sent him a trade gazette, he showed it to Peter and rhapsodized about buying the latest equipment to boost production at Diablo.

Peter's respect for Jigger grew with each passing day. "I'd like to go out with you and learn the work the way you have," Peter told Jigger one evening.

Jigger glanced at McGillacutty's tall, well-built son-in-law with skepticism. "No fear of heights?" he asked speculatively.

Peter laughed. "Not especially." He fingered the leather rigging straps Jigger had been showing him.

"I can always use a good faller."

"Look, all I want is a taste of what it's like out there," Peter said eagerly. "How can I understand the timber business if I don't have any hands-on experience?"

Jigger hung the rigging harness on a peg in Peter's office and stood up, a glint in his eye. "Time to hit the sack. Tell you what, Casey, m'boy. I'll start you out nice an' easy. You kin fill in fer Griswold as a bucker for a few days."

By this time, Peter knew that a bucker sectioned off a tree into logs, preparatory to the oxen hauling them down the skid road into the yard. He nodded his eager assent.

"See you tomorrow morning."

When the nine o'clock lights-out bell rang, Peter locked up the office and set off for his cabin in the dark.

Katherine had left the lantern lit, its warm yellow glow softly lighting his way to bed. Peeling off his jacket, he looked across the bundling board, Kate was asleep already, and no wonder. Every time he spotted her, usually from a distance, she was rushing somewhere. It seemed Al's new cookee didn't ever walk; she ran.

While he undressed, Peter noticed that the new curtains in the cabin windows looked suspiciously like Katherine's plaid dress. She certainly hadn't wasted any time putting needle and thread to work that morning when he had given her a sewing kit from the company store.

It surprised him how accepting Katherine had become of her circumstances, especially since he could understand her initial rage. He was even more amazed by her stamina and her grit. She still flashed him fiery looks in the dining hall; often defiant, sometimes pensive. But mostly she skirted around him, avoiding open conflict. Lately a polite civility had developed. Whether this meant she was just too tired to enjoy a good fight or had given up hope that he'd let her go, he couldn't tell. He rather thought it was the former, although he preferred to reserve judgment until she got her second wind.

In the morning they dressed back to back in silence. Then, at a prearranged signal, his shaving mug sounded the downbeat, and her hairbrush the equally mad maestro's upbeat on their respective sides of the dresser. They squared off and perused each other for possible serious omissions in their individual toilettes. Then they gave each other a curt nod.

If this was marriage, it was deadly, and Peter wanted no part of it. But for now, it kept them civil.

The next morning Katherine crossed the dividing line and headed for the door. Her exaggeratedly long steps told Peter they hadn't reached an armistice, but merely a temporary cease-fire. He opened the door, waved her through, and followed, five paces to the rear.

Like a royal princess bestowing her blessing upon the commoners, Kate gracefully raised a hand in greeting to Camp Diablo's derelict crew.

Peter watched the scene with only slight amusement. Kate couldn't spare him the time of day, yet she exuded friendliness toward these men. Probably only a handful had come within ten yards of a wholesome woman in their lives!

Peter tried to relax. He told himself the men were merely responding to her cordial wave. Why worry? After all, Kate was completely covered, neck to toes. There wasn't a thing seductive about her bulky jacket and wool dress.

So why was he so horny that one look from her tied him in knots? Because he was a ruddy fool, that's why. Old habits died hard.

"Dammit, Kate!" he bellowed suddenly, vowing to break with the enemy within his own soul. Perhaps if he took a truly objective look at her . . . After all, it was only four-thirty in the morning! How many women looked good at such an ungodly hour?

Puzzled by his outburst, Kate turned, the frosty breath of early morn on her rosy lips. Her eyes, paler than precious emeralds, sparkled with health. Her cheeks were nipped a bright rosy hue by air so pure and clean it left him giddy. "Something the matter, Peter?"

Clearly she had no idea that she was driving him half-mad with desire.

Peter stopped in his tracks, realizing how ridiculous his infatuation had become. He needed a legitimate bone to pick, or at least a plausible reason for yelling at her. Pasting a supercilious smirk on his face, he gave Kate a critical once-over. His lips curved in sophisticated amusement, and his eyebrows flew up, almost disappearing into the blond locks flowing across his matinee-idol brow. It was an act he'd used many times with devastating effect.

"Really, Katherine," was all he said.

"Did I do something wrong?" She looked down at herself, wondering what he saw that was out of place. She had all her clothes on and her jacket properly buttoned.

Peter knew he had to come up with something fast, or reveal that he'd been reduced to a complete clown by her stunning beauty. Quickly he reached out and flicked an imaginary bug off the top of her head.

"Stop that, Peter," she protested, flinching.

"It's gone now," he said with a superior smile and walked right on past her into the dining hall.

"What's gone?" Katherine asked, running to catch up. She grabbed his arm to stop him.

"For goodness sake, Kate, you mean . . . you don't know?" O'Rourke bluffed. At least he'd made her drop her Lady Bountiful act.

"Indeed I do not!"

"Poor child," he said condescendingly. "It's lucky you have me to look out for you."

"I don't believe that for a minute," Kate said indignantly. She walked past him and slammed the kitchen door in his face.

"I need more flour," was Al's greeting.

Kate took off her jacket, hung it on a peg, and started toward the storage room. She came back with a scooper full of flour and dumped it in a large mixing bowl.

Peter appeared in the doorway between the kitchen and dining room. He grinned at her.

"Loggers wait in the dining room, or outside," she informed him.

"Is that any way to speak to the man who probably just saved your life?" Peter joked.

"Saved my life!" Katherine stamped her foot.

"I could use some sugar and molasses, Mrs. O'Rourke," Al interjected.

"How many times must I tell you to call me Kate?" she

raged, feeling close to paranoia. She whirled to vent her anger on the man responsible for making her life nearly intolerable. "Peter, you just love to torment me, don't you? Go on, admit it! You plunked me on the head for no good reason."

Peter spread his hands wide. "You're right, Kate. I made it up."

Kate's eyes narrowed with suspicion. Peter had agreed with her too quickly. Maybe there *had* been something on her head. She came up to him and shook her fist under his nose. "All right, O'Rourke, what was it, hmmm?"

"Like you said—nothing." He smiled ingratiatingly, and Katherine felt her heart skip a beat.

Meanwhile Al was muttering, "Sugar and molasses." He went to get them himself.

"I can't believe anything you say," Kate said tartly, tying knots in her apron.

"Would you be happier if I told you that you were about to be attacked by a tsetse fly?" Peter affected a tragic pose. "Deadly carrier of disease. Often fatal."

Kate jammed her fists on her hips and glared. "Will you *kindly* get out of this kitchen?" she yelled. "I have better things to do than flap my jaws with an ornery cayuse like you."

"Good, Kate. You sound more like a Western cowpuncher with every passing day," Peter teased. He ducked as she threw the metal potato masher, which she was trying to *sproing* off his head; it landed in the middle of the dining room floor.

Without bothering to retrieve her weapon, Katherine set the table. After she finished, she went out and sat on the back stoop, slumped against the rough shingles. She was still there, fuming, when O'Rourke rounded the corner and dropped a white fur ball in her lap.

"Peace offering."

"For me?" Shocked, Katherine held up the tiny kitten. It had eyes the color of green moss and a black nose. "It's precious!"

Peter nodded toward the small kitten. "Might give her a bath with some of that stuff Hoss uses to discourage flies and mites on the horses."

"Oh," said Mary Kate, the light finally dawning. "This must be one of the kittens from the bunkhouse."

"Precisely. So give it a thorough going over. We don't want lice or mites in our cabin, now do we?" He reached over and scratched the kitten gently behind the ears.

"She's very pretty. Thank you, Peter." Her fingers rubbing the kitten's fur, Katherine raised her head to gaze at him. "Al says you're trying your hand at logging today, Casey."

"Jigger promised to go easy on me today." Peter pulled on a pair of leather gloves.

"Don't be too sure about that," Kate warned.

Peter winked. "I think he plans to separate the men from the boys."

"Just as long as you don't separate an arm from a shoulder, or a foot from a leg," Kate said with a cryptic smile.

"My sentiments exactly." He hunched his shoulders, driving his collar up around his ears. "Say a little prayer for me today, huh?"

Katherine's eyes twinkled mischievously. "Any special request I should put in for you?"

"Oh, something like 'break a leg' will do nicely," Peter quipped and strode away.

Oh, that I'll do, gladly, Mary Kate thought, watching him join the rest of the lean, hungry 'timber wolves,' a name she used to describe the loggers' voracious appetites.

Then she retracted her ornery prayer. She wasn't about to ask the Lord to give him a broken leg. Then he'd be under foot all the time, instead of only occasionally. *He probably knows that, too, the pest,* she thought, pondering his facetious remark.

Still, it was too bad that he'd beaten her to the punch line.

CHAPTER 14

As the nine o'clock bell sounded the day's end in camp, Kate reluctantly set the last plate on the shelf. It perplexed her that Peter had left right after supper without so much as a nod to acknowledge her. Without fail, he always stayed behind while she finished up, then escorted her back to the cabin. Where had he disappeared to?

She checked through the kitchen window and saw no lights in his office. Nothing about his demeanor at supper had suggested any problem. He had laughed, joked, and joined in the after-dinner tomfoolery as usual. But when the loggers began to disperse, he, too, had vanished.

Mr. Al came in the back door and put down his wash pan. "What say I walk you up to yer cabin?" he asked. "The boss man must be tied up."

"Yes, I suppose you're right."

She and Al trudged through the dark in silence. When Kate reached the steps of her cabin, she spied a dim light through the closed curtains. *Of course*, she thought. *Peter had a hard day. He's already in bed.*

She turned to the taciturn cook. "Good night, Mr. Al, and thank you."

"Night, Mrs. O'Rourke." With a casual salute, four fingers against his knitted cap, he shuffled away into the dark.

On tiptoe Katherine mounted the steps and eased open the latch, not wanting to disturb Peter if he was asleep. She cracked the heavy door just enough to slip into the cabin.

She was correct about one thing at least: Peter was fast asleep. But he wasn't in bed.

Feet and arms dangling over the sides of a huge metal bathtub, Peter lay submerged in water, his head propped against the elevated back of the tub. Next to one lax hand, a script bearing the title *Hamlet* lay on the floor beside an empty glass. A thin cheroot, the smoke still curling lazily toward the rafters, burned in a cracked saucer next to it.

Katherine stood transfixed, her heart behaving like a frog doing somersaults on a lily pad. From the doorway, her eyes zeroed in on the back of O'Rourke's golden head. As she crept stealthily into the room, a set of broad, muscular shoulders came into view, and a mat of blond fur on an equally impressive chest rose and fell in peaceful cadence.

Jolted by the sight of so much exposed masculine flesh, Katherine gradually worked her way around to view Peter's long torso sideways. Curiosity, coupled with deliciously sneaky pleasure, overcame caution. By the time she got within an arm's length of the godlike figure draped over the sides of the bathtub, her heart was pumping wildly. Her mouth went dry. And a strange exultation surfaced that she had rarely felt, except during Handel's *Hallelujah Chorus* one Christmas in Chicago.

For here, slumbering in a swamp of bath water, was the kind of good news created to gladden any foolish young maiden's heart! The temptation to touch was so strong that Katherine had to bite her thumb to keep from screaming out loud.

A soft snore rose from lips that curved in a faint smile.

Mary Kate knew she should close her eyes. She should tiptoe across that chalk line and get into bed before she was discovered. From there, safely under the covers, she should awaken him. But how?—yell, "Yoo-hoo"?

Kate debated furiously with herself. What to do? An opportunity like this didn't come along every day. A cautious glance confirmed that her cabinmate was indeed asleep. Out cold. To her disappointment, her survey of O'Rourke's rippling chest muscles and flat, narrow waist stopped at the water line. Emerging at the opposite end of the tub were sinewy thighs and superbly developed masculine calves, sporting a golden sprinkling of downy hair.

Spotting the high arch in his foot, Katherine stealthily crept toward the feet dangling so temptingly over the tub's rim. From O'Rourke's crown to the tips of his toes, he was an awesome specimen—just waiting for mischief to happen.

When a lifetime of being a proper, predictable, and mostly compliant female is combined with an inherited sense of mischief and easy access to a man's unguarded big toe, almost anything can happen, and probably will. Especially when the young lady involved is inspired by a powerful need for revenge.

Gleefully she hunkered down, her fingers just itching.

A splash of water hit her in the face!

Gasping, Kate swiped away wet strands of hair and cleared her vision. Peter, though he hadn't moved, fixed his fierce green gaze on her.

"Oh, you're awake!" she said brightly. She scooted away and, hoping to convince Peter she was innocent of wrongdoing, she fluttered her eyelashes with an injured air.

"Don't even think it," he warned.

Retrieving his cheroot with a swift, graceful movement, he set it in his teeth, picked up his manuscript, and proceeded to ignore her.

Kate sidled closer, noticing that *Hamlet* now covered his midsection. After a few minutes of uncomfortable silence, she said, "Your bathwater is getting cold, Peter."

"I'm well aware," was his terse reply.

Shrugging, Katherine strolled across the yellow line to her own side. She hung up her jacket and rearranged the toiletries on her side of the dresser, while she snuck nervous sidelong peeks at her cabinmate.

Peter was frowning studiously at the open book held over his lap. Oddly enough, he seemed to have completed his bath, yet made no move to extricate himself from the tub.

"I suppose you'd like me to leave, so you can get out?" Kate finally asked, fidgeting.

"Ordinarily I'd say yes," Peter gritted out, his cheroot wagging madly between clamped teeth. "Tonight, I may require your help."

Katherine did a double-take, instantly alert. "What's wrong, Peter? Are you stuck?"

He put out his cigar in the water, tossed it in the saucer, and raised an eyebrow. "Do I look stuck?"

"No—"

"I am not stuck, Mary Kate. Just paralyzed, dammit!"

Kate's eyes grew round. From where she stood, Peter looked hale and hardy. In fact, she doubted that many males could match his physical perfection.

"Jigger's sadistic sense of humor and my own stupidity are to blame." Flexing one leg carefully, he winced. "I used muscles today I didn't even know I possessed."

"Oh." Kate cocked her head, considering Peter's predicament. Evidently he was more vulnerable than she had realized. Finally! She had Peter O'Rourke at her mercy. How long had she dreamed of this moment? Or one very like it. The possibilities for revenge fired her imagination.

"Poor man," she crooned. "So you've had a bad day. Can I help in any way?"

Gingerly Peter forced himself to a more upright position in the tub. "You could hand me that towel."

"Your wish is my command." Katherine fetched his towel, shaking open its generous, fluffy folds as she advanced.

Peter gripped the sides of the tub and grimaced.

"Do you need help getting out?" she asked, all solicitation.

Peter shook his head stubbornly. He was so stiff he could barely flex a muscle. He had sawn mammoth logs for ten hours straight, taking only a short lunch break. As long as he kept moving in the woods, cutting limbs, and dragging long saws across tree trunks, he'd been able to keep up. But coming back to camp, his muscles had cooled too fast. By the time supper was over, every muscle and joint in his body was writhing in agony.

Katherine retrieved the whiskey flask from O'Rourke's end of the dresser, her mind made up. She would kill him with kindness. It was the least she could do, after all he'd done to her, she reminded herself.

She poured a tall shot of the fiery liquid and handed it to him. "Drink this," she urged. "It will make you feel better."

And, indeed, it did. A moment later, his privates camouflaged by the towel, O'Rourke maneuvered his lanky frame awkwardly out of the tub.

"I must be out of my mind. This line of work is worse than any crazy monk doing penance," he groaned. Peter's muttered imprecations got him as far as the table, where he stopped to shake a tight cramp out of his left calf. "As I recall, there *are* easier ways to make a living."

Katherine bit back a smile; she'd never seen him so miserable! "You just overdid things a bit, Peter. Tomorrow you'll do much better."

"Aye, if I live that long."

Hobbling stiffly, he allowed Kate to help him to the nearest chair. Except for the towel wrapped around his middle, Peter's body was bare. It was all Kate could do to maintain her composure with so much raw animal magnetism within her grasp. In his present state, Peter was harmless, a fact that sent a warm rush of glee coursing through her belly. The pleasure of touching him and possibly arousing him without suffering reprisal brought out all her worst vixenish tendencies.

Testing how far she dared go, Katherine reached for a small towel and dried his hair. Closing his eyes with a moan of gratitude, Peter surrendered himself to her gentle ministrations. Encouraged, Mary Kate expanded her horizons and patted the moisture from his shoulders.

"I can do that," he grouched.

She scoffed at the idea. "After working so hard all day? Nonsense." Warming to her work, Kate knelt and buffed his legs with the towel. She even dried between his toes. Then, rising, she looked at him expectantly, as if awaiting his slightest command. "Would you like your robe?"

Peter nodded, his jaw tight with pain. Kate dropped it around his shoulders, and his right arm reached for the jar of liniment on the table.

"Here, let me do that for you," Katherine insisted. She unscrewed the lid and wrinkled her nose at the liniment's strong odor. Setting his robe on the back of the chair, she daubed salve on his shoulders and massaged it into his muscles.

As Katherine's fingers glided over his skin, heat radiated through his sore body. O'Rourke sighed and flexed his shoulders, grateful for the momentary relief.

"I *could* stand another shot of whiskey," he hinted, desirous of milking as much service as possible from his beautiful nurse. Her eagerness to help left him flabbergasted. Best to take advantage while Mary Kate was in the mood, he decided.

Katherine placed the glass and whiskey on the table within his reach and went back to her brand of physical rehabilitation. Liberally spreading liniment from shoulder to wrist, she worked it into first one arm and then the other.

"That . . . feels . . . wonnnderful, Katherine," he murmured, leaning against the table and pouring another drink.

Sensing O'Rourke was too stiff and tired to offer any serious resistance, Katherine had planned to lull him into a false sense of security and then tickle him unmercifully.

But somewhere in the process of applying the liniment, she changed her mind. Peter's pain from overstressed muscles was genuine. Far better, she decided, to apply another kind of pain.

Deliberately, as she reached for more salve, she leaned her breasts into his back, while she smoothed and rubbed his back in ever-widening circles, always watching for his reaction.

Still Peter remained impassive beneath her teasing touch. Piqued by his lack of response, Kate blew in his ear. His blond curls stirred and tickled her lips, but Peter didn't bat an eyelid.

Frowning now, she began in earnest to explore his strong, elastic skin. Soon she grew bolder, until suddenly she was taking marvelous liberties. She ran her fingertips down his spine in feathery strokes. She trailed the ends of her hair between his shoulder blades and down to his waist. Her knuckles worked like an inchworm doing push-ups all over his muscular back. Over and over, she bumped him with her breasts.

Finally she ran out of things to do to his back.

Sheepish, yet exhilarated that she'd gotten away with so much, Katherine paused to catch her breath.

"Don't stop now," Peter chuckled, raising his head to confront her with a naughty twinkle in his eye.

Kate's fingers tingled, and she felt her face burn. In searching out his vulnerabilities, she had inadvertently dropped her guard. Gazing into his thickly lashed green eyes, she saw her own susceptibility spelled out.

What a time to be muscle-bound from neck to ankles! Peter thought, cursing his rotten luck. The vixen was intent upon torture, and he wasn't in any shape to call her bluff.

"Thank you for your, uh, kindness, Kate," he said, rising to his feet stiffly. He bolted down the last of his whiskey. "If you'll hand me that pair of flannel drawers, I can manage the rest."

Katherine sashayed over to where his flannels hung

halfway out of the second drawer. Handing them over, she went to the fireplace and added a log. She was careful to keep her back turned until she heard Peter sigh and shuffle toward the bed.

She glanced around furtively. He had on his robe, belted tightly at the waist and covering him past midcalf. Since the drawers were nowhere in sight, she presumed he'd put them on.

Smiling, Katherine came toward him solicitously. "Can I get you anything else?" she asked, as he lowered himself carefully onto the narrow edge of the bed.

"Nothing, thanks." Slowly Peter stretched out full length, sorrier than ever that he'd been a legalist in apportioning equal shares of the bed. Considering the difference in their sizes, he should have given himself two-thirds of the mattress.

Katherine fussed with the pillow. "Now, you're sure you're comfortable?" she persisted.

"No, I'm not! Let me rest in peace, Kate."

She clapped her hand over her mouth to stifle a giggle. "That sounds so . . . terminal. Really, Peter! You may be stiff as a board, but you're nowhere near ready for the graveyard!"

"Stiff all over," O'Rourke confirmed, managing a lopsided grin despite his discomfort. "Now get away from me, woman, and let me sleep."

"Maybe if I massaged your legs a little." She playfully tweaked the fur on his calf.

"No!" Peter heaved his carcass over and lay on his belly, his right arm and leg dangling off the bed. All he wanted was to be left alone.

Unfortunately, Katherine had other plans. O'Rourke was even more vulnerable on his stomach. Kate crossed to the lantern and blew it out. Retrieving an aromatic hand lotion from her trunk, she crossed to Peter's side of the bed. Pouring a generous amount into her palm, she smoothed the cool, creamy substance from his right knee down his leg to the ankle.

"That's cold, Kate!" Peter complained, his voice groggy with exhaustion.

Refusing the hint, Katherine applied more lotion to his left leg. Kneeling, she ran her hands up and down both legs, squeezing the large muscles and working out the knots. Groaning helplessly into his pillow, Peter submitted, finding her hands surprisingly strong and supple—and far too sensitizing.

Telling himself she would finish faster if he didn't give her any backtalk, Peter let himself drift along, while she subjected him to long, even strokes. He felt her fingers on the backs of his knees. Soon her hands were playing "This little piggy went to market, this little piggy stayed home," and squeezing his toes. And then she lathered his legs all over again, only this time, it was with gardenia-scented lotion.

Lord, don't let the men get a whiff of this tomorrow, he pleaded silently.

Mary Kate hummed an Irish lullaby—off-key again, but it seemed wondrously gentle to him. Completely relaxed, Peter went limp beneath the mesmerizing rhythm of song and her hands' soothing caress. He slept like one who is newborn.

Somehow Casey O'Rourke made it up out of bed the next morning. Well fortified by a stack of Al's pancakes, three fried eggs, bacon, biscuits, and coffee, he followed Bobbie White Feather and Hoss down the skid road at break of dawn.

His muscles were aching, but his spirits had lifted. This unexpected turnabout in Mary Kate's behavior could only mean a softening in her attitude toward him. His heart felt a squeeze of tenderness as he caught sight of her watching him from the kitchen door on his way to work.

He couldn't keep his eyes off her, especially after last night. Though her actions were a calculated torment, she had unwittingly revealed a gentler, caring side to her nature. Perhaps because she'd perceived his passivity as nonthreatening, she'd felt free to test out her feminine wiles on him. For a man used to taking a more aggressive role in affairs of the heart, Peter found her innocent mischief far more seductive than the careful arts of an experienced courtesan. Whatever Katherine was up to, he meant to enjoy it to the full.

"Good morning, Mary Kate." He nodded to her, a smile in his eyes as he approached.

Just for a second, the sun cast its rays across the camp, spotlighting her in a brilliant halo. As if she knew what he was thinking, Kate blushed and waggled two fingers at him.

"Good morning, Peter," she said softly and dropped the tiny white kitten Peter had given her down inside her jacket with a mysterious smile. "Come, Moriah," she told the kitten, as she turned aside, "let's get a saucer of warm milk from Bessie."

Of course, he could be wrong, Peter reasoned, but Mary Kate actually seemed to be enjoying herself, despite her surroundings.

If McGillacutty wanted his daughter to show what she was made of, she was doing a superb job. That didn't mean she liked roughing it, but neither was she behaving like the spoiled social butterfly her father had made her out to be. In fact, she had settled in much better than Peter had expected. Her hours were as long as his, sometimes longer. Nobody could fault her attitude. She was bright, beautiful, and, like him, a damn quick study.

Aye, Peter had to admit, Katie O'Rourke was starting to grow on him. This innocent might just break his heart, if given the chance. But the way his body felt, it might be days before he could put all his unanswered questions about Kate to the test.

Pain has a way of making a man work smarter instead of harder. Watching Bobbie White Feather, Peter immediately saw how the young Indian set up a rhythm and

let it carry him through the day. Shortly he adopted a
similar pattern, following Bobbie's lead. Whenever the
work became especially strenuous, Bobbie burst forth
with fragments of song or told a joke.

O'Rourke soon learned the wisdom of keeping his
mind as busy as his saw. He swapped tales with Bobbie,
taught him a few minstrel bits and sea chanteys he knew,
and picked up several valuable tips on bucking logs.

Sweat was to muscle what oil was to machinery. During
the day, his muscles gradually eased. They were still stiff
from the new demands made upon them, but it was not
unbearable. Even so, Peter didn't want to risk cooling
down too quickly after work. Instead of sauntering back
to camp, as he had done the night before, he made himself keep up a brisk pace.

"Hey, Jigger! Wait up," he called, loping over to join
Jansen and a group of fallers.

Jigger paused, axe on shoulder, and looked over the
company man with grudging surprise. "Casey, how ya
be? You're looking a mite livelier than yesterday."

"Still working the soreness out," Peter admitted with a
grin. "Another week, and I'll be in the best shape I've
ever been."

Jigger nailed a lizard to the side of a tree with a spurt
of Bull Durham chaw. He was surprised to see O'Rourke
on his feet after the double load of work he'd assigned
him the day before. "We'll make a logger outta you yet."

Peter nodded to Mel and Joe Burns and fell into step
beside Jansen. "Exercise is good for the mind," he declared with more cheerfulness than he felt. "I expect,
after some practical field experience, I should be able to
tear through those books in half the time."

"Half those reports don't amount to a hill of beans."
No respecter of persons, Jigger made no effort to spare
the feelings of Camp Diablo's newest greenhorn.

Peter did a few boxing steps, bouncing around and
feinting at the forest's shadows across the path. He had
no intention of letting Jigger or his crew know he hurt

like holy hell. "I've been going over a lot of things in my mind these past few days."

"Be sure it don't give you no hernia," Mel laughed, nudging his sidekick Smitty in the ribs.

"No, I feel fit as a fiddle," Peter lied. "But I find we lose valuable time hauling logs down the mountain to the yard. We can do better. Spread the word: anyone who comes up with a way to improve the operation gets a hundred-dollar bonus."

"Lor'!" Smitty almost swallowed his tobacco wad whole.

O'Rourke could see there wasn't a man present who didn't think he was throwing away McGillacutty's money with both hands. "I'll be putting up a suggestion box in the dining hall. Just write down your ideas, sign 'em, and hand 'em in at day's end. Rewards for saving the outfit money will be in a man's pay envelope at week's end."

Leaving them in his dust to ponder his latest offer, Peter stubbornly jogged down the trail into camp.

After supper, Peter asked Al to walk Kate up to the cabin at quitting time. He spent an hour on the books at the wangan, while Mason opened the store so the men could purchase personal items. Then, wisely calling it a day around eight, he went back up to the cabin, did a few slow stretching exercises, and crawled into bed.

Katherine was slightly miffed to find her cabinmate asleep when she walked through the door. All day she'd been looking forward to baiting Peter, and there he lay, sleeping like a fallen angel on his side of the bundling board.

Disgusted, she prepared for bed, using the fire on the hearth to see her way around the room. Her mind buzzing with ideas, she ignored his rule and crossed the yellow chalk line.

"Peter?" She reached down and shook him. "Wake up, Peter."

"Hmmm?" Peter cracked an eyelid. "Oh, it's you, Mary

Kate." He yawned and stretched, giving a fair imitation of a man roused from deep slumber.

"Do you want to talk?" Katherine asked, playing with the satin sash on her nightgown.

"It's been a long day, Kate." Although he'd been awake the entire time, just waiting to see what tactics she meant to use on him tonight, Peter groaned for dramatic effect.

Ah, the firelight! he gloated. Unbeknownst to Kate, her diaphanous gown, backlit by the fire, revealed her curves in tantalizing detail.

"I had hoped we might . . . talk." Pacing restlessly, Kate wrung her hands appealingly, as if she wanted to put them to better use but feared he might be out of temper and frustrate her benevolent kindness. She would have made him a great leading lady, he thought.

Peter decided to play along. "Kate, my muscles are still so sore, I can hardly think, much less talk."

"Really, Peter?" Kate considered his words eagerly. "I'd be happy to rub more liniment on you. That is, if you wish it."

"You'd do that for me?" Peter hoped he wasn't grinning so broadly that she became suspicious.

"Of course. It's the decent and charitable thing to do."

"Bless you." Peter gestured weakly toward the dresser. "The liniment. Terrible-smelling stuff, but what can I say? With your soft touch, I can stand any amount of pain."

"I could use my lotion," Kate offered.

"Do you have anything a little less . . . flowery?" Peter asked, letting her roll him onto his stomach.

"Lavender, rose, or gardenia. Take your pick." Katherine peeled back his nightshirt, leaving Peter naked from the waist up. She moved her hands experimentally up and down his smooth back.

"Lavender, then." He chuckled. "It smells a bit more manly than rose or gardenia, and a good deal better than liniment."

* * *

Thus did Katherine practice her nursing skills for several nights. Peter moaned and flinched, pleading for mercy at appropriate intervals. A curious zeal crept into her work, as Kate grew more intimately acquainted with the details of his perfect male body and its most sensitive spots. At times Kate found she was genuinely glad she could ease his discomfort. But then some imp would emerge from her subconscious, inspiring her to tickle, tease, and torment her victim.

The more Peter held back from retaliating, the bolder she became.

Kate never suspected Peter's strategy was to let her seduce herself.

CHAPTER 15

Increased familiarity quickly heightened Katherine's—
and Peter's—senses to the flash point. It got so nerve
wracking that Peter was grateful for the grueling work all
day long, for it gave him a much-needed respite from
his wife, who could hardly wait to get her dainty hands on
him each evening. Intent upon her peculiar brand of revenge, Katherine became proficient at whipping through
a stack of dinner dishes in record time. Most nights, by
the time he left the office and staggered through their
cabin door, she was already in her nightgown, brushing
her long auburn hair.

Peter was almost tempted to burn the midnight oil
over her father's set of crooked books. However, morning reveille came before dawn. Besides, when had he
ever run from temptation?

His sixth day out in the woods, Jigger trusted Peter
enough to assign him to the crew that felled trees.
Around ten o'clock Peter was sent aloft to top a three-
hundred-foot ponderosa. A "big blue," it was called,
because its girth at the ground was enormous, yet it tapered like a giant candle to less than a foot in diameter
at the top.

As O'Rourke sank his cleats deep into the bark and
shinnied skyward in the crisp mountain air, he had

second thoughts about a lot of things. Considering his foreman's ability to dish out physical punishment, he wasn't all that sure Jigger didn't mean for a high wind to send him toppling to his death. Two hundred feet up, the big blue bent and swayed fifteen feet in any direction under his weight.

"A little higher, Casey," Burns shouted from below.

Clenching his teeth till he thought his jaw would break, O'Rourke inched upward. Seven men stood around the base of the tree, urging him on. Watching him test his mettle as a fledgling logger.

Peter knew Jigger held his crews' respect by his constant show of tough, unflappable nerve and his ability to make critical decisions under pressure. This was, in a way, his own initiation, his hazing. He couldn't back down. Anyway, up this high, a few feet higher didn't make a helluva lot of difference. His blood pumping, O'Rourke renewed his vigorous climb upward.

The pine groaned and creaked, and still he moved up the tree. Fifty feet higher . . . then sixty. Only thirty more to the peak, by God! And all the while the tree bowed like some second-rate diplomat at his first state function.

"Hey, far 'nuff, Casey!" Mel yelled. "Get a good toehold."

"Ai-yup, sink those cleats in good!" Isaac Yancey shouted.

Peter secured his position. He tightened the rigging around his waist and stomped his cleats deep into the bark. Then he freed the saw looped on the back of his belt and waved it, testing the leather straps to make sure they bore his weight. Relieved when they held, he notched the tree enough to set the saw teeth. Shoulders and arms flexing, he went at it with all the strength he could muster.

Fortunately the tree sap had already begun to recede with the cooler weather. In twenty minutes, he sent the top twenty feet of timber plummeting earthward.

"Tii-i-i-mmm-m-mmber-r-r-r-r!" he remembered to

yell just in time. The long wood spike had already started its deadly journey toward Diablo's main falling crew.

The men scattered, hurling curses at the inexperienced topper. The top section crashed and careened through the surrounding trees, cracking and sending a shower of smaller branches down to the forest floor.

While the men cleared the area below, O'Rourke lowered himself several feet to the next level and set up another platform from which to cut the second section.

This particular tree was in a tight spot. It was situated where a man was literally forced to pit his strength and wits against the caprice of nature. Tightly entwined branches of several trees had kept the men from felling the tree from below.

Either he had the steel nerves required, or he didn't. O'Rourke was determined to pass the test, even if the Devil should send a zephyr whistling through the treetops. He lopped off a number of branches that wedged the pine in solidly among its neighbors. Now it was time to show what he could do.

Leaning out as far as he dared, Peter freed the trunk from encroaching limbs. The trunk was several inches thicker at this height. Attacking the task with the skills he had already learned as a bucker, he worked furiously. Minutes later, the trunk crashed heavily to the ground, landing where Peter had calculated it would.

Encouraged, Peter performed the same job twice more. Removing branches, he topped the next two twenty-foot sections cleanly.

"We'll take 'er from here, Casey," Jigger called up to him finally.

Sweating profusely but pleased with his success, Peter clambered down. The other men clustered around, slapping him on the back and congratulating him. Their approval meant more than getting a rave review ever had. Peter knew he was a long way from being proficient, but he had mastered his fear in the face of real danger and walked away unscathed. Best of all, he'd won the grudging respect and acceptance of the rugged bull-of-the-woods, Jigger Jansen. With him on his side, Peter felt confident that he could turn Diablo Camp into a successful operation.

"Time to put on the feedbag," van Ecklund said and turned away, the only faller who hadn't shaken Peter's hand. It was several days since Peter had eased Kate out of a nasty situation with van Ecklund, but evidently the man bore a grudge. He might bear watching, Peter decided.

"Sure, let's grab lunch now," agreed Peter, still breathing hard.

A half hour later, Burns and Yancey left to scale trees several hundred yards away, while the rest of the crew finished off the ponderosa pine Peter had topped.

The number of trees they felled that day surpassed the previous three days! Elated over the men's output, Peter strode back to camp as frisky as a new colt. It completely slipped his mind that Kate thought he was still a semi-invalid—until he saw her clanging on Al's big fry pan to summon the men to supper.

Not one to spoil a good thing, O'Rourke dropped behind the other loggers and changed his gait to that of a tired old workhorse on its way to the glue factory. He stopped to slosh cold water over his head at the washhouse, then took his time catching up with the hungry crew.

Clomping into the cookhouse, the loggers took their places with their usual disorder, noise, and ribald good humor. Peter walked in, with just enough of a limp to stir Kate's sympathies without attracting the men's notice.

"Hey, Casey! Over here," Hoss Lauken hollered, banging on the table.

"Thanks." Peter slid in beside the burly wrangler, who smelled as strong as his horses. The whole camp was in a particularly jubilant mood, having outdone themselves.

They subjected each other to merciless backwoods humor, including Peter as one of them for the first time.

"This man of yers did one helluva job today," Jigger called out to Katherine as she brought a platter of venison steaks to the table.

"A total animal up in them trees, he were." Smitty's broad grin made it clear O'Rourke's performance merited high praise.

Katherine cast a suspicious eye at the strapping Irishman she had married in a moment of weak-minded desperation. O'Rourke shrugged modestly and tore off a chunk of sourdough bread with work-roughened hands. But before she could start feeling sorry for him, the men began bragging about his exploits.

"You shoulda seen him today, missus," said Yancey, washing down a mouth of venison and sourdough bread with a swig of milk. "This man o' yers climbed pert near three hunerd feet straight up, and he like to set a record sawin'!"

"Cain't do no better myself," Joe Burns confirmed with a nod toward O'Rourke. "Hell, we'd have never gotten that tree felled if he hadn't shinnied up that big blue an' topped it like he done."

"Best damn boss we've had. Sweats like a real man," Charlie Mason chortled, punching the logger next to him and taking the beans away from him.

"No more yappin'!" Al hollered, fists braced on his hips. "I ain't stayin' up all night washin' no goldang dishes."

The men hunched apologetically and fell on their food like hungry wolves.

Katherine served in silence, covertly studying the man who had feigned helplessness for the past several nights. Why, she practically had to undress and tuck him into bed! The more she reflected on the loggers' enthusiastic praise, the hotter her temper soared. Wait till she got through with him tonight! Peter would not be swinging in the treetops tomorrow.

She watched Peter say good night to the other men after supper. Once they all retreated to the bunkhouse, he got to his feet slowly and limped like a lame horse into the kitchen.

"Al, thanks for seeing my wife safely home after work lately."

Mary Kate whirled around from the stove, a heavy kettle of boiling water in both hands. "Feeling better tonight, are we, *darling?*" she asked, a dangerous gleam in her eye.

"A little," he conceded, hoping his redheaded spitfire of a wife wasn't wise to him yet. "But it's taking longer to get used to all this rugged outdoor work than I thought."

"You poor man," Kate tsk-tsked. "Well, you go rest yourself, you hear? I'll be along directly. What you need is more horse liniment and another long soak in the tub."

"Could you or Al bring more hot water when you come?" he asked, taking the kettle from her hands.

"Oh, I'll see that you get all the hot water you can stand," she promised, trying to calculate just how much water it would take to drown him in the tub.

Peter gave Kate a platonic peck on the cheek. "You're a treasure, no doubt about it." He turned to Al with a wink. "The good Lord gave me a true angel for a wife."

"Don't listen to him, Mr. Al." Katherine turned to pour more water into a bucket for her husband. "He's full of Irish blarney." Burdening Peter down with buckets, Kate pushed him out the door. "Now, try not to strain yourself, Peter," she called after him in the lowering dusk. "I'll be right along to help you."

She turned with a vengeance to the three-foot stack of dinner plates. *It's not enough that I slave all day,* she fumed, sloshing soapsuds and near-scalding water over the dishes. *Now he wants me catering to his every whim! Well, he is in for a rude awakening!*

By the time Kate finished the dishes, she was all geared up for a fight as she marched toward the cabin, a bucket of ice water in each hand. *No more will I allow myself to be the victim of a cruel fate,* she vowed, setting down her burden and shoving open the door. *I am quite capable of*—

Before Katherine could finish her vengeful thought, a pair of strong arms scooped her up and bore her to the bathtub where she had expected to find her prey.

"O'Rourke, what are you doing?" she cried, clutching at him frantically. He moved so swiftly, the room spun, leaving her quite breathless and dizzy by the time he set her down beside the tub.

"As hard as you work, Kate, and after all you've done for me, I just think turnabout is fair play."

"What?" Katherine's initial reaction was shock. Peter's hands were already busily unbuttoning the back of her dress. Kate whirled around to protest. "Wait! You can't do this!"

"Ah, but I can, dear wife," he said, smoothly divesting her of her dress. A second later, her petticoats joined the practical outer garment lying crumpled at her feet. Horror-struck, she watched him pull the slender satin ribbon on her chemise, opening it to the waist.

"Thank goodness!" He chuckled. "You have no idea how I dislike ladies' corsets."

"And why would that be?" she had the misfortune to ask. She looked down to see her breasts bare to his perusal. In a panic, she ducked under his arm and lunged toward her side of the room. "Keep away from me, Peter!"

"Don't tell me a bath doesn't appeal to you after working in that hot, smoky kitchen all day," O'Rourke persisted with a devilish smile. Before she could cover herself, he caught her around the waist. Katherine grabbed hold of the dresser to impede her progress toward the tub.

"Lout! I don't want a bath!"

Peter pried loose her fingers and unceremoniously dumped her into the warm tub, soaking her chemise and pantalettes.

"Now look what you've done!" she wailed.

Rolling up his sleeves, Peter grinned, eying with bawdy satisfaction the blushing pink skin, puckered nipples, and dark auburn triangle revealed through her clinging wet undergarments.

"How dare you!" she cried, struggling to rise.

"Uh-uh." He shook a finger at her. "This will relax you and help you sleep." He soaped the cloth and knelt beside the tub.

Kate glared at him, clutching her chemise together over her heaving breasts. "Don't pretend you give a damn for my comfort, O'Rourke."

"Ah, but I do." He laughed and, capturing her arm, lathered and rinsed all the exposed parts of her upper body. "Thought you'd play the saucy vamp and get away with it, did you?" Clearly he meant to pay her back in kind, *with interest!* Her face on fire, Katherine dropped her gaze to the eloquent hands and wrists resting against the rim of the metal tub. His green eyes gleamed with good humor and sensuality. She gulped, thankful she still wore *any* clothing, although for all practical purposes, her scant apparel scarcely concealed a thing from his bold gaze.

Abruptly Peter broke her train of thought. "Did you bring more water?" he asked.

Without thinking what he was about, Kate nodded. Then, as he retrieved it from the porch, she realized the jig was up.

Testing the water's temperature as he returned, Peter raised an eyebrow in sudden understanding. "Let me wash your hair for you, Kate," he offered, all smiles.

"I washed my hair this afternoon, and I don't want you touching me." Katherine's voice quavered. She didn't dare mention the bucket of cold water, for fear he might dump it over her head. She only hoped he didn't suspect she had meant to use it on him.

Peter leered at her. "But it's all right for you to do outlandish things to me?"

Kate squirmed uncomfortably, as his hand dove

beneath the water and brought up one long, slender leg. "Yes . . . er, I mean, no! That was different. I thought you needed me."

"My need grows stronger every day," he admitted, stripping off her wet stocking and kissing the instep of her left foot. His eyes never left her flushed face.

"Let me go, you . . . you pervert!" Katherine yelled, trying to retrieve her foot from his grasp. "Oh, what am I going to do?" she despaired aloud.

"I don't know, Mary Kate. What are you going to do?" Standing at the foot of the tub, Peter, his hands clasping her ankles, placed her dripping feet against the crotch of his long johns.

Katherine let out a startled whoop, as her toes grazed his hardened male organ.

"Unhand me this minute, you . . . you villain!" she gasped, her eyes round with panic.

If Peter had heard *that* line once, he had heard it a hundred times. In its present context, he found it both endearing and comical. Kate's gaze spelled trouble as surely as a storm at sea, but her curves and flaming tresses were more arousing to his senses than a mermaid's.

Stroking an imaginary mustache, Peter gave her his best stage-villain's laugh. "Unhand you?" he quipped. "But why, fair beauty, when I have you in my power at last!" And he waggled his eyebrows at her.

"Oh, stop it, O'Rourke! This has gone too far." Katherine kicked at him furiously. He let go, still laughing, and dropped into a chair. She lunged over the side of the tub, spraying water like a bad-mannered spaniel spurning a bath. Fixing her tormenter with a snooty glare, she beat a hasty, sodden retreat across the yellow chalk line to safety.

Peter assumed a wounded air. "How can you question my motives? I merely seek to return the good care you gave me these past few nights."

"You tricked me, O'Rourke!" Kate disappeared behind the corner partition. Stripping out of her wet garments, she dried hastily and pulled a nightgown over her head. All the while, she lectured and complained righteously about his treatment of her.

"Here I was worried about you, when all the time you were leading me on," she accused, emerging to deliver a list of grievances.

"That wasn't compassion you were feeling, Mary Kate," Peter threw back at her, for laying all the blame at his feet. "And don't tell me you weren't bent on seduction."

"I wasn't!" Going to sit before the fire, she pulled the pins from her hair and let it fall like a flaming second-act curtain before her audience of one.

An all-too-familiar flood of primal urgency surged through Peter's veins, with the same intensity that pushes a starving lion to make its kill. He took two quick steps toward her before he caught himself. "Ah, sweet Kate, let me make love to you," he said, his voice husky with desire.

Kate jumped to her feet as violently as if a spark had shot under her nightgown and set her on fire. She spun around to face him, her hair fanning out around her shoulders. "No! Stay away from me, O'Rourke." She advanced, brandishing her hairbrush. "Get this straight. I loathe, despise, and . . . and—"

As she came closer, a tug of desire gave a queer little twist in her heart. Unmasked passion stared her in the face, before an invisible veil fell to shield Peter's emotions from her gaze. She caught but a glimpse, but it was enough to shake her deeply.

I can't even lie convincingly to myself, she thought, appalled. "I . . . I don't even . . . like you," she finished lamely and retreated to her side of the chalk line.

You want me, too, his sultry green eyes told her.

"No!" Katherine stamped her foot.

Peter got a grip on himself. There was more than one way to bring down lively game. "Let's not get all worked up about it." Affecting nonchalance, he strolled over and put a last log on the fire before going to bed. Whistling softly, Peter extinguished the lantern.

"Will Shakespeare hit the nail right on the head:

"'Have you not heard it said full oft,
A woman's nay doth stand for naught.'"

"That's only one man's opinion," she snorted and took refuge beneath the covers.

"Let's be done with quarreling, Kate." Peter sighed getting into bed. "Your lips say no, your actions say yes. You can't blame me for getting confused."

"Huh! I suppose you want me to apologize for your stupidity!"

Frustrated by her obstinacy, O'Rourke turned toward the dividing plank. It was but a small barrier, compared with the emotional wall between them. Where to start? How far did he dare take this?

Plagued by desire and a long dry spell, Peter decided to open negotiations with his bed partner. "Katherine," he whispered.

Hearing her stir, Peter peered over the board. Even in the dark, her eyes glowed like a cat's. "We *are* married," he reminded her cautiously.

"So?" She raised up on one elbow, inches separating them.

In the faint moonlight, he found her unspeakably fair to look upon. *All that keeps us apart is this ridiculous two-inch-thick board.* He swallowed hard with erotic longing and took the plunge. "Look, Kate, why don't we get rid of this damn board and . . . talk?"

Without any change of expression, Kate returned her kidnapper-husband's ardent gaze. It was a moment she had dreamed of for days. Her fingers traveled to his face, seeking out the deep cleft in his chin and tracing his dimples with seeming tenderness.

Peter's breath caught in ragged anticipation, his body

tightening. *All the saints be praised!* He would have his bride this very night!

Then the temptress showed her true colors. "I would rather make love to a two-headed rattlesnake," she hissed, her fangs sinking deep. "Good night, O'Rourke!"

Descending once more beneath the covers, Kate smiled, tasting the first fruits of what would eventually be total victory.

But she hadn't counted on Peter Casey O'Rourke having a comeback. Chuckling, the wretch had the audacity to spout poetry to her!

"Oh, serpent! cunning to deceive,
Sure, 'tis this tree that tempted Eve;
The crimson apples hang so fair,
Alas! what woman could forbear?"

O'Rourke laughed softly, improvising on the poet's art. He had no intention of letting her get the best of him, though her rejection stung like bloody hell.

"How pale, how languid, and how dead;
Yet, let the sun of thy bright eyes
Shine but a moment, it shall rise;
Let but the dew of thy soft hand
Refresh the stem, it straight shall stand;
Already, see, it swells, it grows . . ."

His words, though somewhat confusing to her virgin ears, throbbed with emotion. But the full impact of his message soon dawned.

"Really, O'Rourke!" she cried, no longer able to keep silent. "Where do you find such disgusting rhymes! In a . . . bawdy house?"

"Nay, sweet Kate, you are my inspiration," he assured her.

Thoroughly provoked, Kate poked her head over the

board. She saw his profile as he stared up at the rafters. He shot her a sidelong glance, knowing full well whose rapid breathing matched his own sluicing desires.

"Have I upset you, sweet Kate?" His rich voice sounded gentle, even penitent, but Kate wasn't fooled for one minute.

"You seek to torment me," she accused him, squirming uncomfortably under his bold gaze.

"'Forgive . . . It's the tree by which we live,'" he quoted again.

"No!" she shouted and, lying down again, turned her back.

"'Tis God's honest truth," Peter said, glad he could get such a rise out of her. He smiled in the dark. She could deny all she wanted, but Mary Katherine McGillacutty O'Rourke was as red hot as her flaming tresses. "Let's see . . . If you don't like Sheridan, maybe you'd prefer a bedtime story by Lord Wilmot?" he asked.

"I would not! Now hush up, O'Rourke. I'm trying to sleep," Kate snarled, again beneath the covers with her fingers in her ears.

Peter ignored her protests. He had promised not to lay a hand on her, but words, he knew, were a potent seducer. "Close your eyes now, and dream upon these words," he told the huddled figure under the blankets.

"Naked she lay, clasped in my longing arms,
I filled with love, and she all over charms;
Both equally inspired with eager fire,
Melting through kindness, flaming in desire."

Incensed, Katherine sprang up. Hurling herself over the divider, she landed on top and punched Peter in the jaw.

"Don't you *ever* quote to me again!" she seethed.

Their bodies came together like two cosmic forces careening madly off course. Sensing immediately his state of arousal, Kate tried to reverse her mistake by extricating herself from his rude embrace.

Peter's hands grasped her small round bottom, pressing her hips to his loins. Alarmed, Kate arched frantically, prying her breasts from his chest. But now the burning ache his manhood touched off at the juncture of her thighs threatened to undo her altogether.

"My God, O'Rourke, have you no mercy?" Her passions were so inflamed that she feared she would faint.

Laughing, Peter ran his arm up her back and brought her down to him again, while he rocked his pelvis slowly, making her agonizingly aware that, indeed, he meant to offer her the tree of life.

"Self-defense, my dear," Peter told her, nibbling the nerves on her neck. "*You* attacked *me,* remember?"

Kate, trembling and moaning in his arms, felt the fight ebb from her body. His mouth undeniably persuasive, she surrendered her lips to his intoxicating kisses. She wilted against him, returning his probing advances with a hunger that warmed her like a living fire.

Responding to the probe and thrust of Peter's manhood through her nightgown, Katherine braced her right leg on the floor. Guided by blind instinct, she opened herself to him. It was madness, she knew, but she was beyond caring!

Surprised how quickly she had capitulated, Peter's hand skimmed up her thigh, gathering the gown's soft material around her waist. Kate gasped, as his practiced fingers quickly took her beyond any faltering, last-minute change of heart. She arched, pressing against his hand, seeking a cure for the fever that consumed her. Her head flung back, and her hair flew like the torch of an angel, lighting all the hidden corners of his soul. Insatiable passions raged, inflaming them both.

A tiny gasp escaped her softly parted lips, as Katherine pressed on toward the gift Peter offered, wanting it desperately, her body admitting the need her lips denied. She sought the flame, the fuse ignited, setting off a chain reaction. A soft scream tore from her throat, as she exploded in a thousand directions and went into an orbit of glorious rapture.

"Easy, girl," Peter crooned, watching the look of wonder break over her face in savage splendor. He gave her that moment, knowing the power he now held over her, even as she did.

Katherine collapsed on top of him, panting and limp as a jellyfish. He kissed the damp curls on her forehead, feeling a strange tenderness for the fledgling woman in his arms.

Ordinarily, Peter would have followed a decade of habit and spent himself in Kate's luscious body. But the bundling board and his own sudden, insane compassion for the "weaker sex" swayed his judgment. Later Peter was to regret he didn't immediately finish what he started. Still, what man with a beautiful woman in his arms needs hindsight?

Fool that he was, Peter convinced himself not to press selfish advantage. Instead, he let Kate sleep, content that what he'd begun could be accomplished in stages.

Of course, he fully intended to consummate their union after she took a short nap. He just didn't count on falling asleep himself.

CHAPTER 16

At nine o'clock the next day Peter strode past the cookhouse, mentally giving the cookee a good dressing down. Damn that woman! He had overslept, and she hadn't even bothered to wake him. His schedule was completely ruined. It was too late to go out in the woods with the men. Swearing a blue streak, Peter entered the wangan and picked up a stack of neglected reports. He needed to review them before he met with Jigger later in the day.

By midmorning Peter suddenly realized he was squinting over the books. Crossing to light the lantern, he glanced out the window, wondering why the horizon was so dark. A thick haze covered the sky, and he heard what sounded like a great wind roaring in the distance.

He shook his head, started to return to his work, and suddenly halted.

Wind, yet no movement? That seemed odd. For if it was wind, why wasn't a single leaf moving on the trees outside his office window? In fact, the outdoors was deadly calm, except that the noise was growing louder, like the approach of a fast-moving freight train.

Come to think of it, the sound was accompanied by the smell of sulfur and . . .

Smoke! That's what was making his eyes smart.

Thinking they must be in for something of a storm, Peter walked to the wangan door, pulling on his jacket, and stepped outside.

Except for Griswold, who was still laid up with a busted leg, only Al, Kate, the blacksmith, and he remained behind in camp. The crews were out on the slopes, felling trees, trimming and sectioning, or loading and bringing logs down the skid road into the yard.

Out on the office steps, the choking smell of smoke was unmistakable. The overcast sky wasn't ordinary cloud cover, either. Somewhere in the woods there was a forest fire. And if his senses didn't mislead him, it wasn't far off.

Peter knew absolutely nothing about the woods or dealing with a forest fire. But he *did* know how quickly a fire could turn from a blessing to the worst kind of a living hell. As a lad, he had witnessed a fire sweeping through a tenement in Dublin—a terrifying experience he would never forget. Mass hysteria. Grime-streaked faces helplessly looking on while the fire raged out of control. He had watched a frantic young mother fight to get past her neighbors, heard her scream, "My baby's in there!" And then, as her husband reentered the burning building, the whole blazing structure had collapsed, compounding her loss.

He had stood across from the Orpheum Theater in Philadelphia the night six patrons were trampled to death in a panicked crowd. The fire was put out in minutes, but that didn't make the loss of life any less tragic.

Spurred by horrors he would carry with him always, Peter leapt off the wangan porch and turned automatically toward the western slope. There! The darkest part of the fire, directly behind the steep rise. He hadn't seen signs of trouble earlier, possibly because it came from the California side of the Sierras. Diablo Camp was in a direct line with the fire!

"Blackie!" Peter yelled over the din, racing toward

the forge. "Hitch the horses. Meet me back at the wangan—*now!*"

The blacksmith looked out from inside his darkened hole. "What's up, boss?" he called, noting how fast the new man from the head office was running toward the cookhouse.

"Forest fire! Move!" O'Rourke called over his shoulder without slackening speed.

Blackie dropped his hammer and the tongs holding a half-formed horseshoe back onto his anvil. He was so used to the smell of smoke and the dark confines of his forge that he hadn't noticed any fire but his own. It took a second for his eyes to adapt to the outdoors, and another to confirm O'Rourke's words.

"Jeez!" he swore and doused himself with the water bucket standing beside his anvil. He grabbed the mane of the horse waiting half-shod outside his door, swung onto its back, and took off at a full gallop for the barn.

He quickly emptied out the barn and corral, and returned with two strong draft animals hitched to a double-sprung wagon, just as Peter got there with Kate and the cook.

Peter threw the camp ledgers and cash box under the driver's seat. "Start loading," he ordered. "Clothes, blankets, matches, lanterns. Hell, I don't know! Take anything we'll need once the fire burns itself out."

Kate hurried out with a stack of blankets and tossed them in the wagon. Right behind came Al, carrying piles of work clothes.

"Where are you going?" Kate called after O'Rourke, who was already running down the dirt road.

"Got to get Raimey," he hollered and kept on going.

"Can I help?" Katherine screamed after him. The roar up on the hill had grown louder, making her eardrums hurt.

"No! Find the medical supplies. We'll need 'em once this is over."

As Peter disappeared into the bunkhouse, Katherine

turned and ran back into the office. She threw rolled
bandages, liniment, salve, and a half dozen whiskey bottles into a large box. Handing these to Blackie, she
ransacked the store shelves, adding matches, soap, more
blankets, and another lantern to her stash.

"Mr. Al, help!" she cried, staggering under the load.
She gladly relinquished her burden, then snatched up
several pairs of boots by their laces and slung them over
her shoulder. Blackie was just coming back in, muscles
sweaty and bulging, when she spotted a large box of tools.

"Blackie!" Her throat sore, she pointed to the ham-
mers, axes, saws, and files.

"Yes, ma'am!" Working feverishly, Blackie helped her
collect tools, rifles, and cartridges.

When they came back, O'Rourke was back. Half-sup-
porting, half-dragging Raimey Griswold, he and Al laid
the grimacing logger in the wagon on top of the confis-
cated clothing and blankets.

Abruptly Blackie darted back into the wangan and
came back, carrying a huge painting of a half-naked lady
in a gilt frame. "Can't leave without this," he declared,
giving the brightly painted image a kiss on her cherry-
colored lips. "Camp mascot." He laid it in the wagon
next to Raimey. "Holy Mother of God, Casey! That fire's
gonna burn us to a cinder, if we don't git a move on!"

"Let's go!" O'Rourke yelled. He and Blackie grabbed
the horses' harness and headed for the cookshack.
"Three minutes—no more," Peter warned tersely. "Kate,
grab all the pots you can lay hands on. Al, you and
Blackie help me load food supplies."

All four raced the fire. Katherine stacked pots inside
of other pots, making a dreadful clatter in her haste. She
tossed unwashed flatware and plates into a kettle. Both
arms straining under the load, she carried it out to the
wagon.

Relay fashion, Peter and Blackie passed staples through
the kicked-out storage room window to Al. One after another, the heavy sacks sailed through the air, landing in

the wagon. A sack of oats landed on the loggers' favorite objet d'art, creating a hole in the canvas lady's navel.

"Aw, have a heart, boss," Blackie complained.

Peter heaved another sack of beans up to Al in the wagon bed. "You want to save your ever-lovin' arse so you can visit the lady in person? If so, shut your yap."

Blackie forgot his grievance as he saw a ghastly pale-yellow blaze flare amidst the smoke on the mountaintop. "Oh, my God!" he gasped, suddenly white as a ghost. "It's here!"

Al glanced over his shoulder and turned the same ashen color. "Let's get outa here!" He leapt to the driver's seat, released the brake and whipped the horses. The wagon lurched forward, leaving Peter standing in the dirt.

It took him a second to realize Katherine wasn't in the wagon. Nor was she at his side.

"God dammit, Mary Kate, where are you?" he bellowed, competing with the roaring ball of fire surging down the slope.

Suddenly he saw Kate, poised in the doorway, a covered bucket in each hand. He grabbed her arm and took off running. Ahead of them, the wagon lumbered down the skid road toward the lake. "C'mon, Kate, we've got to catch up," he urged, pulling her along. "Why the hell did you go back inside?"

Katherine glared at him incredulously. Couldn't he avoid arguing, even in a crisis? "I had to," she panted, holding onto her buckets for dear life.

"I'm going to wring your neck, first chance," Peter promised through clenched teeth.

"You . . . could . . . help, you know!"

Without stopping and already feeling the wall of fire several thousand yards behind on their backs, Peter snatched one of her buckets from her hand. They kept running, their hearts and legs pumping, their noses and throats seared and parched by the acrid smoke.

What the hell? Peter thought. Al was driving like a

madman, hoping to escape his destiny with the Devil. He
meant to drive the horses right into the bloody lake!

He and Katherine would just have to make it on foot.
Hopefully they could still outrun the fire—if they hadn't
lost too much time.

Red-hot flames shot up to the sky, turning three- and
four-hundred-foot trees into giant torches. The fire avari-
ciously licked up brush and trees, all the while racing down
the slope at a speed more relentless than molten lava.

Going down the skid road was the long way to the
lake, but did they dare leave the barren path? At least
the road wasn't strewn with underbrush, which could in-
cinerate them in seconds. Peter kept one eye on the
lake, one on the fire, knowing it was going to be close.
Lungs bursting, they pressed on, calling upon every
ounce of reserve strength.

The skid road had been constructed by clearing brush
and laying logs over the uneven terrain. Then the wash-
board surface had been filled in with a layer of packed
dirt. A hundred yards above the lake, it crossed a shallow
creek. Katherine had slowed dangerously, bent nearly
double, a cramp in her side.

"Go on without me, Peter!" she gasped, too exhausted
to appreciate how quickly the fire was gaining on them.

"Dammit, Kate," O'Rourke swore, "put that bucket
down. I'll carry you." He set down his own pail and
started to heft her.

"No!" she yelled, drawing back angrily. "I worked hard
making this soup, and I'm not leaving it behind!"

"Soup! You'd risk our lives for soup?" Peter shouted,
almost incoherent over this incredible bit of information.

Kate nodded. She shared her logic. "We *do* have to eat,"

"Dead people don't eat!" Cursing furiously, Peter
dumped the contents of the pail over her head and
slung her over his shoulder. He plunged down the em-
bankment into the creek. Though the lake was closer
this way, cutting through the woods could prove fatal if

the fire caught up with them. But time was running out. They couldn't chance the skid road at this point.

Thirty yards above the lake, Peter tripped over a rock. He staggered, went crashing to one knee, and felt Katherine tumble off his back. He looked up to see a giant wall of flame, not a hundred yards away and moving fast.

"Oh, Christ!" He scrambled up. On all fours, Katherine raised her head, slightly dazed but otherwise unhurt. Together they saw the red fireball descending like an army of demons.

Peter grabbed Kate, thinking that the fire made even her tangled red hair mousy by comparison. He braced himself to make one last desperate run for the lake.

"Say a prayer, sweetheart!"

Splashing down the creek bed, Peter suddenly spotted a small cave opening in the raised bank. Obviously an animal's lair, partially concealed by underbrush. He and Kate were soaked to the skin with sweat and creek water and her damn soup. Dragging Kate, struggling and kicking, by her hair, O'Rourke slid feet first into the hole, raising dust and dislodging rocks.

Not a second to waste! O'Rourke shoved rocks and dirt into the opening to block the raging inferno outside. He yanked off Kate's wet woolen dress, popping buttons and ignoring her protests. The garment, dripping with creek water, might just provide a shield of some sorts or filter the air. He stuffed it into holes in the blocked entrance.

Praying to God this wasn't an exercise in futility, Peter pulled Katherine back from the mouth of the cave and waited. The entrance was small, but the chamber dropped and went deep into the earth. The farther back they went, the larger the cavern became.

In winter, Peter could imagine large bears hibernating in the cave. He didn't care to speculate on whether it was presently occupied. It would be enough just to escape the fiery destruction that roared out of control aboveground.

For long minutes they huddled together in the dark.

They heard the hiss of steam and the fire's deafening howl as it passed overhead. Finally Peter crumpled to the uneven floor, taking her with him. Katherine felt his heart beating wildly against hers. Neither of them could hear anything but the fire overhead.

A long time passed in the hot cavern. The air was smoky, filled with the smell of charred earth and hot cinders. Finding it hurt even to breathe, Kate kept her face buried in O'Rourke's jacket. Though his trousers were wet against her scantily clad body, she clutched him tightly, as one animal seeking comfort from another.

Peter lay still, conserving his strength. He breathed through the singed cloth of his sleeve, still wet with chicken soup, water, and sweat. It was not a particularly agreeable combination, but a damn sight better than dying.

Finally when it had grown quieter, and they could hear themselves think, Kate stirred.

Talking into his jacket, she whispered, "You saved me, Peter."

"We're not out of the woods yet," Peter remarked through a raspy throat. Lord! That had to be the all-time stupidest thing he'd ever heard himself say! Of course, they weren't out of the woods! Realizing it could take awhile before the earth cooled, he wondered when it would be safe to leave their shelter.

Katherine, on the other hand, focused on Peter's heroic actions. Her opinion of him had risen considerably. She was even willing to forgive the way he had dumped her lovely soup all over her. She was proud of her soup, having made it with only minimal supervision by Mr. Al. It saddened her that nobody would get to sample the very first meal she'd ever prepared.

Still and all, O'Rourke had acted with amazing courage and speed. She supposed, compared with her modest culinary effort, his actions on their behalf did tip the scales well in his favor.

"I forgive you, Peter," Kate murmured magnanimously.

She snuggled close, though not for warmth, certainly; the cave was well over a hundred degrees. Strangely secure, she promptly went to sleep.

Peter leaned back against the uncomfortably warm earth and reviewed his newly chosen career dispassionately. So far, he'd watched Diablo Camp go up in smoke, God alone knew where his men were, and McGillacutty would no doubt find some way to blame his temporary son-in-law for costing him tens of thousands of dollars in destroyed timberlands and lost equipment.

On the plus side, Homer's daughter was willing to "forgive" him, although Peter hadn't the foggiest idea what for. And he was still alive.

Any sane man could see how things were headed: the luck of the Irish, at least for this Wexford Irishman, was definitely running out!

Oh, well, O'Rourke told himself, things can't get much worse. He settled his companion on his shoulder and, sighing deeply, closed his eyes.

In his dreams, always, always he was running. He dreamed they made it to the lake, only the fire swept out from the shore, licking up the water and consuming them in a virtual lake of fire. He dreamed that he and Katherine danced, laughing and kissing, while the flames licked at their toes.

Again Peter dreamed. He was carrying Kate deep into the earth, and they came to stand in a beautiful, cool running stream. They were in Ireland with its emerald hills. Silvery brooks rippling through the countryside whispered in his ears like the clear, bright laughter of small children. Intensely happy, Peter caught Mary Katherine up in his arms. He kissed her lips, her swan's neck, her beautiful eyes. Aye, 'twas his very own Kate that he kissed!

And, smiling, she lay down beneath him in the stream, that red hair of hers spreading all around, while the water flowed over her bare thighs and the birds sang sweetly in a willow nearby. She drew him into a warm, wet embrace, and together they tumbled along in the cool brine, their limbs entwined like seaweed.

"Oh, Katherine!" He nuzzled her neck. "Give me your hand, love."

She placed her warm hand in his, and Peter guided it to that part of him where he felt his need of her the most.

"You bastard!"

Peter felt Katherine strike him across the cheek. Still groggy and disoriented, Peter tried to shake off his sleep, only to find himself engulfed in the blackest night. What? Had he been cast into the outer regions, to a place of weeping and gnashing of teeth?

For certain, Peter recognized the unmistakable gnashing of teeth! Oddly, the noise was restricted, or so it seemed, to the vixenish creature presently gnawing the collar of his shirt.

From happier days, he remembered those teeth to be white, even, and beautiful, like pearls. Surely Kate wasn't destined to share such an ignoble end as he?

And what caused her voice—usually as musical as the bright ping of fine bone china—to turn so harsh and shrewish? Was this *his* Mary Kate, uttering words only a fishmonger's wife would deign to say?

"Mary Kate, my own sweet colleen," he murmured sleepily, his lips nibbling her ear, "deny me no longer."

He got a whack on the head for his trouble.

"I am neither yours, nor sweet," the same unsympathetic voice informed him.

Notwithstanding, Peter thought a slight quaver of indecision betrayed its owner. He decided to investigate further. He sat up and, groping his way in the dark, found the swell of a soft, round thigh. "Aye, I knew it was you, my bonny Kate, my superdainty Kate," he said, waxing eloquent.

His heart thumped happily as, moving upward, his fingers brushed the soft curls where Katherine's legs joined. Receiving an instant response beneath his cupped hand, he boldly dipped two fingers into her honey pot and felt her quiver.

Everything in the cave went still.

Katherine held her breath, waiting.

O'Rourke stroked absently, trying to decide if she was real. When the dream didn't blow up in his face, and he felt a tiny bud swell beneath his hand, he knew he was awake, all right.

He had the real thing and the real Kate within his grasp. *At last.* He smiled.

CHAPTER 17

Having held her breath as long as she could without passing out, Kate drew a long, shuddering breath. "Wake up, please, Peter," she pleaded, licking her lips.

Peter chuckled. "I just did." He kissed her neck, and she turned her face into the swell of his shoulder. "My dream was a beaut, Kate, but not this promising."

"We ought to be thinking of getting out of here." Her voice was high and nervous.

"What's your hurry?" Peter asked. "It's still dark."

"It wouldn't be dark, if you hadn't stuffed all those rocks and my dress in the opening!"

"Don't I deserve a little credit for keeping you alive?"

"Of course. Thank you very much," she said primly, pretending she didn't notice what his hand was doing.

Peter nudged her into a probing, open-mouthed kiss, and Kate went down beneath him like a dumb ox hit over the head at the Chicago stockyards. Her legs sprawled, and the tiniest mewl of passion in her throat signaled her trembling surrender.

His left hand left its relentless rhythm and pressed home, while his right went to her breasts. His thumbnail sketching light circles around the tantalizing nub, he eased aside the tiny frou-frou on her chemise and took her soft flesh into his mouth. His lips and tongue teasing her senses, Peter suckled gently while Kate gasped, arching and writhing with delight. As his teeth delicately grazed her, tugging her peaked nipple, Peter's left hand felt her passion flow like warm honey. Her hands slipped beneath his coat and shirt as she pressed against the heat of his caress, her whole body on fire.

Outside the cave, the holocaust raged on, unchecked. Inside, safe from the fury, Peter and Kate felt no desire to flee from the combustion of long-suppressed passions.

"Peter, you're driving me insane," she burst out, moving against the seductive rhythm of his hands.

"Let's go crazy together," he said with a low, reckless laugh.

Suddenly his hands ceased their magic, so abruptly that Kate felt bereft. Her temper flared, furious that he had brought her to such a fever pitch and then abandoned her. "Peter, where are you?" she whispered, coming up on her elbows.

"Right here, love." Peter crawled like a huge cat, crouching above her.

Katherine reached out and caressed the short, crisp curls on his bare chest, the taut muscles on his shoulders. Besotted with emotion, she wrapped her arms around him and, catlike, rubbed her breasts against his chest. Her nipples tightened and her excitement grew more intense as Peter kissed her deeply, savoring the silken sweetness of her mouth. Hearing his moan of pleasure, she smiled in the dark and returned his kiss passionately.

Consuming Kate with a fiery trail of kisses, Peter sampled her body like a gourmand. He tasted every inch of her. He suckled and savored all the delicate flavors of her wild response.

"Who needs food with a feast like this?" Peter asked, his lips nibbling on her breasts, until the faintly rough texture of his tongue made her ache for him all over.

Katherine arched beneath him, mutely imploring him to indulge his appetite further. He played his game until she was mindless with desire, her head thrashing slowly on her long, slender neck. He returned to sample a single tear at the corner of each eye. "Universally the best seasoning," he affirmed, then tasted a smudge of soot on her cheek and protested. "Overcooked. But still tasty!"

"You are shameless!" Kate laughed, forgetting in the heat of the moment that she considered Peter O'Rourke her absolute worst enemy.

"Banquets are meant to be shared, Kate," Peter said, inviting her to indulge herself to the full. "Feel free. What would you like. More tongue? My heart? Whatever tickles your fancy, my dear! Some prime rump roast, perhaps?" And he chuckled at Katherine's indignant gasp.

"I see you can't make up your mind," he teased, continuing his journey along the sweetly curvaceous buffet laid out beneath him.

"Peter, are you always this crazy?" Katherine asked, feeling his hair tickle her stomach as he played games with her navel, blowing and tickling with his tongue. He kissed her hip bones, then started down her left leg.

"I wish I could see you, Kate," he groaned, and Kate thought it was merciful that he couldn't, for she would surely die of embarrassment. This way, at least, everything seemed like a delicious dream, and she could indulge her fantasies without fear of him laughing at her.

Tentatively she arched to kiss his muscular shoulders. He smelled smokey. He tasted warm and salty, like her chicken soup. Meanwhile Peter discovered the goose bumps on her thighs. By kissing them he created more gooseflesh.

"Mmm, spicy and hot." He laughed a second later, sampling her womanly passion. "Specialty of the house."

Katherine was stunned to stupefaction. Her fingers tugged in his hair as she lay panting softly, scarcely believing what he was doing. She felt his lips and tongue and her own throbbing, shameless response. Tiny sparks of pleasure nagged at her, and they both began rocking and thrusting, seeking completion. With even stronger, more urgent yearnings driving her, she gasped his name aloud and, reaching, drew him toward the heart of her deepest passions.

In the darkness Peter crawled the length of her and dropped down between her open thighs.

Kate gasped and nearly fainted.

O'Rourke was naked!

She was entirely bared to him. There was no nightgown, no flannel drawers between them now. Hot blood ran like a fever through her veins as Peter touched her again intimately.

His hands cupped her face, and he drank from her open lips thirstily, all the while probing her. Alarmed, she sought to close her thighs, while she counted his hands in the dark. Two hands were in her hair, his fingers caressing, touching her eyelids.

Oh, help! Katherine gulped, for even a magician had only two hands. She went limp with the thrill of discovery and surrendered herself to his long, possessive kiss. Her scent and the taste of herself on his tongue had a hypnotic effect—that they should bare such secrets to each other.

Her hand left his shoulder, explored his back, his hip, then the front of him. Just as she suspected: his third hand.

Peter's breath blew fierce and hot against her cheek as her inquisitive fingers came to rest. Holding her breath, she touched him experimentally while Peter balanced above her, his turgid member stroking her lightly. He let her grow accustomed to the hard feel of him. Kate couldn't see him, but she imagined him looking deep into her soul. Smiling, she heard his labored breathing and knew that Peter could barely hold himself in check. Finally he dipped his head and kissed her ear; his impatience showing, he pressed against her, a little harder.

Katherine ducked her head against his strong neck and held on for dear life. She now knew what he felt like down there. He was hot and alive and throbbing, masculine power exuding sensual energy from every pore in his body.

"Please," Kate whispered, preferring not to die of suspense, but he held back, touching, making her weep for him down there. Every second seemed an eternity. What was he waiting for? Unable to contain her excitement, she arched her hips.

That was the signal.

Like a jockey holding a racehorse in check at the starting gate, Peter lunged forward, at the same time delivering his mount a resounding slap on the rump.

Momentarily distracted, Katherine cried out at this indignity, unaware that the slap had masked the deeper tear within.

"You . . . struck me!" she pouted, when he finally slowed his initial ride and settled into a slower cadence.

Peter kissed the corner of her mouth. "Better to hear you complain than have you start blubbering all over the place, my dearest darling, my love." He chuckled and began to ride her hard.

"You brute!" Kate railed, trying to throw him off. But he was too deeply embedded for her to escape the unfamiliar fullness. She bucked and thrashed rebelliously. Raising her rump and clashing with him in midair, she shrilled at him, appealing to his better nature. But Peter only laughed and continued to ride her with long, even strokes, penetrating deeply. Twisting one way and then the other, Kate tried to toss him. She simply couldn't budge him.

As she began to lose some of her wild panic, she learned his rhythm and, giving up fighting, followed his lead. His hand gently curved around her derriere, lifting her to accommodate him. To prolong their coupling, he withdrew until all she could feel was the pulsing tip. She squealed with excitement. Making it excruciatingly slow and deliberate, he sluiced into her like a gondola, slipping, sliding, gliding along a dark canal at midnight. Katherine could feel every throbbing, smooth push as his vessel picked up speed and sent them both racing blindly, nearly driven mad with the powerful climax that followed.

An ecstatic cry burst from her lips, followed by wild weeping and joyous panting sighs. Katherine clung to Peter, kissing him rapturously, so overcome that she feared she might be dying. "Don't leave me, Peter, don't ever leave me," she begged, her voice a breathless whisper.

Peter buried his face in her hair, breathing her in like much-needed oxygen. Emotions so rare and strange to his experience that they were frightening rose within him like a strong tower. Suddenly he saw clearly all that had been missing from his life. All the emptiness and deep yearning for connection. An inexpressible joy seized him. It grew inside him like a cleansing fire. He felt it burn deep, like a brand upon his heart. It was as if Kate were the sun, and even his blackest sins couldn't eclipse her healing rays. She was life. She was hope. And she was his!

In that moment of blazing truth, Peter found himself beyond speech. Otherwise the truth might have wrung from his lips a confession he'd never made to any woman, except his mother.

But in his heart of hearts, he knew what had taken place in his spirit. *Katie O'Rourke, I . . . love . . . you!* Then, shuddering in the last wrenching throes of ecstasy, Peter collapsed like a dead man into Katherine's arms.

In the bosom of the earth, instinct and need had catapulted the pair from an emotional no-man's-land into the realm of intense intimacy. During the hours that followed, Peter and Katherine made love almost continuously in that dark cave.

And in the giving and receiving of love, each conjured up images of the other. Katherine fantasized about the vows she and Peter had exchanged at the altar on their wedding day. She recalled her valiant knight-protector,

standing in a halo of sunlight beside her in the back of
the church—a foreshadow of the extraordinary way in
which they'd been spared from the fire, and she thought
of Peter's role in saving her from certain death.

Peter, too, was swept away by powerful emotion. His
appetite was insatiable for his eager young bride, whose
beauty had wooed him away from a life of one-night
stands. In his mind, he rewrote Shakespeare's *Romeo and
Juliet* and gave it a happy ending. He saw Katherine as his
very own Juliet, each time she cast herself breathlessly
into his arms, vowing never to belong to any other. And
in his heart of hearts, he made the same promises to her.

The tender words, the warm embraces, the soft
laughs, and whispered confidences were as sincerely
meant as either knew how to make them.

But at the summit of this joyful discovery, the pendulum
began to shift, subtly at first, and then with pronounced an-
tagonism. They were faced with a very real problem: basic
survival. Memory conspired with self-doubt and physical
deprivation to play nasty tricks, which defiled the new-
found wonder of love. Tempers began to flare, playing
them both false and driving a wedge between them once
again.

As the earth above them cooled, so did the cavern that
had sheltered them from the threat of thermal extinc-
tion. So did ardor, after a cold night without adequate
clothing.

Teeth chattering, Katherine told Peter it was all his
fault she had nothing to wear. Also, she wanted nothing
more to do with him. "As soon as we get out of here, I
want an annulment."

"On what grounds?" Peter's mocking laughter bounced
off the earthen walls of their love nest, which seemed no
better than an inhospitable tomb. "The marriage has
been consummated."

"A divorce then," she argued, glad he couldn't see
how teary-eyed and flushed she had become. *Stop! Stop*

it! she chided herself. *Why do you always say things you don't mean?*

"Come here, Mary Kate." She felt Peter's arm snake around her naked waist and pull her against his partially clad torso.

"Stay away from me, Peter. You're nothing but trouble." Katherine knew she ought to fight him, but she was so cold and miserable, she barely had enough strength to argue.

"Don't be ridiculous," he growled in her ear. He covered her trembling body with his. "You'll catch pneumonia otherwise. I promised your father I'd take care of you." *I also promised God, you stubborn woman,* he thought, exhausted.

"I hate you, Peter. I shall never forgive you. N-never." Her teeth chattered uncontrollably.

"Hate takes too much effort. We need to conserve energy." He nibbled on her earlobe.

Finally Kate agreed to share body warmth. "All right, just so we can stay alive. But I expect you to behave, Peter, just remember that."

"I shall," Peter chuckled and, to her utter astonishment and relief, he went right to sleep.

Sometime during the night temperatures dropped even lower. Peter and Kate discovered that vigorous sex keeps the blood moving and reduces the possibility of chilling.

"Most probably we saved each other's lives," Peter told her afterward, taking most of the credit for suggesting this very practical solution.

Hunger and thirst intruded early in the game. Stomachs growled. Lovers turned grouchy, even after Peter shared the whiskey flask in his jacket.

Next they quarreled over a difference of opinion: neither could agree how long they should remain underground.

A distinct correlation between cooling passions and soaring tempers was demonstrated. Still they valiantly struggled on, determined to maintain a semblance of civility, tortured yet not able to suppress conflict. They negotiated. They used their imaginations. They discovered how alike they were, especially when it came to selfishness. Even so, in the interests of survival, they decided they could put up with each other a while longer.

"Let the future take care of itself," said Kate, shaking hands in the dark with her nemesis.

"Agreed. Now what shall we do to keep our minds off food?" Peter asked.

They made love on an empty stomach and found it a rather effective distraction from their problem. But only temporarily. When Katherine got cranky again, Peter did the decent thing: he generously brought her to repeated climaxes, until she was too relaxed to badger him about *anything*. She gave up complaining about the lack of food, his scratchy beard, their rotten sleeping accommodations, and what a bad influence he was on her.

They made excuses for being on edge. "It was such a silly, inconsequential thing," Katherine admitted after one squabble.

"I'm glad you're willing to admit it," said Peter, assuming a superior position, as he often did. To keep from debating the issue any further, they made love. It was amazing how resourceful they became, when faced with crisis.

By the time they agreed that it might be safe to venture forth, each was secretly convinced that the other was impossible to live with—or without.

Clinging desperately to their fragile fantasies about each other, they crawled out of the cave on the third morning. The moment of final disillusionment came when they saw the object of each other's delight in bright daylight.

Mary Kate clutched what was left of her dress across her breasts. "Oh, my God! Do I look as bad as you do?" she asked.

Peter blinked like a mole. In his opinion, Mary Kate didn't look half-bad, considering what they'd been through. Mud and leaves stuck to her everywhere. Her hair was impossibly ratted and stuck out in spikey disorder. She had a black smudge on the tip of her nose. A bruise on one cheekbone—from knocking heads during a heated wrestling match—was mercifully disguised by a daub of clay. Even so, Peter found the creature standing before him, whose virginity he had unabashedly taken, utterly enchanting. Perhaps he wasn't thinking coherently, but just seeing her alive and whole was enough after their ordeal.

Peter scratched his ear. "You undoubtedly look *much* better than I do."

"Well, that's a relief!" Kate declared, brushing ashes off her skirt.

They were standing in the creek bed. All the water had dried up in the fire. A few patches of smoldering earth and blackened tree trunks were all that remained of the forest.

"Do you suppose we're the only ones left?" Katherine asked, looking around at the black and gray wasteland.

"No, of course not." Peter took her hand and started down toward the lake. The water reflected the smoke-filled sky overhead—a murky gray. They carefully picked their way through the charred debris, avoiding hot spots.

"Careful, Katherine. These stones are still hot," Peter warned. He reached out and helped her jump over the tangled remains of two trees. "Big blues. They must have caught fire and fallen together."

Katherine sought the comfort of his arms while they viewed the wilderness that was no more. "Imagine. We would have met a similar fate, if it hadn't been for you, Peter."

Peter grinned at her. "You and your damn chicken soup."

"So we're back to that, are we?" she snapped defensively.

"Nearly did us in."

"All right. I shall never make chicken soup again."

"Let's not get melodramatic. What soup I sampled on you tasted quite delectable." He gave her a look that kindled a small fire in her nether regions.

After all they'd done in the cave, she couldn't believe she would ever blush again, but she did, a fact that his wicked grin and her hot face confirmed. Peter laughed and gave her a quick buss on the cheek, making her color up even more.

The only two visible survivors in a vast ravaged wilderness, Peter and Katherine stepped carefully through ash and crumbling debris. The skid road was impossible to traverse, having disintegrated into an unstable mess of dirt, rocks, and burnt timbers.

Heartsick, they passed the logging yard. Not a stick of usable material remained; the equipment looked damaged beyond repair.

Higher up the hill, they could see Diablo Camp, completely razed.

Reluctantly they took the last few steps to the edge of the lake. Through the gray ash and silt, the water reflected their images back to them. Nothing could have been more sobering.

They hated what they saw.

My God, I am a fright! He could never love me the way I look.

Hellfire, I look bad enough to play King Lear's father. She could no more love me than a dirty sheepherder!

They exchanged furtive glances and quickly looked away.

Why kid myself? Peter thought. *Kate never wanted this marriage anyway.* Heartsore, he scanned the perimeter of the lake as far as he could see in either direction. A number of giant boulders to the right and a sheer thirty-foot drop-off on the left obstructed his view.

He waded into the lake a few feet and retrieved a floating beer bottle. Skimming pollutants from the surface,

Peter scooped water and quenched the worst of his thirst. Then, cleaning the bottle the best he could, he handed it to Katherine, who drank greedily.

"We need to find the others," he told her.

Kate nodded, still drinking. Finally she paused and spat what tasted like foul sand from her mouth. "The sooner we get rescued, the better. I'm famished," she said, eying a floating dead fish with regret.

Peter saw what she was looking at. "Don't eat anything that isn't alive unless we catch it. Come on, let's see if we can find Blackie and Al and Raimey." He headed around the bend to his right. The terrain was so altered, he could only guess where the skid road had come out of the woods. He stopped to yell, "Halloo-oo-o-o!" Maybe someone would hear. The sound of his voice rolled around the basin created by the mountains and dropped into the lake with a lonely thud.

Katherine trailed along behind him, stumbling, light-headed from hunger.

Peter stooped to examine a set of wagon ruts right before they disappeared into the water. He turned to Kate with a baffled look. "Where the hell do you suppose they went?"

Shivering in her torn dress, Kate looked around at their desolate surroundings. Across the lake was a small island with tall trees growing on it, untouched by fire.

"Maybe they swam to the island," she suggested, struggling to hold back her fears.

As if confirming her words, the high whinny of a horse carried across the water.

"Halloo-o-o-o!" Peter called again, using all the lung power his stage training had developed.

A second later, a rifle shot sent back the answer they desperately needed to hear.

Katherine's green eyes sparkled up at Peter through her tangled hair. "Found! We're not alone anymore."

Interpreting her eagerness as a desire to shed him altogether, Peter waded out and filled the bottle with water again. "Let's hope some of the food survived, along with the men. We could use a good hot meal."

"O'Rourke! That you?" came a shout from the island.

"The same," Peter returned, trying to make out the caller's voice over the distance. "That you, Jigger?"

"Hell, yes! Hold on. I'll send a boat."

Almost at once, two men dragged a small rowboat out of the brush. One fellow stepped into it and set off, rowing smoothly.

"It's Bobbie White Feather!" Kate exclaimed, clutching his arm excitedly.

Peter glanced down, trying to discern Kate's true feelings. She was laughing and crying and hugging his arm. When she became aware of his serious regard, she ducked her head and wiped her tears on his dirty sleeve.

"I'm sorry, Peter," she said self-consciously.

"Who wouldn't want to be rescued?" Peter managed. He peeled off his jacket and placed it around her shoulders. "Here, you wear this."

Kate looked up, puzzled. "But, Peter, you need it! The wind—"

"Cover up, Kate," he snapped. "You don't want to give these loggers an eyeful." And his eyes fastened on her torn bodice.

Her face flushed with embarrassment. Kate let him button the warm, fleece-lined jacket around her. When he finished, their eyes met. "I owe you so much, Peter. Including my life."

O'Rourke turned away, hunching his shoulders against the brisk, chill wind. "Think nothing of it. I guess it sort of evens the score."

"What do you mean?" Katherine followed him along the edge of the shore, staring at his back.

He couldn't bring himself to face her. "I didn't stick to our agreement. I'm sorry," he said, staring out at the lake. "But don't worry, Kate. I'll see that you get every last dime back that I owe you."

His words struck her like a punch in the stomach. Oh, God, she was right! She meant nothing to Peter. But she hadn't expected the truth to hurt like this. Badly shaken, she lowered herself carefully onto a rock to wait.

O'Rourke raised his arm in a wide, sweeping gesture to the grinning Indian, as the boat reached the shallows. "Hey, Bobbie, over here!" Then he waded into the cold water and helped Bobbie pull the boat in to shore.

CHAPTER 18

As they made for the island, Bobbie pulling furiously on the oars and Peter frowning from the stern, Katherine carefully kept her eyes on the water, watching the boat skim through the tenacious ash that choked the lake's surface.

Behind them on the mainland, a deathly stillness had settled over the blackened forest and the rocky shore. No birds sang. No rustling pines; only the smell of scorched earth drifting on the heavy air. The sun, barely penetrating the sooty haze, played among the charred giants, creating elongated slashes of light and dark upon the ground. Almost surrealistic, the landscape seemed as unfriendly and uninhabitable as a distant planet.

As the rowboat skimmed through the cattails and landed in the thick ooze, Kate fought to control the shaking inside. She dreaded what lay ahead. Why had she demanded a divorce? What made her say such things? She despised herself for every word she'd flung in Peter's face. She hadn't meant half of what she'd said. It was just her way of saving her pride.

"Kate?" O'Rourke's voice interrupted her self-flagellation. "We've landed. Give me your hand."

Raising green eyes brimming with tears, Kate saw his lips tighten. Probably impatient because she'd made no move to get out of the boat. To avoid any cryptic remarks, she clambered nervously to her feet, nearly upsetting the boat. Peter caught her just before she toppled into the marshy grass and water. He set her feet on solid ground, his arm taut around her waist.

"Don't, Peter," she said softly. Avoiding his inquiring gaze, she pulled away, knowing he couldn't love her. Feeling already the pain of standing in his arms, unloved. Knowing it was nothing compared with the pain she would feel when he turned away from her for the last time.

Bracing herself against any emotional display, Kate walked over to the few ragged men who waited to greet them. "Mr. Jansen, what a relief to see you! You, too, Mr. van Ecklund. Blackie, how are you?" For their sakes, she tried to sound cheerful. "We were so worried! But it appears you all made it to safety."

"All but Joe Burns and Mickey Bannon, ma'am." Jansen looked over her shoulder at Peter. "The fire doubled back, cut 'em off."

Shocked, Katherine fell silent. Wordlessly, she continued through the ranks, shaking hands with each one in mute consolation. Peter, his hand at the small of her back, calmly spoke with the men, praising their quick action.

When they reached the place where the men had set up camp, Katherine was relieved to see that things were not as hopeless as she'd feared. The men had cut down a number of small trees and thrown up several crude temporary shelters.

Presently Peter left her side to greet those who were unable to meet them at the water's edge. He hunkered down beside Jeffers, who was too severely injured to do more than shake his hand. "What happened?" he asked Bobbie White Feather, who sat on his heels beside his friend.

"He was hauling timber down the mountain. His team smelled fire an' went crazy with fear. Sluiced right down on top of him," Bobbie said." Me and Hoss dragged him out from under that dumb ox."

Although Jeffers had escaped being burned, he had been badly crushed; might even be hemorrhaging internally, judging by his pallor.

"We're getting you to a doctor, Jeffers," Peter told him.

"Hell, I . . . been stomped before, Casey." The man coughed from the effort of talking. "Hurts like blazes, but ain't no need . . . fer a sawbones."

"He ain't got enough brains left to know the difference between brave and stupid," Hoss said, dropping into a squat beside the man he'd rescued. "C'mon, man, drink this soup. Dammit, buddy, you gotta try."

Peter left the two loggers with Jeffers, knowing friendship would win out. He spotted Griswold, propped against a tree, peeling potatoes. "How's the leg, Raimey?"

"Mending slower'n I'd like." Griswold flipped a peeling into the fire. "Wish I was more use, with winter around the corner. I can smell it in the air."

"We'll have you out of here long before the snows come." Peter pointed to the white kitten, Moriah, playing with Griswold's leather shoelace. "Mind if I borrow her awhile?"

"Sure, why not? Not much use anyhow. Always in the way."

Peter scooped up Moriah and took her over to Kate, who stood musing before the cook fire. "Thought you might need this to warm your hands, Mrs. O'Rourke."

As he dropped the kitten into her hands, Katherine hugged it to her and exclaimed, "Oh, Peter! You found her!" Raising up on tiptoe, she gave him an impulsive kiss.

"Nothing to get worked up about," he said, already envious of the attention she was giving the kitten. "I figure a good little mouser should serve you well anywhere."

Then, before she could say anything, he walked away.

***

That evening, his belly growling, Peter stared morosely into the fire. Except for the crackle of burning twigs and the wind's soft moan, the forest was as hushed and eerie as an Irish graveyard.

Trying to shake a growing sense of dread, Peter drew the men into conversation, and inevitably talk gravitated toward the women in their lives.

Suddenly Charlie Mason came over to share a private burden he'd never talked about before. "I was wonderin', Casey. Would you mind checkin' on my wife and kids in Virginia City?"

"I'd be happy to."

"I worry sometimes, y'know?" Mason went on. "Suppose one of my kids got sick, or Emily? I wouldn't find out till the spring blow-in."

It didn't take long before several men began sharing similar concerns. Most felt keenly the long separations from loved ones. "My wife had our first baby all by herself," Bobbie revealed. "Little Betsy was five months old before I got to hold her."

Listening intently, Peter saw how a lot of the tension he'd noted among the men might be eliminated. "Once we settle on a suitable location for a sawmill, maybe we could build a few houses, instead of barracks," he said. "What do you think? Would your wives be willing to move up here?"

Bobbie's dark eyes lit up. "Mine would come!"

"I like things just the way they are," said Yancey, tossing another log on the fire.

Sucking on a toothpick, Jigger threw his first wet blanket on the scheme. To him, it seemed best not to get his men's hopes built up for nothing. "I doubt McGillacutty will put up the money to build a logging town and bring families into the woods," he said flatly.

Instantly Peter saw the crew choose up sides, the bachelors against the married men.

"Huh!" Blackie sneered, "women are nuthin' but trouble."

Mason laughed. "Spoken like a confirmed bachelor! What you need is some good home cookin'!"

"Think what else you're missin' by not havin' a pretty gal around to fuss over you." Thoroughly enjoying himself, Bobbie propped his boots against a rock and winked at O'Rourke.

"I'd like my own woman," Martinez volunteered quietly.

"If we had a bunch of women around, we'd all have to take baths and wear hair tonic and worry about how we smell," Yancey snarled.

"Whoo-o-ee! Maybe all us bachelors better live downwind of the married folks," Jigger drawled.

Peter laughed. "We'd better decide where to put the sawmill before we worry about bathing."

Yancey rose and stretched. "Hell, I'm turnin' in," he said in a bored voice.

As the men dispersed in the dark, Jigger lingered for a private word. "Casey, listen, I hear Charlie Crocker has been sendin' survey teams over Donner's Pass since last July, mapping out a route through the mountains," he confided. "A bunch of Sacramento businessmen want to bring the railroad across the mountains. If it goes through, we stand to make millions."

Peter sat up, his interest piqued. Selling railroad ties could bring in more revenue than the mines did. "Any suggestions where we should relocate?"

"West of Truckee would be my choice. Or Verdi—that's good, too."

"There's a reliable source of water power?"

"Yep. The California outfits run whipsaw mills. If we set up a waterwheel, we'd beat all the competition, hands down," Jigger said.

"But we could convert to steam later, when the engine I ordered from Topeka arrives?" Peter asked.

"Hell, we can make the changeover in a day," Jigger shot back.

Peter clapped a strong hand on Jigger's shoulder.

"Jigger, you know the territory. Find yourself the best spot for a sawmill and start building. Meanwhile I'll head back to Virginia City for more men, money, wagons, and supplies."

"You really think McGillacutty will refit this crew?"

"Aye! The Old Man's tight with money, but he's no fool."

Jigger nodded. "Better take Griswold and Jeffers with you. They're no use to us, the shape they're in."

"Aye." Peter gazed north, picturing thick stands of ponderosa and fir on the mountains. "We start tomorrow. There's much to accomplish before winter sets in."

"Hmmm!" Jigger scratched his head. "How are we gonna keep these men from takin' off for work in the Redwoods?"

"Jigger, I'll do whatever it takes to keep them here. What do you say to full wages and a share of the profits?"

"Casey, the men will back you a hundred percent, as long as you see their side of things."

"You find the spot to build. I'll find the means," Peter promised.

"I know just the spot," Jigger revealed. "It's gonna cost McGillacutty a bundle, though." He whipped out his stash. "Have some snoose," he offered.

Peter surveyed the tin box with raised eyebrows. "Snuff!" he chortled, hardly able to believe a tough bull-of-the-woods like Jansen would use anything that tame.

Jansen winked. "My own private blend."

Humoring his foreman, Peter took a pinch of damp snuff and placed it under his lip.

An inscrutable smile on his face, Jigger waited. McGillacutty's son-in-law didn't disappoint him. A second later, O'Rourke's eyes watered, then bugged out. For a moment Peter thought the top of his head would blow off.

"Sonuvabitch, Jigger! What are you trying to do to me?" he yelled, spitting out the vicious concoction.

Jigger roared with laughter and pocketed his Scandi-hoovian Dynamite. "Enjoyable, huh?"

"Vile," Peter said truthfully. "I thought I'd tried everything, but that stuff caught me off guard."

"Cleared your head, didn't it? I use it as a little pick-me-up after a drinking bout," Jigger confided cheerfully, noting to himself that O'Rourke had passed the test with flying colors. Anyone who wasn't knocked on his can after a jolt of snoose was all right in Jansen's book.

"A bloody hangover might be preferable." Peter laughed, wondering why his cantankerous foreman would choose such a singular way to demonstrate his friendship and acceptance. Or maybe it was a warning—that he'd better keep his word to the men. Whatever it meant, it was a send-off he wouldn't soon forget.

Hearts racing, they catapulted down the mountainside straight into the rising sun. Katherine, leading her plains-bred mustang, followed close behind Peter's roan. Dislodging earth, pebbles, and small plants, the horses dragged Jeffers and Griswold on a travois down the steep slope. Holding on for dear life, Peter and Kate dug in their heels, carried forward by the sheer momentum of earth moving under their feet. Several times they barely missed jagged outcroppings of rhyolite and scrubby sagebrush.

Kate had never seen Peter so relentless. The more torturous the terrain, the more insistent he was that they keep moving. Mercifully, Jeffers had lapsed into unconsciousness. Griswold still had enough life in him for a few well-chosen expletives to express his opinion of the route they'd chosen—almost straight down. But at last they spotted the sleepy Mormon settlement of Genoa in the distance, just as Jansen had described it.

"Oh, thank goodness!" Trembling with exhaustion, Katherine let go of her horse's reins and sank to her knees.

Her horse went right on past.

"Stop this runaway!" Raimey shouted, bouncing on his travois.

Reacting fast, Peter grabbed the reins as the tough-mouthed mustang skittered erratically over the rocks. "Katie O'Rourke, get over here," he yelled.

Through her tumbled hair, Kate spied her husband being pulled in two directions between his horse and hers. Scrambling to her feet, she ran and snatched her horse's bridle. Yanking him around, she brought him to a stop.

"Thank you." Peter's voice crackled with sarcasm. "I appreciate not being drawn and quartered."

"I'm sorry! My legs gave out." Casting an anxious glance toward her horse's litter, she bit her lip. "Are you all right, Mr. Griswold?"

Raimey nodded. He was covered with dust, but his eyes retained a twinkle. "Fine, missus, though I'd kinda like to make it home with only a broken leg."

Peter led his horse over and gave the logger a visual check. "We'll get you home to the wife and children yet," he promised with a grin, then steered his drooping wife over to a fallen log.

The first icy blasts of winter blew down the jagged heights above. Rubbing her hands together, Kate huddled beside Peter amidst the boulders and gnarled trees, using his body as a shield against the wind. "It's heartless to take injured men over such rugged terrain. Poor Mr. Jeffers will be dead before we reach a doctor."

"He's tough." Peter broke out a canteen and a few biscuits, fed Griswold, then returned to offer Kate a piece of jerky. "Trust me: we're all going to make it."

"It's a wonder we didn't fall off a cliff or get buried in a rock slide." She sniffed.

"Tenderfoot." His shoulder bumped hers gently. "A few more hours roughing it, and who knows? I might be able to swap you to a Paiute brave for a few sturdy ponies."

"You'd like that, wouldn't you?" Kate asked.

"You did say something about wanting a divorce,"
Peter reminded her. Producing a flask from his pocket,
he took a swig and replaced the cap. His lips quirked
with ironic humor. "As you'll be looking for a new husband anyway, I could use the ponies."

Katherine spat out her jerky. "I'm not looking for another husband," she said, cursing him under her breath.
"We made a deal."

"I thought we had," he said, glancing out of the
corner of his eye at her. She was breathtaking with that
wild mass of auburn hair, snapping green eyes, and
pearly white skin. Heavy in his heart, he stood, pulling
her to her feet. "Time to push on, Kate. We need to get
Jeffers to that doctor Jigger recommended in Genoa."

They left Jeffers with Dr. Reeves, who turned out to be
a bona fide frontier doctor. While he examined Jeffers,
he told how, fresh out of medical school, he had received a contract in 1859 from the U.S. Army to handle
casualties during the Indian uprising. Once peace was
restored, the demand for his services had dwindled, he
explained.

"This man is pretty broken up inside. Better leave him
with me," Reeves concluded, putting away his stethoscope.

Taking their leave of Jeffers, Katherine and Peter
mounted up. Still dragging Griswold's travois behind
Katherine's horse, they started out across the Washoe
Valley toward Sun Mountain. Riding behind, Katherine's
gaze was drawn to O'Rourke's hair. Long overdue for a
haircut. His clothes had seen better days, too.

A gust of wind whipped into a miniature twister
around his horse's hooves and, following in Peter's wake,
Katherine caught the sudden updraft of desert sand in
her teeth. Spitting, she raised her jacket collar to shield
her face. Ahead of her, Peter's pace never slackened.

For a man who was usually so talkative, he was extremely
quiet about his past. True, he considered himself a re-

formed prodigal, but he never mentioned his family or how he made a living before her father had hired him. What did she really know about him? Only that he was tall and handsome and brave. He had an Irish temper and a good sense of humor, she mused. And he made her crazy sometimes, made her love him and hate him—all at the same time.

He rode with the easy grace of a man born to the saddle, she observed, yet surely few of his countrymen owned horses. Hayburners belonged to people with money. Could he have worked as a stable boy? Not likely. His speech and manners suggested a better upbringing. Whatever his past, he was surely *the* perfect lover. But she didn't want to dwell on that. Their go-rounds were so physical, so rousing! But, then, she found everything about him fascinating: the way his hands cupped to light a cigar, the hidden laughter in his voice, even a fleeting glance, when he didn't think she noticed, could stir her passions.

Suddenly a cold lump of fear settled around her heart. Peter was going to see her father. After he gave a full report about the fire, what else would he divulge? That she'd slept with him? Katherine drew up on her reins, nearly turned around. Would her father still try to make her marry his foreman? Who could ever tell about Papa? He had such an unpredictable temper.

She wasn't the least bit sorry she'd lied and schemed to outsmart her father. A girl had to do what she had to do. But she *did* care about her shabby treatment of Peter. Even if he had a wicked past, she should never have dragged him into this mess! Yes, Peter was right not to love her. She was just a burden to him. But, God help her, she did love him so.

Kate had no idea how long she spent reflecting on her own shortcomings, but when she finally became aware of their surroundings again, they were on the outskirts of Virginia City, in front of the Griswold's modest two-room cottage. As always, Katherine couldn't get used to

the lack of lawns and landscaping around the houses in
these barren hills.

"Remember, you're still on the payroll," Peter told
Raimey Griswold, after being introduced to the logger's
wife and children.

Raimey's wife, Anna, stood listening, their three children clustered around their father in the tiny kitchen.
"You're a good man, Mr. O'Rourke," she said.

Peter patted her worn hand, and she blushed at his
handsome smile. "No, I'm practical. I need this man of
yours back working for us in a month's time." He slung
a casual arm around Kate's shoulders and drew her close
as he confided to Mrs. Griswold, "Knowing how much a
good wife means to a man, I'm counting on Raimey to
persuade you and the children to join him in the spring.
By then, we should have homes built for the married
men. Talk it over together," he urged. "I'll drop by
before I head out of town, in a day or two."

"Thanks, Casey, for everything." Raimey and Peter
shook hands.

Back outside, Katherine flounced over to her horse
and mounted. "Wasn't that a charming scene?" she
flared, snatching the reins away from Peter. "I suppose
you plan to sell that poor couple on the joys of living in
a log cabin. Mrs. Griswold will think that tiny hovel she
lives in now is a palace, when she sees the kind of place
I had to live in!"

"Keep your voice down, Kate," Peter warned. "I have
no intention of dragging that woman out to a life of
misery in the woods."

"Oh, but it was good enough for me?" Seething,
Katherine kicked her horse in the ribs and left Peter in
the dust. It was all she could do not to try out a few of the
oaths she'd learned from Diablo's loggers on him.

Crossing C Street at the corner of Union, her eyes
were irresistibly drawn to the Bucket of Blood Saloon,
where first she had met Peter Casey O'Rourke—worst
luck! Katherine tossed her head to show her disdain for

the tall blond rider behind her and turned onto B Street.

When she reached the cavernous entrance to Ferguson's Livery, she stopped and got down unassisted. Her derriere felt the way Mr. Al's pulverized venison steaks would, if they had feelings. Nose tilted to the sky, she stalked past Peter, who was talking to the livery boy.

O'Rourke caught her arm, swinging her around. "Wait." He frowned. "We need to talk."

After he paid for both animals' care, he strode back up Union Street to C Street, ignoring her attempts to yank free.

"Where are you taking me?" Kate demanded, running to keep up.

"How about a sarsaparilla, or are you grown-up enough for a glass of wine?" He paused outside the International Hotel, waiting for her answer.

"I-I'm not fit to be seen in public." Kate caught sight of herself in the hotel's dining room window and shuddered. To think she'd come to this! She wore a lumberman's jacket over a filthy woolen dress, and her hair was a scrambled mess.

Seeing two fashionable ladies and their escorts come out of the hotel, Katherine wanted to crawl into a hole. Who among her friends in Chicago would look twice at her now?

Her life was a shambles. And Peter wanted to "talk." She supposed that was how men usually discarded their mistresses. Only in her case, they'd have to settle a few legalities before he went his merry way.

Grinning, Peter gestured to his own clothing. "You may not be dressed to the nines, but if it's any consolation, I'm no better off."

"Humph! You'd look good even if you were thrown into a . . . a barrel of mud!"

"Why, thank you, wife," he replied. "I'm amazed you didn't mention that infamous horse trough we shared, but as usual you've outdone yourself in handing out the compliments."

"Very amusing, and the answer is no. I don't want a sarsaparilla or wine," she snipped. "That's what got me in all this trouble in the first place."

Suddenly a very stylish brunette clothed in rich maroon velvet stepped out of the hotel. Katherine bit her lip in pure envy. The woman's hat, decorated with blue and silver plumes, set jauntily atop several fat, sleek curls. Such a gorgeous hat. She eyed the woman's wardrobe hungrily, wishing she owned anything half as chic.

As if reading her thoughts, Peter's head swiveled in the woman's direction. Kate froze, seeing his gaze lock with a pair of soulful gray-blue eyes. Holding her breath, Kate saw a look of warm recognition pass between the two.

"Peter, darling!" the woman exclaimed in a voice so rich with emotion that people stopped on the boardwalk to watch the exchange.

Peter's face lit up. "Nina? My God, Nina! What are you doing here?"

Katherine, her stomach doing flip-flops, reeled back against the brick wall, watching in horror, as the petite brunette threw herself into Peter's arms. She had to dig her fingernails into her palms to keep from scratching the woman's eyes out. She wanted to scream, pull her hair! It was so unfair! She could never hope to compete for Peter's affections against such a sophisticated vamp.

Not that I would lower myself to try, she told herself. Even so, she couldn't bear to watch her husband return the woman's embrace.

"How could he!" she agonized.

As Peter bent his golden head to kiss the brazen hussy on the cheek, Kate turned her travel-grimed face to the brick wall and wept bitter tears.

CHAPTER 19

Nina L'Ambourghetti laughed up at her former leading man. "Henri and I are here for a week's engagement. We open tonight."

"I'll be there!" Peter promised, his smile growing broader every second. He squeezed her hand lightly. "Nina, let me introduce you to someone very special." He turned to include Kate in the conversation and found that his wife had vanished into thin air. Surprised, Peter turned back to the beautiful actress he'd worked with back East. "She was here a minute ago."

Nina smiled knowingly. "The tall redhead in the, uh, unconventional attire? I saw her watching us. You still have a taste for excitement, I see." She winked.

Peter grinned. "This one, I fear, is more excitement than even I can handle. I married her in a moment of deranged *je ne sais quoi.*"

Nina took in his appearance and delicately brushed a straw off the shoulder of his jacket. "Have you two been rolling in the hay?" she teased. "I've never seen you so carelessly dressed—or so healthy, for that matter."

"Sober, you mean? It's a long story, Nina, but I'm a changed man. Wholesome outdoor living, early hours and—"

"Desperately in love?" Nina's lips curled in a mischievous smile, and she shook her finger coquettishly. "Didn't I tell you?"

"You issued a stern warning, as I recall."

"So I did. And I'm glad to see you caught in the same love trap as the rest of us. Married love is the best, am I right?"

Peter shrugged noncommittally, not wanting to spoil her smug enjoyment. "I'm new at this, Nina. Ask me in a year or two, when I'm settled into a rut."

"Who says you have to get in a rut, silly darling?" Nina poked his arm playfully with a perfectly manicured nail. "Look at Henri and me. We've been married twelve years, and still no regrets."

Clicking his heels together, Peter made a cavalier bow over her hand. "You and Henri shall be my inspiration," he promised with a smile.

"Peter—" Nina hesitated, then decided to take him into her confidence. "Peter, might I ask a great favor?"

Though her face bloomed with mature beauty, Peter saw a cloud of distress drift across Nina's features. "Of course. I can catch up with my wife later. Did I mention her name is Mary Katherine?"

Nina smiled up at her young friend. What a remarkable change in him! Why, he was fairly glowing! Her instincts had always told her that Peter was more lost than bad, despite his long nights of debauchery and casual affairs. It did her heart good to see him so healthy, especially now, when she needed cheering up.

"I shall adore to meet your Mary Katherine," she assured him. "But for now, why don't we have a cup of coffee and catch up on old times?" Again a faint suggestion of worry touched her beautiful eyes. "Henri's upstairs in our suite, gravely ill. I'm so afraid, Peter! He's always had a bad heart. Rheumatic fever as a child." She indicated the dining room with a graceful wave of the hand. "Shall we?"

After they ordered coffee, she leaned forward across the

linen tablecloth. "Dr. Vintner, I believe his name is, blames Henri's problems on the altitude here in Virginia City."

Peter reached over and gave her hand a little squeeze. "What's wrong, Nina?"

"Shortness of breath, and his legs are badly swollen. Difficulty with his lines this afternoon during rehearsal." She sighed and shook her head, eyes pleading. "When he became confused and couldn't remember we were running over the third act, I summoned the doctor."

"Good God, Nina! How could that be—a man in his thirties?" Peter met her helpless gaze, wishing he could give her more than words for solace.

"Actually he's forty-seven," Nina confided. "Anyway, there's nothing to be done. Henri is confined to bed rest." She looked on the verge of tears. "Peter, I honestly don't know what to do."

Peter spread his hands in a shrug. "That's easy. The show must go on, right?"

"Yes, the show must go on—without Henri, until we get back to sea level." She looked at him hopefully. "Peter, you've played Paolo in *Francesca da Rimini*, haven't you?"

Peter nodded. "I understudied the role in Philadelphia."

"Then you could help me!" Nina exclaimed happily.

"I'm not an actor anymore." He gave her a rueful smile. "I'm in the lumber business now."

"No! Lumber? Dear God, you can't be serious." Nina stared at him, saw that he was indeed serious, and pouted for a full two seconds before lifting her coffee cup to her lips.

"People buy more lumber than theater tickets," he said with a laugh. "I guess I like money more than acting."

Nina fixed him with one of her winning smiles. "You can take the actor out of the theater, Peter, but you can't take the theater out of his blood. I dare you to deny it!"

"Maybe so, but it's been over a year since I even looked at that particular script."

"I have no one else to ask," Nina said, tearful. "We have no understudy for Henri's role."

"All right, Nina, you've got yourself a poor man's Paolo. I'll never do the role as well as Henri, but if you can put up with me, I'll do it."

"Oh, thank you, Peter!" Nina threw her arms around his neck, pulling him toward her across the table, and kissed him full on the lips.

Gently unwinding himself from her embrace, Peter pushed back his chair and stood. "First I'll need a script—and a bath." He glanced apologetically at his rough clothing. "Sorry. I just got into town."

Nina was already fishing around in the large brocaded knitting bag she carried. "Here's the script, darling."

He tucked the thick, dogeared pages under his arm. "I'll be at the theater early," he promised. "Say hello to Henri for me. I'll drop by after the show—I presume he's able to see visitors?"

"I'll tell him." Nina stood, raised up on tiptoe, and pressed her cheek against his rough beard. "You won't forget to shave?"

"What? Play a love scene without shaving?" Peter pretended shock. "I wouldn't dream of insulting my favorite leading lady. It'll be like old times, eh?" He pinched her cheek flirtatiously.

"Old times!" She laughed gaily.

They parted company in the lobby, agreeing to meet again at the theater at seven.

His nose already in the playbook, Peter strode out the front door of the International Hotel and sailed right into Katherine. Recovering her balance, she fell into step beside him.

"What was that all about?" Kate demanded.

"It seems I am the answer to her prayers," Peter said.

"That's disgusting!" Kate said. "I saw what went on in the restaurant. How can you stand a woman kissing and fawning all over you like that! She made a complete fool of herself!"

Peter began walking toward her father's house on B Street. Glancing up from his quick perusal of the first scene, he couldn't resist giving Kate some of her own back. "'A woman like that'? Nina could give you a few pointers. God knows, you need a few lessons on being a wife."

Stung by his remark, Katherine stopped in her tracks. But only for a second. Recovering, she ran to block his progress down the street. Peter lightly brushed her aside. The amused smile on his lips was the only sign that he took any notice of her at all.

"How dare you suggest I seek advice from your mistress!" Kate stormed and launched herself at him, intent upon blackening his seductive green eyes. "I am your wife, lest you forget, and I refuse to be made an object of public pity."

"She's an old friend, not my mistress." Peter stepped back, leaving the wooden sidewalk, rather than duke it out with his wife in broad daylight.

"You expect me to believe that?" Katherine dissolved into tears. The violence of her feelings frightened her. She was losing Peter, and she didn't know what to do.

"Katie O'Rourke, you are without a doubt the blindest, most thick-skulled woman I ever met!" His green eyes bored into her like a diamond drill point trying to penetrate solid granite. "Otherwise you wouldn't go jumping to conclusions about a perfectly innocent friendship. Now get yourself on home. I'll deal with you later." He pivoted on his heel and headed back to the hotel.

"Where are you going, Peter?" Kate hollered, her fists held rigidly down at her sides.

"Where I can get some peace and quiet," Peter growled.

Kate ran after him. "I don't want you to see that woman again!"

"'That woman' is Nina L'Ambourghetti, and in all the time I've known her, she has always behaved like a perfect lady. That's a damn sight more than I can say about a certain redhead I know!"

"Well, if Miss L'Ambourghetti is a lady, I never want to be one," Katherine raged, too incensed to note the lightning-swift change in his demeanor.

"She is a happily married woman," Peter told her.

"Really! Is her husband as blind and stupid as your wife? How cozy for you both!"

"That does it!" Peter made a running tackle, his shoulder connecting with Katherine's heaving diaphragm. The wind went out of her sails with a loud *whoof!* and for a moment she hung over his broad shoulder, gasping. Peter wheeled about, this time marching toward the McGillacutty's mansion.

"You brute! Put me down," Katherine yelled defiantly, by now thoroughly exhilarated.

"With pleasure, madam," Peter deposited her on the swing on her father's veranda. Stabbing a finger at her, Peter drew his brows together in a fierce scowl. "Don't leave this house until I give you leave."

Kate stared up at him in disbelief. "Just because we're married—" she began hesitantly.

"Ah, yes! Do trot out that interesting little contract you love to punish me with!" Peter's cleft chin jutted forward, and his eyes flashed a message as feral as any predator on four legs. "Till death do us part, isn't that how it goes?" He leaned menacingly over her, his hands gripping the ropes on the porch swing. "Aye, well, don't tempt me, Kate."

Kate shrank back, her green eyes snapping. "You can't intimidate me, O'Rourke. You know the agreement we made."

His green eyes glittered dangerously. "I won't apologize for forgetting myself and acting the part of a husband. It was as much your doing as mine. No, Kate, it's high time you decided whether the vows we made before God mean anything to you, or not." He straightened, the manuscript tucked under his arm. "Look," he said, more gently, "let's talk about this after we've both slept on it."

"You're going back to Nina, aren't you?" Kate ducked her head, convinced her marriage was over. Great tears rolled down her cheeks.

"I promised to help Nina this evening at the theater."

"What kind of help?" she asked resentfully.

"Backstage," he said evasively. Now wasn't the time for candor; he had so little time before the curtain went up. "Nina's husband is ill, and I agreed to stand in for him."

"Well, have a good time," she said, dejectedly raising her hand in a faint-hearted wave.

Peter rolled his eyes toward the sky and groaned. "Still don't trust me! Well, believe it or not, I will be out there tonight, sweating worse than I ever did logging trees!" He started down the steps, then realized his vagueness about his acting chores might add fuel to the fire. Over his shoulder, he gave her an earnest look. "Look, Kate, I don't want a divorce."

Katherine raised her chin and stared at him through troubled green pools surrounded by damp, spikey lashes. "Don't look so forlorn," he said. "I'll be at the hotel, if you or your father need me. See you tomorrow."

Not waiting for an answer, he rushed down the street and booked a small room in the hotel. He had to concentrate on his role! He ordered a bath and luxuriated for an hour, studying the script. Then he slipped across the street for a shave, manicure, and haircut, using the time in the barber's chair to again review his lines.

Boker's play consisted of five long acts in blank verse, and although his role as Paolo, the ill-fated lover, came back to him with a rush of memory, there were differences between the Philadelphia production and the script this company was using. He knew Nina was an exquisitely intuitive, if somewhat emotional, actress in the romantic style. He would have to play their scenes together in a complementary fashion, even though he leaned more toward the neoclassical technique himself. This was Nina's showpiece, and Peter intended to give her the support she needed. Aye, Nina L'Ambourghetti's star would shine brightly tonight! *Francesca da Rimini* was a fabulous vehicle for an actress with her range.

As Peter crossed the street again to the hotel dining room for a light meal, he was struck by the extraordinary events that had taken place during the past few days. He still had to bring Homer McGillacutty up-to-date on the fire and reach an understanding with Mary Katherine, but both would have to wait if he was to play a halfway credible Paolo.

While he stirred his coffee, Peter forced himself to focus on the evening performance. Even so, his mind kept returning to Kate. He supposed she would give her father the facts about the fire and, no doubt, a few choice embellishments about her husband's conduct. If that didn't get him fired, he'd be very surprised.

Perhaps it was providential that this acting role had dropped into his lap, he mused, taking it from the top of Paolo's love scene with Francesca.

Sporting a dust cloth over her dark curls and brandishing a feather duster, Madeleine McGillacutty whirled about her husband's study, singing, "'Drink To Me Only With Thine Eyes,' . . . and I will drink with mine."

Homer was expected home any minute, and she hoped to surprise him. Through diligent effort, she had eliminated layer upon layer of dust, of a type found only in a desert mining town. She had polished his desk with lemon furniture oil and straightened his college diploma on the wall. And she knew he would be pleased to find his favorite cigars restocked in the box where he kept them. And to add to his comfort, she had hired Billy Forester to fix the broken caster on his red leather swivel chair.

Madeleine surveyed her tasteful rearrangement of his office, then whisked off her kerchief and shook loose her glossy curls. She hadn't had so much fun since she was a young bride!

"I do declare, Homer hasn't changed a bit. He is still the same forceful, dynamic man I married twenty years ago," she said aloud with a merry laugh.

Of course, Homer had changed over the years; so had she. But in the weeks since her daughter left for Diablo Camp with Mr. O'Rourke, Madeleine's life had undergone singular changes. For the first time in years, she felt restored—a new woman. Being cherished and loved had done what all the beautiful clothes, social acclaim, and charitable good works on hospital auxiliaries never could accomplish.

For the first time in years, Homer felt settled and complete as a man. Money, success, power, and prestige, a pretty mistress, and material blessings hadn't been able to fill the void left in his heart when Madeleine and he had separated.

Madeline marveled at the changes in her life now. She had dreaded coming West, fearing that Homer's pretty mistress and the life he had carved out for himself in Virginia City would only add to her heartache after all these years of separation. But Homer was tired of his makeshift life and wanted only her. They were reconciled at long last, and they were madly in love again!

Probably she would have packed up and left town as quickly as her daughter if Homer hadn't come to his senses in the nick of time.

He had simply swept her off her feet again! That one night in the International's honeymoon suite had done what years of faulty diplomacy had not: it had enabled them to overcome all the grudges and slights, set aside their need to demand and receive apologies, and realize how much they still loved and needed each other. Extraordinary! In the full bloom of maturity, the experience of being together was even more powerful than before. She never wanted it to end.

Noticing the time on the clock in her husband's office, Madeleine scurried down the hall to the kitchen to check on dinner. She was preparing another quiet

candlelight dinner for her husband. These days the
McGillacuttys had the whole house to themselves and,
like two naughty children on a lark, they were making up
for lost time.

What a sweet, adorable man! she thought. Riding high
on their resurrected love affair, Madeleine basted the
roast and stuck it back in the oven for another twenty
minutes.

Dear Homer will be home any minute, she reminded herself for the umpteenth time.

Gathering her best china plates and silver, she bustled
into the dining room to set the table. As she passed the
front window, she thought she heard a soft, childlike
whimper. Curious, she glanced across the street to her
neighbors, but saw no children out playing. Strange,
there it was again. There was only one person, besides
herself, whom Madeleine had ever heard make that
woeful noise.

Madeleine walked into the foyer and opened the front
door.

Mary Kate fell across the threshold into her mother's
arms. Blubbering all over Madeleine's freshly starched
lace collar, she clutched in a fierce hug the small woman
who had given her life. "Oh, Mother, what am I going to
do?" Kate wailed.

Madeleine dearly loved her daughter, of course, but at
that particular moment, she wasn't entirely pleased with
this impromptu visit. In fact, she rather resented it. With
a mother's unerring gift for clairvoyance where her
child was concerned, she sensed that all her carefully
laid plans for the evening had just been destroyed.

"I don't know, darling," she said with a sigh. "That depends on what you've done to bring yourself to such a state."

Katherine broke off in the midst of pouring out her
grief. "Of course," she said, regarding her mother sadly,
"how could you possibly know?"

Madeleine smiled tolerantly. "I know a good deal more
than you give me credit for. And I know my own daugh-

ter. Would you care to tell me what's wrong?" She led Mary Kate to the parlor settee. "Shall I get you some tea?"

Kate suddenly noticed how politely restrained her mother's greeting was. "Aren't you glad to see me, Mother?" she asked, wiping her tear-streaked cheeks with the back of her hand.

"Well, yes and no," Madeleine McGillacutty said with perfect candor. "If this were a happy drop-in visit, I would be overjoyed. Judging by those tears, you may be planning a somewhat longer stay."

Kate studied her mother's face. "Oh? Have I come at a bad time? How's Father?" she asked, wondering uneasily if the Unforeseen had happened during her absence.

"Never better." Madeleine smiled tenderly, then sighed. "We *were* planning a quiet evening at home tonight, just the two of us. I suppose you plan to stay for dinner?"

Katherine wasn't used to being treated like an outsider. She and her mother had always been close, so it was only natural to turn to her in time of trouble. Now, Kate wasn't so sure it was a wise idea. "A lot has happened since I left, Mother," she began, wondering how to break the terrible news.

Madeleine looked at her daughter's gown. She surveyed the untidy hair, the broken fingernails, the smudge of dirt on her daughter's chin. And peeking out from beneath the dark woolen skirt, a pair of worn, dusty boots. "You've neglected your appearance since I last saw you," she observed quietly.

Katherine rolled her eyes toward the ceiling and uttered a mirthless laugh. "I just survived a forest fire, Mother. All my clothes got burned up. On top of that, I've worked my fingers to the bone in a logging camp—as a cook's assistant."

"That must have been quite a challenge." Her mother smiled, thinking of her own struggles with domestic chores.

"Most of this is Papa's doing." Hands behind her back, Kate began to pace, her boots flapping.

"Yes, I know," Madeleine said, feeling compassion for

her beautiful daughter. "Your father was a bit tactless, but"—she waved an eloquent hand at Kate—"I must say you seem to have survived splendidly." Her lips curved in soft amusement. "With the notable exception of your wardrobe, of course."

"Mother, I married Peter O'Rourke to get away from Father, not because I loved him." She hung her head, knowing how disappointed her mother must be with her.

Madeleine drew a deep breath at this bad news. "Oh, my dear child! If I'd known that, I would certainly never have permitted—why, your father assured me that you and your handsome young man were as taken with each other as he and I were some twenty years ago."

"That's not exactly true, Mother," Kate confessed, dropping to her knees before her mother. "Peter knew why I was marrying him, and that I planned to get an annulment the minute I got to San Francisco. I even paid him a thousand dollars to marry me." She buried her face in her mother's lap and howled.

Slipping a slender hand beneath Kate's chin, Madeleine raised her daughter's perfect, though tear-streaked, face. "I'm not going to scold, Mary Katherine, but really! Bribery? I thought you had more pride and good sense. I'm sure your dear Peter would have married you anyway."

Kate gave her mother a gloomy look. "You have no idea how hard he tried not to go through with the wedding."

"Did he now?" Her mother smoothed the tumble of unruly hair back from Kate's forehead. "Your father was pleased enough with your choice."

"Oh, what does Papa know?" Katherine sniffed.

Madeleine rose and lit the gas lamp against the approaching dusk. "Don't underestimate your father." She laughed softly, and when Kate shook her head in confusion, Madeleine only waggled her finger at her. "Sweet lamb, your father was one step ahead of you all the way."

CHAPTER 20

"I don't believe you!" Katherine shot to her feet, shook out her skirt, and followed her mother's lithe step down the hall to the kitchen.

"He knows how your mind works, darling. What he didn't hear through that dreadful laundry chute in his office, or from Peter, he figured out for himself." Madeleine calmly picked up the whistling tea kettle and rinsed her best china teapot with boiling water. Bustling about, setting tea cups, saucers, and spoons on a silver tray, she added, "You're so alike, your father and you. All that fiery red hair and tempers to match."

"And he let me go through with this . . . this sacrilege of a marriage?" Kate tried to deny that inheritance, of which her mother was so fond of reminding her. How humiliating! All her efforts to outwit her father had been in vain!

"Outsmarted by your own impetuous nature," her mother blandly affirmed, and poured boiling water over her favorite blend of Ceylonese tea leaves.

Kate groaned. "Well, I guess that saves me from having to explain what's been going on."

"Ah, but I'm fascinated! What have you and Peter been doing since your father and I saw you off on your honeymoon?" Madeleine asked, carrying the tea tray to the front parlor.

"Some honeymoon," Kate said, trailing along behind. Silently she admired her mother's beautiful watered-silk gown; she did have the most exquisite taste. "Peter kidnapped me, Mother. He dragged me into the woods and forced me to work from dawn till long past sundown. He said if I didn't work, I didn't eat."

Her mother raised her eyebrows. "I see. That doesn't sound very romantic." She made sympathetic clucking sounds, and handed Mary Katherine a tea cup.

"That's not the half of it."

Madeleine's mouth twitched. "I'm all ears," she said.

Kate launched into a full exposé of Peter's crimes. During her narrative, little things like the white kitten, Moriah, began to creep in. To her surprise, it hadn't been all terrible, she realized in retrospect. After all, she *had* learned to cook. "I can milk a cow and cook breakfast and chicken soup. Everyone loved my venison steak," she bragged, getting completely off track.

Glancing at the clock, Madeleine suddenly jumped to her feet. Dashing to the kitchen, she hastily rescued the roast from the oven. Nearly burning her finger on the pan, she covered her latest culinary effort to keep it warm. When she returned, she settled herself on the settee again in a rustle of crinoline and silk. "Sorry, darling. Where were we?"

"I just finished telling you what a disaster my marriage is."

"No, actually you only told me how well you adapted to a difficult situation. Your father will be so proud," said Madeleine, munching on a macaroon. She shot a quizzical look at her daughter. "You barely mentioned you and Peter."

The moment of truth, Kate thought with a shrug. "He saved my life in the fire, of course—"

"Remind me to thank him," said her mother, calmly sipping tea.

Katherine set down her cup and resumed her restless

pacing. "Then he dragged me into a cave, and we made love for two days, and I told him I wanted an annulment."

"Wait, wait!" Madeleine waved a daintily jeweled hand to interrupt. "You made love? I presume, from what you've told me so far, that was the first time?"

Kate nodded, her face crimson, thinking about all she had experienced in the darkened cave. "Actually we did it several times."

Madeleine studied the tea leaves in her cup with a mysterious smile. "Did you enjoy yourself?"

"Mother!"

"Ah! You did, didn't you?" Madeleine smiled at her daughter's scandalized expression. "It's all right. I understand about such matters." She waited, a twinkle in her eye, and Kate suddenly noticed how young and happy her mother appeared.

"I'm sure all Peter's lovers enjoy . . . that is"—Kate ducked her head—"I mean, Peter is very experienced and worldly."

"So was your father when I met him," said Madeleine dreamily. "But I must have missed something, dear. You and your very handsome caveman"—she laughed softly—"had sexual relations. It wasn't unpleasant, yet you wish an annulment?"

In her ruined black wool dress, Kate looked like a spinsterish schoolmarm, not a cherished bride. "Don't be dense, Mother!" she snapped, exasperated. "Peter and I had an agreement. The marriage wasn't supposed to be consummated."

Her mother sighed. "I don't see how you're going to get an annulment. Why don't you just accept the fact that nature took its course, and you're married to a thoroughly charming man?"

"I never thought my own mother would turn against me!" Kate said. "I told Peter . . . Well, since it was too late for an annulment, I insisted on a divorce."

A terrible silence fell. Madeleine stilled the rattle of her cup on the saucer with both hands and stared at her beautiful daughter. For the first time, she saw that she had seriously erred by raising Kate without a father's firm hand. "Well." She set her cup on the silver tray. "You shall simply have to apologize to your husband."

"What? Crawl?" Katherine's lip curled.

"On your knees, if necessary, young lady." She faced her daughter with stern dignity. "Your father and I have had our differences, even sinned grievously against each other. But never have we carelessly hurled about threats of divorce. Though we came close a few times, I admit."

Katherine froze, truly stunned by the reprimand. "I know Papa saw other women, but you never—?"

Madeleine shook her head, and her dangling black-beaded earrings danced. "I never invited another man into our marriage bed. But I'm no saint, Katherine." She bit her lips. "A woman gets lonely, too, after so many years." She took a deep breath. "But, thank God, we came to our senses in time!"

The mantel clock chimed, alerting Madeleine to Homer's imminent arrival. She reached out her hand in appeal. "Mary Kate, I don't want to see you throw away your best chance for happiness."

Katherine clasped her hands around her knees, rocking slightly, and gazed toward the window. "It's too late," she said. "He and his mistress are at the hotel right this minute."

"How can you possibly know that?"

"I saw them kissing in front of everybody in town," she said brokenly.

Madeleine reeled mentally. "Perhaps you misjudged the situation," she said cautiously.

"Oh, he'd like me to think she's just an old friend," Kate said. "She's a married woman, Mama, and she took my husband away from me, just like that!" She snapped her fingers.

Oh, dear saints above! Madeleine reached out to comfort her daughter. Pressing her lips to Kate's pale forehead, she closed her eyes and prayed for quick inspiration.

What was it, when everything else went wrong, that kept two people together?

Instantly she knew that she needed to know how her daughter truly felt about her husband. Mary Kate was usually a sensible girl. For her to carry on this way, there had to be deep feelings between the two.

"Mary Katherine, how did you feel when you saw Peter with his lady friend?"

"I wanted to scratch her eyes out!" Kate snarled, her green eyes blazing. "Oh, Mama, she's so beautiful and sophisticated! I just wanted to die."

"How do you feel about Peter?" her mother asked, gently stroking her daughter's tresses.

"I hate him! He made love to me, and I—" Katherine lifted her beautiful face, made blotchy with tears, and gazed into her mother's shining blue eyes. "I had really started to hope that he and—" Kate dropped her face against her mother's shoulder and sobbed.

"Ah! So you *do* love him," Madeleine said thoughtfully. She pulled Kate close and patted her back as she would a child. "You have a bad case of jealousy, my darling. Nobody is jealous of something they don't want." Lifting Kate's chin, she looked her straight in the eye. "You love this husband of yours very much."

"What am I going to do?" Kate asked forlornly.

"My goodness! I do believe that's the same question you asked when you first came through my door," Madeleine smiled and handed her daughter a handkerchief. "We've been going around in circles, but I do believe we've made some slight progress."

"Even if I do love Peter," Kate wiped her eyes, "he's with her, not me."

"When may we expect him? I presume he plans to join us for supper?"

"No, we had a big fight. He's staying at the same hotel as Nina L'Ambour . . . oh, whatever her name is! She's an actress, and he gave me some lame excuse about helping her tonight backstage."

Madeleine's eyes lit up with recognition. "Nina L'Ambourghetti? Oh, my darling, you do have stiff competition. She's appearing at Maguire's tonight." She picked up the tea service. "Come to the kitchen and freshen your face. We'll talk while I finish preparing supper."

Looking down at her shabby dress and boots, Kate nodded. "I do look like something the cat dragged in, don't I?"

"More like a grizzly bear." Madeleine teased. "Don't worry. A hot bath will make you feel much better. Come along now."

Clad in her mother's Chinese silk robe, she stood with her mother in the parlor. Together they had made a little ceremony of depositing her black dress on the hearth fire and drinking a toast to her mother's scheme. "Good-bye, scarecrow clothes!" And they both laughed.

Then Madeleine returned to fixing dinner, and Kate retreated to the small room off the kitchen for a long soak in the bathtub, brimming with her mother's favorite bubble bath. Dribbling warm water over her breasts from a fat sponge, she soon felt her spirits begin to rise.

"We must get you ready to send into the lion's den," her mother called from the next room. "The right clothes will do wonders for your confidence! I declare, you will make Peter so hot and jealous, he will drop this actress. He will never look at another woman, Kate! Trust me. Everything will turn out beautifully."

Waiting for her mother to stop fussing with the roast and come rinse the soap from her hair, Katherine drank a second glass of her father's sherry. She thought her mother overly optimistic, but the wine gave her courage to go along with her mother's plans for the evening.

Soon her father arrived home, stomping through the hall, calling lustily for his wife. And she heard her mother's feet patter swiftly to greet him. It seemed so strange, after all these years, to hear their laughter, instead of strained silence and slammed doors.

Leaning her head back against the tub, Katherine felt beneath her eyelids a sudden rush of tears. She was happy for her parents—truly! But why had it taken them so long? Out in the kitchen, sounds of a friendly tussle and a light smack were followed by her mother's sudden squeal. "Homer, sshhh! Mary Kate is here. She'll hear us," came her mother's frantic whisper, amidst more muffled laughter.

"Mary Kate? What's she doing here?" Homer's voice boomed, and Katherine cringed in the bathtub. "She should be with her husband."

"Peter's in town as well. I'm sure he has a great deal to report." The commotion with pots and pans told Katherine that her mother was having difficulty keeping her father's mind on supper.

"Come here, wench," her father told his wife, getting back to his original game. There were more laughs and soft slaps and then a noisy kiss.

"There's plenty of time for that after supper, Homer darling," her mother teased.

Kate sat up, listening intently. It was the first time she had ever heard her parents do anything but fight. She felt almost jealous, because they were happy and she wasn't.

"Mother!" she called petulantly. "Could you rinse my hair? The water's getting cold in here."

"Just a minute, dear." Madeleine rushed in, carrying a pitcher of rinse water. "Your father's home," she said breathlessly.

"Yes, I know. I heard."

Her mother blushed in pretty confusion. "You have so much hair, Mary Kate. I'll fetch more water. Be right back!"

Finally Katherine's hair was rinsed and perfumed. She slipped out of the tub and toweled off. Dripping on the linoleum floor, she wondered what she was going to

wear, since she and her mother had burned the last
dress she had from the logging camp.

In answer to all her worries, her mother said mysteri-
ously, "I've sent your father on an errand," and shooed
Kate up the back stairs. "We are going to the theater
tonight!"

Kate sped on long legs down the hall to her bedroom.
While she awaited her mother, she checked the closet.
Her wedding dress hung alone, covered by a muslin
sheet. She'd done too good a job of packing. The fire
had destroyed everything she owned.

Hurry up, Mother! she fretted.

Another half hour passed before her mother came
upstairs with a dinner tray.

"Eat. You'll need your strength." Seeing Kate's high
state of agitation, Madeleine warned, "It's going to be a
long night."

"I'm not hungry." She rolled her eyes. Mothers were
always urging their children to eat.

Madeleine tied a linen napkin around her daughter's
neck. "Nobody should go into battle on an empty stomach." She set the tray in Kate's lap and stood back to
watch, her slender arms folded across her bosom like a
female general.

"All right, all right!" Katherine said. She wolfed down
the roast beef and carrots, then stuffed a dinner roll in
her mouth. "Satisfied?"

Her mother smiled. "Drink your milk."

"God! You treat me like such a child." Kate swore
softly, then caught herself. "Sorry, Mother," she blushed,
"I guess I've been away from polite society too long."

"You're forgiven," Madeleine said warmly.

"This isn't going to work, you know," Kate said, slurping
her milk. The tip of her pink tongue passed over her
milky mustache. "By the way, you're a pretty decent cook."

"Thank you, dear." Kate's mentor leaned forward
until their eyes locked. "And, yes, this *is* going to work.
Trust me."

"Mother, I haven't a thing to wear. I can't very well attend the theater stark naked." Her gaze turned to the near-empty closet, and Madeleine's gaze followed her daughter's. She took down the wedding gown and ran her fingers lovingly over the white satin.

"Remember how lovely you looked in this?"

Katherine stabbed a forkful of baked apple. "Nobody wears a wedding dress twice."

"If we remove the train and the boa, nobody will know it was your wedding dress."

"It's white," said Katherine, diving into her potatoes, since her dessert was gone and she was still ravenous. "White is for virgins, which I definitely am not. Not anymore."

Madeleine raised her chin to challenge such foolish talk. "I wear white all the time. Now, if I lend you my tiara and matching eardrops, you'll look like a queen, dripping in pearls and white satin," she whispered for dramatic effect.

Kate paused, about to shove a bite of lumpy potatoes in her mouth. She set down the fork and, wiping her fingers, dropped her napkin on the plate. "Let me see that dress, Mother."

Together they spread the beautiful creation across the bed. As the lustrous pearls, lace, and satin winked up at them, they saw as if by magic what it could become with a few adjustments.

Her mother raised her brows at Katherine. "Are you prepared to become a seductive woman of the world?"

A delicious shiver coiled low in Katherine's belly. She threw a slender arm around her mother's neck and hugged her close. "As Peter would say, 'Hell, yes!' Whatever happens, Mother, thank you."

"Just don't demand a divorce when he's carrying you off to bed," her mother advised with a twinkle in her eye.

Katherine's face turned crimson. "I won't make that mistake again."

Madeleine sat her daughter down and began the transformation process that would hopefully bring

O'Rourke under her spell. "We have less than an hour before the curtain goes up at Maguire's Opera House. Let me see what I can do with your hair." Deftly she began to brush out Kate's hair and arrange it in an up-sweep of curls.

Suddenly Kate realized how selfish she was being. Her eyes met her mother's in the mirror. "You and Papa haven't had any dinner yet."

Madeleine smiled. "Your father will get fed, don't you worry."

"I'm to face Peter alone?" she gasped, clutching the bedpost while her mother cinched her unmercifully in one of her own corsets. "What's keeping Papa, anyway?"

"Your father is inviting his foreman, Mr. Simpson, to escort you. You and he are simply going with your parents to an opening-night performance at the theater. All perfectly innocent, you see." Madeleine fastened the petticoat tapes and took out her pocket scissors to make a few minor alterations on the wedding dress.

"Mr. Simpson?" Katherine asked, suddenly suspicious. "But he's the man Papa wanted me to marry in the first place."

"What difference does that make? You're married to Peter now."

Snip snip snip. The boa came off. Next the satin train was detached and set aside. Careful of her coiffure, Katherine slipped into the gown and stood docilely while her mother laced her tightly. Then her mother secured the tiara on the rich auburn tresses. She laid a jeweled choker around Katherine's white throat. Nodding her approval, she watched Kate adorn her pretty ears with heirloom eardrops that had been in the St. Yves's family for three generations.

"If all this doesn't get your Mr. O'Rourke excited, I don't know what will," she said.

Katherine stared in amazement at the sorceress who gazed back at her from the mirror. "I look like a . . . a . . ." She lowered her lashes, unable to say "courtesan," although that was the word that popped into her mind. "Do you think Peter will like me this way?" she asked.

"If he's a man of the world, how can he resist?" Her mother's blue eyes sparkled. "As for your competition"—she shrugged disparagingly—"remember, she is much older than you."

"And much more experienced." Biting her lip, Kate twisted this way and that, inspecting herself.

"Trust me, darling. He will go mad for you in this gown." With that, her mother whisked out of the room to change her own dress for the theater.

Katherine stared after her, all preconceived ideas about her mother crumbling. Going downstairs to await her father's return, she giggled, envisioning how Peter would act when he saw her at the play. If he was backstage, she must be sure to visit the cast after the show. He would rue the day he ever flaunted his affection for Nina whatever-her-name-was, she thought.

Suddenly a gust of cold air interrupted her delightful reverie.

"Papa! You're back!" Mary Kate exclaimed and rushed forward eagerly to greet him and his guest.

"Mary Katherine, I'd like you to meet my foreman, Lew Simpson," Homer told his daughter.

Katherine stared up into a pair of the most striking brown eyes she had ever seen. Lewis Simpson lacked Peter's height, but he was every bit as handsome. His wide, sensual mouth broke into a friendly smile upon seeing her all dressed up in her finery. His hair was blue-black and freshly trimmed. But the most outstanding feature were his Byronic eyes, almost brooding in their intensity.

Kate felt her brain whirl dizzily. Were she forced to decide between this man and her husband, solely on the basis of physical attractiveness, it would be hard to choose. For one crazy moment, she wondered if she hadn't put herself through a lot of misery for nothing.

Her father's choice had not been some ragtag, consumptive miner after all!

"We meet at last," Simpson said, displaying perfect white teeth. He didn't have Peter's dimples or cleft chin, but there was no denying his Black Irish charm.

My goodness! Kate thought, her hand in Simpson's, gawking at her father's foreman.

He's gorgeous. What do I do now?

"Where's your mother?" Homer wanted to know. He stepped to the bottom of the staircase. "Maddy, get a move on, or we'll miss the first act!" he hollered.

Her mother called down: "I'll be right there, sweetheart."

In minutes they were out the door. Homer handed his wife and daughter into his carriage and then took the driver's seat, while Lew Simpson joined the ladies.

"A lovely night, Mr. Simpson, don't you agree?" Madeleine remarked, to fill Kate's stunned silence.

"So it is, ma'am." Lew looked at the beautiful redhead sitting opposite him and couldn't think of a thing to say. *So this is the boss's daughter,* he thought, swallowing hard. He knew she had married O'Rourke, the fellow her father had hired to handle his lumber holdings. It had all happened so fast, before he even had had a chance to meet her. But that was so often the way of it out here, where men outnumbered women thirty to one. By the time a man got off his shift, any eligible woman fresh off the stagecoach was usually spoken for.

"The play's nearly sold out," Homer said, puffing on his stogie and longing for his supper. He didn't much like being drawn into Maddy's hare-brained scheme. Let Mary Kate salvage her own marriage, he'd told his wife. But Madeleine had insisted. He hated dragging poor Simpson into this, after Mary Kate had turned up her nose, sight unseen. From what Maddy had told him, this no-account O'Rourke was up to his old tricks with women. Though why his daughter wasn't enough trouble for the man was beyond his ken.

"I'm so glad you could get tickets, Homer darling," Madeleine cooed, as if she had nothing in mind but an evening's entertainment.

"How nice of you to join us on such short notice," Kate added, flashing her escort a smile.

"I've only been to the theater once in four years," Lew confessed.

Madeleine glanced at the good-looking young miner thoughtfully. "I suppose your work keeps you too busy for such pleasures."

"Yes, what *do* you do in your spare time?" Kate asked.

Lew flushed, knowing most of his off-hours pursuits wouldn't pass muster with these genteel ladies. "A game of cards, a glass of whiskey, that sort of thing," he said evasively, omitting his passion for the ladies at Julia's Palace up on D Street.

"My guess is Mr. Simpson spends most of his time working," Madeleine told her daughter. "Am I right?" She gave the foreman her most charming smile.

The carriage stopped in front of Maguire's theater, and McGillacutty produced four tickets from his inside vest pocket. He snuffed his cigar in the receptacle by the door and took his wife's arm. The crowd was rowdy, and he was glad he had hired a box. He didn't much relish subjecting his family to the indignities of main-floor seating.

"Let's find our seats," he grumbled.

The gaslights dimmed twice, signaling that the play would begin in three minutes.

Homer and Simpson elbowed and pushed through the crush of miners, doxies, businessmen, and wives, giving Katherine and her mother safe conduct to a private box at the side. Once there, Kate found herself and Simpson wedged tightly between her parents.

"I doubt I'll notice a thing on that stage tonight," Lew whispered in Kate's ear, as the houselights dimmed and the crowd hushed in anticipation. "I can't keep my eyes off of you."

Overhearing his remark, Madeleine reached past Lew to hand Kate an ivory fan. "For luck," she whispered.

"Thank you, Mama. I'm going to need it." Katherine nervously glanced at the dark-haired Irishman seated beside her. She could only imagine Peter's reaction when he saw them together.

The footlights went up, as the house plunged into darkness. Theater owner Maguire stepped through the garish maroon velvet curtain and held up his hands for quiet.

"Ladies and gentlemen, your attention, please!"

A murmur of excitement swept through the crowd.

"Due to illness, there is a change in tonight's program. In the role of Paolo, we are privileged to present an actor who appeared recently on our stage. You may remember him in the production *Camille*, put on by the Irish Players.

"Will you welcome, please, back for a return engagement, that distinguished leading man—Mr. Peter O'Rourke!"

CHAPTER 21

"And now, on with the play!" Maguire exited stage right into the wings amidst a ripple of polite applause.

The curtain parted noiselessly to reveal a stage flooded with artificial sunlight, and strolling to center stage in thirteenth-century Italian garb, Peter O'Rourke spoke the play's opening lines.

Still in a state of disbelief, all three members of the McGillacutty family strained forward in their seats.

Homer's cheek twitched convulsively. "An actor!" he hissed, his meaty hands clutching the ornately carved balustrade on the front of the box. He collapsed back in his seat. "Maddy, aw, Maddy," he moaned, "how could this be? I've been bamboozled by my own son-in-law!"

Masked by applause, Homer's dragonlike snorts of outrage went unnoticed by all but his wife and daughter.

Already tired after a long day in the mines, Lew Simpson stretched out his legs. The program change meant nothing to him. One actor being pretty much the same as the next, he yawned, closed his eyes, and settled back for a thinly veiled catnap in the darkened theater.

But for the McGillacuttys, the revelation of Peter's professional status as an actor was no laughing matter.

Homer saw it as a personal betrayal, a blatant attempt to pull the wool over his eyes. Why, he had hired

O'Rourke off the street! Even welcomed him into his home, and approved him as a son-in-law! *What unmitigated gall!* he fumed. To think that he'd taken O'Rourke into his confidence and finagled the scoundrel into marrying his precious Mary Kate! How could he have been so blind!

Madeleine McGillacutty, too, was shocked, but her main concern was for the two people she loved most in all the world. What Peter O'Rourke did for a living wasn't nearly as important as her daughter's happiness. Considering how Homer was puffing and snorting like a steam boiler about to explode under too much pressure, she feared for the delicate balance of his health.

"Give me that!" Katherine filched her mother's opera glasses and trained them on the man playing an Italian count. It was Peter, all right! As overwhelmingly handsome as ever. Masculine, long legged and lean, Peter was the perfect specimen to play the role of Paolo. Onstage and off, he was a natural-born charmer, capable of weaving a soporific spell to ensnare any woman's soul.

As Paolo, the handsome brother of Count Lanciotto, a hunchback ruler of noble character, Peter was sociable and romantic; he was also possessed of a poetic soul.

As the tragic love story began to unfold, an undertow of romantic expectation quickly cast its spell over even the most ribald rowdy in the audience. Throughout the theater, people sat forward with baited breath, hanging on Peter's every word.

In one box in particular, three out of four ticket holders held their breath, not because they gave a damn about the fate of Francesca da Rimini and her lover, Paolo, but because of who was out there, trouping the boards.

No wonder he drove me wild, quoting poetry half the night! Kate groaned inwardly. How Peter must have laughed up his sleeve. No doubt he did it to keep in practice—never mind her feelings! *Ooh!* And to think she had been completely taken in!

McGillacutty wrestled the opera glasses from his daughter's grasp and watched his son-in-law strut his stuff. Tights showed off a pair of long, muscular legs to perfection. *He looks like a goddamn gigolo!* Homer ground his teeth, certain he had fallen for the biggest con job ever perpetrated in the history of man. The fellow deserved to be horsewhipped! *He has more dadblasted nerve than I do,* Homer admitted grudgingly. Who'd have believed it? An upstart actor, making fools of them all!

Angry as he was, Homer might have chalked it off to experience if it wasn't for what O'Rourke must have done to Mary Kate. *Poor, unsuspecting lamb! Probably never knew what hit her.*

Katherine stared in fascination at Peter. Refusing the deformed brother's suggestion that Paolo marry Francesca himself, Peter made even Kate believe his sincerity when he demurred, "I'd rather see you smile than see the sun shine."

The snake! she thought, remembering his glibness with her. She had fallen in love with a man whose every word probably came from another man's pen.

All over the theater, people were brought to the edge of their seats by his rich, ringing baritone. A certain animal magnetism flowed from him across the footlights, capturing the grudging admiration of males and making female hearts flutter.

With consummate skill the players set the scene for full-blown tragedy. Mr. Davenport, the New York actor playing Lanciotto, received enthusiastic applause as the curtain fell on Act One.

First Intermission. Lew Simpson rose gracefully, refreshed from his nap and smiling. "That was some acting, wasn't it?" he enthused.

"Extraordinary," said Madeleine, tucking her hand in Homer's.

"He's very good, don't you think, Papa?" Katherine asked, willing to give the Devil his due. "I'm as surprised as you are, but—"

"He's a revolting playactor, Mary Kate!" Homer exploded, his face beet red. "How can you say, 'He's very good, Papa'?" he mimicked. "Wait till I get my hands on that young scoundrel!"

"Now, Homer, why don't you and I go home?" Madeleine asked. "You'll feel much better after a quiet dinner. I'll even give you a back rub," she added with an inviting smile.

"Don't try to manipulate me, Maddy." McGillacutty pounded his fist on the railing. "I trusted that fellow with my daughter—!" He couldn't finish, he was so choked up. He got up and started for the door, pushing through the crowd.

"What do you mean, Father?" Katherine asked, suddenly anxious.

"It's not so much what O'Rourke has done, as what he is!" He paused outside to light up.

"I was looking for a good, rock-solid husband for you, Mary Kate. All I want is a few sensible grandchildren. Was that too much to expect?" He glared at Katherine's midsection. "I suppose there's a tiny little actor in the oven right now."

"Now, Homer, what a thing to say!" Madeleine gasped.

Homer ran a freckled hand through his red hair, leaving it standing straight up. "What did I ever do to deserve such a fate? Kate, how can I ever make it up to you?"

Katherine was upset with Peter, but her father's attempt to pass himself off as a martyr made her giggle. "Oh, Papa, really! It's my life, not yours. I'm the one who has to live with Peter, not you or Mama."

"I'm sure their children will be perfectly splendid looking," said Madeleine, trying to help.

"But will they be sensible?" Homer persisted.

"Papa, stop talking about hypothetical grandchildren," said Katherine.

"Homer, you've been under too much pressure lately, what with the mine flooding and having to close down operations on the lower levels," Madeleine said, smoothing her husband's silk tie. "You mustn't get yourself so worked up."

"I'm contacting my lawyer first thing tomorrow," McGillacutty threatened, chewing violently on his cigar.

"Oh, dear! I'm sure there's a perfectly logical reason why Mr. O'Rourke didn't divulge his true profession," Madeleine went on, nervously trailing behind her husband, as he took to pacing the boardwalk.

"Will somebody please tell me what is going on?" Lew Simpson demanded. He still hadn't connected the thirteenth-century count onstage with the O'Rourke he'd met several weeks back in Shaft No. 9.

"My husband is an actor," Katherine explained, huddled miserably in her mother's black-velvet cape. Chill winds coming down from the snow-capped mountains sent an icy shiver down her back, and she couldn't control her chattering teeth. Her shock was compounded by a very real fear of what her father was planning to do. She had never seen him so angry, not even when she refused to marry the man standing at her side.

A hawker passed through the crowd, announcing that Act Two was about to begin. "Two minutes. Take your seats, folks. Two minutes."

Simpson glanced up at the marquee, finally catching on to the family commotion. "You mean your husband was on that stage tonight?" he asked.

"He's playing the romantic lead," Kate admitted.

"I thought the fellow onstage looked familiar."

"Your mother and I are going home," Homer growled, expecting Katherine to take her cue and accompany them.

Not having any real desire to spend the evening listening to her father rant and rave, Kate was determined to stay. She flashed her best smile at Lew Simpson and was rewarded by an appreciative gleam in his brown eyes. "The play's a rather good one, don't you agree? Even if Peter *is* in it, I'd like to see how it ends. That is, if Mr. Simpson is willing to be my escort?"

"I would be honored," Lew said with a slight bow.
"Rest assured, Mr. McGillacutty, I'll see your daughter
safely home."

"Thank you, Simpson," Homer mumbled. "We'll leave
you two the carriage. I need to work this out of my
system, and walking will help. C'mon, Maddy."

Kate placed her glove on Simpson's brawny arm and
followed the audience back inside. "Hurry, Mr. Simpson," she said, "I do believe the second-act curtain is
going up."

The scene was already in progress as they slipped into
the empty box. Simpson helped her remove her wrap,
and they settled into the imitation Louis Quatorze
chairs, upholstered in blue velour. Another backdrop of
scenery greeted their eyes, and Katherine remembered
the evening Peter had taken her backstage and shown
her how everything worked. In retrospect, she was
amazed that she had watched him demonstrate his familiarity with props and scenery and never once suspected
a thing!

Shrill catcalls and stomping feet accompanied a thun-
derclap of applause as the female star made her first
appearance of the evening. Enviously Katherine turned
her attention to the exquisite tragedienne who swept onstage, a creature of noble character and incredible
beauty.

Through her opera glass, Kate examined the actress
for flaws. The makeup looked harsh under the blazing
footlights. A trace of umber cork outlined her large,
soulful eyes, and her eyebrows rose on a pale brow like
the wings of a sorrowing dove. Glancing over at her
escort, Katherine laughed to herself. Lew Simpson was
on the edge of his chair, enthralled. To him and almost
every other male, Nina L'Ambourghetti was a goddess.
Her gentle imprecations, as she begged her father not to
marry her to Lanciotto, brought out the protective instincts of every man present. Kate could identify with
Francesca's plight, to a point, for her own father tried to

force her into marriage. But Francesca—*poor, spineless
ninny!*—was willing to sacrifice her happiness to her
father's wishes.

Of course, Kate could see that her father's choice, who
sat beside her, practically drooling over the gorgeous actress onstage, was totally unlike Francesca's true love,
Paolo. Completely different. For that much she was
grateful. Looks weren't everything, she was beginning to
realize.

Kate and the play's heroine caught sight of Peter simul-
taneously, as he made his next entrance. During the
exchanges between Francesca and Paolo, Kate studied
Peter's character closely, comparing his actions onstage
with the offstage Lothario she knew. Poor Francesca!
Unable to help herself, she fell in love with the wrong
man although—at least she had an excuse for her misery:
her prospective husband, Lanciotto, was a grossly disfigured, though kind, individual.

In sorrow, Francesca turned to the man she desired:
"So, Count Paolo, you have come, hot haste, to lead me
to the church, to have your share in my undoing?"
Nina's musical voice trilled with tremulous accusation
and longing.

Along with hundreds of enthralled spectators, Katherine sat riveted to her seat, scene after scene, absorbing
the drama. Tearfully she nibbled her fingernails. Alas,
the lovers stood at cross purposes. Her own marriage
seemed equally hopeless.

Kate sobbed quietly when Paolo, unable to speak of his
love without dishonoring his sworn duty to his brother,
protested to Francesca, "No! Stand still! You stray around
the margin of a precipice. I know what pleasure 'tis to
pluck the flowers that hang above destruction, and to
gaze into the dread abyss, to see such things as may be
safely seen. 'Tis perilous."

Peter's anguished gaze left the petite brunette onstage
and roamed the darkened theater. Katherine sat tensely,

his words directed like an arrow straight to her
own heart.

"The eye grows dizzy as we gaze below," he intoned
passionately, ". . . a wild wish possesses us to spring into
the vacant air. Beware, beware! Lest this unholy fascination grow too strong to conquer."

Ah, too late, Peter, too late! Katherine gulped back a sob.
Why couldn't Peter speak such beautiful words to her
and truly mean them? Again she trained her glass on the
pair of ill-starred lovers. They were so impassioned in the
clinches! So anguished at the thought of losing each
other's love. As she watched them kiss deeply, Kate bit
her lip and tasted blood. It was more than she could
bear! The man she loved was actually French-kissing another woman! Damn him! In public. With a married
woman. What sort of husband would allow such a thing?
Maybe Nina didn't really have a husband in the wings.
Peter might have lied about that, too.

The play had turned into a nightmare. Her world was
suddenly collapsing, and there wasn't a thing she could
do to make things right.

During their torrid love scene in Act Five, Peter and
Nina pulled out all the stops on their lovemaking.
Katherine writhed in vicarious anguish and ecstasy. The
actors' ardent declarations heated her own blood with
fervent longing. At one point, Francesca drew Paolo's
head down to her breast and cried in rapturous tones,
"Take me all, body and soul!"

Peter swept her into his arms, circling as he captured
his costar's lips in a lengthy, impassioned kiss that set the
males in the audience to stomping their feet with approving whistles and cheers.

Kate seethed with rage. *No, Peter! You should be kissing
me, not that . . . that hussy!* The spectacle of her husband
performing before this rowdy crowd left her reeling. If
she'd had a gun, she, like Lanciotto, would have finished
off both Nina and Peter.

The lovemaking continued for five minutes—*at*

least!—with scorching words and caresses. A woman in the box next to Kate's screamed and fainted; her husband had to carry her out.

Serves her right, Kate thought bitterly and returned to catching Peter at his seductive best. *Wait till I get my hands on him!* She promised herself sweet revenge.

At last the final curtain closed to wildly uninhibited, thunderous applause. The stage lovers lay dead in one another's arms; the grieving brother collapsed in grief beside them.

Katherine, her head cradled in her arms, sobbed out loud.

Simpson stirred in his seat, made uncomfortable by her emotional display. "It was a good play," he admitted gruffly, "but not that good."

Her head came up as the curtains parted again and the players came forward for more curtain calls. She rested her chin on the railing, watching Nina and Peter walk forward together, their hands clasped, to acknowledge the standing ovation.

Mr. Maguire came from the wings, bearing a large bouquet of silk roses for the female star. Kate remembered seeing a similar bouquet in the prop room. Peter had told her real roses were so scarce that Maguire used silk ones at every performance.

Nina accepted the tribute, as gracious as a queen.

Katherine sniffed, thinking, *How fake can you get?*

The actress curtsied to the miners, who made up eighty percent of the theater patrons. Then she stepped back, throwing kisses. At that point, the crowd went wild. A rain of silver dollars hit the stage. "Bravo! Bravo!" the miners shouted.

Nina alone, and then Nina and Mr. E. L. Davenport stepped forward to receive the crowd's accolades. Then Nina reached out and drew Peter forward to take another curtain call with her.

After several minutes, the curtain closed for the final time. The houselights went up; it was time to go home.

Oblivious to the noisy chatter and the press of bodies
pushing to exit the theater, Katherine sat, her chin
propped against her fists, staring at the closed curtain.

Simpson touched her shoulder lightly. "I think we
should go, too."

As Katherine got to her feet, she glanced down, remembering the lengths to which she had gone to make
herself look irresistible. The whole point of the evening
was to make Peter realize that Nina couldn't hold a
candle to her. If she didn't put in a brief appearance
backstage, the evening would be a total waste.

"Mr. Simpson, I wonder if we might stop backstage for
a moment?" She smiled sweetly at her companion. "I want
to tell my husband what I thought of his performance."

Simpson frowned slightly. "As long as we're not too
long," he allowed. "I have to be back at work by five in
the morning."

"Oh, this will only take a minute," she promised.

Caught in a surging tide of men pushing toward the
exit, Kate held onto Lew Simpson's arm for dear life and
let him elbow a path to the sidewalk outside. Breathing
deeply to rid her lungs of the stale smell of sweat, tobacco, and alcohol, she tugged on Simpson's sleeve.
"This way," she gently urged, starting toward the alley
and the open stage door. Nobody was watching the door,
so she boldly mounted the steps and mingled with the
throng backstage.

Emerging from behind a black-velvet drop, Peter was
surrounded by a bevy of admiring females. His shirt was
open, and Kate could see the perspiration streaming off
his torso, staining the waistband of his thirteenth-
century pantaloons. He mopped his face with the towel
around his neck, leaving it streaked with cake makeup
and sweat.

Katherine winced, as a pretty blonde pressed up
against him, exclaiming over his performance. "You
were so convincing, Mr. O'Rourke," she gushed.

Peter patted the girl on the shoulder casually. "Takes

practice—offstage and on." His laugh infuriated Katherine. The girl and her friends were obviously infatuated.

He handed the towel to his dresser, who offered him a cigar. "Thanks, Nelson." Peter let the man light it before he turned back to his eager fans. "Ladies, I hate to spoil your fun so early in the evening, but I'm a married man now."

Faces fell as if a death notice had been nailed on the stage door. One saucy creature with corkscrew brown curls spoke for all her sisters in sin: "You can't be serious!"

"Ah, but I am," he said with a smile and a wink. He turned and looked directly at Katherine as she hurried forward. "Here comes the light of my life now, no doubt to rescue me," he chuckled.

Drawing herself to her most regal height, Kate surveyed her competition coolly. "I hope I'm not in your way?" she asked archly.

Peter grinned obligingly at his followers. "Will you excuse us, ladies?" He bowed to his clinging-vine admirers. Taking Katherine's arm, he started toward his dressing room, but stopped when he spotted Lew Simpson waiting in the shadows nearby. "Or perhaps I'm the one in the way?" He raised an inquiring eyebrow.

Kate tossed her head, wishing he wasn't so blasted attractive. It would be so easy to let herself forget his disgraceful display onstage. One kiss, and she feared she might throw herself in his arms like Francesca, crying, "Take me, I'm yours . . . All that I call life is bound in thee."

Before that could happen, she drew back defensively. "Must you flaunt yourself so obviously?"

He grinned, deliberately baiting her. "My fans seem to expect it," he said and blew a smoke ring over her head.

"Well, you certainly outdid yourself tonight," she returned.

He stuck his cigar between his teeth and adjusted her tiara just a tad to the right. "You're putting on a pretty fair performance yourself," he said knowingly.

Katherine flushed. His green eyes seemed to stab right through her outer trappings to the part of her that stood quaking inside. "Not as convincing as the show you and Nina put on here tonight."

"Why, thank you!" He put his hand over his heart and bowed.

"There is no way in hell you and she are mere friends," Kate blazed. Forgetting the image she had worked so hard to produce, she sprang at him, both fists raised to strike. "A performance like that should be grounds for divorce!"

His cigar clenched in his teeth, Peter grabbed her wrists and yanked her hard against him. "Threatening me again, Kate?"

If her tiara was slightly askew before, it was dangerously tilted now. "Let go, you seducing rogue!"

"I will when you calm down."

"How can I be calm? And don't expect me to sit by meekly while you kiss and fondle other women in public!"

Peter's lip curled. "I don't consider what I did on that stage an adulterous act."

"Then how do you perceive it, pray tell?"

"When I'm onstage, I envision a glass wall between me and the audience." Peter gestured with his hand to illustrate his invisible-wall theory. "People pay for a good show and honest emotion. I try to make art as true to reality as I can."

"And what did you think about while you were making love to a married woman?" Kate was sure she had him trapped into an admission of guilt.

"You want to know—honestly? I thought about a red-headed witch I made love to in a cave not so very long ago," he whispered, and touched the distracting curl on her bosom.

"Liar!" her trembling lips blurted out.

"Liar yourself." He jerked his head toward Simpson, who hung back discreetly. "Are you looking for an excuse to add another heart to your collection?" He glared down at her like some incredibly handsome, wrathful deity.

"No, I'm not!" Kate's heart swelled and churned with sudden fright. The fear of losing him made her weak.

Peter pushed her to the wall, trapping her with his body. The acrid smell of cigar smoke seared her nostrils as he pressed against her. "Your father hasn't lost any time, has he? Introduced you to Simpson the minute you were back under his roof." Angry, he shoved Kate away.

"That's not true, Peter!" Katherine clutched her cloak around her, suddenly icy with fear. "Naturally Father is upset to learn you're an actor, but—oh, Peter, why didn't you tell me?"

He swore, his green eyes blazing. "Why? I was broke, stranded, and needed a job. Don't you remember? I knew damn well your father wouldn't hire an actor to run his lumber business."

He uttered a bitter laugh and gestured toward her handsome black-haired escort standing in the wings. "Maybe you're having second thoughts. Want to marry Simpson?"

Shaking her head, Kate blinked back her tears. "I-I would have married you anyway."

"The hell you say!" Peter towered over her, making her hold her breath. "Anyone handy would have suited your purposes. All you wanted was to run off to San Francisco."

"No. Not just anybody," Kate said softly, her stomach giving a queer little lurch.

"Yes, you would. Well, maybe you ought to reconsider your Papa's choice. Go on, if that's what you want," he said roughly. "I won't stand in your way."

"You'd like to be rid of me, wouldn't you?" Kate cried, almost paralyzed with fear that Peter meant to abandon her.

"I didn't say that." A queer flicker of emotion came and went in his sultry gaze, before she could define its meaning.

She lifted her chin defiantly. "I know my rights. You

can't just dump me on my parents' doorstep, while you play up to loose women."

His sensuous mouth twisted with humor. "Kate, those are just infatuated, empty-headed theater hounds. The only woman I want is you. Can't you get it through your head?"

"Hah! I wasn't the one kissing Nina L'Ambourghetti tonight!"

"Well, I sincerely hope not!" a low, melodic voice said behind Katherine. "So this is your beautiful wife, Peter, darling," Nina said with a warm smile.

"Nina, allow me to present my wife, Mary Katherine. Kate, my love, this is the lady whose beauty you've been envying all evening."

Katherine ignored his unkind, though painfully accurate, assessment of her feelings. "How do you do, Miss L'Ambourghetti?" she asked stiffly.

Nina's blue-gray eyes twinkled up at Peter mischievously. "No wonder your love scenes lacked their usual fire, Peter. You were holding back for someone else, *n'est-ce pas?*" She laughed, her finely trained voice trilling with merriment. "It's so good playing opposite you again," she enthused. "Now hurry, and don't forget to bring your wife to the party. You will make everyone green with envy!"

Having delivered her exit line, the actress sailed out the stage door into a patiently waiting throng of admirers.

Katherine stared after her rival in surprise. "What was that all about?" she asked Peter.

He shrugged. "There's a cast party in the hotel dining room. Care to come?"

"No, I'd better not." She hesitated. "I've kept Mr. Simpson long enough. He was kind enough to wait and see me home. Besides, Papa will be waiting up."

On impulse, Peter leaned down to steal a kiss from Kate's soft lips. "Stay with me tonight, Katherine." *Stay with me tonight . . . Stay with me forever,* his eyes pleaded.

Tonight, gladly . . . But what of tomorrow, and all the days and nights to follow? she wondered. How could she trust a man with Peter's ability to twist her heartstrings around his silken words? "I really must go, Peter. Otherwise my parents will worry."

Peter's eyebrows rose in disbelief. "*You're* worried that *they'll* worry if you're out late with your own husband?"

"It sounds absurd, but . . . yes." She stared at the mat of golden hair on his chest and swallowed hard. Her fingers curled inside her gloves, longing to touch him all over.

"Take it from me, love: 'tis a poor prodigal who dances to a parent's tune." He shook his head, as if disparaging her ever breaking free of parental injunctions.

"I'll dance to whatever tune I choose," Kate said with more bravado than she felt.

In an almost desperate move, Peter seized Kate in his arms and before she could utter a word of protest, ravaged her mouth. His eyes glittered with sultry seduction, and Kate whimpered low in her throat, knowing she could never fight the insane attraction she felt for him.

Their eyes met, and Peter's lips curled in a knowing smile. "We'll pursue this tomorrow, then. Sleep well, love—if you can!"

CHAPTER 22

Homer McGillacutty came stomping off the mine elevator in muddy boots. He had been down in Shafts 4, 5, and 7 since five o'clock that morning—all flooded out below five hundred feet. He had laid off another crew yesterday, and now it looked as if he would have to shut down another shaft.

"I wouldn't mind so much if the veins of the Lucky Strike mine were played out, goddammit!" he growled, lighting up one of his stogies as soon as he stepped out into the pale daylight. It was only eight o'clock in the morning, and already he felt the heavy burden of discouragement. He likened the sensation to being buried alive under a crushing weight of silver tailings. He felt helpless to control the situation. And angrier than a bull being fed salt peter during mating season.

All because of water seepage. He had the pumps going full tilt day and night but, in spite of everything, he was losing ground daily. There was small comfort in knowing he wasn't the only mine owner plagued by flooding. Most of the mines in the Comstock Lode were experiencing similar problems. The value of stock certificates had plummeted to rock bottom, and San Francisco securities brokers were clamoring for the mines to sell out, so they might recover at least part of their clients' money.

No two ways about it: Virginia City was on the verge of going broke in the late fall of 1864. Men were being laid off in droves, mines were closing, and owners were spending most of their remaining capital and efforts to come up with a way to lower the water table. Incredible, rich silver-ore deposits lay buried in the earth, but until an engineer came up with a workable solution, flooding was going to make paupers of them all.

McGillacutty was feeling the pinch. Just to man the pumps cost him a hundred cords of wood a day. That represented a sizable sum of money. Why, in three weeks he hadn't produced enough ore to make one thin silver dime!

Work had virtually come to a screeching halt and, with every passing day, the pressure to stay afloat increased. Now the pump in Shaft No. 7 had broken down. He needed another loan from the Bank of California.

"Lew, send Adams down to the bank. I need to get hold of Bill Sharon," Homer growled, shoving his hard hat back from his sweaty forehead. He pulled out a red kerchief and mopped his brow. "Lord, it gets hotter down there every day!"

"Maybe we should talk to Sutro," Simpson suggested for the third time that morning.

"Hell, by the time he builds that tunnel he keeps talkin' about, we'll all be flat broke." Homer kicked a coal bucket, thoroughly exasperated. "Lew, dig out the books. I'll take 'em home and work there for the rest of the day." He spun on his heel and left.

"Sure thing, Mr. McGillacutty." Simpson dispatched Adams, the office clerk, to flush out the bank agent. Then he carried the ledgers outside to his boss.

McGillacutty was frowning up at an overcast sky. "Just what we need—rain," he said morosely.

"It'll blow over, boss."

"Huh!" Homer grunted. "With my luck, we'll have a flash flood."

In Virginia City when it rained, it poured, turning the streets to gray muck.

O'Rourke had gone to bed around four, after seeing his friend Henri Lyons and putting in a brief appearance at the cast party. Even so, by ten o'clock that morning, he was up, shaven, and dressed in the only clothing he had left from the fire. He dawdled over breakfast in the hotel dining room, not eager to get down to business with the Old Man.

Peter never had much stomach for being the bearer of bad news—had a history of skirting it. After last night, McGillacutty was not going to welcome him, either as an employee or a son-in-law. And so he procrastinated over second and third cups of coffee in the hotel dining room, watching the rain muddy the unpaved street through the hotel's dingy, spattered window and reviewing his options.

He could take the easy way out, of course. Kiss Virginia City and his marriage good-bye, and board the stage for San Francisco with Nina and Henri Lyons at the end of the week. A quick solution to a painful episode in an otherwise catch-as-catch-can, self-centered existence.

He could go back to living out of a trunk, unreflecting, unattached, filling his nights with empty applause; giving no more thought to his tomorrows than he ever had. He saw one very good reason for choosing that road: he wouldn't have to hash it out with Homer McGillacutty.

This option he rejected the instant it occurred to him. He couldn't find it within himself anymore to treat life as if it was one big joke.

It might have been different if other people weren't counting on him.

He was married now . . . though for how long he had no idea.

Loving Kate had turned his life around. He had made promises to her, promises he still hoped he would get a chance to keep.

And no less binding, he realized, were the promises he had made to Jigger and his men. They were counting on him. Even if Old Man McGillacutty fired him, Peter knew he had to take up the men's cause.

"Rain like dis ain' nevah gwine stop till it wash away all dem shanties on de edge of town," the mulatto waiter said, chuckling, and filled Peter's cup for the fourth time.

Glancing up, Peter caught the hint behind the grin. "Guess I'd better get moving before I have to swim for it," he said good-naturedly.

"Yassuh, I spec so," the waiter said.

Minutes later, Peter was slogging along the boardwalk toward the McGillacutty domicile. An ox-drawn wagon, heading up the hill from the mines, sprayed his trouser legs with gray-brown sludge.

Peter drew the collar on his lumber jacket up around his ears. Damn, it was cold! The wind turned his nose red, and the rain came down in a torrent. Almost as bone-chilling as a winter storm on the coast of Ireland, he thought, surprised to find his thoughts so far adrift. It had been years since he'd been home yet, all of sudden, the blustery winds he'd braved as a lad on the sea cliffs came back to haunt him.

Splashing his way down B Street, Peter realized that Kate had come to mean everything to him. She was as saucy a colleen as ever he'd laid eyes on. Aye, and her eyes were as green as a shamrock. He was courting trouble, he knew, but he couldn't let her go. She was the Devil's own daughter, with hair the color of flame and a spitfire temper to boot, yet he wanted no other. Kate had tampered with his very soul. She had come into his life at a time when he felt the candle of his existence starting to gasp and sputter, as in a dark and airless room.

Aye, she was as necessary to him as earth, fire, water, and air! *Ah, Katie, Katie,* he thought, *if you only knew. I've been searching for you all my life!*

He scraped the mud from his boots on a flagstone and ran up the McGillacutty's porch steps. At his knock, Kate's dark-haired mother opened the door, impeccably dressed.

Smiling, she reached forth and grasped Peter's cold, wet hand. "Come in, Mr. O'Rourke," she exclaimed. Standing on tiptoe, she brushed his cheek with a kiss. "My husband is busy with Mr. Sharon from the bank. The minute they're finished, I'll let him know you're here."

"Thank you, Mrs. McGillacutty. I've come on rather an urgent matter. Kate no doubt told you about the fire." Peter surrendered his outer garments, relieved to find himself ushered into the parlor, where a fire blazed brightly on the hearth. He stood before the grate, thawing his hands.

"Thank the Lord you both are safe," she said.

"We lost two men," he said. As he gazed into the flames licking tamely around two yellow pine logs, his thoughts flashed back to the fire.

"I understand your heroic efforts saved Mary Katherine." Madeleine's eyes were shining. "May I offer you a cup of coffee while you wait?"

Peter, still feeling the effects of potent coffee, shook his head. "None for me, thank you."

"Perhaps you'd prefer chicken soup?" a familiar voice teased from behind the paneled door that closed off the parlor from the dining room.

"Mary Kate!" Sliding open the tall partition, Peter discovered his wife, clad in a warm woolen wrapper and nibbling petit fours at the table. "You look even more fetching than last night," he said, eagerly coming toward her.

Kate blushed. "I'm not exactly dressed to receive company."

"You mustn't stand on ceremony with your husband."

Her mother's blue eyes twinkled. "Mary Kate's wearing my robe, until we can replace what she lost in the fire," she explained.

Peter's fingers reached out to caress the long auburn curl that tumbled across Kate's left breast. "There's no Titian goddess can rival the one I see before me," he said huskily.

The panel door quietly slid shut, leaving them in privacy. Instantly they were in each other's arms. "Oh, Peter, you came!" she cried, drawing his head down for her kiss.

"Forgive my dampness, Kate," he said coming up for air and noticing that his rain-soaked clothing was getting her wet. "I've missed you, my bonny Kate, more than I can say."

"You were wonderful last night, Peter," she said breathlessly. "I am so sorry for losing my temper."

"We've both been on edge," Peter agreed. "After all we've been through lately, the main thing is that we're together—"

Whisking around him solicitously, she began touching him here and there, and tugged at his shirt and tie. "I'll get you one of Papa's shirts to wear while these dry."

"Stop, Kate!" he laughed at her wifely airs, and rescued his sodden shirt from her clutches. "I need to see your father first."

"I just am so glad to see you—" She stood in front of him, buttoning him up, obviously nervous and wanting to please him.

"Kate, you don't have to fuss over me. I'm in fine fettle! Just look at me," he said, spreading his arms and turning around for her perusal.

Just then a loud banging fist shook the paneled doors. Uttering a horrified shriek, Katherine clutched at Peter and buried her face in his shoulder. Reluctantly they turned, as the dividing panel slid opened with a boom.

Both her parents were there, with shocked expressions on their faces.

From Homer's perspective it looked as if his daughter was the aggressor. Madeleine, peering from behind her husband's burly mass, had already seen enough to consider it a draw.

"O'Rourke, what's the meaning of this?" Homer roared, advancing with clenched fists, all his protective instincts coming to the fore. The veins in his florid forehead popped out angrily. "Have you no sense of decency, to be making love to my daughter in broad daylight?"

Peter managed a look of innocent surprise. "It was only a harmless kiss, sir."

"You're half-dressed, man!"

"That's my fault, Papa."

"She has this terrible effect on me, sir," Peter said with an infectious grin. "I do apologize, if we startled you."

"I don't care if you two are married." Homer growled. "I was in the midst of a serious business deal. What if my banker had walked in here?"

"The point is, darling, Mr. Sharon did not get an eyeful," Madeleine interceded, coming to the young lovers' rescue. "Homer, look how young they are, and so very much in love." She cast him a meaningful glance. "Surely you haven't forgotten what it is to get carried away by passion."

Homer's face reddened with indignation. "And what's that supposed to mean?" he growled, although he knew full well. "Maddy, leave these two to me." He fastened a baleful glare on his only child. "Mary Kate, take yourself upstairs this instant. O'Rourke, you and I need to have a serious talk."

"Aye, that we do," Peter agreed. Reluctantly he relinquished his hold on his favorite redhead and followed her father into his office.

"Come along upstairs, Mary Kate," Madeleine urged. "They'll be in there for some time. Then perhaps Peter can take you downtown to do a little shopping."

Katherine waved her mother away and went to stand at the foot of the staircase, where she could eavesdrop on her father and Peter. As her father absorbed the full impact the fire had had upon his lumber business, the low rumble of male voices behind the closed door sounded like a council of war.

Peter's voice started out quietly reasoning and calm; her father responding in muffled tones. Suddenly Homer exploded. "No . . . no . . . and no!"

"I won't accept that answer, sir!"

A loud thud sounded, presumably her father's fist on his desk. It was a sound Katherine knew well enough from past experiences with her father's temper.

"You can't turn your back now, sir. Those men and their families are counting on you."

"I'm not shelling out another nickel on that burned-out, worthless piece of land!" A heavy fist fell against the desk, and then another in angry response.

"There's plenty of untouched timber to harvest," Peter countered with equal vehemence.

"Not one nickel, y'hear? I've poured my *blood* into the mine, and I've got nothing left to spare. The mine is bleeding me dry."

A deadly silence settled over the office for several heart-stopping seconds. Mary Kate and her mother exchanged a nervous glance, hoping their spouses weren't about to come to blows.

"I gave my word. You have to back me on this," Peter insisted. His voice rose and fell as he described the need for a sawmill along the Truckee River. He related how the men were already hard at work, cutting trees and preparing housing for themselves and their families.

"Awful high and mighty with my money!" Homer shouted.

"It was either let the men go, possibly lose a season's work, or keep them busy. You need them as much as they need your backing!"

"The hell you say! If the mine shuts down, I won't need timbers to shore up the tunnels, and I sure as hell won't need a hundred cords of wood a shift to run machinery, either!"

"With all due respect, sir, even if the mine folds, you can still make a fortune selling to the railroad and to settlers along the Donner Trail."

"Well, that's not the way I see it!" the old redhead said, chuffing away on a smelly cigar. "I *know* I've got a fortune in the ground, and that's where I'm staking what's left of my savings."

Peter's voice rose in furious accusation. "You would abandon those men, with no thought of the hardship to their families?"

"You want to be a bleedin' heart? Then you scrape up the money, O'Rourke. I've got my own problems."

"I wish to God I had the money."

Katherine sank down on the stairs, listening to Peter condemn her father's callous disregard for his men. His language was strong enough to strip the varnish off her father's desk. She cringed as another series of thumps resounded.

Madeleine, too, strained to make sense of the ensuing bedlam. She feared fighting. Clutching her voluminous skirts, she dashed forward and pounded her small fist on the sturdy door. "Homer? Are you two all right in there?"

Homer wrenched open the door and nearly bowled over his wife. "O'Rourke, you're fired!" he bellowed, turning back to Peter. "I don't like your way of doing business. You'll never amount to a hill of beans. Now get out of my house, and don't come back!"

His shoulders filling the doorway, Peter braced off against the older man, his face a mask of impotent fury. "I hope to God I never have to walk over other people to make my fortune." His fiery gaze flashed in Kate's direction. "Mary Kate, maybe you can talk some sense into your father. I sure as hell can't."

Kate rose, her bare toes crimped on the edge of the riser. "Peter—"

"Good day, Mrs. McGillacutty," Peter said, his jaw set

as stubbornly as his father-in-law's. "Kate, you know where to reach me." He grabbed his coat and hat from the hall tree and strode out onto the porch.

"Good riddance!" McGillacutty shouted, slamming the front door.

"Homer!" his wife cried in gentle outrage.

Katherine caught a glimpse of her husband's rigid back going down the walk. She swung around, her eyes flashing with temper. "Papa, you should have listened to Peter."

"Don't you defend that glib-talking actor to me!" Homer's bellow reverberated off walls, high ceilings, and delicate female eardrums. "I hope to God he hasn't gotten you in a family way."

"That's quite enough, Homer!" Madeleine said, prepared to do battle, if necessary.

"Stay out of this, Maddy. I regret ever inviting that snake-in-the-grass into my home."

"That's not fair, Father!" Kate said. "Peter didn't want to marry me, remember? It was *my* idea."

"Oh, was it, Miss Smartypants?" His hard gray-green eyes stabbed at her through a wreath of foul cigar smoke. "He used us, Kate!"

Kate threw up her hands. "Then all I can say is, there's a God in heaven, because we both got what we deserve!"

"Which is?" He stuck out his jaw, waiting.

"Exactly nothing! Oh, damn you, Papa! I hate you for ruining my life." She dashed away her angry tears. Peter was gone. Her life was over!

Homer clumsily patted her shoulder. "I'll find you another husband," he offered.

"I don't want another husband," Kate sobbed. "Did it ever occur to you I might love Peter? Not that it matters, after what you just did."

"Maddy," Homer yelled, "I won't have our daughter talk to me like this!"

Madeleine raised a delicately arched brow. "Go upstairs,

Mary Kate," she urged quietly. "Let me deal with your father."

"Gladly!" And she ran bawling from the room.

Maddy McGillacutty turned to the man she loved but had such difficulty keeping halfway civilized. "Homer, darling, we can hardly complain because things didn't turn out the way we planned."

"It's in the genes," he said darkly, slouching toward his office in weary resignation.

"Nonsense." Madeleine's arm circled his thick waist in a quick hug. "You know perfectly well why you're angry. Peter O'Rourke is as pig-headed and opinionated as you." Removing the cigar from her husband's mouth, she brushed a light kiss across his leathery lower lip. "And he is the right man for our Mary Kate."

"Over my dead body," Homer growled, closing the study door. He leaned back, letting his helpmeet console him. He had suffered a major financial blow minutes before his blow-up with O'Rourke. It was good to know at least one female in his family cared a damn for him. "I still prefer Simpson as a husband for Mary Kate," he said like a true die-hard.

"No, dearest," Maddy murmured against his massive chest.

"O'Rourke's all wrong for a sweet, delicate child like Mary Kate. I shall see my attorney this afternoon."

"I don't think so," his wife said. "Let nature take its course."

"Don't you have some housework to do around here?" he asked, appealing to her sense of guilt.

"I dusted yesterday," Maddy said, calmly examining a hairy mole on his sun-reddened neck through her thick black lashes.

"How about fixing me lunch, then?"

"Oh, very well." Madeleine sighed and got up to leave, since her efforts to bring him around weren't working. She leaned over and kissed him. "You stay right here, promise? I'll be right back with your steak sandwich and coffee."

As soon as she disappeared into the hallway, McGillacutty heaved himself out of his chair. He put on his frock coat and gathered up a stack of papers, muttering revenge.

He was long gone when Madeleine returned with his lunch.

She shook her head, thinking, *Homer McGillacutty, for all your orneriness, this is one battle of wills you're not going to win.* Then, feeling completely justified, she opened the lower-left desk drawer and took a nip from his private stash of Southern Comfort.

CHAPTER 23

Peter shivered, trudging back to the hotel. High mountain winds and near-freezing rains buffeted him every step of the way. Notwithstanding the miserable weather, by far his spirit felt a bleaker chill. How was he going to break it to the men? A helluva thing to be out of work just as winter swept over the High Sierras, blanketing them in snow. McGillacutty hadn't even given his request a second's consideration. He felt like such an abysmal liar, promising the men his support and not being able to deliver.

Seeing Mary Katherine, huddled in a blue down comforter in the upstairs window as he left, had only added to the dull ache of discontent inside. She had looked so lost, her eyes red from crying. So much unfinished business! Would they ever know where they stood with each other?

Bracing his shoulder against the heavy outside door, Peter pushed his way into the hotel lobby, carrying the tempest inside with him. He paused briefly to greet Davenport, the guest star appearing as Lanciotto, and the company stage manager, Enoch Laskey.

"Walk-through rehearsal this afternoon at four," Laskey said.

"I'll be there," Peter promised. "God knows, I'm rusty."

"You're drenched, darling," Nina L'Ambourghetti

scolded, turning from the front desk with a tidy pile of mail in her jeweled hands. "Be sure you drink plenty of strong tea with honey and lemon."

"Yes, Mother," Peter teased, and dodged her light slap of affection.

"Incorrigible pest!"

He stood drumming on the counter, waiting for his key. The assistant desk clerk sidled over, his face crimson with embarrassment, and slid a thick envelope across the desk to Peter.

"Mr. O'Rourke? I apologize for not giving you this when you checked in yesterday. I had forgotten all about it."

"For me?" Peter's voice reflected his surprise. "Now who could possibly know I'm staying here?" His fingers closed around the fat envelope, addressed to him in an unfamiliar, rather pinched scrawl. Postmarked Belfast, Ireland, June 17th, and forwarded twice. Peter raised his eyebrows, seeking clarification from the clerk.

"It came several weeks ago, when the Irish Players were in town. You were staying somewhere else, and Miss Dooley said she'd let you know it was here."

"My God, man! This is late October, over four months since this was posted."

The clerk's brow crinkled worriedly. "I am truly sorry, sir. After you checked in yesterday, I had only the vaguest recollection, but it was enough to send me searching through the manager's office this morning."

"Thanks." Peter tapped the envelope on his thumb nail, mentally weighing it. A lengthy letter, judging by the heft. Registered and insured. Again he checked the handwriting. It seemed odd that, months after his last contact with his family, this voluminous correspondence should suddenly catch up with him. He found it especially hard to believe his father would relent and send word through his Belfast attorneys.

Pocketing the envelope casually, Peter exchanged a few witticisms with other cast members in the lobby.

"I'm going upstairs and soak in a hot tub," he said

presently, cutting short the light-hearted banter. He
flipped the bellhop a silver dollar. "Bring me whiskey
and a pot of black coffee," he said. "Room 208."

"Make that lemon tea," Nina interjected in her musical voice.

"All right, send that up, too," he told the fellow, acced-
ing to her wishes with an easy chuckle.

"Right away, sir." The youth scurried toward the hotel
kitchen through a rear corridor. Meanwhile Peter
headed for the stairs. Suddenly he was hungry for news
from his family. Damn! He should have written, even
though his father had cut off his allowance months ago.

As soon as he reached his room, he tore open the envelope with impatient fingers. Several sheets of stationery
imprinted with the firm name of McDermott, Smythe
and Glover were folded around a bank draft drawn on
the Bank of London in the amount of . . .

"Holy merde! Two hundred thousand pounds sterling!"

Peter dropped the check like a hot brick. What the
hell? He'd never received more than a few hundred
pounds at any one time from Father. There must be
some mistake. His father was much too tight to have sent
such a sum of his own volition.

Peter stooped to retrieve the bank draft and carefully
set it aside. A prickle of apprehension made the hairs on
the back of his neck rise. He turned to the attorney's de-
tailed four-page letter for answers. In seconds, a sickening
shock coiled in his gut, as the truth hit home.

Enclosed with the attorney's letter was a handwritten
copy of his father's last Will and Testament. *Ah, Christ—
no!* The handwriting jumped erratically before his eyes.
His father, dead? *Oh, God, not like this! Not now, when I'm
halfway round the world.*

Peter steeled himself against jumping to rash conclusions. His father had been in robust health the last he
heard. Nobody in his family died before they reached
their eighties or nineties.

He sat at the small desk in his room and turned up the

gas lamp. Starting with the letter from a Mr. Gerald Mac-
Donald, he read of the death at sea of his father *and* his
older brother, Sean.

Closing his eyes, Peter swallowed deeply. He shivered in
his damp clothing, a terrible premonition tearing at his
throat. This couldn't be, he thought, staring in disbelief at
the letter, the legal document, and the bank draft. A mean-
ingless jumble of words swam before his eyes. Suddenly all
the reasons he'd ever used to justify leaving home seemed
unimportant, the ultimate in self-serving rhetoric.

Sean, too. Ah, God! Sean should have been the next
Earl of Wickstead, not him. Sean and he had raised hell
and caroused as teenagers, chasing girls and sneaking in
late together. In his mind he could still picture the time
his big brother brought him home, falling-down drunk,
laughing like a loon after his first visit to a bawdy house.
Lord, how zany and carefree it had all seemed then! But
they'd soon landed in the soup, Sean taking the lion's
share of the blame, because he was older.

Abruptly, Sean had been sent to school in England.
Father had been adamant. They must learn to conduct
themselves as young country squires, not behave like
hooligans.

Peter had escaped a good deal of the punishment that
fell to Sean as an elder son. But with Sean gone from
home, and no longer acting as a buffer, Peter had begun
to chafe under the heavy hand of discipline. Eventually
he ran off to visit his brother at school and never came
back. Later, when Sean returned to Wexford to take up
his duties, Peter had continued to roam.

Sean, Sean! he grieved. Why Sean? He had everything
to live for. Finally, his hands still shaking, Peter forced
himself to focus on the main details of MacDonald's
letter:

Your Lordship,
    This is to inform you of the change in your
family's fortunes. On May 29, 1864, your father and

brother both went down aboard the *Silver Dolphin* while crossing the Irish Sea. At a time estimated around two in the morning, she was struck broadside by a barge and took on water through a deep gash below the water line.

Your brother leaves behind his wife and three children, all cared for under a trust established by your father two years ago.

The title and lands of your father's estate automatically pass to you as the surviving male heir of majority age . . .

Peter scanned two pages outlining his father's various holdings, including both real property and liquid assets deposited in Belfast, Wexford, London, and Boston banks.

As he came to the bottom of the fourth page, he broke down and wept.

Needless to say, your mother has been heartbroken over this sad turn of events. It is her devout wish that you return to Wexford at the earliest possible moment, as it would give her great comfort to see you again, safe and well.

Please advise as to your wishes in all the above matters as soon as possible.

I remain,

Your ob't servant,
Gerald MacDonald

Peter was still sitting, his head buried in his hands, when a knock sounded at the door. Supposing it to be the bellboy, he called, "Come in."

The door opened quietly.

"Mr. O'Rourke?" a timid voice asked behind him.

Without looking around, Peter gestured to the nightstand. "Aye, just set the tray down, and get out."

An uncomfortable silence was followed by an awkward clearing of the throat.

Peter glanced around to see a small man blinking at him from behind wire spectacles.

"Uh, Mr. O'Rourke, I've come from Judge Turner's courtroom to serve you with a restraining order." He tapped Peter with a rolled document, dropped it on the desk, and fled.

"Here now! What's this?" Half-rising, Peter marked the man's hasty retreat into the dim corridor. He stared incredulously at the legal injunction lying atop the litter of legal papers from Ireland.

Quickly he unrolled the brief missive from the local court. He saw his name at the top listed as the Defendant, below Homer McGillacutty's name as Complainant, and groaned. This was not his lucky day.

"Kate's Old Man is suing me?" he questioned the air. His eyes went to the first paragraph, and he went deeper into shock.

So much for promises made in good faith. He was being ordered not to set foot on the McGillacutty's premises or make any attempt to contact their daughter.

The second paragraph explained the first:

Whereas the above-named Defendant is estranged from his wife, Mary Katherine McGillacutty O'Rourke, this petition is entered before the City Magistrate of Virginia City, Nevada, this 27th day of October, anno Domini 1864, pending further legal action.

Signed,
Judge Turner

Peter balled up the piece of paper and pitched it into the waste receptacle with an earthy expletive he reserved

solely for use in the most rare and trying of circumstances. He crossed to the bed and cast himself, still in
his damp clothes, across the pale blue chenille
bedspread.

So Kate considered herself estranged, did she? Damn
the little hypocrite! She'd seemed eager enough to get
her hot little hands all over him this morning. Peter
passed a hand over his face, wondering how he should
interpret this latest injunction. Exactly where *did* he and
Kate stand? Were they really finished? Or was this just
the Old Man's way of keeping them apart?

He lay there, staring up at the ceiling, emotionally
wrung out. Bloody hell! What was a man to do when so
much bad news hit, all at once? Immediately he rejected
the first idea that popped into his head: getting roaring
drunk would only make him feel worse when he sobered
up. Besides, he still felt an obligation to Nina and Henri
to finish out the week at Maguire's.

Another knock sounded at his door. Peter tensed,
then swung his legs off the bed; the mattress springs
giving a twang of protest. In two long strides, he reached
the door and nearly wrenched off the knob in his haste.

The bellhop and another boy stood in the hall, surrounded by buckets of steaming hot water. They gaped
up at his scowling face, clearly intimidated. "Uh . . . your
bath, sir."

Relieved that they weren't the bearers of more bad
news, Peter waved them toward the private cubicle off
his bedroom. "In there." He rummaged in his pockets
and came up with some jingle, figuring he might as well
be miserable in style. "Here, lads! Bring me a roast beef
sandwich," he said, "and a box of the hotel's best cigars,
while you're at it."

"Yes, sir!" The boys dumped their buckets into the tub
and rushed out the door, colliding in their eagerness to
carry out his orders.

As Peter dropped soap and a cloth in the steaming
water and gathered toiletries, he realized he'd never

been faced with so many important decisions, all at the same time. A prestigious title and a fortune in English pounds—but what did that matter? No amount of prosperity or acclaim could soften the terrible blow he'd just received. Besides loving his father and brother, he'd also failed his mother in her time of sorrow.

The inconsolable ache of a misspent past rose up to accuse him again. In his mind's eye, the years spent away from his family rolled past him like a moving diorama. So many wrong turns! So much unfinished business between him and Sean and his father.

His knees crumpled, and he wept. A wall of silence closed around him, forever separating the damned and the dead. His life was heavily scored with regrets, the latest having to do with breaking the sad news to Jigger and the Diablo Camp crew. He had let everyone down, badly.

And Kate. What of her? For all he knew, she had turned from him as well. Yet to lose her was to be cut off from the sun. She flowed like liquid fire in his veins.

Though pulled in every direction, he must decide. Should he cut his emotional losses in Virginia City, take the first ship out of San Francisco, and sail for Ireland? Running his father's estate had never appealed to him, and he felt strongly averse to taking it over now.

Deep down, Peter sensed that his restless heart would find peace only in this far country, not in the land of his birth. He couldn't deny the problems he faced, if he stayed, but neither could he walk away from Kate.

Aye, he decided; it was a poor time to let guilt override his understanding of what he was about. Life had proved a hard schoolmaster, but he had learned not to fit molds other people sought to impose.

Peter stripped and bathed vigorously, as if to cleanse away more than the mud and grime of the storm raging outside. He stood on the brink of a bold new beginning. If he wanted to look back ten, even twenty years from now without regret, he must give free rein to his gut instinct.

Shaving again, since he wouldn't have time between rehearsal and performance, Peter tried to picture what the last few months must have been like for his mother and Sean's widow, Patsy. He would write them tonight, explain his situation, and express his condolences. He credited his mother with wisdom; he had inherited the same independent streak that infected her.

If anything, Patsy and her three fatherless children had the greatest need. Most likely, his mother had invited Patsy and her children to move into the main house; that would be so like her! Perhaps he could see to his mother's ongoing needs by setting up a life estate, while placing the estate in a conservatorship for Sean's children. After all, they would have been the rightful heirs, if Sean had lived.

Aye, Peter decided, he would give his mother full reign over the handling of his affairs in Ireland. Better that she keep herself occupied. It was quite understandable that she wanted to see him, and he had no doubt he would, in time, return for a visit. At this point, however, Peter saw his future clearly mapped out for him in the American West.

He and Kate might never make a go of it. He had no crystal ball. So far, the cards seemed stacked against them. Even so, he'd been dealt an exceptional hand and, God willing, before he cashed in his chips, he hoped to make a bloody fortune in lumber. If for nothing else, he could thank his father-in-law for educating him to that fact.

The young boys he'd sent off to get his lunch returned. He ate, surprised to discover he had a voracious appetite, despite the news he'd just received.

Descending to the lobby later, refreshed physically, if not emotionally, Peter borrowed an umbrella from Mr. Davenport's dresser and crossed C Street to the Emporium halfway down the block, with a mind to replenish his wardrobe.

Using money McGillacutty had handed him along with his walking papers, he purchased two pairs of whip-cords, a pair of canvas coveralls, three shirts—one a fine white wool, the others heavy wool plaid—plus socks, long johns, a pair of sheepskin gloves, and a muffler.

As he plunked down his money on the counter, thoughts of his father-in-law's parting gift to him, the re-straining order, returned to rankle him. *No, godammit!* he thought. No sonuvabitch was going to write off Peter Casey O'Rourke. And no worthless piece of paper was going to keep him away from Mary Kate. Not as long as she was his wife. Not without a fight.

A steely glint entered Peter's pale green eyes. It was time he let Kate know that she was solely his responsi-bility. Turning, he surveyed the racks of feminine ready-made delicacies with an experienced eye. He se-lected a half dozen silk chemises, choosing the most provocative in stock. Nothing pure and chaste for that little spitfire! Everything that went next to her skin should send a message, loud and clear: his claim on her, body and soul, was irrevocable. She belonged to him, "till death do us part," and he had no intention of letting her forget it.

A dozen pairs of silk stockings, including black ones with embroidered clocks, and lace garters in three colors joined the pile of fripperies on the counter.

Peter continued to fish around, heartily dissatisfied with the cotton pantalettes on the shelf. He intended that Mary Katherine should look every inch a lady on the outside. But by God, those svelte curves deserved to be covered by something every bit as sensuous as she is!

A chicly dressed whore from Julia Bulette's Palace swept past him, her expensive Parisian perfume beckon-ing. Like a bird dog, Peter drifted behind the woman to the back of the store, to a rack of lingerie not on general display. Peter grinned, watching the woman zero in on an outrageous pair of black and purple lace drawers. A

little risqué for Kate, but more helpful to his cause than
the stony-faced woman behind the front counter.

Elbow to elbow with the infamous Julia's employee,
Peter sorted through laces, satins, and silks in every
imaginable size, design, and color. It was easy to see why
Virginia City's red light district prospered, Peter laughed
to himself. The items on their exclusive little rack were
far more exciting than those on display for the store's
more respectable ladies!

Peter transferred a revealing teal blue chemise from
the collection to his growing pile. Next, four silk pantalettes with daring drop drawers and loads of garters
sailed through the air. Each garment was chosen to em-
phasize the warm tones in Kate's pearly white skin. He
wanted everything to remind Kate how she felt when he
caressed and possessed her.

Indulging a personal whim, Peter added ivory hair
combs, a silver hairbrush set with matching mirror, delicately scented dusting powder, and lilac-scented imported
soaps.

Never before had Peter embarked on such a shopping
adventure for a woman. As it progressed, he found himself infused with new gusto. A sense of mischief crept
into his buying as well. He wanted to surprise, even
shock Kate a little.

He also wanted to send her father a strong message:
that Mary Katherine wasn't his little girl anymore. She
was a grown woman with all the appetites and needs of a
healthy, venturesome female! Let McGillacutty stick *that*
in his cigar and smoke it, by God!

Finally even Peter recognized he had overdone his se-
lection of gossamer sheers, silks, and peep-show laces. If
he ever hoped to get her out of her father's house, Kate
needed something to wear over all this. Moving over to
the racks of current fashions, he started by selecting
three warm dresses for everyday wear. For entertaining
at home or visiting, he chose an emerald taffeta shot
through with gold and silver threads, and a light blue

wool trimmed in velvet. Surely that was enough, he thought, to help Mary Kate escape the confines of her father's house in proper style!

As he pulled out his purse to pay, a high-necked pearl gray faille with pearl buttons from throat to waist caught his eye. The tucks and ruching, the nipped-in waist, and high bustline would set off her figure to perfection, just as an understated but elegant frame set off a Gainsborough or a Reynolds portrait.

It followed logically that she would need a matching wrap. Peter threw in a silver fox capelet, then rolled his eyes as he made a quick tally of his extravagance thus far. Thank God his next stop was the Wells Fargo Bank!

But he was on a roll, and he wasn't quite ready to stop. Peter decided he needed one more little something to top it all off.

On impulse, he tried on a saucy straw hat, piled high with tulle. Delicious forget-me-nots, white rosebuds, and lilies of the valley dripped over the brim. It was a fun hat. He could easily picture Mary Kate in such a creation.

"How does it look?" He winked at the scandalized clerk behind the counter. The hat was a trifle overstated, but surely every woman needed one totally outlandish bit of whimsy? Aye, just the right chapeau to raise a young wife's spirits.

Wearing the flowery creation with the price tag dangling over his left ear, Peter made one more quick survey. "Do you have this in pale yellow? he asked, holding up a low, square-necked gown for the woman's inspection.

"Yes, I believe we do," she said and disappeared into the back storeroom. A moment later, she returned in triumph with the required item. "For your sweetheart?" she asked.

Peter shook his head. "Wife." He snagged a sheer lavender lace peignoir with a matching nightgown from a window display. "I'll take this, also," he told the clerk, whose eyes steadily grew larger with each item added to his shopping spree.

"While you tally up the bill and box everything," Peter told her. "I'll just step next door to the bank. I think I may need a bit more coin than I brought in with me."

Succumbing to his dimpled charm, the woman beamed. "Your wife must be very beautiful for you to be so generous."

"Aye, that she is," said Peter. "Here's a deposit, and I'll be right back with the rest." He peeled off some bills. "Send everything to Mrs. Peter O'Rourke. She's staying with her parents, the McGillacuttys on B Street."

"Of course, Mr. O'Rourke." The woman busied herself with calculations, clearly overwhelmed by her good fortune. Usually people stayed home on a rainy day, but her business today was better than it had been in a week!

Peter pointed to a sewing kit and cookbook on the shelf behind the counter. "Those, too." He squinted through the smoke from the cigar clenched in his white teeth and added, as an afterthought, "Would you have a copy of Knowlton's *The Private Companion of Young Married People?*"

The clerk blushed to her eyeballs, looked swiftly around to make sure none of her other customers had overheard his request. Wordlessly she produced from beneath the counter a medium-sized volume wrapped in a plain brown paper.

"Our last copy," she whispered, glancing furtively at a woman in widow's weeds, who stood glaring at the fripperies and laces piled high in plain view.

Peter removed his cigar from his lips and bowed graciously to the widow. "My wife and I are just starting out," he announced, dimples flashing. "'Tis best to break a wife in right, I always say."

"Humph!" The woman turned her back on the scallywag, certain that she'd spied his photograph in the *Territorial Enterprise.* Probably a criminal, despite the extraordinary looks his Creator had endowed him with, her attitude declared.

The clerk finished adding everything up. "That comes

to a grand total of . . . let me see"—she placed her decimal point with a flair—"seventeen hundred eight-nine dollars and thirty-seven cents."

"The wisest money I've spent on a woman," Peter quipped without batting an eyelash. "Here, let me autograph that cookbook."

Using the salesclerk's pen, Peter wrote in a bold, sweeping hand:

To the woman I want to see over the breakfast table
for the rest of my life. A belated wedding gift.

Love,
Peter.

He blotted the flyleaf. "Wrap everything carefully so it won't get wet," he cautioned, surveying his purchases with satisfaction. "I'll be right back."

Peter picked up his own clothing purchases, which had cost under seventy-five dollars, and headed for the Wells Fargo Bank. Sidestepping the teller's cage, he sought out the manager.

Introducing himself, he laid the draft in front of the manager, whose bored indifference immediately changed to fawning cooperation. "It will take a few days to verify the current rate of exchange from English pounds to American currency, Mr. O'Rourke."

"I'm in something of a hurry," Peter explained. "I'll be making a sizable investment and trust you can advance me a few thousand on this?"

"Of course," the manager said. "How much will you require?"

"Right away, eighteen hundred. I'd like an additional thousand in cash first thing tomorrow morning. And a bank draft for—let's say, fifty thousand—by tomorrow afternoon. I plan to make an offer on some land," Peter said, his plans taking shape even as he spoke.

"That shouldn't pose a problem," the manager said. His manner clearly indicated that he didn't find Peter's demands out of line. "Can the bank assist you in any other way?"

"I shall require the services of an attorney," Peter said, "a man who can hold a client's business in strictest confidence."

"Our bank uses a very fine attorney," said the manager, pleased to make the recommendation. "Mr. Daly. His office is located next to the assay office."

Peter rose and shook the manager's hand. "Now, if you will write out a receipt and give me eighteen hundred dollars, I shall be on my way. I have other pressing business at four."

"Certainly, Mr. O'Rourke." The manager quickly produced the cash, a bank draft, and a handwritten receipt on bank stationery. "What time will you drop by for the thousand dollars tomorrow morning?"

"You open at nine o'clock?" At the manager's nod, Peter smiled. "I'll be here at nine fifteen." He headed for the door that separated the manager's office from the outer public area, then paused. "By the way, I'd like that thousand dollars all in nickels."

CHAPTER 24

"Come in, Mr. Daly," Mrs. McGillacutty greeted the lawyer, and whisked him through her front door speedily to avoid filling the entire downstairs with a polar blast. "My husband is with Mr. Sharon, but he should be able to see you soon."

Mr. Daly self-consciously followed the slender matron across a fine wool carpet into the parlor. He tried not to muddy the muslin runner she had spread from the front door to the hearth. A great many visitors had been coming and going, judging by the smudges on the runner.

Madeleine smiled graciously at the small man shivering in front of her fire. "You look as if a cup of tea might be just the thing, Mr. Daly."

"Yes, ma'am," he brightened appreciatively. "'Tis a mite c-c-cold out there this morning."

"I won't be gone a minute," she said and rustled away to fetch him a cup.

While he waited for McGillacutty to be free, the door knocker sounded again.

"I'll get that, Mother," a fluting young voice rang out from upstairs. She came racing past the open parlor door, her flaming hair flying loose about the shoulders of an ill-fitting green dress. Catching sight of yet another guest, she slowed up long enough to say, "Oh, hello. I'm

Katherine O'Rourke. I hope my mother has made you comfortable?"

Daly bowed, interested to see his client's wife in person. "Thank you, ma'am. I am Tom Daly, a local attorney. But don't let me delay you in answering the door."

"Yes, of course. Please excuse me. Whoever is knocking is certainly persistent!"

She flung open the front door. On the doorstep, surrounded by two dozen wrapped boxes and bundles, stood two freckle-faced young deliverymen.

"Special delivery for Mrs. O'Rourke," said the duo.

Mary Kate's green eyes grew wide with surprise. She turned from the deliverymen to summon help. "Mother, come quick!"

All the way at the back of the house, Madeleine could feel sub-zero temperatures whoosh through the hallway. "For pity sakes, Mary Katherine, close that door!" Wiping her hands on her apron, she rushed toward the front door.

Katherine pointed to the huge stack of packages on the veranda. "Did you and Papa buy all this?"

Madeleine stopped in her tracks, dumbfounded. She looked at the two young men standing like early Christmas elves, while all the heat in her house was sucked right out the door.

"We're from the Emporium, ma'am."

Madeleine looked at the young fools on her porch, who in turn were gawking at Mary Kate as if they'd never seen red hair before. Her daughter, in a similar state of paralysis, gaped at the mysterious boxes and bundles. On each her name was clearly marked.

"Don't just stand there," Mrs. McGillacutty said, gesturing to the two. "Bring everything inside."

Katherine and her mother stood back, while the pair and Mr. Daly carried in garment bags and cardboard boxes of every conceivable shape—flat, long, narrow, short, and just plain enormous! Stacked around the vestibule and taking up half the parlor besides, the assortment was impressive indeed.

"Sign here, Mrs. O'Rourke," said the taller one, as he stuck an invoice under Madeleine's nose.

Katherine stepped forward. "I am Mrs. O'Rourke." Taking the man's pencil, she glanced at the invoice on the clipboard and felt her knees buckle. The price was staggering. "Are you certain you have the right house?" she asked in disbelief.

The man rechecked the address at the top of the invoice and nodded. "Yes, ma'am." He fished around in the large pouch slung over his shoulder and produced two books. "I was told to deliver these to you, personal."

Katherine took the volume in brown paper and a copy of *The Pioneer Woman's Gourmet Cookbook*—the title seemed such a contradiction in terms—and clutched them to her breast.

"We'll be goin' now, ma'am." The men ducked their heads and backed out the door, stuffing their hands into woolen mittens.

"Thank you for coming," Mary Kate called after them. She grinned at her mother, who looked equally puzzled by such extravagance, when the mine was going broke. "Now who do you suppose—?"

Madeleine shook her head. "I'm sure I don't know. This snowstorm has kept us housebound since yesterday, and your father's been busy trying to negotiate a loan."

Katherine walked around the boxes, nibbling the tip of her finger, her brow furrowed. Hesitantly she touched the wrappings on a large box. "Maybe . . . Oh, I just— well, I should hate to open everything, in case it's all a big mistake." She glanced uncertainly at her mother.

Mr. Daly smiled. "How can you find out who sent them if you don't open them?"

Her mother picked up a hatbox. "What possible harm could there be in opening one?" she asked.

With a nervous laugh, Kate set down her books. Opening the box, she brought out a straw bonnet piled high with

tulle and gay spring flowers. "Oh, this is darling!" she ex-
claimed and rushed to preen in the mirror over the mantel.
She caught Tom Daly's admiring look over her shoulder.
"Do you like it?"

"Just what's needed on a day like this," he said. "A bit
of spring cheer. And I've never seen a lady better suited
to wearing it," he added gallantly.

"Thank you, sir!" Tossing her curls, Kate felt her spirits rise. She rummaged around for another package to
open. "Just one more, in case it all has to go back to the
Emporium," she told her mother and selected a stylish
box decorated with a purple and yellow bow.

Opening the lid, she tore through layers of white
tissue and drew forth a lavender peignoir and matching
nightgown. Blushing, she turned to her mother.

"Perhaps it's from your husband?" Madeleine suggested.

"Really, Mother! Peter couldn't afford all this." Katherine put the lovely apparel back in the box with a reluctant
sigh and sat down on a small chair in the midst of the
boxes. "We shall just have to wait and ask Papa."

Madeleine remembered her duties as a good hostess.
"Oh, Mr. Daly! I forgot your tea."

Kate sat examining her manicure and avoiding Mr.
Daly's look of amusement. For something to do, she
picked up the cookbook and fanned the pages, most still
uncut. Who could have sent her such a wonderfully frivolous hat? And a peignoir set and a cookbook. It seemed
an odd assortment of gifts, and highly improper, too. A
girl simply did not accept such things from an outsider.
Her eye fell on a recipe for opossum stew. She turned
the page. Beavertail soup and johnnycake and sorghum
bread and winter bean porridge sprang off the pages at
her. She giggled, scarcely believing the instructions for
preparing marinated elk's tongue.

"Oh, this is classic!" She snorted through her nose and
nearly fell off her chair laughing. "Three jiggers of
whiskey, wild sage, salt and pepper, jalapeno chilis, and
a dash of Tabasco sauce." She rolled her eyes and con-

tinued reading. "Combine with water and simmer one elk's tongue, thinly sliced, for four hours. Save the drippings and serve with mashed potatoes on the side."

"Myself, I'd take the whiskey straight," said Mr. Daly with a poker face.

Madeleine leaned over her daughter's shoulder and tapped the recipe on the opposite page. "Now this one I heartily recommend: pork chops baked in a slow oven with apples and potatoes. Your father really likes it."

Katherine closed the book and offered it to her mother. "Here. A gift for you."

"I have a copy." Madeleine smiled. "Keep it, dear. You never know when a cookbook might come in handy."

"Oh, fiddlesticks," said Kate, flipping through the table of contents. Just the names of the dishes were entertainment enough. "Oh, look!" she cried as she spied the flyleaf. Glancing up excitedly at her mother, she said, "It's from Peter!" Silently she read Peter's salutation. Her eyes misted and her throat tightened as she came to the words "Love, Peter."

"Excuse me," she said quietly and stood up. "Mother, I'll be upstairs for a few minutes." Taking the cookbook and the book done up in a plain brown wrapper, Kate walked out into the hall and up the stairs in a daze. She couldn't imagine what had possessed Peter. He had practically bought out the Emporium! Where did he get the money? Nearly eighteen hundred dollars, the invoice said. Somehow she doubted actors earned that much.

There must be a logical explanation. Maybe he won a large sum in an all-night poker game. Or—why, of course! He must have used the money she bribed him with to marry him, as a down payment!

But that still didn't explain why he sent her a silly old book full of indigestible recipes. She was no pioneer woman. Still, it *was* sweet of him to be thinking of her.

He should stick to hats and nightgowns, she thought, and cast herself lengthwise across her bed, still clutching the books to her heart. Clothes were ever so much more practical.

Rolling onto her stomach, she stared down at the book wrapped in brown paper. Probably a book about polishing silver, scrubbing floors, and cleaning oven grease. What else would come in such a drab wrapper? *Better get this over with,* she decided, gritting her teeth. *If he wants a domestic goddess, so be it.*

Rip, tear, out it came.

Katherine turned over the red leather-bound copy, prepared for some of the dullest reading this side of the Continental Divide. Expecting another charming inscription on the flyleaf, Kate opened the cover and read, "*The Private Companion of Young Married People. An Authoritative Explanation of the Medical Facts,* by Dr. Charles Knowlton." Underneath was an innocuous sketch of two heads, male and female, with their lips pressed together in a chaste kiss.

"Oh, drat!" she said, instantly frustrated, for all the pages were uncut. Determined lest the pursuit of knowledge be thwarted, Katherine scrambled off the bed. Soon a sharp pair of scissors was clearing the way for further education.

Feeling like a cat with her tail set on fire, Katherine glanced guiltily toward her bedroom door. What if her parents caught her reading such a scandalous book? They would be livid!

She raced frantically through the first twenty pages with growing anxiety. There were chapters on birth control, fertility, the prevention of disease, and other "inconveniences" of marital relations. The rest of the book described pleasures a couple could give each other in the privacy of their bedroom. *Oh, my word!* Mary Kate gulped, and her face grew hot, and then hotter still. Without even touching her, Pete had set off a shockwave of deeply erotic longings. She began to hyperventilate, more and more with every page she turned.

Suddenly she heard her father's voice through the

laundry chute out in the upstairs hall. "Mary Kate, get down here this instant!"

Katherine grabbed the offending book, wondering where to hide it. Quick! She stuffed it under her mattress and smoothed the lace bedspread.

Her heart pounded as she heard his footsteps on the stairs. If only she was half the actor Peter was! Kate took a quick peek at her flaming face in the mirror. She looked guilty as sin! It would not take a genius to know what wicked thoughts lurked in her head. One look, and her father would know all!

Her bedroom door flew open, and her father's beaming face appeared. "Daughter! Quit your moping! Our money problems are solved!"

Kate looked startled, not comprehending his joviality. Had he not come upstairs to give her a lecture? She glanced guiltily toward her bed and then decided to try looking nonchalant.

"Come downstairs, Kate. I want you to join your mother and me in a toast."

Grateful that some extraordinarily good news had saved her hide, Katherine followed her father downstairs. In the parlor, her father's attorney, Jacob Morrell, stood next to Mr. Daly, whom she'd just met. Everyone was smiling.

"May I present my daughter, Mary Katherine," Homer said genially to one and all. His warm hand at the small of Kate's back propelled her across the room. "This is Mr. Morrell, whom you already know," he said, "and this is Mr. Tom Daly, a sharp new lawyer in town."

Katherine extended her hand. "We've already met. How are you, Mr. Daly?"

Her mother entered with a tray of wineglasses and an open bottle of sherry, which she set on a small side table. "Darling! Did your father tell you? Mr. Daly has brought your father an offer that will keep the mine open."

"That's wonderful." Katherine managed a smile. "How did this come about?"

"Mr. Daly represents a wealthy client—a naturalist, I believe," Homer enthused, as his wife served claret to Mr. Daly and Mr. Morell. "Imported. I hope you like it."

"I represent the Earl of Wickstead," Tom Daly explained with a smile. "A man of many interests and talents. Recently he fell in love with the High Sierras during a hunting trip. He has decided to settle in these parts, more or less permanently."

"Where is your client from?" Madeleine politely asked.

"Ireland," said Daly. "Always had a bit of the wanderlust, he told me, until he came out West."

"Fascinating," said Katherine. Everywhere she turned lately, she was bumping into more Irishmen. She accepted a glass of claret. "Obviously the Earl of whatchamacallit—"

"Wickstead, Mary Kate," her mother whispered, almost as if they were in church.

"Oh, yes, Wickham. So what did you do, Father? Sell this wealthy but slightly addled gentleman some of your burned-out timberland, sight unseen?"

McGillacutty shot his daughter a warning glance. "Not at all, daughter. Seems the Earl took a fancy to owning a two hundred-and-forty-thousand-acre parcel of land along the Truckee River. Offered me a handsome price for it, too. Forty dollars an acre."

Attorney Morrell chuckled. "A helluva price, just so he can build a hunting lodge."

Mr. Daly held up his glass to the light. "Ninety-six thousand is a mere pittance in the eyes of a true outdoorsman like my client."

"I propose a toast," said Homer, raising his glass. He winked at Maddy, touched his glass to hers first, then each of the others in turn. "To the Earl of Wickstead, a very fine fellow indeed."

"Here, here."

Katherine sipped her wine, pleasantly warmed by the spirits and the crackling fire on the hearth. She only half-listened to her father and the two lawyers chat about plans for the Lucky Strike mine. Although she was happy for her father's sudden good fortune, she wished her father's guests would stop making small talk, so she could haul all those intriguing boxes upstairs and see what else Peter had bought for her.

Soon Mr. Daly took his leave, and Katherine suddenly realized that her father and Jacob Morrell were waiting to speak with her.

"Too bad that old chap Wickstead already has a wife, Kate," her father laughed. "Otherwise I'd be tempted to marry you off."

Katherine gave him a scathing look. "I already have a husband, in case you've forgotten."

"Only until Mr. Morrell can arrange an annulment," Homer corrected.

"I believe I should have some say in the matter," Kate said, her cheeks burning.

Jacob Morrell cleared his throat discreetly. "Annulments require time, Homer. Sometimes years, since the Church must be petitioned to set aside the vows."

Katherine smiled triumphantly at her father, refusing to bow to his interfering tactics. "Annulment on what grounds? Nonconsummation? Really, Father! Surely you realize what a waste of time that would be." She gave a toss of her head.

"Perhaps we can prove fraud, then?" Morrell offered, trying to be helpful.

"The only fraud has been mine and my father's," Kate said. "Perhaps, since my husband is the injured party, he should be the one seeking your services, sir."

"Saints preserve us!" Homer put his wineglass down on the tray his wife held. "O'Rourke misrepresented himself when I hired him to supervise my lumber operations. If that's not fraud, I don't know what is."

"Then you *sue* him, Father!" Kate blazed, turning with tears of outrage to accuse her domineering parent. "The problem is, you and I were so busy trying to trap him into marrying me that we didn't think to ask why a man of his obvious intelligence would consent to getting mixed up in such a scheme."

"Mary Kate, this is neither the time nor the place for a family discussion," Homer cautioned, the veins standing out on his forehead.

Madeleine gracefully interposed herself between her two favorite battling redheads and handed Mr. Morrell his hat and coat. "Mr. Morrell, thank you for coming today to lend your assistance to my husband. I'm certain that if Kate requires legal assistance"—Maddy gave her husband a warning look—"she, and not my husband, will seek you out."

Mr. Morrell looked relieved. "I'll be on my way, then. Good day, Homer. Ladies."

Homer and Katherine barely noticed as Madeleine escorted the attorney to the door.

Mary Kate started picking up her packages. "These are from Peter," she informed her father. "He didn't have to send them, but he did. Considering how you've treated him, I think he's behaved very decently, don't you?"

"I won't have a damned actor for a son-in-law!" Homer roared. "And you're going to send all this stuff back."

"I am not." Katherine clutched a huge garment bag to her like a shield. "I love Peter O'Rourke, and you are not to interfere with my marriage. I don't know why Peter would even want me, after the way we've all behaved, but it's up to *us* to decide the future of our marriage, not you, Papa," Kate said, surprised how calm she felt under pressure. "If and when I need your advice, I shall let you know."

Madeleine entered the parlor in time to hear her daughter's declarations. It was the first time she'd ever heard Katherine speak her mind so decisively. For once, Mary Kate wasn't throwing a tantrum. She was defiant, but firm.

"Homer, I think our Mary Kate has come of age," she said, placing a gentle hand on her husband's arm.

"I think I know what's best for our daughter, Maddy," Homer growled, disguising his displeasure behind the business of lighting another cigar. "Anyway, I doubt that worthless, skirt-chasing husband of yours will be around town much longer," he predicted, a triumphant gleam in his eye.

Katherine stopped in her tracks, her arms piled high with the packages from the Emporium. "And why not, pray tell?"

"Because I had Morrell serve him with a restraining order. If he steps foot on this property or tries to see you, he goes to jail. Thirty days." He blew a smoke ring, glad to set his feisty daughter back on her fancy bustle.

"Then I shall go see him!" Kate said. "Or do you plan to throw your own daughter in jail, too?"

"Give it up, Kate. He's all wrong for you."

Katherine passed her gifts to her mother, burying the smaller woman beneath a stack. She sidled up to her father, hips swaying, and poked his big barrel chest with her forefinger. "You put Peter in jail, Papa, and I'll join him there. I shall swear on a stack of Bibles to the judge that you put an innocent man in jail. You will wind up a laughing stock in this town."

"Be sensible, daughter!" Homer ran his fingers through his hair making it stand on end. "Do you think I worked hard all my life, just so you can throw your life away on some worthless charmer? Kate, as an actor's wife, you wouldn't have a roof over your head. No security, cheap boarding house rooms, immoral companions. What kind of a life is that?"

Kate paused, seeing the pain in her father's eyes and knowing she had hurt him deeply. "It's my life, Papa," she whispered. "Can't you understand that?"

Madeleine's beautiful blue eyes darted back and forth, the only part of her that was visible above the parcels. "My two dearest darlings, let's not argue. All your father and I want, Kate, is your happiness." Her eyes pleaded with Homer. "Please, let's give this time."

"I'd rather rot in purgatory with an extra thousand years tacked on, than see Mary Kate ruin her life with

O'Rourke," said Homer with a deep scowl. "I'll not rest till the man's safely out of her life." He consulted his watch, needing an excuse to escape these two termagants who plagued him worse than a hive of maddened bees. *Women, bah!* he thought.

"No, Father!" Kate's face turned pale with fright. "Let me talk to Peter and see what he says. If he wants an annulment or a divorce, I-I won't say another word."

"I forbid you to see him, Kate," Homer said, looking fierce. "You're not to leave this house without my permission."

Oh, yes, I will, Father. Beneath carefully lowered lashes, Katherine thought: mutiny! She *would* go to Peter, even if she had to sneak out to do it!

"If you two are quite finished," sighed Madeleine, "I'd like to tidy up. Mary Kate, will you help me carry some of these packages up to your room?"

Homer flicked his ash into the fireplace with a snort. He deplored the unfair tactics females resorted to. Striking mine workers, union toughs, and knock-down drag outs he could handle. Tears and accusing looks never failed to tear him up inside.

"I think I'll catch a late lunch downtown," he muttered, heading for the hall coatrack. "But Kate better not think she's off the hook."

As he left the house Katherine glared out the window at his broad back. "He refuses to listen," she said glumly.

Madeleine went to her daughter and put a comforting arm around her. "He means well, but he's dead wrong. You and I both know it, Kate."

Katherine burst into tears. "He's ruining my life!"

A mischievous smile played around her mother's lips. "Let's unpack all these lovely things, and then I'll send for the liveryman to return one of these boxes to the Emporium."

"I'm not giving anything back," said Kate, thinking she would have to fight her mother as well. "They may be all I ever have to remember Peter by."

Madeleine laughed merrily. "Of course you'll keep

everything. But this large box, once we empty it"—she pointed to one nearly her daughter's height—"this must go back."

"Empty?" asked Kate, failing to understand.

"Of course, or you'll never fit inside. Once you get inside the Emporium's storeroom, you can just slip down the street to the hotel and see Peter."

With a wild shriek, Katherine threw her arms around her mother, lavishing her with hugs and kisses. "You are a positive genius, Mother!"

"Thank you," her mother said, recovering from Kate's affectionate onslaught. "Now hurry, before your father gets back."

"I love you so much!" Kate burst out. "I promise you, I won't disgrace you and Papa."

"I know that, darling." Madeleine patted Kate's cheek. "Follow your heart, Mary Kate. And leave your father to me. I can handle him." She smiled and then went down to the kitchen for a pair of scissors and a strong cord suitable for resealing a sturdy cardboard packing box.

CHAPTER 25

The trip in the back of Mr. Ferguson's wagon didn't go exactly according to plan.

For one thing, the driver, Willard Ellis, suffered terribly from chilblains. Like many old-timers around the territory, he relied heavily on spirits to keep his blood properly thawed, and a horrendous thirst was upon him that blizzardy day in late October 1864. For another, he could see no earthly reason for that uppity society woman Mrs. McGillacutty to bring a man out in subzero temperatures just to return a few dresses to the Emporium.

Ellis's irritation was further compounded when he found himself saddled with nearly a hundred and twenty pounds of merchandise to be returned, all in one oversized box. Staggering under the weight, he lurched unsteadily and slid down the McGillacutty's icy steps. Landing in a snowdrift, he cursed loudly.

"Thank you very much, ma'am," he sarcastically told the lady of the house. He picked himself up and dusted the snow off his backside, not at all convinced her three-dollar gratuity made it worth the effort.

"Have a care, Mr. Ellis. That merchandise must be returned within the half hour," said Madeleine, following him out onto the veranda to make sure her daughter's destiny wasn't about to suffer an odd turn of the screw.

"Ain't the first package I ever delivered," said Ellis. Shouldering the slightly dented box, he continued down the icy, snow-packed walkway and heaved the rejected merchandise into the back of his wagon.

Cursing like the former muleskinner he was, old Willard commiserated loudly with his horse and headed straight for Gallagher's Saloon at the lower end of D Street. It would take a pint of white lightning, straight, to keep his blood moving on a nasty day like this, he told himself. Mrs. McGillacutty's merchandise be damned!

For forty-five minutes, Ferguson's livery wagon stood parked in the alley behind Gallagher's. Meanwhile Willard sat with his drinking cronies around the potbelly stove, warming his heels and buying a round of drinks with Mrs. McGillacutty's three dollars.

By the time the old man had properly cleared his sinuses and thawed his chilblains, his cargo had vanished. At least the contents had. Scratching his head over the torn-up box left propped against the saloon's trash barrel, Willard decided to call it a day. Hell, it never was much of a day, anyway. He staggered back inside, in time to hear Old Man Merriwether talk about the time he outfought a grizzly bear in Gizzard Gulch eight winters ago.

Right away Mary Katherine knew her mother's plan had gone awry. Ten minutes of listening to honky-tonk piano playing, raucous male laughter, and the frequent dumping of glass bottles into a nearby trash receptacle convinced her of that. Well! She wasn't going to freeze to death in a back alley, while some rum-soaked driver guzzled a gallon of firewater.

Fortunately, Mary Kate had dressed warmly, or she might never have survived to fight her way out of the sturdy container. In record time, she kicked, punched, and tore her way to freedom. She emerged from the

Emporium's sturdy packaging a complete shambles, but nevertheless triumphant!

Ignoring the pair of doxies who eyed her silver-fox cape and brand new gray faille, which was nowhere near warm enough for the blustery winds, Kate collected her belongings and started heading toward the center of town, a half mile back.

Shouts of "Hey, Red!" and "Baby, come on in, and keep me warm," and "Lost, sugar?" followed her through the red light district. As Kate hurried along, the sky grew even more ominous under lowering storm clouds; it would soon be dark. She rushed past seamy barroom doors, dodging around the few unfortunates who shared the slippery sidewalk with her.

Quickening her pace, Katherine crossed the street, head down against the biting wind. Her only thought was to escape her sordid surroundings and find Peter.

The next moment, a pair of steel arms in a heavily quilted jacket caught her around the waist, knocking the breath out of her. Swept off her feet, Katherine gasped indignantly and dropped her overnight case in the snow.

"Put me down this instant!" she hollered, struggling. Spitting and snarling, she tried to move her face away from the man's full and vile-smelling beard.

With a hearty guffaw, the man lifted her high and planted a whiskey-saturated kiss on her mouth. Dizzy from the fumes, Kate felt her stomach roll. She thought she would throw up. Then she wished she could; it would serve the man right.

"You filthy blockhead, unhand me this minute!" She kicked him in the legs with the sharp toes of her new boots. To her relief, he released her. She staggered off balance and landed in her backside in the snow next to her overnight case and its scattered contents.

"Aw, sweet thing, I was only funnin'," the man said. He saw her lace fripperies scattered in the snow and advanced with a fresh gleam in his eye.

Katherine scooted back hastily. "Stay away from me!"

she cried. Frantically she began to stuff her belongings back into her case, careful to keep an eye on him.

"Come on," the man wheedled. "Hell, I'll even shave and take a bath for a cute trick like you."

"Keep your distance, sir," Kate warned, wishing she had a gun.

Three other men had come out onto the sidewalk to watch the exchange. All around her in the gathering dusk, the street started coming alive with those who catered to the fleshpots of sin. Kate cringed inwardly, seeing the flicker of desire in the men's faces. She drew herself to her full height, determined not to show fear. "My father is Homer McGillacutty," she told the men.

"Sure he is." A man snickered in the shadows.

Seeing it was useless to debate the issue, Katherine picked up her case, ready to use it as a weapon, if need be, and set off down the street, only to have another man grab her arm. She swung around to give him a clout.

"Mrs. O'Rourke?" said a low, well-modulated male voice, full of surprise.

Katherine looked up and found herself staring into the kindly face of Father Manogue. "Oh, Father!" She was so relieved she nearly cast herself headlong into his arms. "What are you doing here?"

The priest smiled. "Another lost lamb," he said without batting an eye. He tucked her hand under his arm and began walking. "I find my flock scattered about in the strangest places."

Katherine blushed. "I've never been so glad to see anyone in my life," she admitted fervently, clinging to his arm.

"It's much too cold and dark for you to be out alone, my child," the priest said. "May I see you home?"

"No, please, Father. My father would skin me alive if he knew where I am headed."

Father Manogue moved at a steady pace, condensation streaming from his nostrils, as he guided Kate toward the center of town. They descended the hill toward C Street. "I must take you somewhere," he said practically.

"I was on my way to see my husband," Katherine said, "when I took a wrong turn."

"Ah, I see." The priest nodded with an understanding twinkle. "An interesting young man, that husband of yours. I spoke with him only two days ago."

Katherine's jaw dropped with surprise. "You did?"

"Quite concerned about his marriage, he was," said the priest. "If there is any way I can help . . . ?"

"Perhaps there is," Kate said, hope welling up from within. "Could we talk?"

"Of course, Mary Katherine." Without asking, he entered the International Hotel and headed for the dining room. "Will you join me for a cup of coffee? After my rounds this afternoon, I could do with a bit of thawing out. How about you?"

Confronted by the understanding cleric's warm brown eyes, Katherine burst into tears. "Father," she said, "I fear I've made a terrible mess of things."

Manogue leaned close and patted her half-frozen little hand. "Nothing that can't be fixed."

By the time Katherine finished pouring her heart out to Father Manogue, she felt a tremendous burden had lifted. She was ready to leave behind all her nagging guilt about vows spoken without love. She also had his assurance that Peter wanted their marriage as much as she did.

"I'm sure he'll meet you more than halfway, Mary Kate," the priest told her with an understanding smile. "Vows exchanged before God are not meant to be broken."

Katherine's eyes grew misty once again as the priest's thumb brushed her forehead in a quick parting benediction. Inside she was still trembling. With all her heart, she wanted to spill out the secret of her love to Peter. She wanted to beg his forgiveness and begin anew.

Crossing the lobby to the desk clerk, she introduced herself and inquired after Peter's whereabouts.

"He's been in and out all afternoon," the clerk said. He reached for the extra key to Room 208. "Perhaps you'd prefer to wait for him in his room?"

Katherine's face lit up. "Yes, I'd like that very much," she said eagerly. She would surprise Peter. "Perhaps you could arrange a late supper for us? Around eight o'clock? And a bottle of your best wine?"

The clerk beamed. "Happy to oblige."

Taking the key, Katherine ascended the stairs, planning how she would surprise Peter by wearing the peignoir set he had given her. Her heart was thumping with happiness as she glided along the dim corridor. This evening would mark the true beginning of their lives together.

Kate trembled with excitement as she reached the second floor. It wasn't the honeymoon suite where they'd spent their wedding night playing poker, but Room 208 would be forever etched in memory as the place she gave herself—mind, body, and spirit—to the man she loved.

Suddenly she heard a great deal of racket on the stairway, as if someone was dragging very heavy luggage up the stairs. Darting around the corner from Peter's room, she peered down the stairwell and saw Peter and another man, their backs to her, as they hauled a small trunk and several leather pouches up the stairs.

"Thanks, Merrick," she heard Peter say. They were dressed in bulky lumber jackets, with wide-brimmed hats pulled down over their eyes, a light dusting of snow on their shoulders. She didn't get a good look at the man with her husband.

Both men were clearly straining as they laboriously dragged the weighty pouches over to Peter's door. Peter propped two rifles against the wall and fished in his pocket for the key.

"Keep a sharp eye out," he told the other man and, with a slight grunt, threw two pouches over his broad shoulder.

The man called Merrick looked furtively up and down the corridor, and Kate saw that he stood, back to the room, one hand on his revolver at all times. *What in the world?* she wondered, mystified by the obvious tension in the stranger's stance. She shrank back into the shadows, listening to the drag and *chink* down the hallway.

"That should about do it," Peter said with a note of satisfaction in his low voice. "We'll get an early start in the morning."

"I'll have the wagon ready to go at daybreak."

Because Peter wasn't alone, Katherine retreated around the corner. She wondered if perhaps Peter was involved in something she wasn't supposed to know about.

A few minutes later the door to Peter's room opened and closed again. Then she heard quick steps going down the stairway, and knew the two men had left.

Kate so wanted her first moments alone with Peter to be special. As soon as she was certain they weren't coming right back up again, she made a beeline for Room 208. She rushed inside, locked the door, and set down her overnight case.

The dim glow of gaslight over the desk cast eery shadows across the floor. A couple of heavy tarpaulins, an old horse blanket, and a bridle had been tossed in the far corner beyond the bed. Kate turned up the gas lamp and surveyed the room. The two rifles leaned against the wall next to several crates of shells, two dozen medium-sized traps, some axes, and a box of assorted hand tools. A case of long knives with savage-looking scalping blades sent a shiver up Kate's spine. The articles that lined the walls looked more like the trappings of a primitive mountain man than an actor or even a lumberjack.

Oh, Peter, what are you doing? she worried. *Remember,* she told herself, *your love and loyalty are to the man, not his vocation.* But as she speculated on the mysterious items he had spirited up to his room, she felt a dread chill start to creep into her bones. Surely Peter wasn't planning to become a mountain man?

Except for a small box of books, she saw no sign that a civilized gentleman occupied the room. This odd turn of events tested every fiber of her being. She could not imagine anyone but a desperado skulking around with so many guns! Something terrible must have happened. Why else would Peter surround himself with such strange gear?

She gave her brain a mental cudgel, reminding herself of her original mission. She was there to tell Peter she wanted to be part of his life. To pledge her love and loyalty. To share his bed, bear him children. To go with him to the ends of the earth, if necessary. After her encouraging chat with Father Manogue, she had felt well satisfied that she could make such a commitment without fear.

Now she started entertaining serious second thoughts. She remembered the strange cookbook he'd sent her. Elk lips! Badger-tail stew. Seven recipes for rabbit stew. Pioneer recipes that virtually turned her stomach. This had to be a joke!

Katherine sank down on the edge of the bed, doubting herself even more than she did her husband. She wanted Peter to take her in his arms and promise that none of this strange equipment was going to be a part of their lives.

There must be a perfectly logical explanation, she told herself.

As for the guns and traps and knives—lots of men left such things lying around, didn't they? Well, didn't they? They must! Nobody she had ever met did. But that was no reason for rushing to wrong conclusions. She must simply—*gulp!*—trust Peter; she must hear him out.

With renewed determination, Kate carried her overnight bag into the bathing alcove, where she snapped open the tiny case and laid out her lavender peignoir. Pulling out a hairbrush, she set about preparing herself to greet her husband. Everything must be perfect, she thought, preening in front of the mirror.

So as not to let the room's rough gear detract, Katherine turned down the jet light and added a log to the fire for warmth. The dinner and champagne she had ordered arrived at eight. Still no sign of Peter, so she paid the waiter with coins from her purse. Finally, ravenous, she gave up stewing over Peter's whereabouts and polished off the entire supper for two.

Another hour passed and Peter still hadn't returned. Katherine began to pace. Perhaps she shouldn't have come unannounced. What could have delayed him? She knew the theater was dark, due to the storm. Father Manogue had told her the troupe had played their final performance last night to a small house; they had packed up and left that very morning.

Katherine left the champagne chilling on ice and sauntered into the alcove to change into her nightgown. She hung her gray faille behind the door, then debated whether to remove the pretty lace camisole and pantalettes, delicately clocked gray stockings, and lavender garters. But then Kate envisioned Peter undressing her, his hands praising and caressing her skin, so she slipped the sheer nightgown over her undergarments. The faint whisper of silk against her skin made her tingle with anticipation. Tonight . . . Tonight she and Peter would celebrate as never before.

A riot of uncertainty and questions raced through her mind as she waited, impatient for his return. She was about to give up and go to sleep when she heard a key turn in the lock.

Peter!

Katherine smiled in the dark, barely able to contain her excitement.

The door widened, and she watched him enter quietly. He locked the door from the inside, then tossed his hat and key on the desk.

Rubbing his hands, he shivered. "Must be twenty below tonight," she heard him mutter. He slouched across the room, still wearing his jacket, and threw two more logs on the fire, then stood a moment, moodily staring into the fire.

Poised on tiptoe, Kate was about to rush from her hiding place when Peter turned his head sharply. He frowned, his green eyes like hard glass in the firelight, and his hand went to the revolver lashed to his lean, muscled thigh.

Holding her breath, she watched Peter stealthily cross to the closet. Finding nothing, he visibly relaxed, though still on guard. Going to the window, he drew back the drape, checked the fire escape, and headed toward the horse blankets and canvas in the corner.

Katherine swallowed nervously. If Peter suspected a prowler, he might shoot at anything in the dark. Including her. Ask questions later. Kate knew she should step out and make her presence known, but she was suddenly afraid. Peter's manner seemed so sinister. She crouched, hearing her own heart thunder. She could only hope Peter wasn't trigger-happy.

She heard him rummaging in the corner under the tarp. There was the unmistakable jingle of coins being poured out. A great number of coins, by the sound of it. Followed a second later by Peter's satisfied, "Huh!"

He had money stashed in the room. Instantly a wave of fear invaded her. She listened to the tumbling of coins; as they were restored to the pouches on the floor, Peter's unexpected extravagance came surging back to haunt her. Earlier this evening he and his furtive companion had brought a great deal of money up to his room. Their actions had been shrouded in secrecy, almost the sort of thing criminals—of course! Why else would Peter prepare for a trek into the wilderness? Suddenly everything became perfectly clear: Peter had done something desperately wicked.

And now he was on the run. Of course! That explained

the weapons and mountain gear. He was planning to hide out until the coast was clear.

And unwittingly she had driven him to it.

Oh, if only I'd told him how I felt; been more supportive! Kate castigated herself bitterly, He had thought her incapable of loving him for himself. And now what chance they might have had for happiness was gone. Out the window. Lost forever.

That was why he had lavished her with all those clothes. He had foolishly thought to win her heart with material things.

Peter heard her strangled sob behind him and whirled. In the nick of time, he stopped himself from drawing his Colt .45. He braced himself as an ethereal negligeed nymph darted from the alcove and hurled herself into his arms.

"Oh, Peter darling!" Kate cried, and her arms closed around his neck in a wild stranglehold.

Startled, Peter frowned at the trembling beauty in his arms. "Kate! What on earth? How did you get in here?"

"Oh, Peter, I shall never forgive myself," Kate blubbered, clinging to him. She wept so inconsolably that Peter stood there dumbfounded.

"I see you got my gifts," he noticed instantly, and his hands skimmed over the filmy fabric that separated her warm flesh from his questing fingers.

With a howl of anguish, Katherine tore herself from his arms. She whirled, unaware that the firelight danced revealingly against her pearly skin. "How *could* you?" she demanded, stalking over to the tarpaulin. She pulled it back to expose the damning evidence. "You might have at least considered how this would affect me!"

Peter folded his arms across his chest. A puzzled frown marred his handsome brow. "I planned to see you first thing in the morning, Kate."

Katherine uttered a snort of disbelief. Stooping down, she tore open the pouches and ran her fingers through the coins, then looked up at him, her expression pale and troubled.

"Don't lie to me, Peter. I heard you and your partner-in-crime. You plan to sneak out of town tomorrow morning."

"Not before I said good-bye."

"Good-bye? How dare you? I came here tonight to tell you how much I love you, and that I'll follow you to the ends of the earth, if need be. Nothing matters except to be your wife." She overturned a pouch of coins onto the floor and threw the empty leather pouch at his head. "Wells Fargo Bank," she stormed. "You would do this to me?"

"I thought it was what you wanted," he said slowly.

"Peter, I cannot believe you said that!" Katherine felt desperate; her world was falling apart. Behind his clever mask of nonchalance, Peter still didn't seem concerned that she was so upset. "Money doesn't mean a thing to me. It can't make us happy. If you had given me half a chance, I could have told you that!"

Peter stood studying his wife. For all his dealings with the fairer sex, he was having difficulty fathoming her indignation. She was magnificent, towering in her rage! But not making a helluva lot of sense. Suddenly he realized that she hadn't made the connection yet between the money pouches and the thousand dollars she had paid him to marry her.

"Kate, I swear I was coming over in the morning," he said, "to give you every last nickel of this."

"You robbed the bank, and now you're telling me it's my fault?" Kate asked, both fists flying at him.

Peter caught her wrists and dragged her up against him, squirming and panting. "Robbed a bank?" he asked, confused.

Lips parted, she stared up at him. She nodded earnestly. "Peter, we have to give it all back! Before they notice it's missing."

"I can't do that," he said. The fact that Kate actually considered him capable of such a rash act brought out a

devilish streak that wasn't ever buried very far below the
surface anyway. Here she was, telling him in one breath
that she loved him, and in the very next, accusing him
of holding up the Wells Fargo Bank!

Thoroughly bedeviled, Peter decided to string his wife
along. When would he ever have a better chance to test
her love? Besides, she deserved a little of her own back.
She'd given him a rough go of it; it was time to turn the
tables. Just how loyal would she be if their backs really
were to the wall? he wondered.

Peter regarded her sadly and shook his head. "Ah,
lass, I took it this afternoon in broad daylight. The bank
clerk would recognize me in a second."

"No!" Katherine sagged against him. Her eyes grew
wild as she took in the numerous pouches. "There must
be thousands," she groaned.

"We shall just have to make a run for it." He held her
damp cheek against his throat and smothered a mischievous smile. He patted her back comfortingly and listened to her snuffle.

"I know! I'll get my father's lawyer to help us. He
seems to know all the right people. We'll give the money
back and take our chances." She gave him a little smile,
intending to be brave; she couldn't quite keep her chin
from wobbling, though.

Peter kissed her perky nose. "Would you wait for me,
if I went to prison, dear heart?"

"Of course, I would," Katherine said, and her body
shook at the thought of being separated for years and
years from this wonderful, utterly foolish man.

"I couldn't let you do that," Peter insisted. "You're
young. I want you to have a happy life, children, and a
loving husband to care for you."

Katherine pounded her fist against his chest. "No, no,
no!" she cried. "How could you even suggest such a
thing? I could never be happy with anyone but you!"

"You say that now . . ." His green eyes sparkled with

bold amusement, and she saw that he still doubted her sincerity.

"Peter," she proposed, a clever plan beginning to take root in her brain, "if you're worried about getting caught, we can leave the money with my mother. In fact, that's exactly what we shall do! I'll have Mother contact Papa's lawyer. He'll straighten this out. I know he can."

Peter sighed. "You make it sound so simple. What if there's a price on my head?"

"Then we'll hide out in the woods. Eventually they'll stop looking for you." Kate started to pace, her mind searching desperately for a way out of their predicament.

"Wait for the statute of limitations to run out?" Peter suggested helpfully.

"Exactly." She stopped in front of him, wishing she was better at solving such vexing legal problems. "Or we can leave the country. Go to Ireland!"

"I never knew I was married to such a remarkable woman," Peter said, taking her into his arms again.

"Oh, Peter, I feel partly to blame! If only I hadn't been so cold and heartless."

Peter nearly choked, for if there was one thing Katherine was not, it was cold. He buried his merry chuckle behind a coughing spasm.

"You're catching a cold!" Katherine said, even more alarmed.

"No, no, I'm fine," he assured her, catching his breath. He allowed her to soothe his brow with her long, slender fingers.

Katherine started pulling off his coat and shirt. "If we are to escape at daybreak, you must get some rest," she said, all efficiency. She stripped him down to the waist, pushed him down on the edge of the bed. "Let me help you get those boots off, darling."

Peter smothered a laugh. "I'm not tired," he insisted, trying to pull her into his arms.

"Don't lie, Peter. Robbing banks must be exhausting work." She pulled off his boots and started on the waistband of his trousers. "Promise me you'll never do such a thing again."

"I promise." Weak with silent laughter, he let her undress him. As she tugged on his pants legs, Peter eased his lean buttocks off the bedspread.

Up until that moment, Katherine had been busy managing her errant husband as if he was a little boy who required a firm hand. As she pulled his pants down to his knees, the sight of him sprawled beneath her changed all that. Her breath caught. The hearth's amber fire popped and sizzled, dancing over his body like an ancient Aztec spirit. It was the first time she had seen her husband in a fully aroused state.

For a second, she thought she might swoon. Or scream. He was magnificent! Katherine tried to still the dizzy, weak-kneed wobble of wallowing lust that assailed her. From the top of his golden head to the pulsing tip of his manhood, Peter was a compelling sight.

He lay there, watching, revelling in her reaction.

Katherine herself could scarcely breathe for fear that the last remnant of self-restraint would fall away. She trembled, feeling very wanton for wanting to pounce.

"Oh, Peter," she whispered, her eyes half-closed in dreamy longing. Her long mane of auburn hair tumbled about her shoulders like a fiery shimmering sunset.

His lips curled seductively; his tongue darted across them. "Kate," he said in a husky voice, and touched her breasts.

"We may never have another night like this," she reminded him, a trifle forlorn. She felt quite primitive as she arched toward his seductive caress.

Peter pulled her down on top of him. "Then let's make it a night to remember."

CHAPTER 26

While the wind outside howled and rattled the windowpanes, inside, suspended in a time warp beyond their ken, Peter and Katherine gazed with rapt absorption into each other's green eyes.

"Quote poetry to me, Peter," Katherine whispered daringly.

"Nay, sweet love, words cannot express the true depths of my feelings for you," the lazy, lean blond giant assured her. "You are Juliet, the sun, and I am the moon."

"More!" Like a soft kitten seeking heat from a hot brick hearth, Mary Kate curled herself against the hard-ridged muscles of his chest, their bodies forming two halves of a perfect whole.

Spellbound, they remained locked in a tender embrace, each yearning for the full expression of their love, yet too caught up in the moment even to move. Scarcely did they breathe, as the truth fully dawned: that from the beginning, this had been their destiny, the inevitable conclusion of Peter's prodigal wanderings and Katherine's most restless yearnings.

This is where I belong, Peter's heart thundered against Kate's warm breast.

Kate's gentle sigh answered, *I am yours, Peter, now and forever.*

Sparks flew upon the hearth as a log burned through
at the midnight hour. Roused by the swirling wind in the
flue, Peter lifted his head and marveled, watching the
burning embers reflected in his wife's crimson tresses.
Kate lay softly panting in his arms, her eyes glazed with
sexual desire, her lips moist and ripe from his kisses. He
uttered a besotted chuckle and drew her even closer.
Even to himself, he couldn't explain the depths of his joy.

"We've been kissing for hours," he said as it dawned
on him. He couldn't seem to get enough of the simple
pleasures of her mouth. He buried his lips against the
long, swanlike curve of her throat and breathed in her
scent. "How can this be? he asked, fingering her negli-
gee. "You're still wrapped up in all this."

Kate was swimming in liquid fire, the sheer lavender
between his hard, hot body and hers totally forgotten.
Now she reached for him, her breasts arching in mute
invitation. "Undress me, Peter," she whispered. "I don't
want anything between us."

And with her words, the final barrier fell away, both
aware that they were crossing an emotional frontier that
had little to do with the removal of clothing. They were
twin spirits, unmasked, no longer holding back from
each other.

"Take me, Peter," she whispered, surrendering herself
totally to her husband. "I want you to kiss me all over. I
want to feel you inside me, a part of me, filling me."

"Ah, Katie, my life, my love." Peter felt a lump rising in
his throat. The love he had for her drove him to wild distraction. His hands swept feverishly over her soft flesh,
skimming lightly from her slender feet over silk stockings
to the garters at her knees. Peter lifted her long leg, kissing the inside of her knees, licking the tiny indentations,
as he peeled away her stockings. He plied her with a trail
of hot kisses until she erupted in delicious gooseflesh.

Giggling, Kate gasped in protest. "I—stop, Peter,
before I perish," she laughed, making a grab for him.

But he was too quick. He kissed and nibbled his way

down to her toes. Ignoring her breathless entreaties, he sucked on the tender pad until she thought she'd climax in a wild spasm of ecstasy. She shrieked and writhed beneath his teasing.

"I love every inch of you, Katie O'Rourke," he said, straddling her.

"And I you." Eyes gleaming, Kate decided that two could play the same wicked game. Rubbing against him with saucy abandon, she reached out and latched onto the virile blade thrusting above her. Her fingers closed over the hot, throbbing tip. "Mine," she declared with a cheeky smile.

Before Peter managed more than a groan, Kate wriggled lower in the bed beneath him. "Mine," she repeated and took him into her mouth. Her wet, greedy sucking and wild giggles threatened to drive him over the brink of sanity.

"Kate!" Erotic fantasies spiraled through Peter's brain, and his whole body surged forward. Hearing her sensual moan, he shuddered as she milked his slick member inside her throat. His hands clutched her flowing tresses, his thumbs stroking her flushed cheeks. The intimate caress of her lips and tongue plunged him into a vortex of wrenching physical intoxication. Peter realized he was going to lose it completely, yet he was powerless in his wife's greedy grasp.

"Unhand me, woman!" he begged, growing desperate.

A smile broke around Katherine's rosy lips, and she grinned up at him, her tongue curled possessively around the throbbing warmth in a tremulous smile of triumph.

"I'm warning you, Kate," Peter gasped.

Kate released him and collapsed beside him in helpless laughter. "You are a randy rogue," she informed him, amused by his struggles to rein himself in.

"And you are a vexatious vixen," Peter confirmed.

"We deserve each other." Squirming higher on the rumpled bed covers, she sat up, braced on her elbows, and thrust her breasts at his chest with a wild toss of her hair—a clear challenge. "What are you going to do about it?"

"Drive myself crazy," Peter groaned, pulling her night-gown up over her hips.

"Let's go wild together," Kate rejoined.

Eager fistfuls of filmy lace floated upward, leaving them momentarily engulfed in the transparent folds. Peter didn't bother to extricate himself from the flimsy veil that settled over them but buried his face in her silky flesh, his tongue touching her navel in a light tickle. He nipped and nuzzled, revelling in her incredible feminin-ity, delighting in her rich, musky scent.

"You are so utterly . . . wonderful," he told her with the fervor of a true worshiper. "Beautiful from the inside out." Suddenly his hands were everywhere on her. His mouth and skin and hair praising her body in bold adulation.

A moan caught in Kate's throat. She had never known such pleasure. Slowly she opened herself to him, her body unfolding like the trembling petals on a rose, wel-coming him into the very center of her being.

Peter stretched above her in a leonine gesture, exer-cising his dominance with a gentle strength that was more exciting than force ever could be. In a single stroke he swept to possess her, filling her up, right to her very soul. In that instant, Kate knew that no force on earth could ever drive them apart. She felt their union with such intensity that she climaxed at once. A sudden series of wild near-deaths pulsed through her, urgent and sweetly torrid. Life-giving.

Her body tightened, drawing Peter deeper, deeper. They flirted with danger, loving it. The ebb and flow be-tween them defied all reason as, teeth bared against her temple, Peter moved over her, his thrusts set to the rhythm of a life force older than time. Another glorious wave of rapture flashed through her, and Kate gasped at its splen-dor. Over the roar of hot blood pounding in her brain, she heard her own small, evocative cries, as Peter deeply ex-claimed the wonder of their love. They collapsed in each other's arms in a final paroxysm of ecstasy, and in that voluptuous moment, Peter embodied the sum total of her existence, her *raison d'être*.

Like a great comet burning out on an extralong vapor trail from outer space, they slowly descended to earth. Laughing and giddy with discovery, they clung to each other, thoroughly spent and spun out.

"Remind me to thank your parents," Peter murmured and pressed his lips to her left eyelid.

Katherine brushed back a mass of damp auburn curls and studied her husband's blissful expression. "My parents?" she echoed, mystified. "What have they to do with this?"

"They had you, silly. Where would I be without you?"

Katherine snuggled closer, loving the way their sweaty bodies stuck together. "Mmmm," she agreed happily.

Peter's finger explored the tip of her breast. "Just think, I was seven before you were even a figment of your father's imagination."

"A poor Irish boy, just pining away." Kate giggled, trying to picture Peter as a venturesome schoolboy.

She wondered if their children would inherit his lips, which were presently quirked in a lazy smile, as if he found the world enormously pleasing. Or would they have his classical profile? She leaned closer to examine the dancing gold flecks in his twinkling gaze.

"Even then I had begun my quest," he taunted. "Somehow I knew I'd find the woman of my dreams under a pile of petticoats, if I just kept looking long enough."

"That's hardly how you found me," Kate reminded him.

His eyebrows lifted, and he laughed. "Right in the middle of C Street, I was, when I spied the most beautiful redhead standing over me."

"Love at first sight?" she prompted hopefully.

"I thought I'd died and gone to heaven."

"Spoken like a true romantic." She closed her eyes and gave him a tender kiss with plenty of tongue in it.

"Sweet," said Peter, his appetite instantly revived.

"Pure poetry," said Katherine, and upon his body she wrote a love sonnet too beautiful to be set to a precise meter.

This time their lovemaking assumed a less frenzied pace, though they ventured into uncharted waters. Peter's care of her, body and soul, surpassed Kate's wildest fantasy. She in turn gave to him, desiring only that he find pleasure in her every response. Once again the night exploded in a silent meteor shower, forging an almost alchemic bond between them.

Near dawn, they went into orbit again, Katherine astride, her back arched and breasts bouncing freely. In the throes of ecstasy, the strength of their climax came upon them in the same blazing second.

Together they shouted out, "Yes, yes! Glory to God, yes!"

A curse and loud pounding on the wall next door startled the pair back to full awareness.

"Don't you two ever sleep?" a male voice bawled.

Startled, Katherine looked about, making sure they were still alone.

A series of disgusted thumps shook the paper-thin wall near the headboard. "Shut up, or I'll sic the house detective on you," the man threatened.

Dissolving into silent laughter, Katherine clapped her hands across Peter's mouth to stifle his loud guffaw. "Don't laugh, Peter," she warned, her cheeks burning with embarrassment.

The strapping Irishman beneath her shook all over with merriment. "Ah, Katie," he whispered, his lips and teeth nipping at her hand, "I've got to shout it from the house top." Ignoring Kate's disapproving frown, Peter threw back his head. "I love you, Katie O'Rourke!" he bellowed.

Panic-stricken, Katherine tried to smother his declaration

with both hands across his mouth. "Stop, Peter," she hissed in his ear. "If the house detective arrests you, he will surely hand you over to the sheriff."

Peter went still beneath Kate's frantic efforts to squelch his enthusiasm. "Sheriff? Oh, yes, nearly forgot." Chuckling, he struggled upright. Clearly it was time to let Katherine know her husband wasn't quite the desperado she believed him to be.

Kate clung to his neck, dragging him down in the bed again. "We must escape before daybreak," she whispered, gazing at him earnestly.

"See here, Kate—"

Katherine hopped off the bed and, searching for her clothes, got down on all fours to peer under the bed.

The sight of her wriggling bare bottom inspired him to new mischief. Clearly Kate believed he was a bank robber, so why disillusion the minx? Since she was determined to prove her staunch loyalty, who was he to deny her the pleasure? She loved him, and that was all that really mattered.

Besides, he never could resist a bit of harmless fun.

Solicitously Peter helped Kate retrieve her clothing and sent her into the alcove to wash. Meanwhile, dressing quickly, he gathered his legal papers, the new set of ledgers, and the strongbox full of operating cash. In minutes, he had his gear reorganized to conceal his role as the new owner of the Diablo lumber mill and logging operation.

Kate, still clinging to slightly misguided ideas about her desperado husband, was adamant about going with him—a fact that delighted him greatly. Even so, she would need warmer clothing and a horse. Peter decided to send Merrick on ahead with fresh supplies and the dozen new men he'd hired. Meanwhile he would tend to last-minute details and then, to spare her pride, he would return to make their escape look convincing.

He glanced at the Wells Fargo pouches. The money had arrived on the stage from San Francisco the previous afternoon. It had taken the bank manager three days to collect a thousand dollars in nickels.

All along, Peter had wanted to return the blood money Kate had paid him to marry her. He wanted the money out of the way, no longer an issue between them. To make his point, he had planned to dump the entire sum—all in nickels—in her lap.

But the whole idea had lost its appeal once he realized how much it weighed. In all, there were over two hundred pounds in nickels—nearly twice Kate's weight. He couldn't do it; the weight would have buried her.

But he *had* intended to have it out with her, once and for all. On his way out of town, he had planned to go to her house, drop the contents in the doorway, and deliver an eloquent plea for her to join her ragtag lumberjack of a husband. He wanted Kate to love him as is, not because he'd fallen into an inheritance.

As it turned out, his elaborate scheme wasn't necessary. Kate had come to him instead.

She loved him without a nickel to his name, her actions told him. Peter treasured that knowledge more than all the gold and silver in the Comstock Lode.

"We must return those, before we go," she said, slipping her arms around his waist from behind.

Peter turned to meet her troubled gaze. "I'll take full responsibility," he said. "After all, I took it out of the bank."

"Peter, no! It's too risky."

"There's a man coming within the hour," he cut in smoothly. "He can drop it off at your parents' house, and they can return it to the bank during normal banking hours."

"No, let me, Peter. I need to pick up my clothes anyway." Kate gave him a look of reproach. "Oh, Peter, if only you hadn't gone wild and robbed a bank."

"It's only a thousand dollars, Kate," Peter said.

She raised her finger to his lips. "Every word you say only gets you in deeper. You know there must be twenty thousand in those saddle bags—at least! If you needed only a thousand, you could have used the money I gave you," she told him with a wise nod and headed for the door. "Stand aside, Peter, so I can go tell my father where the money is. After we're gone, he can take it all back."

"There's no need to drag your father into this," Peter insisted. "Don't forget, he issued a restraining order, lest I seduce his daughter—my wife!" He let out a huff. "Besides, I have better things to do with my time."

"Like spending the next twenty years in prison?" Kate whirled indignantly, hands on hips. Sparks flew from her eyes. "Then how, pray tell, do you plan to talk yourself out of this mess?"

"I'm in no danger of going to jail," he said, ready to make a clean breast of it. Damn! He should never have let this get so blown out of proportion.

Her toe tapped impatiently against the carpet. "Don't be bone-headed, Peter. Can't you see? I'm your only hope! Trust me. I'll be right back, with the best legal counsel in the territory."

As she grasped the doorknob, Peter seized her shoulders and spun her around to face him. "No, Kate. The money is yours—honestly, it is. I was planning to return it to you this morning."

"I won't have a thing to do with . . . stolen money!" she gasped, looking mortified. "I will not be your accomplice."

"I thought you said you love me."

"I do. Desperately." Kate's green eyes swam in a flood of tears. "But the money's going back to the bank. Nothing you say will change my mind."

"Very well." Peter ground his teeth. Never had he seen a woman so stubborn. So Kate knew beyond a shadow of a doubt that he was guilty, did she? "All right! *I* will take the money back."

He swept her up, struggling in his arms, and tossed her on the bed. He loosened his string tie, wound it several times around her wrists and tied her securely to the bedpost.

"Peter, what are you doing?" Kate swore at him in a fury, kicking and bucking to get loose. "You can't leave me here!"

"Just watch me." Peter pinned her with green eyes so full of tawny fire that she quailed. He picked up two jingling pouches and strode to the bed. "You stay put, while I make arrangements to redeposit this money."

"I'll get loose," she threatened, sticking out her jaw.

Peter began to pile heavy leather money bags over her limbs. Each weighed nearly thirty pounds. Very quickly Kate found herself trapped. Soon she couldn't move a muscle.

"I'll scream!"

"I guarantee the house detective won't thank you for creating a disturbance at this hour," said Peter, continuing to weigh her down. "Trust me, Kate. This is for your own good."

"Ooh!" She raised her head from the pillow and glared at him. "I'll get you for this!" She tossed her head.

O'Rourke leaned down and kissed her. She tried to bite him. "Still love me?" he taunted.

"I—" Kate was tempted to tell him she hated him, but she couldn't lie. Rather, she despised herself for being such a weak-willed, pathetic excuse for a woman. One night of love, and she was lost—utterly. All her good sense and proper upbringing, flown out the window. Peter was a bank robber, a scoundrel. He dared laugh at her. And *still* she loved him—more fool she! "If only I didn't love you," she gritted out, wishing it was not so.

"You won't be sorry." He smiled, curiously jubilant, and swept her a courtly bow from the doorway.

"I'm sorry already," Kate sobbed. She lay there, staring at him; weighted down by two hundred pounds of Peter's ill-gotten gains. She couldn't help herself; Peter needed her, now more than ever. She couldn't abandon him in his time of gravest peril. She would devote herself, until he was a rehabilitated man, once more a man worthy of her unqualified love and respect.

The aroma of Wells Fargo leather chafed her spirit, reminding her that before long they would ride out across the mountains together, with the law in hot pursuit behind them.

"Hurry, Peter. I'll be waiting."

Peter threw back his head and roared with laughter. The absurdity of his wife, pinned to the bed, informing him of her intention to wait for him, brought tears to his eyes.

"Ah, Katie, you're priceless!"

Chuckling, he closed and locked the door. After he found his accountant, Merrick, O'Rourke stopped at the livery stable, where he woke up a groom and purchased Mary Kate a horse. Next he woke up her father, explaining that he was leaving to work for Diablo's new owner, and that Kate would be going with him.

He was fully prepared for Homer's blow-up. "You've got moxie to ignore that restraining order, O'Rourke," McGillacutty yelled, his face as red as the plaid wool dressing gown he wore. Nevertheless, he opened the door and let Peter in.

"Kate came to me, sir," Peter said.

"I'll get her things," Madeleine said, yawning, and slipped upstairs.

"Where is she now?" Homer demanded, striding down the hall to the kitchen, his fists clasped behind his back.

Peter smiled. "She's watching over the dowry she insisted on paying me. I had hoped she'd put it to better use, but she insists that it go right back to the bank."

"Humph!"

Peter regarded his father-in-law with a mischievous twinkle. "She has a right practical attitude about money. Must take after her Old Man."

McGillacutty grudgingly picked up the coffee pot. "Share a cup of coffee with me?"

"Thank you sir, I'd like that." Peter straddled a chair at the kitchen table and accepted a cup. McGillacutty's brew was stout as molasses and twice as bitter.

Homer cleared his throat, studying his son-in-law with a prejudiced eye. "So, you're giving up acting?"

"Yes, sir. With a wife I need a steady income. That's where lumber come in. Pays better. I have you to thank for steering me in that direction."

Homer scratched behind his ear. "Strange. You've got your old job back with the same outfit, you say?"

"Not so strange. I heard the new owner was hiring."

"What's the Earl of Wickstead like?" Homer asked.

Peter shrugged noncommittally. "A regular bloke. Matter of fact, I went to school with him."

Homer grunted. "Small world. About your age, is he?"

"More or less. He always had more money than was good for him." Peter grinned, rationalizing that he couldn't stop McGillacutty from leaping to conclusions, any more than he could Kate.

"Whereas you've had to make your own way," Homer said, falling in with Peter's deception. "Well, good luck, O'Rourke. I hope everything works out for you."

"Thank you, sir. For Kate's sake and mine, I sincerely hope so." Peter watched McGillacutty pour and stir a second cup of his lethal brew. He wondered how the old redhead would react if he knew his own son-in-law had bought him out of the lumber business.

Quickly he dismissed any idea of making a clean breast of things—yet. First, he had to make good.

A few minutes later, Madeleine summoned both men upstairs. Together they hauled down two trunks full of the clothes Peter had purchased.

Madeleine rose on tiptoe and gave her son-in-law a conciliatory peck on the cheek. "Stay in touch, Peter."

"I shall." He handed McGillacutty Kate's key to Room 208. "Kate would consider it a great kindness if you'd deposit her dowry in the Wells Fargo Bank later this morning, sir. We'll leave it on the bed."

"I'll see to it," Homer promised, shifting his cigar to the other corner of his mouth. "Take care of my little girl, y'hear?"

"You can count on it, sir." Peter shook Homer's hand in farewell. "And who knows? Maybe you and Mrs. McGillacutty will see your way clear to pay us a visit, once the mountain pass opens up next spring."

Quickly he covered the distance between the house and the heavily laden wagon in the road. He threw Kate's trunks in the buckboard and swung up to the seat beside Merrick, who sat hunched against the cold behind a team of four.

"See you in the spring," Peter yelled, waving to his in-laws and signaled for Merrick to drive off.

Standing in the open doorway, McGillacutty felt his wife's slender arm circle his stout waist. He drew her close and pressed his leathered cheek against her warm dark curls. "What have I gotten our Mary Kate into?" He shook his head, all of a sudden feeling old, as he watched O'Rourke disappear down the road.

"I wouldn't worry too much about our daughter," Maddy said calmly. "She's a lot like her father. She can survive anything."

CHAPTER 27

Diablo Camp on the Truckee River
Early June 1865

Mary Kate burst out of the woods, her cheeks flushed a bright, rosy hue and her eyes sparkling with vitality. She whirled about, swinging her basket of wild strawberries, and let out an exuberant sigh, satisfied in every way with her new life.

Breathing in the pristine mountain air, she thought about the cascading waterfalls and ice-cold streams that lay behind her on the slopes. Life was springing forth everywhere from the cool, damp earth. Tandem dragonflies drifted over the trout pond at the bottom of the dammed stream, and bees drifted with the gentle air currents, sampling nectar from the two apple trees Peter had planted beside their cabin.

It was here that she and Peter had spent the past seven months in idyllic bliss. She could scarcely believe the contentment she had found in this primitive country.

It hardly seemed possible, yet every day with Peter she felt happier, more certain of herself, and certainly more hopeful. When they first rode into Truckee in the dead of winter, they arrived half-frozen, flat broke, and with a future as bleak as the snowy forest.

My, but life had changed since then. The miracle of spring had come to the High Sierras, and to their lives. She was madly in love and fairly bursting to tell Peter the good news.

Taking a shortcut across her struggling vegetable garden, Kate bent to pluck a vagrant weed. Chipmunks and squirrels chattered in the trees, and half her garden was eaten by deer, but she had never felt happier. Coming around to the cabin, she noticed the quiet curl of smoke from the chimney with satisfaction and laughed out loud.

Wouldn't Peter be surprised when he sat down to a supper of rabbit stew! Raimey Griswold's young son had come by after breakfast with a brace of blacktail jackrabbits. She skipped a step, recalling how she had skinned, gutted, and dressed the carcasses, then braised the delectable "critters" in her big black skillet. Even now they simmered over a low fire with vegetables from her own garden. And strawberries for dessert, and salad greens, just picked.

Once she would have been appalled by the idea of being a backwoods wife. In Chicago, she had never even set foot in a kitchen! But thanks to her pioneer cookbook, she had relatively few culinary disasters now. Stripped to the bare essentials, she was constantly reminded how fortunate she really was.

And by some miracle, Peter's brief transgression of the law had been smoothed over. She no longer lived in dread that the sheriff would come along and drag him off to jail.

Initially when the pass cleared with the spring thaw, Kate had experienced a few uneasy moments. But as travelers appeared with more regularity, going back and forth between California and Nevada, she soon realized that by Eastern standards, the law of the West was lax. Men seemed more willing to let bygones be bygones, to let a man pick up the pieces of his life and move forward.

Peter had turned over a new leaf. By making himself invaluable to Diablo Camp's absentee owner, they were

saving money from his modest salary every week, and
they'd made a very presentable home for themselves out
here in the woods. He was simply amazing!

And if she reminded him that all his hard work was
making the absentee owner a very wealthy man, it didn't
phase him in the least. "Just being faithful to the task,
Kate," he'd say with a broad smile on his handsome face.
Then he'd stick his hands in his pockets and go about
the day's business, whistling a tune.

Under the guidance of Peter and Jigger Jansen, the
camp ramrod, the men gave a hundred percent. And
thanks to Peter's powers of persuasion, Diablo's new
owner had built fourteen houses for his married employ-
ees. Several wives and children had come to live in camp
recently. There was even talk of hiring in a schoolmaster
next year, and this, too, had attracted reliable workers.

Yes, life was good. Peter had a steady job. Her father
had forgiven her for marrying a penniless actor-turned-
lumberjack. And best of all, Peter's legal difficulties had
been smoothed over. The money he'd stolen was safely
in the bank, and only last week the Wells Fargo agent
had dropped by on his monthly trip to San Francisco.
After being closeted for an hour in Peter's office, the
agent and Peter had parted on the most cordial terms.

Obviously all had been forgiven. Now fully assured of
that fact, Kate's heart rejoiced.

No wonder his men love him, she mused. Peter was enthused about everything he did. Nothing daunted him,
not even the Earl of Wickstead, whom Peter dismissed as
an elusive playboy. The sawmill, using the latest equipment, had outstripped the competition from five other
sawmills between Donner's Pass and Verdi. And now
Peter was building a narrow-gauge railroad trestle. His
ideas for expansion seemed limitless.

Occasionally railroad surveyors stopped by for supper.
There was talk of forging the final link between Sacramento and Salt Lake City, but that was still "a far piece
down the road," Jigger claimed. Crocker and Hartford

were names often mentioned around the supper table, but until the bureaucrats in Washington got down to business, people still had to rely on the Overland Stage.

Hanging her basketful of strawberries on the garden post, Kate ran around the corner of their three-room cabin, chasing away a deer from the garden. Her bright hair flew behind her, ablaze with the variegated colors of a sunset over the Pacific.

Suddenly Katherine's prancing stopped amidst a flurry of petticoats as she saw on the heavily wooded road a sleek black carriage with brass trim come wheeling smartly up to the front door of their cabin. A pair of perfectly matched bays, lightly flecked with foam, came to a stop, leaving Kate flabbergasted.

Who could be coming to call? she wondered.

To say that their home was totally off the beaten path was a complete understatement. Hastily Katherine smoothed her skirts. Her apron was stained with strawberries, and her hair was beyond any semblance of order. Knowing she looked a fright in her gingham dress, she hung back, watching the driver swing down. Impeccable in gray livery adorned with red and gold braid, he rounded the carriage with the fluid grace of an experienced coachman—no stagecoach driver, this fellow! He opened the carriage door with a flourish.

A small, elegant hand reached forth to grasp the coachman's gloved hand.

"Thank you, Mr. O'Hara." The woman's voice floated like music across the yard to where Katherine stood, fascinated. Short and slender, garbed in deep purple and emerald green velvet, she stepped down, her heavily jeweled hands carefully lifting her skirts to avoid the red powdery clay beneath her small feet. The lady— obviously high born and incredibly beautiful despite middle age—spotted Katherine before she could vanish around the corner of the cabin.

"Ah!" she exclaimed, staring at Katherine's windswept appearance with the most compelling green eyes. "You must be Mary Katherine." Her shrewd gaze swept over Katherine in a lively blend of curiosity and friendly speculation, as she held out her hand in greeting. "Permit me to introduce myself, my dear, I am the Countess of Wickstead."

"I'm sorry, ma'am," Kate stammered. "I don't believe we've met—?"

Kate's elegant visitor walked up onto the porch and turned to survey her surroundings.

"Mr. O'Hara, please take my bags to the hotel in Truckee, and then return to me," the lady commanded her driver. "I wish to stretch my legs a bit, if that is acceptable with you, my dear?"

"Certainly, milady," Katherine curtsied, awed by the woman's friendly yet commanding air.

Her elegant guest chuckled. "I trust I haven't come all this way for nothing. Where *is* my errant son?" she asked, looking around the premises.

Mary Katherine blinked. "I have no idea. I've never met him."

"Come now. Where is he hiding?" Seeing Kate's confusion, she patted her arm confidingly. "It's all right. You can tell me. I'm Peter's mother."

"Peter?" she said, confused. "Peter who?"

"I daresay I can produce a baptismal certificate, if it comes to that," the countess joked. "Peter Casey O'Rourke. My son." Her emerald eyes twinkled, regarding her daughter-in-law's look of utter consternation. "He's about six feet four—blond hair, green eyes? An outrageous rapscallion— for which I do sincerely apologize! Not that I could ever curb his antics." She laughed at her own witticism, and Kate knew at once who her husband took after.

"Oh. *That* Peter," Kate said, feeling as if her brain had been cudgeled.

The countess took Kate's hands in her own and smiled. "I see you weren't expecting me."

Katherine gave a little shake of the head, and Anne O'Rourke waved a jeweled hand in a grand gesture toward the cabin. "And this is where you live. Charming! No wonder it appeals to Peter. He's such a romantic!"

Kate clasped her hands firmly in front of her to disguise their trembling. She could not believe she had been so gullible!

Inwardly seething, she mounted the steps and escorted her mother-in-law inside, her bare feet padding across the wooden floor. She felt self-conscious having so stylish a guest visit their modest home. It was a cheerful and sturdy shelter against the cold winter nights just past and the hot, dry summer months to come. But it was certainly no palace. To one used to the refinements of cultured society, it must seem like a downright hovel!

Braided rag rugs and bright candy-striped muslin curtains brightened the dimly lit room. Large clay Indian pots full of spring flowers and herbs sat on tables catching the sunlight, which poured through the window's wavy glass panes and onto the floor near the hearth. In the rafters hung the antlers of mule deer that Peter and other men at Diablo had shot for meat during the long, hard winter. Baskets made from native materials hung on pegs, the products of Leila White Feather's busy, creative hands. Dried flowers, cattails, and driftwood added color and design to the cabin's sparsely furnished main room.

A kerosene lantern stood on the low table beside Peter's favorite chair, giving off a soft yellow glow. Another sat on the sturdy table where they took their meals.

Until that moment, Katherine had accepted her surroundings without a qualm. This had been a love nest for her and Peter, their home.

She had been happy here. And obviously totally deluded.

While her mother-in-law politely inquired about their life and how Katherine prepared meals over an open hearth, Kate bit her lip to keep from giving vent to her displeasure with Peter.

His mother was beautiful, totally gracious. Kate couldn't detect a single critical attitude, and although that fact eased her initial misery, Katherine felt Peter's betrayal to the bone. How could he have left her in the dark? She had thought their relationship had gone far beyond the keeping of secrets.

"Milady, please take a seat," she said, motioning to the overstuffed, tanned-cowhide chair next to the fire. "I imagine a soothing cup of tea will do us both a world of good about now."

The Countess of Wickstead smiled, settling herself into Peter's chair as best she could. The chair was so deep it nearly swallowed her up. "Please, call me 'Mother.'"

Katherine moved the iron crane supporting the tea kettle closer to fire. "I must apologize for my appearance. I've been gardening, as you can see."

"I have a weakness for gardening myself," the Countess said with a twinkle in her emerald eyes.

While Katherine prepared the tea tray, they chatted amicably. Kate found a tin of tea on the shelf, made the tea, and settled into a chair opposite her mother-in-law.

"You seem gifted in the domestic arts," Anne O'Rourke observed, accepting a dollop of honey in lieu of sugar.

Kate laughed and shook her head self-consciously. "Before Peter kidnapped me and dragged me up into these mountains, I couldn't boil water."

"My son did *what*?" The countess' jaw dropped. "Oh, my dear. I had no idea."

Katherine blushed. "It's not as bad as it sounds," she hastened to explain. Before long she had spilled out the details of her tawdry scheme to escape the marriage her father wanted to force upon her. "So you see, getting married was my idea. I paid him a thousand dollars." She smiled with modest pride. "Basically, Peter was opposed to my running off to San Francisco, so he brought me to the High Sierras instead. I was not very happy about that!"

Mrs. O'Rourke kept her eyes carefully on the steam rising from her tea cup. "So Peter wanted to keep you safe from the evils of San Francisco," she mused, a tiny smile hovering about her lips.

"So he said."

"He must have been very taken with you, even then," the Countess Anne said. "And you, dear Kate, do you love Peter so very much?"

The question caught Kate off guard. She gulped down a swallow of scalding tea, avoiding the older woman's shrewd gaze. "Oh, yes," she whispered, drawing a deep breath at last. "But—"

"I suspect he's been playing a little trick on you by hiding his true identity," Mrs. O'Rourke said.

"He did. He totally misled me," Katherine said, blinking furiously.

Anne O'Rourke set down her teacup and, leaning forward, took Kate's hand. "Let me tell you a secret I learned a long time ago: love isn't always enough."

"Oh, Mother O'Rourke!" Kate slipped to her knees with an anguished cry and buried her face in the older woman's velvet lap. "What should I do? He deceived me. Yet I love him so! I was willing to do anything, go anywhere, just so we could be together."

"There, there. Everything is going to be all right." Her jeweled fingers lifted Katherine's beautiful face; she wiped away her tears with a delicately scented scrap of Irish lace. "My son always wanted to be loved for himself. And it appears"—she nodded, indicating the cabin's simple interior—"he has gone to extreme measures to test your love."

"If I truly loved him, then why am I so angry?" asked Katherine, feeling like a failure. She couldn't reform a flea, much less a charming Irish earl.

"Au contraire." The countess laughed. "I would say you've passed the test with flying colors. You didn't marry my son for his money, or a title, or a life of privilege."

Katherine swiped her wet cheeks with the back of her hand. "I thought he was poor," she said sorrowfully.

"Without you, Peter would be poor indeed," said the wise woman from Wexford.

"But you said, 'love isn't always enough,'" said Kate.

"Precisely. A good marriage requires two very good forgivers."

Katherine felt a resurgence of rebellion. "I don't feel like forgiving him just yet."

Anne O'Rourke laughed. "That's understandable. But when he's properly repentant, forgive him. Your love means the world to him."

After Peter's mother returned to her hotel for a brief rest, Kate dashed off to her bedroom. There were subtle ways to make a man suffer, infinitely better than a quick death.

All this time Peter had been amusing himself at her expense. He had played on her sympathies. He had let her suffer the tortures of the damned. She had worried about the law catching up with him—*ooh!* It was unconscionable what he had done.

Of course, he hadn't exactly *lied,* as she recalled. He had just let her imagination work overtime. And blindly and gladly, she had sacrificed her creature comforts to prove her love.

Yes, Peter was going to pay for this deception. When she got through with him, she vowed, he would happily dance on hot coals!

Delving into her trunks, Katherine began to devise the most perfidious torture: she would parade her perfumed body before Peter in seemingly sweet submission, yet deny him access to the pleasures he had come to expect as his husbandly right. She would remain aloof. Untouchable, yet tempting to the point of madness.

Chuckling to herself, Kate went over to her trunk and took out a whalebone corset of her mother's. Positively medieval, she chortled. Perfect for teaching Peter a lesson.

She ignored all the lovely things Peter had bought her in Virginia City. Soon her patchwork quilt was littered with petticoats, a nubby linen shift, and a woolen camisole—God only knew where her mother had found *that* monstrosity!

To be safe, for she knew Peter's sexual thermostat always ran hot, Kate opted for an ill-fitting pair of men's red flannel underdrawers with a drop seat. That should squelch any lascivious tendencies! On top of it all, she would wear her favorite gown: the teal blue shimmering one with silver metallic threads.

Dressing quickly, she stepped before her mirror. Outwardly she looked gorgeous. Underneath, she was a veritable fortress. Even the Mexican army would have had trouble penetrating her armor!

She was ready.

Bring on the mighty Earl of Wickstead, the wandering son from Wexford. Poor Irish lad, indeed!

CHAPTER 28

"Katie, I'm home!"

Katherine raised her head and smiled. Peter was his old jubilant self. *Perfect*, she thought. He was totally off guard. *Now, to take the wind out of his sails.*

The jingle of lumberjack cleats and his springy step set Kate's pulse to racing. She tried to squelch the eager rush of excitement. *Be still, my heart!* she told herself. He really was a scoundrel, and for once she wished ice water flowed through her veins. How would she carry off her revenge, if she couldn't stay mad at him?

Quickly she checked the mirror, then quit the bedroom, confident that her get-up would do the trick. During their chat, her mother-in-law had created an elaborate hairstyle for her—all the rage on the Continent! It was sure to set Peter's blood on fire. Knowing his randy appetite, Kate meant to drive him wild, then leave him high and dry. It was his turn to suffer.

As she swept majestically across the living room to greet him, Peter felt a surge of pleasure and pride. Katherine looked juicy as a plum as she lifted her invitingly moist, softly alluring lips to his. Her Titian tresses, swept up on the sides and tumbling down her back, shimmered in the soft lantern light. Instantly randy, he sailed his broad Stetson across the room to land in his favorite chair.

"Darling, you're home," Katherine said in a low, vampish voice.

"Something smells good," Peter rumbled, making straight for her. "I'm starved, sweetheart."

Katherine braced herself. As Peter swept her into his arms, she screwed up her lips and gave him a dutifully dry kiss. "Where've you been all afternoon, darling?" she asked. She took his jacket and bustled past him, giving him a seductive whiff of her perfume.

"You look mighty fetching, Kate," said Peter, bent on recapture.

"Thank you, sir." Katherine skillfully eluded his reach, her skirts rustling like dry leaves across the floor. She smiled, feeling his eyes feast on her low décolletage. "I dressed just for you. How do you like my hair?"

Ignoring his growling stomach, Peter followed her like a hungry wolf in pursue of a lone ewe lamb. "You didn't have to do anything special. You always look beautiful to me."

His hands circled her narrow waist, and Kate read the hot look in his eyes. She gave him a come-hither smile, while she leaned away to avoid his eager embrace. She placed a hand on his chest to maintain distance. "Peter, please! Restrain yourself," she chided, lightly slapping his exploring hands. "I didn't get all dressed up just so you could maul me."

Maul? That's a new one, Peter thought. He backed off, taking a more critical look at his wife. This was definitely *not* the welcome he'd grown accustomed to after work.

"You look fine," he said and started emptying his pockets out on the dining room table. "Did you have a good day?"

"Lovely." Kate sashayed over and began scooping up everything he placed on the table as fast as he set it down. She handed it all back to him. "Sweetheart, really! Can't you put this clutter somewhere else?" Kate drummed her fingers on her hips and gave him an aggrieved pout.

Peter frowned. "You never minded where I put my keys and money before."

"I'm not one to complain, darling, but just once I wish you could appreciate how hard I work around here." One arm raised to straighten an imaginary flaw in her coiffure, she said, "I slave all day to make our home perfect, and then you tromp in here, and instantly the place looks like a wild bull came charging through the door."

Peter rocked back on his muddy cleats and gave her a bold stare. "Come off your high horse, Kate. You never minded the bull in me before."

Kate's cheeks reddened. Peter was earthy but usually not coarse.

Peter leered, clearly intent upon putting her in her place. "Give yourself a fancy hairdo, and right away you put on airs. Maybe if I showed you a bit more *bull* in the bedroom, you'd be in a better mood when I came home."

"What language!" said Kate, trying to ignore Peter's fingers playing along her rib cage.

Suddenly he scowled. "Kate, what's this—a steel corset?" he exclaimed, never one to mince words about his likes and dislikes in women's apparel. "That contraption must be downright painful."

"Nonsense. Corsets make the fashion." Stoutly Kate defended her cast-iron armor with perverse enjoyment. "You wouldn't want me to neglect my figure, now would you?"

"What the hell?" Peter scrutinized his wife. "There's nothing wrong with your figure," he told her flatly.

"I am positively bursting at the seams!"

Long legs slightly spread, he put his hands on his hips and cocked his head to one side. Kate was testy as a wild boar. The thought crossed his mind that women sometimes acted touchy around the time of their monthly flow, but he knew damn well it wasn't that. Something else was responsible. "Anything happen around here today that's put your nose out of joint?" he asked after a lengthy silence.

"Nothing you don't already know about." Kate turned up her nose pertly and started setting the table. She came over to his side of the table, barely acknowledging his presence.

Out of long habit, Peter stood aside. He pondered why Kate might be putting on such airs. *Aye,* he observed, *my lady's much too high in the instep for her own good.*

Fixing Katherine with an insolent stare, he lounged his hips against the table and stretched out his long legs to block her progress. When she reversed directions, he scratched his lean belly, took in a huge gulp of air, and let out a loud belch.

"My, we're couth," Kate said, plunking down three plates on the table. She returned his devilish wink with a snooty survey of his person. "At least change that disgusting flannel shirt."

"Disgusting?" Peter's green eyes flashed, always a dangerous sign. "What's the matter? Does a little honest sweat offend my wife?"

Kate wrinkled her nose, as if she smelled something. "Better still, why don't you go soak your head in the trout pond?" she suggested.

"Thanks, I just may do that!" Halfway to the door, Peter stopped, spotting the extra place setting. It reminded him what he'd meant to tell her when he got home. "We're having company."

"That's right," Kate said.

"I'm sorry," Peter apologized quickly. "I meant to mention it earlier. We'll need to set two more plates for dinner."

"One," Kate said argumentatively.

"No, two," said Peter. "I invited your parents. They should be arriving around six."

"They're coming here tonight?" She regarded him with alarm. "You're certain?"

Peter gave her a confident smile, believing a visit from her parents to dinner would cure her orneriness. "Yes. I ran into them in Truckee when I went to the bank this afternoon."

Frowning, Kate marched to the cupboard. Turning on her heel like a martinet, she bought two more settings of china to the table.

"Two, Kate, not three," Peter told her, growing perturbed. "Or would you prefer to take them out to dinner?"

"I didn't waste my entire afternoon cooking, just so I can eat boiled pot roast at that lame excuse for a hotel." Kate pushed him aside and set out her best candles.

"What are we serving?" Peter asked, and Kate heard the hint of a challenge in his voice. "I want this to be a particularly pleasant evening."

Kate turned on him in a fury. "You still don't think I cook worth a damn, do you?"

"Never mind. I'll check for myself." Striding to the hearth, Peter grabbed the blackened lid. "Sonuvabitch!" he howled. He dropped the lid with a clatter and stuck his finger in his mouth.

Katherine handed him a tea towel and stood back.

"Burn yourself, Peter?" she asked politely.

"No, and a damn good thing for you I didn't." Peter turned a glare on her. "Mary Kate, I don't know what crawled into your drawers to put a crimp in your disposition, but you'd best calm down fast, or so help me—"

"Oh, I see," said Kate, folding her arms over her breasts. "I'm to play the perfect, docile wife." She eyed his work clothes critically. "What about you? Aren't you going to dress for dinner? You do want to make a good impression, don't you, darling?"

"I only want to be myself," Peter growled.

"Just a poor, simple Irish boy, right?"

"No, just a dumb Irish lumberjack, who'd be forever grateful if his wife reverted to being the sweet Scotch-Irish lass he married," Peter muttered.

"Really?" Her words dripped sarcasm. "Dumb like a

fox, you mean. What an actor you are, Peter. You fooled me completely."

"What the hell are you talking about?

Katherine played her trump card. "I met your mother today!"

Peter flushed, taken aback. "My mother?" he repeated softly.

"The one and only Countess of Wickstead." Kate wrinkled her nose at him like a smug little cat and returned to her housewifely duties. "You have heard of her?" she inquired over her shoulder.

"So that's what this is all about. This whole ridiculous act is because my mother—why, you little—"

"Me, milord? I have done nothing," Kate said, affecting an injured air. "I am merely a walk-on, a stooge in this comedy of errors. You're the one who wrote this farce!"

"You, Katie O'Rourke, are a damn prima donna!" Peter snapped, his brows lowering. "But make no mistake, once our guests leave, I am going to strip you of a damn sight more than that corset!"

Kate shrugged. "We'll just see about that!"

Peter glanced around. "Where is my mother now?"

"Over at the hotel, resting."

"I can barely wait to see her," he said, rubbing his hands together.

"Oh, you're a cool one! You lied through your teeth to me, and it doesn't even phase you."

He grinned sheepishly. "I did plan to tell you."

Katherine followed Peter to the bedroom. "After all these months, there was no hurry, right?"

"I apologize," he said lightly, unbuttoning his shirt. "I trust you made my mother feel welcome?" Peter removed his soiled shirt, tossed it on the floor. He threw her a look that sent a tingle down her spine. His long arm shot out past her nose, snagging a fresh linen shirt. Kate swallowed, watching the play of golden muscles on his chest and shoulders. Her attraction to him made it nearly impossible to focus on revenge, but she saw her duty.

"You really are a cad, Peter."

"I know," Peter said with a dimpled smile. "But I understand you better than you think." He chuckled. "Really angry at me, aren't you?"

"I cannot begin to tell you."

"You were happy enough as long as you thought I was a poor working stiff," he reminded her. Sitting on the bed, he unlaced his cleats, kicking them into the corner. Then he crossed to pour water into the porcelain basin on the chiffonnier. Katherine watched Peter splash his face, hands, and chest with water. Coming up, hair damp, he grabbed a towel and dried himself briskly.

Suddenly, a boyish grin lit his face. He spread his arms wide, displaying his raw sexual vitality. "So where's the problem? I'm still the same lovable fellow you married."

Kate stamped her foot. "You lied to me!"

"Did you ever once think how *I* felt?" Peter's cleft chin jutted at her, placing her on the defensive. "You accused me, your own husband, of being a bank robber, for God's sake!"

Katherine winced. "What was I supposed to think? You deliberately tricked me."

"No such thing! You wouldn't let me explain." He uttered a caustic laugh and leaned his palms against the wall, pinning her to the spot. "So I humored you, just to see how far you'd go."

"*Humored* me!" Kate ducked beneath his arm, grabbed her hairbrush from the dressing table, and hurled it at him.

Peter intercepted its flight and threw it on the bed. "Spitfire! Try again, if you dare." Dropping the towel, he stalked her, forgetting that their parents were coming to dinner. He forgot everything except the hellcat flying around the room, pelting him with perfume vials, pillows, and folded socks.

"Oh, I dare! I dare very much," Katherine yelled.

Climbing onto the bed, she took a flying leap and grabbed a fistful of his long hair. Peter caught her with a reckless laugh and set her none too gently on the floor, then ducked around the bedpost to escape a flurry of fists.

"Stand still, Peter!" Kate shrieked, her heart banging wildly against her corsetted rib cage. "I'm going to . . . pulverize you, you poetry-spouting rogue!"

"Put up your dukes, Mary Kate!" Peter startled her by throwing up his fists. He circled her, lightly stroking his thumb against his nose in a mock pugilistic stance.

Her jaw dropped. "You . . . You're bigger than I am," she pointed out, eying him warily.

"You started this." Peter grinned, adopting a shuffling gait. He threw a couple of punches in the air, dancing around her on the balls of his feet.

Katherine jerked backward, imitating his stance. She regarded him nervously, her eyes rolling wildly. "Peter, don't you dare strike me. I won't stand for it!"

Peter slammed the bedroom door shut, as he circled counterclockwise. The noise jolted Kate. He stood between her and escape! He was bigger and stronger. As angry as she was, she knew better than to test his patience.

"Open that door, Peter," she demanded, her voice quavering.

"Nay, sweet wife. You wanted this discussion. In fact, you insisted. Well, you're not getting out of this room until we have it." Peter rolled up his sleeves and started after her.

Thoroughly alarmed, Kate also felt strangely exhilarated. "Good." She stood her ground and narrowed her eyes at Peter, hopefully in an intimidating manner.

"What have you to say for yourself?"

"Not a damn thing." Peter folded his brawny arms and gave her breasts a lusty male look of approbation. "Discuss away, wife."

Clearing her throat, she ignored his lecherous smile. "Th-there's nothing left to discuss."

"Wrong," said Peter. "Please remember that I had every reason to doubt your sincerity after our—what shall we call it?—marriage of convenience."

"You knew I changed my mind," Katherine said in a barely audible voice. "I-I slept with you."

"Many women have slept with me." Peter shrugged. "Doesn't prove a thing."

"It didn't mean anything to you?" Kate asked, incredulous.

His gaze fell to her flushed face, and he smiled ruefully. "It meant everything to me. By then, I wanted your love desperately. Not just physical pleasure. I wanted you to love me, too. Ah, God, Kate!" He threw back his golden head, and she saw his throat constrict. "It was hell loving you, knowing you had but one desire—to leave me as fast as you could get to town."

Katherine's defenses nearly crumbled. She was tempted to throw her arms around him and beg forgiveness for ever doubting him. "Oh, Peter—" She stopped, remembering what a liar he'd been. Was he playing on her sympathies again? After all, he *was* an actor of the first magnitude.

"It was a rotten trick to play on me." She sniffed, watching his face for any sign of false emotion.

Peter shot her an accusing glare. "You were threatening divorce all the way back to Virginia City," he reminded her.

"But I never meant it!"

"Kate, if I could have walked away from you, I would have," he said earnestly. "I didn't want to give you up, but neither could I force you to stay."

"You would have left me!" Katherine cried.

Shaking his head, Peter stepped closer. "Kate, when I got that restraining order, I felt as if the roof had caved in. You were the most precious thing in my life, and I thought I'd lost you. I was desperate, looking for a way to let you know how much I needed you." He grinned sheepishly. "I was ready to cram those damn nickels down your throat—"

"Now, that was certainly a brilliant idea." Arms akimbo, she tapped her foot.

"I was out of my mind."

"Indeed." After his ridiculous confession, she smiled, in spite of her resolve not to weaken. "What was I supposed to think? Except that you didn't even want my money?"

"No, you goose. You were supposed to know that I wanted *you*, not your money! It was supposed to signal a new beginning, the two of us starting off on equal footing."

"Equal—hah! I hardly think my measly thousand dollars is any match for your fortune."

A triumphant gleam lit up his dazzling green eyes. "Ah, but you didn't know about that!"

"I do now. You behaved abominably. Money and a title cannot begin to make up for what you've put me through these past few months."

Peter shrugged. "Nothing's changed. You love me, Kate. Don't deny it!"

"You won me with trickery."

He smiled, acknowledging his villainy, and tried to take her into his arms.

"All's fair in love and war."

Katherine pulled away, careful to keep the bed between them. "Stay away from me, Peter. You lied, not in so many words perhaps, but you let me believe—I shall never trust you again."

Exasperated, Peter let rip with a salty oath. "This must be the first time in history that a wife objects to being married to a law-abiding citizen, instead of a bank robber. As for the other, I made no misrepresentation. I *am* in lumber. Fact is, I work damn hard! All for you," he added, hoping to win his way back into her good graces.

Katherine shook her head. "Sorry, Peter, that's not

good enough. You would have let me go on indefinitely, believing you were a forty-dollar-a-week lumberjack."

"That's absurd." His face flushed angrily. "I was just waiting for the right moment to tell you. Tonight, in fact. That's why I invited your parents to dinner. This was supposed to be a night of celebration." His eyes twinkled seductively. "I figured we each had something to tell your parents. I was going to tell them that I own the Diablo Lumber Company and Sawmill and—"

"And that you're the sneaky, underhanded Earl of Wickstead? Don't leave that out," she reminded him tartly.

"Aye, that, too. And you would tell them about the baby." Peter's gaze softened, seeing her eyes widen with surprise and her face turn crimson. "How long did you think you could keep it from me?" He pulled her against his bare chest with a chuckle.

Kate drew back and scowled at him. He knew her secret all along. "You nervy Irishman," she fairly choked, because he was so cocky. "Anyway, you are mistaken."

"Oh, aye," he said sarcastically. "I've known for nearly two months," and he began to button up his shirt with an amused air.

Her senses heightened, just smelling the sunshine on his sleeve. Quickly, lest he note her weakening resolve, Kate darted around him and made for the door. His long arm shot out, and he spun her slowly into the circle of his powerful arms and kissed her hard. Katherine squealed, as his ravaging mouth came down on hers.

"I love you, Mary Kate," Peter said gruffly, wrestling to hold her squirming curves still. "Don't be angry, love. I wasn't laughing at you. It was just a joke that got out of hand."

"Just let bygones be bygones, right?" Katherine gave her curls an angry toss.

He looked somewhat relieved. "Right!"

"Even though you made a fool of your wife."

"That was never my intention."

Katherine whirled and gestured toward the main room. "How do you think I felt when your mother showed up? I stood there, yammering like the village idiot!"

Peter's lips quirked. "Sorry I missed it." And he had to duck when she came back at him with balled fists. Katherine jumped on his shoulders and pummeled him.

"Dammit, woman! Hold still." Peter made a grab. "By God, this is intolerable," he growled, grabbing a fistful of petticoats and whalebone stays. He flung her on the bed. Her body swallowed up in a mound of crinoline and silk, Kate glared up at him, panting, watching him advance, as slowly Peter pulled a long-handled bowie knife from his belt.

"This time, woman, you've gone too far!"

Her eyes rolled wildly. "I-I'm sorry, Peter. I never should have struck you."

Peter, his knee pressing against her hip, towered over her, knife in hand. Kate raised her head off the quilt. *Oh, help!* She swallowed, knowing this time she'd provoked him beyond all reason. Peter was probably sure their marriage would never work, and now he was going to—

Till death do us part. Oh, dear, she thought. It had come to that. "M-m-must you do this, Peter?" she whispered, frozen to the spot.

Peter crawled over her and straddled her hips. "Damn right," he said. Fiery golden flecks glittered like savage fire in his green eyes. He gripped the bodice of her gown, his knife poised against the rigid corset.

Kate moistened her lips, wondering how one reasoned with a madman. Peter looked so tan and powerful. His sun-streaked blond hair flowed like a lion's mane around his shoulders. Gazing up at him, she felt herself go limp, her insides puddling with fright and desire at the same time. *How can this be?* she asked herself. *How can I even think about making love at a time like this? I must be as crazy as he is!* Visions of an Indian massacre made her brain swirl. She felt dizzy. Oh, surely Peter wouldn't—Kate prayed he still felt a tiny scrap of tenderness for her.

Peter began to saw away at the layered cloth. His tongue balled in his cheek as he concentrated on his task.

"I-I'll be good, Peter. Give me another chance," she pleaded, then scrunched her eyes shut. She couldn't bear to see the fatal blow plunge home.

"Lie still, Mary Kate," he ordered, slicing her bodice from neckline to waist. Though she felt the cold steel against her skin, it surprised her that she felt no pain.

Cautiously Katherine opened one eye. She watched Peter cut the string that held seven petticoats around her tiny waist. In seconds, he had reduced her beautiful gown to tatters. She lay naked to her hips.

"There," Peter said, putting the knife between his teeth. Kate, her shoulders raised tensely up around her ears, scarcely dared to breathe. He grasped the remnants of her steel corset and yanked it out from beneath her. He pitched it out the open window, sheathed his knife, and got off her. "If you ever wear a corset again, I'll do worse than that."

Kate laughed defiantly, realizing at last that Peter never had murder in mind.

"I shall wear what I choose."

Peter was already busily digging through her wardrobe. "Where's that little thing you wore this morning?" he demanded.

"In the wash. I stained it butchering rabbits, cooking over a smoky fire, and picking strawberries for your supper." Kate sat up, regarded her shredded clothing with disgust, and hopped off the bed. She stalked over to where he stood fingering a silk camisole.

Peter looked at her, startled. "What the devil?"

Kate gave him a catlike smile. She turned, displaying the red flannel underdrawers, her full breasts bare and thrusting impudently. "Since you disdain feminine fashion, surely you don't object if I wear this tonight?"

She swept him a curtsy. "By your leave, milord," she exclaimed, in fair imitation of a lowly serving wench, "I shall go see to dinner now."

Nose in the air, Katherine sailed past him toward the bedroom door.

CHAPTER 29

Peter pounced. "Katie O'Rourke!" he thundered.

Kate had her second wind.

Round Two, she thought, looking up at him over her shoulder. She glanced pointedly at his restraining hand on her arm, then up to his stormy gaze with an arch smile. "Yes, dear?"

"Don't carry this too far, Kate." They were now nose to nose. "I love a good joke in private, but for God's sake, not in front of our parents." He planted his body between her and the door.

"Bully!" Her blood up, Kate pushed her bare breasts up against his shirt front. "You ruin my dress. My hair's a complete wreck, thanks to you. Why shouldn't I parade about? What's to stop me?"

Peter saw her game. She wouldn't dare walk out that door! He stepped aside and motioned for her to precede him. "Go right ahead, be my guest," he invited.

Kate tossed her silken tresses, watching his eyes roam over her breasts. She smiled, recalling her father's bluff several months before, and how she'd met Peter. And though she had no taste for folly now to take another dare, she wasn't averse to making Peter sweat.

"Don't think you're off the hook," she warned, stalling.

"Never," he promised and extended his elbow as if to escort her. "Truce?"

"Oh, all right."

"We'll sit down after everybody's gone and have a sensible chat. Agreed?"

"Agreed." Katherine took his arm as if she was totally serious about traipsing into the living room nude. "Shall we?"

"Oh, hell," Peter groaned and swept Kate into his arms. Walking over to the bed, he set her down and kissed her breasts. He buried his face against her warm flesh, feeling his own body grow turgid with desire, even as she arched beneath him.

"Katie, love, please let's not fight. You're so damn beautiful." He finished his entreaty by delivering a barrage of sensual messages to her neck.

Katherine moaned, returning his hungry kisses with her own. *This keeps happening,* she thought. *He just touches me, and I melt.* Somehow she knew she had to put up a fight if she was to retain even a shred of autonomy. "No, Peter, we can't just kiss and make up!"

Despite her protest, Kate knew she'd met her match as Peter began the slow, seductive adulation that always left her reeling with intoxication. She uttered great sighs, her body already heaving helplessly with womanly desire. Resisting Peter was like trying to put out a blazing warehouse with a fireman's peashooter! She was simply over her head where Peter was concerned.

Oh, damn, damn, damn! Kate groaned. Would it always be thus between them? This powerful attraction and fiery clash of wills? Would their marriage forever be a battleground?

Kate loved it. And yet she denounced her weakness for loving it. It was shameless! Complete and utter madness! She could not conceive of happily married people fighting the way she and Peter did. Where was the ideal she strove for? She despaired that life with Peter would ever be calm and staid and—well, *dignified*, the way a marriage should be.

And even as she struggled with her better nature, Peter had the red flannels off her before she could blink, and she was just as busy with his buttons.

"I can't keep my hands off you, Kate," Peter confessed. His tongue greedily licked the saucy breasts she cupped invitingly for him to taste.

"I'm mad at you, Peter. I shall probably never—"

Katherine gave up. Actions spoke louder than words. If she was ever to make him appreciate her viewpoint, she must be more forceful. Wriggling out from beneath him, she pushed him on his back and overpowered him.

Her breasts bounced against his nose, and Peter latched on, sucking and tonguing the cockled rosy tips. Kate pulled and twisted, striving against him. "You're in my power now," she gloated, since he was quite powerless to resist.

"Aye, Katie," Peter laughed, goading her into her revenge. "Punish me, lass. I deserve it."

"I shall make you cry out for mercy," the auburn-tressed vixen promised her victim. She grabbed hold of his rigid manhood and impaled herself in a single fluid movement.

Bed springs twanged like a serenade on rusty old guitar strings, amidst their yelps and sighs and groans. Katherine threw herself into the fray, sparing neither herself nor her partner; utterly ruthless. Swollen breasts swaying, she thrashed her prisoner with a vengeance, swearing she would wring the full measure of justice from him. Warming to the task, she rode and harried him without pity or pause.

Sensing her fury, Peter cooperated fully in his own redemption. It was the least he could do, after all the grief he had caused her. With a truly repentant heart, he moved his hips at her command. He agreed wholeheartedly with her vigorous chastisement of his body.

And as love's fiery tempest grew, Katherine felt her revenge grow sweeter still. Her world exploded like fireworks lighting the sky. Amidst her rapture, she felt the pulsing radiance of Peter's cannon burst. It was a shattering, liberating, drenching experience.

"Let that be a lesson to you, Mr. O'Rourke," she whispered, breathing heavily in his ear and collapsing happily into his arms. They lay plastered together, listening to each other's heart thunder.

"'Tis a lesson I'll take to my grave," Peter admitted. The corners of his mouth twitched as he tried to suppress a smile.

"I'll be here, in case you're ever tempted," Kate threatened with a giggle. She traced his lips with her index finger, and he lazily nipped at her fingertip.

"Good. I need you to keep me on the straight and narrow." And his eyes pleaded for her understanding.

"Hello?" his mother called from the front of the cabin. "Anyone home?"

"Oh, cripes!" Peter whispered, bounding off the bed. "It's my mother."

"Oh, dear Lord!" Katherine ran to her wardrobe. "Quick! Help me dress, Peter."

Peter already had on his trousers. He threw on his shirt and went down on one knee, searching for his shoes. "What's this, Kate? Not putting in an appearance in the buff after all?"

"Don't be ridiculous," Katherine hissed and threw a chemise over her head. She scurried around, picking up her lace pantalettes, stockings, and garters from the floor.

Peter stuck his head out the bedroom door, calling, "Be right there, Mother," and went to help his wife. Finding a simple but elegant yellow silk in the wardrobe, he laid it across the bed. "Let me," he said and pulled Kate to him. In minutes, he and Katherine were ready to receive their company. Her hair was caught up on the sides with combs, and Peter had tied a narrow satin ribbon in her topknot of curls.

Peter regarded his wife with a satisfied air. "Ah! The new Countess of Wickstead, I believe."

"Don't joke, Peter." Kate frowned.

He stroked the cleft in his jaw consideringly. "No, you're much too saucy a wench to be a countess, and much too American."

"Thank God for that!" Kate wasn't sure what to make of him. He was dressed very simply in tan trousers, a fine linen shirt, and a string tie. Kate decided Peter's casual dress suited him well. His elegance had less to do with clothing than with personal style.

Ready, they went arm in arm to greet his mother.

At the hearth, Anne O'Rourke straightened from stirring the rabbit stew, the ladle still in her hand. "Ah, there you are, Peter and Kate! Am I too early?"

Her eyes twinkled, as she regarded her tall son and the radiant blush on her daughter-in-law's face.

Peter rushed forward to sweep his mother into his arms. "Mother!"

His mother pulled his face down for a hearty buss on the lips.

"This is a wonderful surprise!" Peter exclaimed. Eyes glowing, he turned to include Kate, who stood watching the affectionate reunion with a thoughtful look on her face. "Why didn't you write and tell us you were coming?"

Anne O'Rourke reached out and pulled Kate into the embrace with her son. "What, and spoil half the fun?"

Peter gave both women a bear hug. "Well? What do you think of her, Mother?" he asked eagerly.

"I am overjoyed. Mary Katherine is everything I could ever wish for you, Peter." She gave him a playful nudge. "And she's beautiful, too!"

Deeply moved, Katherine ventured over to the hearth. "How does dinner look, Mother O'Rourke?"

"I'd say it's about done. It smells absolutely delicious!

Reminds me of when Peter's father used to go hunting."
Anne O'Rourke studied the fire, momentarily lost in a
tender memory.

Peter gave his mother's narrow shoulders a gentle
hug. "Aye, Cook used to outdo herself."

His mother raised her head to study her son. "And
now you're the hunter, just like your father."

"On occasion perhaps, but not this morning," he said
with a significant glance at Kate. "I was busy working on
a surprise I've planned for Mary Kate."

"Another surprise? I wonder how I shall survive," Kate
said.

"You'll like this one," he assured her.

Kate turned to her mother-in-law, meaning to change
the subject. "Peter tells me that my parents will be dining
with us tonight as well."

"Splendid! I could not have timed my arrival better."

Peter fetched a comfortable ladies' chair with French
cabriole legs that he'd bought from Maguire's for Kate.
Installing his mother close to the fire, Peter collapsed
into his own chair. "Tell us about your trip," he urged.

While Peter's mother gave them a thimble-sized de-
scription of her harrowing voyage around the Cape,
Kate put the finishing touches on supper. Soon the
rumble of carriage wheels outside interrupted their
conversation.

"That must be your parents," Peter told Kate. Four
long strides took him to the front door. He flung it wide
and stepped outside.

"Hello, Peter. How's that daughter of mine?" Homer
McGillacutty's voice boomed.

"Come right in, sir. Mrs. McGillacutty, 'tis good to see
you looking so fit!" Peter said.

Madeleine entered on her husband's arm. "Thank
you, Peter. I feel fit. My, what a charming hideaway," she
said, looking around.

"Kate's done wonders with the place." McGillacutty winked at Peter.

"Oh, Mary Kate, it's good to see you!"

Kate and her mother kissed warmly, and suddenly her father and her mother were both giving her hugs.

"Welcome, welcome!" Peter said. "I want you to meet my mother, just arrived from Ireland, all the way around Cape Horn. Mother, may I present Kate's parents, Mr. and Mrs. McGillacutty from Virginia City."

Homer bowed to the tiny blonde woman, who came forward to shake hands. "So this is the Countess of Wickstead. A pleasure, ma'am!"

"Please, I hope we won't stand on formality," said Peter's mother, lavishing her Irish charm on Kate's parents. "My friends all call me Anne."

"You told my parents," Kate whispered to Peter, while their parents exchanged pleasantries.

Peter's dimples leapt out at her. "A wife's always the last to know."

"Always the practical joker," she muttered and returned to the hearth to regain her composure. As she placed a batch of biscuits in the Dutch oven, she glanced furtively at her parents. They acted as if Peter being the Earl of Wickstead was a lark. Indeed, she had rarely seen her father so cheerful.

Katherine rushed to inspect the table one last time before she lit the candles.

"Everything looks so homey," Madeleine said, giving Kate a quick hug. "I'm so glad you and Peter are happy."

"Mother, we fight all the time," Katherine muttered.

"Adds to the spice of a marriage," her mother said without a trace of sympathy.

Kate rolled her eyes toward the ceiling. "Mother, really! I don't suppose you and Papa will ever grow up?"

"I certainly hope not!" her mother said. "Now, tell me what I can do to help get supper on the table."

Katherine handed her mother a large bowl of strawberries and a pitcher of cream. Maddy placed them on the table with an approving nod. "Everything looks delicious, Mary Kate."

Homer came to inspect Kate, not the table, for reasons of his own. "Well, daughter, you're looking well," he said in an approving way.

Peter chuckled, and Katherine made a fish face at him.

"Am I missing something here?" asked the Countess Anne, rescuing the biscuits. Using a heavy mitt, she carried the fragrant tin to the table.

"All right," Kate sighed. "I thought it was my secret, but as usual, I'm the last to know anything around here." She looked up and caught Peter smiling at her. "Go ahead, Peter. Don't keep your mother in suspense."

"Kate's expecting our first child in the fall," Peter said. The warm caress in his gaze made his wife blush.

"Oh, I feel so blessed!" Mrs. O'Rourke dropped her pot holders and rushed to give Katherine more hugs. "Peter, your father would have been thrilled."

Peter nearly burst his buttons with pride. "No one could be more excited than I."

Everyone looked at the mother-to-be with expressions bordering on lunatic happiness. Homer McGillacutty recovered first. "This calls for a toast. Got any imported sherry in your cellar, Peter?"

"No, sir. I've got something better. Be right back." Peter bolted out the door, vaulted off the front porch, and disappeared in the direction of the trout pond.

His mother followed Kate to the window. "Where's Peter off to?"

"Hopefully not for a swim," said Katherine, turning back to her parents. "Why don't we come to the table?" She seated her father on her left, her mother and mother-in-law to the right, leaving Peter's place at the head of the table.

Peter came bounding through the door with two bottles

of champagne, his bucket still dripping from the ice-cold mountain stream. He raised a bottle in triumph. "Kate, glasses, please!"

He ripped off the seal and, tongue in cheek, clamped the bottle between his muscular thighs. His strong fingers worried the cork back and forth.

Katherine's eyes followed the action. *Here we go again,* she thought, watching his tapered hands at work. A familiar lump rose in her throat, as the capped foam burst forth. Peter's eyelids drooped seductively toward Kate's bosom. She knew they were remembering the same things: the honeymoon suite and the wagers he had made for her clothes. His gaze met hers for a fleeting second of tender devilry.

"Warm enough, Kate?" he drawled, conjuring up a myriad of mental images for her.

Kate nodded, watching him pour the effervescent wine into glasses. Toasts were made.

Peter raised his glass to her parents. "Here's to my in-laws, who gave me the greatest treasure in the world—my wife."

Madeline sampled her glass gingerly. "Here's to you and Katherine and to a fine family. May all your little ones have green eyes. For luck!"

Peter's mother raised her glass high. "As green as the Emerald Isle."

As the evening wore on, Katherine felt singularly happy. Without a trace of rancor, her father and Peter chatted about business and politics. The Comstock Lode was going full tilt again. "Virginia City's on Easy Street," Homer chortled. "Now that the War Between the States is over, things will soon be booming," he predicted.

Peter shared his dreams for the future, too. There was talk of the railroad and California investors. Both men agreed that soon the railroads would be moving passengers and freight all across the country.

"When that happens, Mother," Peter said, making sure

the ladies were included in the conversation, "going around Cape Horn will become a thing of the past."

"That will be my most earnest prayer." His mother ivered, recalling her voyage through hurricane-force winds on a westbound clipper.

"If you want to invest in a sure thing," Peter told her, "buy railroad stocks. The West is in its infancy, and there's a fortune to be made out here."

"Goodness! It sounds as if the Earl of Wickstead plans to put down roots," Madeleine said with a smile.

"Aye." Peter leaned forward on his elbows. "That's my surprise, Kate. I applied to Governor Nye this morning for American citizenship. It will take awhile, but it's in the works." He gazed intently over the dancing candlewicks at Kate. " 'Tis here I found my bride, and 'tis here I plan to work, raise my children, and eventually plant my bones."

A tiny pucker of concern formed between his mother's brows. "What about your title, Peter?" she asked softly.

"The title and lands go to Sean's eldest when she comes of age. I think it's only right." Smiling, Peter plucked a strawberry from the bowl before him and toyed with it. Impulsively, he tossed it in Katherine's direction, where it landed with a splash in her champagne glass.

"Peter!" his mother gasped, startled by his breach of etiquette.

His eyes never left Kate's. "I have everything I need right here," he said in no uncertain manner.

Katherine felt a warm surge of relief. From the moment she'd learned he was an Irish lord, she had feared his desire to roam might return. That Peter would give up his homeland for her and this rugged wilderness left her speechless.

"Besides," Peter went on, "titles aren't my style. I never felt comfortable with all that stuffy protocol."

Homer nodded approvingly. "Out here we don't stand

on ceremony. A man makes his way by deeds, not bloodlines."

Anne O'Rourke's chair scraped as she stood up. "Well, Peter, I have traveled a long way to catch up with you. And my heart is too full of joy to argue with anything that's been said here tonight. I believe you know where your destiny lies." She looked pointedly at Katherine. "Your father would have been so proud to see how well you've chosen." Her green eyes glittered with sudden tears at the memory of her husband. "I, too, am happy," she added softly.

Hearing his mother's praise, Peter found himself, for once in his life, too choked with emotion to speak. He sensed it was for this moment that she had traveled so far.

Her golden head held high, Anne O'Rourke looked to each person at the humble dining table, including even Katherine's parents in her loving gaze.

"The prodigal has come full circle," she announced with a faint smile, "as I always knew he would. And he is *so* much richer for the journey."

She walked around the table until she stood behind Katherine. Giving her son a level gaze, she laid a jeweled hand on Kate's right shoulder. "This, as you have discovered, is the only treasure worth having. Love is all," she said, giving her new daughter-in-law a gentle pat, "and you, Peter, are wise enough to see it."

Facing her son over Kate's head, Anne drew a soft suede pouch from the pocket of her gown. "Even so, my wonderful, wandering son, I would be remiss if I failed to bestow a proper gift upon this beautiful young lady, who has become the jewel of your life."

Every eye was riveted on the fair Irishwoman, every breath suspended. The Countess Anne beckoned imperiously. "Come, Peter. I need your help for this."

Stunned, Peter rose hesitantly and came around the table, deeply moved by her wholehearted acceptance of Katherine.

Anne took Peter's hand and looked up at her tall son with tears in her eyes. "Peter, your generosity to Sean's children meets with my full approval. Your decision to remain in this country is a bit more difficult to accept, I admit. It will be hard leaving part of my heart here when I return to Ireland."

Peter's dimples sprang into bold relief, as he realized how incurably sentimental his mother was. "Aye, Mother, how you do carry on."

She gave him a little pinch on the arm and went on. "That's why I wish to present my diamond necklace and matching earrings to your wife as a belated wedding gift."

From the pouch, Peter's mother drew forth a large, glittering diamond pendant necklace, set in a heart-shaped cluster of blood-red rubies and smaller diamonds.

Wide-eyed, Katherine and her parents stared at the exquisitely set jewels the countess held out to Peter. "Go on, Peter, put them on your wife."

Peter's hands trembled as he placed the cool stones around Kate's throat. "These have been in the family for three centuries, Mary Katherine," Anne said. "They shall be yours, as a token of my love, even though my son refuses the title that goes with them."

Kate sensed the great honor bestowed upon her, yet words failed. And though his mother's gift was generous, it paled beside Peter's love. Unhesitatingly Peter had announced his intention to stay in the United States. All evening, he'd been making his commitment to her and their unborn children unequivocally clear.

And she had wanted revenge against such a man!

All of Kate's resentment and anger evaporated. Surrounded by so much love, she could not imagine life without him.

Peter raised Kate from her chair and planted a warm kiss on her softly trembling lips. "Mother, you've stolen my thunder," he complained cheerfully. Fishing around in his pocket, he grasped his wife's left hand. "Close your eyes, Kate!"

Astonished at being the focus of so much attention, Katherine obeyed. Just in case, since Peter had such a merry twinkle, she reserved one tiny slit to keep an eye on him.

"Pucker up, wife," he ordered, and Kate heard her father guffaw. Her mother drew an excited breath, and Mrs. O'Rourke said, "My son—always so romantic!"

Peter's lips brushed hers as subtly as a swallowtail's wing. Kate's eyes flew open as his right thumb and fore-finger slid a delicate wedding band onto her third finger.

"'Look how my ring encompasseth thy finger, Even so thy breast encloseth my poor heart; Wear both, for both of them are thine,'" he said.

"Oh, Peter!" Kate threw her arms around his neck.

Peter laughed at her impetuosity. "About time I gave you a proper wedding ring, wouldn't you agree?"

Katherine turned the ring, examining its simple purity in the candlelight. She thought no ring could be more precious than the solid strength in the arms around her waist, pressing her to his heart.

But then she remembered that their parents still looked on. She bit the ring and eyed it critically, then raised a questioning brow. "Is it likely to turn *green* on my finger?" she quipped, leaning back so that their hips rested against each other.

Peter sighed deeply. "Ah me! Such sentiment touches off the poetic magic in my Irish soul." He clutched his breast like a lovesick swain and dropped comically to one knee before her.

Not to be outdone, Katherine planted her hands on her hips and regarded her husband's pose with amusement. "Sir Knight—or is it Sir Clown? For you are more poet than I can bear." Without warning her eyes grew moist, and her voice turned soft as the caress of a moonbeam.

"Peter O'Rourke, I love you with all my heart. No bond is stronger than the love that binds my heart to yours, you dear, sweet, wonderful man."

With an exultant shout of "Aye!" Peter leapt to his feet and crushed Kate to his heart.

Katherine reached up and her fingers curled possessively in Peter's golden locks. Her wet lashes brushed his cheek as she opened her shining eyes. Like the mirrored image of her soul, Peter's eyes reflected a love that was almost frightening in its intensity.

"Katie O'Rourke, will you wear this ring as a token of my love?" Peter asked, his voice low and none too steady, but never more passionate.

The words had been a long time coming, but Kate didn't hesitate to speak them now.

"Till death do us part, you poetry-spouting, lovable man," she whispered against his smiling lips.